OPERATION KARAKORAM

OPERATION KARAKORAM

Arvind Nayar

Arvind Nayar

Rupa & Co

Published 2005 by
Rupa & Co
7/16, Ansari Road, Daryaganj,
New Delhi 110 002

Sales Centres:
Allahabad Bangalore Chandigarh Chennai
Hyderabad Jaipur Kathmandu
Kolkata Mumbai Pune

Typeset in 11 pts. Revival by
Nikita Overseas Pvt. Ltd.
1410 Chiranjiv Tower
43 Nehru Place
New Delhi 110 019

Printed in India by
Gopsons Papers Ltd.
A-14 Sector 60
Noida 201 301

For Vineet
who is the epitome of courage and
fearlessness in adversity and

for Aryan
who made me realise the worth of simple
pleasures of life

Acknowledgements

My inspiration to attempt a novel of this genre has come from legends such as Frederick Forsyth, Robert Ludlum and Jeffrey Archer. It is their amazing works and their genius that opened a window of thrills and excitement to a fascinated child. I would like to thank them and all the other authors who have provided inspiration to me. If this effort is even a fourth as gripping as their many amazing books, I would consider myself lucky and privileged in having succeeded in what I set out to do.

Today, as I write this note, I realise the tremendous importance that Indian sociology places on family, as it is their inspiration that results in achievements thought to be beyond one's potential. I thank my parents for pushing me: my father Justice C.M. Nayar who, despite his very busy schedule, never once forgot that I had a target to meet and constantly reminded me in his simple yet hard-hitting manner; and my mother Mrs Asha Nayar, whose calm and composed guidance helped me to plunge headlong into this task, that I had originally begun only as a whim.

I also thank my wife, Tarang, whose unstinting support and advice has been a major source of strength and a vital contribution to the completion of this novel.

I would be ignoring my obligation if I failed to mention the scores of friends and acquaintances who have been either an inspiration for characters in general or character traits in specific.

Lastly, the entire team at Rupa & Co. for their support and cooperation to a debut work.

Prologue

NEW DELHI, OCTOBER 17, 1995

It was an unusual night. The capital city of India is famous for indulging in hide and seek with rain. Rain cannot be usually forecast with any accuracy even in the peak monsoon season. And that night in October it was actually pouring. The airport had recently been fitted with the latest technology that enabled international aircraft to land and take off in the dead of night irrespective of the weather. Over the years the load of flights that had been grounded or delayed due to poor visibility, and bad weather in the autumn and winter months had become overwhelming. As the attacks by various industrial and consumer lobbies on the civil aviation ministry increased, highlighted by the ever-vigilant press, the minister in charge, a young and energetic person belonging to a group of flamboyant politicians tipped to lead India into the twenty-first century, had finally ordered urgent upgrading of the international airport.

The automatic clock in the arrival lounge showed the time to be 3.15 AM. The British Airways flight 471 from London to New Delhi touched down on the tarmac five minutes before the scheduled time of 3.20 AM. Most of the passengers were British tourists while the rest, apart from a few business travellers, were Indians settled in the UK arriving on their regular 'visit home trips'.

As the passengers made their way towards the Customs counters in the inner halls of the arrival lounge, a clear division was formed as all the British tourists headed towards the large green channel signboards. The majority had come with small and handy knapsacks containing their clothes and other bare essentials. They would return with their bags full of Indian souvenirs. On reaching outside the main terminal building they were surrounded by crowds of hotel agents whose spirits had obviously not been dampened by the downpour. For the Indians the situation was starkly different. The immigrants visiting India were loaded with gifts ranging from electronic items to cheap cosmetics picked up at sales for their extended families, who, woefully unaware that their gifts had been manufactured in Dhaka and neighbouring Moradabad and only assembled and repackaged in England, would then fawn over their more 'fortunate' relatives. The other category of business executives and government officials carried Montblanc pens and Armani perfumes.

One Indian was conspicuous as he joined the flood of westerners rushing toward the green channels. He carried a small briefcase and a few files and was spared the ritual mobbing by the hotel and travel agents and taxi drivers. The Indian was well dressed and on closer examination appeared tense. He was of average height, and was dressed in the worn-out tweed coat so typical of England, and dull corduroy trousers. His eyes, partially obscured by a pair of wide-framed old-fashioned spectacles darted in all directions as if he were expecting someone.

He waited for around ten minutes for the rain to stop, after which he hurriedly crossed the road and ran to the car

2

park opposite the arrival terminal. He went to the row of parked black and yellow taxis and, after glancing around, tapped the windowpane of one of them. The driver who was dozing woke with a start and rubbed his eyes for a few seconds. Barely awake, he looked at the man, rolled down his window and asked, 'Where to Sahib?'

'Chanakyapuri,' replied the man.

'I will charge you double the meter rate,' said the taxi driver, taking advantage of the weather. His voice was hesitant, as if he had doubts about his demand being accepted. In response the man opened the door of the taxi impatiently, saying that he would pay whatever was asked of him.

The taxi began to slowly glide out of the car park. The driver was slightly disappointed. He had anticipated that his demand would not be agreed upon and some hard bargaining would follow. Perhaps the rain had been responsible for the ease with which his passenger had agreed to the upgraded fare. He was now thinking that he should have quoted more.

'Sahib, was your flight delayed or was it on time?' asked the driver.

The passenger looked up, almost startled by the sudden question. 'On time,' he replied curtly.

'Do you live in India?' persisted the driver.

His passenger again looked up and remained silent for some time. In the rear view mirror the driver noticed that he was clearly irritated. 'Hmm,' the man said, realising that the driver was studying him in the mirror.

Forget it, thought the driver, if he wants to be dumb and read his papers. He had only been attempting the customary small talk. After a few minutes the passenger turned his face towards the window. They were now cruising on the Delhi–Gurgaon road. The traffic was thin though there were a few trucks and lorries. As the taxi approached the intersection of

Ring Road and Rao Tula Ram Marg, an Ashok Leyland truck which had apparently stopped for a tyre change, gunned its engine and began to rapidly gather speed, negotiating a lightning U-turn on the broad road, its tyres screeching with the strain. 'What's the fool doing?' the taxi driver shouted in panic. Whatever he said next was drowned in the loud noise made by the heavy truck ramming headlong into the taxi. The car was crushed like paper by the impact. The truck, with only a few dents to show for the collision, turned right towards the Gurgaon road.

The following day the *Indian Express* carried a small news item on the left-hand corner of the front page with the headline 'Diplomat killed in accident'. The report was brief:

'Mr Mohan Bhargava, the Assistant Cultural Attaché at the Indian High Commission in London, was killed in a late night collision near the international airport. He had just arrived in India on an unscheduled visit. The taxi driver was also killed.'

The report added that the bad weather could have led to the accident and that the police were trying to trace the hit-and-run vehicle.

1

ISLAMABAD, AUGUST 17, 1995

The city was buzzing with activity. It was forenoon, the peak hour for commercial and business activity. The capital of Pakistan is a fairly well planned and modern city with its wide and smooth roads and streets, its numerous office complexes and commercial areas. Only the signboards and hoardings in Urdu and Punjabi gave it an Asian hue. However, to the unobservant eye, it is not very different from European cities.

One distinguishing feature of the city was the strong presence of police. The presence of Big Brother had become regular since the coup in which Gen. Asad Mehmood, the last army chief of democratic Pakistan, had toppled the elected government of Chaudhary Nusrut Beg and had seized power. The coup had not been very violent, in fact it had been almost bloodless but for the scattered skirmishes around Beg's residence. The coalition government headed by Beg had been rattled by allegations of corruption and its inaction over the separatist movement in Sindh province. Gen. Mehmood, as chief of the authoritative Pakistani military, had led a delegation of service chiefs, along with the Lahore police chief and a few other men who had been the overlords of Pakistan during the almost decade-long reign of Gen. Zia-ul-Haq. These men of influence had approached the President, Sajid Alam Khan.

Except for the initial period of honeymooning between Alam Khan and Beg subsequent to the dismissal of the Pakistan People's Party government by Alam Khan there had been no love lost between the two. Alam Khan had been delighted by Gen. Mehmood's proposal to dismiss the Beg government and to become a partner in power. The President, though, had given his approval knowing how little choice he had; he had refused to outright dismiss the government and dissolve the national assembly pleading that this would infuriate the people and would trigger a backlash. Instead he had said that the generals could attempt a coup which, in the event of its failure, would be followed by his dismissal of the government.

Within the next three days the military had seized power, with Gen. Mehmood assuming the title of Premier. He had dissolved the national assembly on charges of abetting the Beg government in the looting of the country. Sajid Alam Khan had been rewarded for his support by retaining his position, though his powers had obviously been pruned. To the surprise of the military the people had not reacted as they had been expected to, though isolated protests had taken place. Prime Minister Nusrut Beg had termed his upheaval as illegal and had appealed to the United States of America to intervene. In response there had first been mild criticism of the coup and then, after a few weeks, the US had recognised Gen. Mehmood's government. With the American public strongly disapproving of America's foreign policy as the country reeled under a severe recession, the US President had seen no reason to intervene in Pakistan and hurt his already plummeting popularity ratings. There had been assurances by both

President Alam Khan and Gen. Mehmood that the state of emergency was only a prelude to fresh elections. Two years had gone past, the emergency had been lifted, but the promise of elections had been forgotten.

In this militarised Islamabad, in the middle of the biggest commercial market, a meeting was about to begin. The huge multi-storeyed building at the corner of Gen. Ayub Khan Street had a signboard with the letters IOC on it—Islamabad Oil Corporation, a government-owned behemoth that imported oil for the army from Iran at subsidised rates. The rear of the IOC building faced the Pakistan Defence Ministry from which it was separated by a small dark street, closed to vehicular traffic but open to pedestrians. No one could have ever guessed that beneath that street existed a tunnel connecting the basements of the Defence Ministry and the IOC building.

The spacious basement of the corporation building housed the headquarters of one of the most vital wings of Pakistan's military intelligence, the ISI. For reasons of security, the staff working in this wing could not be seen entering it. They entered through the Defence Ministry with special security passes. Those entering this heavily guarded tunnel had to pass through the offices of the three deputy chiefs of the army, one being Lt. Gen. Ghulam Hussain who held the additional charge of chief of ISI. A charge which made him the second-most powerful man in Pakistan. In the annexe to his office the security passes would be rechecked, the purpose behind the visit questioned and verified, and only then was the pass stamped with an all-clear sign.

Lt. Gen. Hussain had once been a batchmate of Asad Mehmood and had been close to him in the days when both were embarking on a military career. Though a very efficient man in his own right, he had some crucial shortcomings. Unlike Gen. Mehmood he was not well-versed in the art of

7

power politics and was notorious with the military brass for his violent and frequent outbursts of temper. This had proved to be a major obstacle in his career. Hussain had often been shunted from one post to another from station to station for repeatedly annoying his superiors. In fact, but for the Afghan crisis, in all probability Ghulam Hussain would have died an obscure army colonel.

At the time of the discontent in Afghanistan and its subsequent occupation by the Soviet Union, and primarily because of his strained relations with the army brass, Ghulam Hussain was, in 1979, posted as a lieutenant colonel in the North West Frontier Province in Peshawar. Soon he received orders from Islamabad that total support was to be provided to the rebel Afghan Mujahideen. Fully aware of the fact that this could be his last chance to distinguish himself before he was sidelined forever, Ghulam Hussain had plunged headlong into the assignment, which had brought his remarkable organisational abilities and tactical skills to the fore. Under his exemplary guidance the Mujahideen had inflicted tremendous losses on the Russian-aided government forces of President Najibullah. The Afghan campaign proved to be Hussain's crowning glory. He never looked back. From Colonel to Brigadier, then Major General and finally Lieutenant General. But the fiery temper, though toned down, remained.

After coming to power, the first step Gen. Asad Mehmood took was to remove Irfanullah Khaliq, a nominee of Nusrut Beg, from the post of Director General of ISI. At this stage Gen. Mehmood had thought of his old friend. Hussain's candidature had not been smooth, in fact almost all the senior officials privy to the decision had opposed it. However, no one had understood the mind of the wily General. Apart from wanting to use the efficiency and skill of Ghulam Hussain, he also wanted to ensure that the chief of ISI would never be able to depose him because of his inability to carry all the factions of the army with him.

In a large conference room of the ISI office, around a magnificent round table, sat a number of men. Most were from the services. At the helm of the table was Lt. Gen. Ghulam Hussain. Next to him sat Brig. Qayyum Nazir who was the chief of the Cell for India Operations, a service within the ISI. Unknown to the world and even to most Pakistanis, the CFIO had been, for years, carrying on operations to undermine Indian sovereignty.

Lt. Gen. Hussain rose to address the gathering. 'Gentlemen,' he began, 'Some of you have been attending regular meetings in this room. To them and to those who are here for the first time, I have to say that today's meeting has unparalleled significance. I must also add that what is said here is said in the strictest confidence and must not be repeated outside this room under any circumstances.'

Lt. Gen. Hussain paused for a moment, and then looking toward his right where Brig. Nazir was seated, he continued, 'Before we begin the discussion formally, I must congratulate Brig. Qayyum Nazir under whose leadership the CFIO has been carrying on pioneering work for the attainment of its final goal—the annihilation of India. Now I will hand over charge to Brig. Nazir.'

Brig. Qayyum Nazir rose rapidly from his seat and walked to the raised platform in the centre of the room. He began, 'In today's report on the working of Project K2, I must first tell you that the project was launched in the Eighties with the eventual aim of creating turmoil in India and its gradual balkanisation. Till a few years ago, the project was proceeding smoothly, but lately its progress has been hindered. One of the foremost reasons for this is that as the project moves towards its climax, the work of our agents both in and outside

9

India has intensified and has come to the repeated notice of the Indian government which now claims to have clear evidence of our involvement. The Indians have been trying desperately to mobilise international opinion against us. But the silver lining is that they are still not aware of the existence of CFIO, nor are the Americans, who have been keeping a strict watch on us. The second reason is the increasing pressure being put on the Indian government to take action against us by their political rivals, especially the right wing Rashtriya Ekta Party. This party thrives on Pakistan bashing and one of its demands has been to bomb the camps we run for training Indian insurgents. It has been exerting continuous pressure on the government and as its popularity is now on the rise, some of its demands are being met. One step which has been very alarming has been the mining and electric fencing on the border of Azad Kashmir with IOK.'

At this juncture Brig. Nazir stopped and motioned to one of the men at the table. A short, stocky bearded man got up. He was Abdul Ghani, a member of the Kashmir Liberation Party and the liaison agent between Azad Kashmir and IOK. 'I must add to what the Brigadier has said,' he began. 'Because of mining and fencing of the border it has become very difficult to induce youth from the Indian side to cross over to Azad Kashmir for training. They are getting disillusioned and frustrated with us and as the Indian government is making repeated efforts to woo them, some of them are keen to leave our movement. If things do not improve in the immediate future, I am afraid we shall be left with no option but to look to other quarters for support.'

At this a man in civilian clothes interjected, 'Mr Ghani, are you threatening us?' It was Mohd. Shujaat who owed his presence in the room to the fact that he was Gen. Mehmood's son-in-law.

10

'No my friend, Ghani is not threatening us or giving us an ultimatum, he is merely stating the facts, we cannot turn away from the facts.'

Shujaat seemed pacified, so Lt. Gen. Hussain turned towards the podium and told the Brigadier to continue. Lt. Gen. Hussain abhorred Mohd. Shujaat who he thought was uncouth and coarse. He tolerated him only because he was aware that his own position as chief of ISI was not yet secure and that he needed Gen. Mehmood's full support.

'The REP is turning out to be a big irritant in our work. However I would like to assure this assembly that, during this period, we have not been sitting silently over this problem. In the past few weeks some of my best men have been working on it and they have compiled a voluminous document on the subject.' Here the voice of Brig. Nazir was rudely and suddenly interrupted by a shrill bell that echoed through the conference room and the flashing of a red light on a brightly lit panel on the central wall.

The headquarters of the CFIO had an extensive security network which, among its other amazing facets, included a computerised schedule to be followed down to the second by all its members, whatever their rank or position. There were two breaks daily for lunch and dinner during which period the security panels were deactivated. This enabled inter-departmental movement which at all other times remained prohibited. The food packets were also prepared in the complex itself and were served in the main refreshment centre, which had the capacity to hold 1500 persons. Irrespective of rank, all personnel had to proceed to the main centre for lunch and dinner. At all other times any movement from one wing to another was prevented by automatic alarms sounding off throughout the complex. During the breaks specially trained men took over and supervised the movement of personnel from their office to the main centre and back.

'Gentlemen we shall now break for an hour for lunch,' Lt. Gen. Hussain said, getting up.

2

NEW DELHI, AUGUST 17, 1995

As the meeting in Islamabad was breaking off for lunch, a meeting of a different kind and magnitude was in progress in the Indian capital. The centre of Lutyen's Delhi was a sea of humanity with the entire stretch from the Boat Club lawns to the National Stadium choked with men, women and children.

For years the Boat Club lawns have been the venue of political rallies, one of the faces of democratic India. Today, it was the venue for another rally, but one with a difference: the numbers that had turned up was staggering, with separate estimates by journalists ranging anywhere from ten to fifty lakh. The rally had been sponsored by the right wing Rashtriya Ekta Party. The REP had been a late entrant on the Indian political scene, having been created only fifteen years ago. But after its formation it had made rapid strides and was now a leading contender for power. It owed much of its success to its disciplined and united party cadres. But the credit for widening its mass appeal and making it a truly national party lay with its charismatic and firebrand founder leader Prof. Vijay Krishna Kapre.

Fifteen years ago Kapre had been a professor in the National Science College in Pune. He was an upright man, widely respected by the city's academic fraternity. The city unit of a regional party which was then in power in Maharashtra had approached him with an offer to join them and contest the approaching elections to the state assembly. Prof. Kapre had agreed but was soon dismayed by the political machinations and intrigues around him. He decided he could not be part of such a system.

A fortnight before the scheduled elections, Prof. Kapre left the party, announcing that he would contest the elections as an independent candidate. This had brought him into direct conflict with the Maharashtrawadi Party, which he had just quit. The party, in order to keep its image intact, had lost no time in announcing an alternative candidate. It had also thrown all its resources against Prof. Kapre. During that period Prof. Kapre discovered a side of himself he had never imagined existed. He was threatened and attempts were made to bribe him to withdraw from the fray. Had he cowed down he would have ended up as a nondescript professor, but destiny willed otherwise.

Pushed as if by maniacal fervor, Kapre persisted. He was now determined to fight, and win. He faced the might of an old and structured party. Deriving his vigor from his ambition to construct an alternative system, an institution that would outlive him, he matched his rivals. His brief stint with his adversaries gave him an understanding of the complex whirlpool of Indian politics. It had taught him how to meet all kinds of allegations, charges with countercharges of his own, and how to duck controversies and pre-election press exposés. He won, and thus began his career in the murky cesspool of the Indian political system. He was in his late thirties then. He celebrated his victory by launching the REP, initially only a small group confined to Maharashtra, but Kapre had dreams of occupying the top seat at New Delhi. He knew this could be achieved only through a party with a mass base. Kapre's planning was elaborate and detailed. He laid utmost importance to party discipline and grassroot work.

The REP consisted mainly of educated youth and the young professional class looking for distraction from their monotonous lives and to fulfill their desire for experimentation. They poured all their enthusiasm into party work. After two years, elections to the Parliament were held. These coincided with the assembly elections in Maharashtra. The extensive groundwork brought the REP rich dividends, something which had not been expected nor predicted by seasoned political analysts. It swept to power in the state with Kapre becoming the chief minister of Maharashtra. In addition, the REP captured two-thirds of the seats from Maharashtra in the Lok Sabha. This upset the calculations of all other parties. The unexpected windfall made the REP a significant, albeit small, rival of the Congress (I) which had been in power at the Centre ever since India gained independence.

Around this time, two important developments occurred. First the support base of the REP began expanding rapidly. It crossed the border of Maharashtra, with the rise being spectacular in the North Indian plains. Second, the party started moving toward a rightist ideology with the views of its leaders becoming almost militant on several issues. With the next elections, the REP more than doubled its strength in the parliament, but suffered a setback in Maharashtra. It lost in the state elections to a coalition of the Congress and the Maharashtrawadi Party. The loss of power in the state of its birth was not as much due to a fall in its popularity as to the lessening of the curiosity factor. A large number of people

15

who had earlier voted for the Congress or the Maharashtrawadi Party, and had shifted their loyalties in the previous elections, reverted to their traditional voting patterns. This proved to be a blessing in disguise. The loss of stewardship of a key state made Prof. Kapre free to devote his energies to the national scene.

During the period leading to the general elections of 1985, the REP further broadened its influence over the country at the expense of the Congress. Till then the major opposition to the ruling party was the combine of the leftist parties. When the 1985 elections were held the REP made no substantial gains in the Lok Sabha though it came to power again in Maharashtra.

All this while the personal stature of Prof. Kapre continued to grow. He was now beginning to be looked upon as a man of unwavering integrity, one whose views were different from other national leaders. He was now becoming an absolute radical, and the party, totally rightist. Its philosophy began to appeal to many sections of Indian society that had yearned for an alternative. The REP started advocating immediate and stringent action against the insurgents in Punjab and Kashmir, action against Pakistan for abetting terrorism in these states, closer ties with the US and increased cooperation with Israel on counter-terrorist operations. Professionals and ex servicemen joined the REP in large numbers in the years between 1985 and 1990. In 1989 the elections brought the REP a step closer to its eventual goal of governing India. It won 107 seats out of 496, increasing its strength approximately five times since 1985. It became the single largest party after the Congress and the main opposition.

The years after 1990 were the real test for the REP. It had now begun to attract another section of society, the hardliners in the police and other paramilitary forces as well as the defence services. These people began to identify with the discipline prevalent in the party and joined it in large numbers. The names of many retired generals, air marshals and admirals started figuring prominently in its ranks which gave the party respectability amongst the educated classes of India.

On this day in 1995, the rally at the Boat Club was in preparation for the approaching general elections, the dates for which were to be announced in the near future. It was widely believed that the elections would be held in December that year or in early 1996. The people were getting restless. From the huge rectangular twenty-feet high platform at one end of the Boat Club lawns, the voice of Gen. Ranjit Dutt droned on. Gen. Dutt had been the chief of the Indian army from 1986 to 1988 and he had joined the REP in 1989. Now he was one of the general secretaries of the party. Though he spoke well, the people were getting bored. They wanted to hear Prof. Kapre. The others on the platform were the members of the central board of the REP. The blue and gold star, the emblem of the party, was visible in the background.

Gen. Dutt was in the process of rounding up his speech. As he ended, and it was announced over the several hundred loudspeakers in the area that the next speaker would be the president of the party, a roar of anticipation arose from the crowds. This was followed by an excited silence. There was some movement of people towards the platform to catch a glimpse of Kapre as he came to the microphone. The tall and gaunt figure was easily identifiable. Soon the electric atmosphere was resonating with his deep voice. He dealt with various issues ranging from corruption to inflation and the people listened with rapt attention. The professor was an excellent orator and knew exactly what to say to hold attention. He had been an excellent debater as a student and when teaching, had always enjoyed the full attention of his class. This ability had been honed to perfection on entering politics. The secret of his stupendous success in speech-making was that he never prepared in advance, but gauged the mood and the pulse of the audience. He knew exactly what they expected to hear and always presented it in a simple yet hard-hitting manner. Kapre's speech on this occasion was liberally tinged with humour and sarcasm as he moved towards his favourite issue—the worsening law and order situation in the country, and the lack of political will on the part of the government to take action against the rising tide of insurgency and terrorism in certain states. He began castigating Pakistan and—as the crowds cheered—advocated war as the final solution once and for all.

3

ISLAMABAD, AUGUST 17, 1995

The break for lunch at the CFIO complex of the ISI was over. Numerous shutters of wrought iron and steel clanged noisily back into place as the passages between the various departments of the complex resumed their impregnable state. These passages and shutters would now be out of bounds for six hours till the next scheduled break at 8 P.M. The delegates had returned to their seats in the conference room. Brig. Nazir stood at the podium at the centre of the round table. The room grew silent as he rummaged through his files and resumed from where he had left off. 'Gentlemen, now I am going to read a document prepared by the best minds of CFIO, after months of research and analysis. The contents of this document analyse the obstacles in the path of Project K2 and the dangers to its disruption as well as some of the projected solutions.'

'Brigadier why must you always be so vague, we are not schoolchildren here, can't you tell us clearly what you are going to read?' Mohd. Shujaat, interrupted, leaning back in his chair.

Damn him, the blasted idiot, thought Lt. Gen. Hussain, furious with the son-in-law of the premier. He motioned Nazir

19

to continue with his report, determined to mention Shujaat's behaviour to Gen. Mehmood, perhaps even ask that he be barred from future CFIO meetings.

'From the information provided by our field agents in India, and the groundwork done here,' continued Nazir, 'the conclusion is that the primary obstacle to the success of the project is the REP. The REP, however, is not yet in power. As we all know, the elections in India are to be held soon. It is almost certain that if the elections are held on schedule, the REP will win with a massive majority and will certainly form the government in New Delhi. I would also like to tell this esteemed gathering that this projection of ours is not based on casual journalistic predictions but on very accurate and laborious computer analysis. This analysis is of course based on data fed to us by our numerous field agents stationed in India.'

Mohd. Shujaat was on his feet again. 'Why are we so afraid of one single political party, what can they do to us?'

Good god, thought Hussain, the man didn't know where to stop. Well, this time he would put him in his place. He thundered, 'You sit down. If only you would listen to the Brigadier with a little patience, things would be much clearer to you, but you won't stay quiet. You keep interrupting him after every two minutes like a six-year-old child at his first day at school!'

Shujaat was astounded. He remained standing.

Hussain continued, 'You heard me, this is a military conference and my office, you will do as I say. Please take your seat.'

Shujaat was stunned. Hussain had dared to raise his voice at him, that too in the presence of others. To one who was used to sycophancy, this was a bolt from the blue. His first impulse was to give the General a piece of his mind and walk

20

away from the meeting, but he knew that he could not leave the room until the end. But he would soon show the General who was the boss; let him enjoy his brief period of triumph. Mohd. Shujaat sat down slowly.

Brig. Nazir started speaking again, 'Let me come to the consequences of the REP forming the government in New Delhi. An REP government in New Delhi and an REP prime minister would mean that there would be a large scale crackdown on our men in that country. It is very possible that the Indian government would take aid from the Mossad, the Israeli secret service. Need I add that howsoever dedicated and well trained our boys may be, they would be no match for the Mossad. Besides, it is near certain that the REP would launch a military offensive against us. In the current global scenario, the REP thinks that the Indian forces would at the most get a week. After a week, the United States and other countries are sure to intervene.' Nazir paused for a second and then continued, 'We all know that our relations with the US are not what they used to be and even if the US responds immediately, the proceedings in the UN would definitely delay its intervention.

'A short war lasting a week or a fortnight is going to be very beneficial to India. And if war does result, we shall not be able to use our nuclear arms because they will retaliate with a strike of much greater magnitude, and the territory of Pakistan being less than a third of India, such a risk is not feasible unless we wish to fight till the end. So where does that leave us? The alternative would then be to use only conventional weapons which may ensure us parity very effectively for a couple of days provided India does not use its ballistic missiles. If these missiles are used, our forces will not be able to hold the advancing Indian army and there is a very real danger of Pakistani territory being occupied by India.'

Brig. Nazir stopped to gauge the reaction of his audience. The majority of the delegates were old hands from the armed forces and knew the bitter truth. After the 1971 war, Pakistan had aspired to make its military strength greater than India and repeated propaganda had proclaimed the attainment of this superiority but now...

'Brigadier can you explain this in detail to Mr Shujaat and some of our other delegates here,' said Hussain, in an obvious attempt to placate Shujaat. Although not a very bright man, Shujaat understood this. Ha, the old fool was chickening out, he thought gleefully.

Nazir started again, 'I believe that almost all of you have heard of the extensive missile programme launched by India. Its attention was focused on their surface-to-surface missile Prithvi which has a range of 200 kilometres or more depending on the size of the warhead. The most dangerous of the Indian missiles is Agni, their IRBM. Work on Agni was started to counter the threat from the Chinese missiles which had targeted major Indian cities. Agni was designed to be able to reach the Chinese capital and important cities such as Shanghai and Guangdong.

'Gentlemen,' Nazir paused momentarily for effect, 'herein lies the catch. Sino-Indian relations are at their best at present and there is not even the remotest possibility of war between them, but we can't say the same about our relations with them, so Agni is an immediate threat to us and not to the Chinese. I must add that there is not a single inch of Pakistani territory which is safe from Agni and even though the Indian authorities say that Agni is still in the testing stage, our intelligence reports indicate otherwise. We have information that there are at least four prototypes of Agni ready, which could be deployed by the Indian army even tomorrow. To shed further light on the issue, I shall request Gen. Waheed to address the gathering.'

All eyes in the room turned to Major Gen. Aslam Waheed. He was the deputy commander of all the Pakistani artillery divisions, and a popular man. The tall and thickset Gen. Waheed got up and made his way to the podium, adjusted the microphones and started speaking. 'Gentlemen, I will come to the point straightaway. It was to counter the launch of the Indian missiles programme that we also began work on ballistic missiles, both short and medium range. Our programme concentrates on developing three missiles based on French rocket technology. The three missiles under development are Hatf-1, Hatf-2, and Hatf-3.

'The most important missile of our programme, Hatf-3, is designed to have a range of 800 kilometres with a conventional warhead weighing over 500 kilogrammes. While Hatf-1 and 2 can cause considerable damage to nearby cities of India like Amritsar and Jodhpur, it is only Hatf-3 that can reach the Indian capital and is our answer to Agni.' Gen. Waheed looked up from his paper to see the effect of what he had just said. Yes, everyone looked a bit relaxed now. He carried on, 'There are two versions of the Hatf-3 on the line. The first version being developed has a length of about twelve metres and a booster with a diameter of eighty-two centimetres. In the second version, the Hatf-3 has a length of about ten metres and a booster with a 100 centimetre diameter.

'Now I come to the results of our programme. The Hatf-1 was deployed in 1991, the Hatf-2 at the end of last year and Hatf-3, according to our schedule, should be deployed after a period of approximately fourteen months or early 1997.' So saying, Gen. Waheed dismounted from the podium and went to his seat at the round table, conscious of the disappointed faces of his colleagues on hearing the closing statement of his speech.

As Brig. Nazir stepped in front of the microphone again, there was a murmur about the possibility of using Pakistani air power to counter Agni. Aware that everyone in the military knew of the tremendous superiority in both numbers as well as talent of the Indian Air Force, Nazir didn't even bother to discuss that option.

'Gentlemen, your disappointment is not unwarranted but it is slightly premature. This meeting has been called to discuss the solution of the dilemma we face. In fact let me correct myself, we have already come up with a solution.'

'Who's *we*?' That had to be Shujaat, thought Nazir, and it was. Nazir first looked at Shujaat and then at Lt. Gen. Hussain, who once again wore a disgusted look. However, he kept silent and with a slight movement of his eyes urged Nazir to answer the query.

'*We* refers to the best brains in the IS and CFIO,' said Nazir turning to Shujaat, 'my best men, some of whom are geniuses at political as well as military analysis.'

'And what makes them such geniuses?' retorted Shujaat, enjoying having such senior officers answer his silly question.

By now Ghulam Hussain was almost wincing, his efforts to control himself noticeable to everyone in the room. He got up from his chair slowly, deliberately went to the refrigerator and poured himself a glass of water, hoping that it would quell the storm that was brewing within him. Here were absolute professionals, devoted and brilliant men who had spent their entire lives, sacrificed their youth at the altar of Pakistani glory, and sitting with such men was this oaf, this namby pamby fellow who was not even fit to be an orderly in the army. At that moment Hussain felt a searing contempt for the 'great' Gen. Mehmood. How could he tolerate having such an idiot around him?

As the freezing water coursed through his lungs and throat, Hussain seemed to regain his balance and the faces in the room looked relieved. But Mohd. Shujaat was disappointed. His attempt to bait Hussain had failed. Had Hussain reacted as he had expected, Shujaat would have had enough ammunition against him by the end of the day. But the wily old fox had escaped the trap. He is not as rash and foolish as he is rumoured to be, thought Shujaat.

Meanwhile Brig. Nazir fumbled through a file and started enumerating the credentials of his research team to Shujaat.

4

The rally at the Boat Club was reaching its climax. As Prof. Kapre ended his speech, the surcharged atmosphere erupted amidst thunderous clapping and cheers. The noise seemed to reverberate between Rashtrapati Bhavan from one end to the National Stadium at the other. The applause was music to the National Council of the REP but had a menacing ring to the ears of the old and extremely tired Hitesh Singh, Home Minister of India.

Sitting in his plush office in North Block, Hitesh Singh was a worried man. The reports he was beginning to receive about the REP's show of strength did not augur well for his party. His thoughts were interrupted by the ringing of the phone. It was the private line of the home minister, direct access to which was restricted to the three service chiefs, the prime minister, the chief of the Intelligence Bureau and the chief of the Research and Analysis Wing. He picked up the receiver.

'Hello.' It was the tired voice of Anand Kishore, the director of IB. A couple of minutes later Singh replaced the receiver. The IB director had called to tell him that he was sending the comprehensive report of the day's rally to him.

26

Singh's thoughts went back to the previous year's events when Kishore's predecessor had retired. Though the seniormost officer in line to be director, Anand Kishore had not been backed by any political lobby. Hitesh Singh himself had not been inclined in his favour, but the PM seemed to have thought otherwise. Overruling him and the entire cabinet, the PM had plumped in favour of Kishore. Looking at his performance over the year it appeared that the PM had spotted something more than just his seniority, something which he and the other ministers had missed.

ISLAMABAD

That should satisfy him! thought Gen. Hussain, as Brig. Nazir finished listing the credentials of his research team. The Brigadier looked visibly fatigued, not by his speech or the meeting but by Shujaat. Shujaat, on his part, had hardly paid any attention. He was not interested in anything but piling up ammunition against Gen. Hussain. He would get his chance again, he thought.

Brig. Nazir delved into the pocket of his belted tunic and took out a large and crumpled handkerchief with which he wiped his face.

'Brigadier you have done an excellent job so far,' said Hussain, indicating that Nazir should continue with the report. Mohd. Shujaat wondered, this time genuinely, what had been so extraordinary about the report. In his opinion it could have been compiled by an ordinary desk officer. Trust these defence men to see nothing beyond their uniformed noses, he thought.

Brig. Nazir addressed the gathering again. 'It is now obvious to all of you that for Project K2 to reach its logical and desired end it is imperative that the REP not win the next general elections in India. And the REP is surely going to win with a thumping majority unless some change in circumstances is brought about or an event takes place to substantially alter the existing political equations in India.

There was a brief silence in the room as the magnitude of the meeting began to dawn on everyone present. Shujaat was particularly excited. He loved being witness to major policy decisions. It gave him a sense of power.

'After considering and discarding numerous alternatives my team has come to the conclusion that there is only one way to prevent the REP from sweeping the elections and forming the government.' Nazir paused for effect as ten expectant and impatient faces looked up at him silently.

'We have to finish him friends. Only the death of Prof. Kapre can save Project K2 and fulfill the dream of every Pakistani, of seeing our flag fluttering atop Lal Chowk, Srinagar.' Nazir did not stop to see the reaction of his audience but continued, 'Kapre is as close to natural death as any other man present in this room so the answer is assassination. Gentlemen, Prof. Vijay Krishna Kapre will have to be assassinated if Kashmir is to be won, if forty-eight years of humiliation of our nation, of the Quaide-e-Azam, of Chaudhry Liaqat Ali Khan, of Marshal Ayub, of every citizen, every living person who calls Pakistan his home is to be avenged.'

This melodramatic end to Brig. Nazir's speech left everyone dumbfounded. In their attempt to concentrate on every word, they had lost track of when a cool, clinical and professional military man had donned the mantle of a political leader. The intensity on his face, the sincerity in his voice, the conviction, distinguished Brig. Nazir from a rabble-rouser and turned him into a man of stature.

NEW DELHI

It had been over half an hour since Prof. Kapre had ended his speech yet the crowds had not departed. The sea of humanity would not move till their leader passed in his car through the roads leading out of New Delhi's favourite rally spot. Prof. Kapre's motorcade was moving at snail's pace as the Delhi Police, the CRPF, the BSF, the home guards and other paramilitary units fought with the crowds to restrain them and to keep them behind the barricades.

The people did their best to catch a glimpse of the man they believed would be the next prime minister of their country, the first man whose ideas were at such odds with the founders of independent India.

ISLAMABAD

Brig. Nazir was prepared for the volley of questions that followed his statement about the REP supremo's assassination. The questions ranged from demand for the blueprint, who would do it, when it would be done, how it would be done, whether the ISI could do it without blood spilling into Pakistan and above all, could it be done at all?

'Patience my friends! My team has considered every question, every consequence. You must understand this was not just a random statement. This is the conclusion based on research, and by the best brains of the ISI.' After his long monologue, Nazir was somewhat out of breath, his irritation based not on the questions but the expressions of disbelief and ridicule, specially on the face of Shujaat who looked as if he had just heard a good joke. The questions in themselves were logical, not the mocking tone they were being asked in.

Lt. Gen. Hussain noticed his discomfiture and spoke up. 'Brigadier it's not you or your team we are doubting, it's the magnitude of the task. We all worry about the possibility of this being achieved without fingers pointed at us. I personally feel that what you suggest has very slim chances as it is, but after the Bombay blasts and the long trail blazed by the Yakub Memon family and Dawood Ibrahim it becomes practically impossible.'

Lt. Gen. Hussain's words helped Nazir understand what it would take to convince the top bosses of Pakistan to sanction the assassination. All this time he had been so involved in the preparation of the report, he had almost forgotten the paranoia generated after the Memons and Dawood, and subsequent diplomatic reverses and strengthening of the Indian point of view in the world community. For almost two years now Pakistan's tactics in Kashmir had boomeranged consistently. Whether it was Geneva, London or New York, support for India was growing, and Pakistani involvement in terrorism was being increasingly suspected and disapproved of. Leave alone the turnaround of the primarily Christian West, Pakistan was not even getting the required support from the Organisation of Islamic Countries. Brig. Nazir sighed heavily. He realised the next session of the meeting was going to be the most important briefing of his life, in front of the most sceptical and intimidating audience he had ever faced.

5

ZURICH, AUGUST 17, 1995

Walther Krantz entered his well-furnished office, walked around the desk and seated himself on his leather chair. He rotated his chair so it faced the small computer on his desk which was linked to the 3-zero section of the main computer terminal of the bank. Krantz was a tall slender man with aquiline features and neatly combed grey hair. His day had begun with a routine and seemingly mundane visit to the communications section in the basement of the red stone building that formed the zonal headquarters of the Hoffman & Handel Bank.

In the basement Krantz had been informed by Marie Stossel, the clerk who had been on overnight duty at the communications section, of the arrival of faxes from London. She had tried twice to reach Krantz. Now as Krantz sat in his office on the fourth floor with its huge glass windows overlooking Zurich, he thought that there could be only one reason for the midnight faxes. Patrons in London generally contacted Krantz on the fax machine in his office. In the event of his not being available in his office, the faxes were directed to the basement. Krantz's thoughts were interrupted as the

31

computer screen flashed the fax number of the London contact. He got up from the leather chair and went to the small mahogany desk at one corner of the office. He rapidly punched the code on the fax machine and sat down on his couch to wait.

Though Krantz could understand the lengthy procedure prescribed by Herr Darrel he was beginning to get irritated by it. He remembered Darrel's condition, that they would deal with only one officer at the bank. Four years ago the request and the circuitous procedure seemed routine as the transfers had been frequent, but in the past one year the frequency was much less, about three times a year, and the transfers and the long criss-cross of communications threw Krantz's entire schedule into disarray. His reflections were interrupted by the shrill beep of the fax machine. He took out the printed sheet and read the message. Yes, as he had suspected it was a query about whether an amount had been transferred in the last twenty-four hours to the account. If yes, the exact figure and the time of the transfer was wanted.

Krantz punched the keyboard of his computer and all the 3-zero account numbers started flashing on the screen. He stopped as the access codes of the Darrel account flashed. Krantz punched the key to open the access codes, and waited. The next instant the entire screen went blank except for the Darrel account number. Krantz took out his spiral pad and started jotting down:

Account: *Zero-Eight-Nineteen-Eleven-Zero-Fourteen-Thirty six-zero*
Name: *Restricted to legal instructions and owner*
Access: *Restricted*

His writing done, Krantz exited the programme. For any other account, all the information was stored in the computer and all incoming and outgoing transfers could be determined in a few seconds. But in the case of the Darrel account, the only information that the computer gave was whether there had been a transfer, and if there had, the specific amount and the transferor bank, and this only after secret codes known only to the director and himself were keyed in.

Krantz walked up to the imitation Mona Lisa that hung on an otherwise bare wall and gently touched the left eye. The wooden frame swung soundlessly to its left revealing a small steel safe built in the wall. He pressed the combination of the dial, then turned the golden dial nearly 360 degrees, took out two envelopes from the safe and went to his desk. He opened the first envelope and looked at the security codes. He entered the codes and there it was—first the screen flashed 'yes' and then the amount flashed and the name of the transferor bank.

The huge amount of rials from the Royal Bank of Oman, Muscat did not surprise him as the 3-zero accounts only dealt with substantial amounts. The rials converted into US dollars amounted to an exact figure of five million. Noting the amount, Krantz picked up the other envelope. It was a large white envelope with the Hoffman & Handel seal on the reverse. Printed on the envelope in clear terms was an access restriction warning. The simple words prohibited anyone other than a Ray Darrel of Walter Simpson and Associates from access to any information pertaining to the account.

Krantz opened the envelope and took out the sheaf of papers—a record of all transactions on the Darrel account. He checked the current funds excluding the last transfer—there was nearly 124 million US dollars in the account. As was his habit now, Krantz read the past record before recording the last transfer. There were numerous statements of entry, the sums extraordinary and all going back to four years, the original payments ranging from Egyptian dollars to Lebanese pounds, rials from Qatar and Oman and other middle-eastern currencies converted into Swiss francs and US dollars. The other statements described the monetary traffic between London and Zurich, with the destination in London always the same—Walter Simpson and Associates. After recording the latest transfer Krantz punched in the specific codes that only he had in the bank. The screen flashed the information: Roscoe Craig; unlisted adress; British citizen.

Who was Roscoe Craig? The question entered Krantz's mind for the millionth time. He was an Englishman with a Saxon name, that much was clear. He looked at all the rials and dirhams and thought that the man might be some sheikh's right hand man or an industrialist based in the Middle East with business interests in Europe as well. I am getting carried away! thought Krantz. It was a possibility that there was no man of this name, it could just be a fictional name used by Herr Darrel and his firm—it was a perfectly legal ploy used by some of the bank's patrons from time-to-time.

Anyway, thought Krantz, all this was not his business, he was a manager and one of the best ones at that! After all, confidentiality and secrecy were the hallmarks of the Swiss banking industry. If someone wanted to go to these lengths to protect their identity, they were welcome to do so. Krantz got up from his leather chair and walked over to the fax machine. Herr Darrel would have his answer and he his commission, for the extra trouble he took over this account.

MUSCAT, AUGUST 18, 1995

It had been a good day for Amal-al Mansour, the desk receptionist of the Viscount Grand. And why not? He wasn't manning the desk of some third grade hotel. The Viscount Grand was one of the best in Muscat, probably the best in the Gulf. The prestigious *National Tours* weekly had mentioned that arguably the best hotel in the entire Mid East had to be a toss up between the Grand and the Al-Hijaz in Baghdad. But operation Desert Storm had settled the question. The Al-Hijaz had suffererd extensive damage in the war and was now mangled beyond immediate repair. The Grand was the jewel in the crown of Astor de Miles, the man who had replaced Warren Buffet on the top of the Forbes millionaires list. De Miles owned three hotels in Oman and two each in Aden and Basra apart from the many properties he owned all over the world.

Al-Mansour's day had not yet ended and it would become even better after the generous tip from the gentleman in Room 666. In his seven years in the hotel industry Mansour had never met a more charming man. It wasn't just his physical presence, but every facet of the man's personality which was overpowering. The way he walked, the fluency in languages all added up to this suave gentleman with enormous panache. He was warm, informal, the type of man one could talk to, a welcome exception to the crisp and curt Englishmen Mansour generally met.

Tonight the tip would be even better. All Mansour had to do was relay the message from London to Room 666, and fifty pounds would follow.

The subject of Al-Mansour's thoughts was just waking up on the sixth floor of the Viscount Grand from a satisfying nap. It always pleased and surprised him, the ease with which he could fall asleep, but then his calm nerves had been discussed in half a dozen nations. Years ago, in the ambushes in the minefields of war-ravaged Beirut and the smouldering cauldron that was the Middle East, he had learnt that nothing was ever achieved by loss of sleep. Sleep and rest were weapons nearly equivalent in force to carbines and machetes.

His vanity never bothered him. This too was an integral part of his deadly arsenal, an arsenal which made him the most efficient man in his line. He believed what the Bible said— everything is vanity—but the quote was tempered by his belief that 'talent and vanity go together'. If talent was authentic then vanity had to follow. And to doubt his own talent would be the most profound insult, not only to himself but to the men who had come in touch with him, those who felt his hand on their lives and the audience, men of impeccable credentials, men not given to frequent and frivolous judgements. After all, Merlin Kramer, the living legend, survivor of Auschwitz and Treblinka, leader of the team that had brought Adolf Eichmann from Argentina and the longest serving chief of the best intelligence agency in the world, Kramer himself had acknowledged his genius less than a decade ago. And time had only honed his talents.

The white and black telephone that linked Room 666 to the reception desk began ringing. He picked up the phone, listened, said a soft thanks and replaced the receiver. To Al-Mansour the message from London had made absolutely no sense, the words being twenty-five thousand five hundred and nineteen. Decoded it meant simply the word YES. The code was perfect, the man in Room 666 thought, its strength lay in its simplicity, a beautiful cover which the self-congratulating jerks sitting in cellars in Langley and Cheltenham would never crack.

6

Now draped in traditional Arab robes, the man from Room 666 walked rapidly down the paved edges of the wide arterial road known as the Hassan al Kabir Avenue. After leaving the Grand he crisscrossed the Muscat suburbs till he came through to the ruins of the old Portuguese settlements located on the periphery of the Muscat waterfront.

He was soon in the area of the city that housed the vast wholesale markets from where cartloads of vegetables and fruits would be sent to several countries in the Gulf. The large fruit market, appearing to be in the grip of a time warp, was teeming with people. It was a market place far more structured than a bazaar, with well kept shops lining the square, the architecture a bewildering amalgamation of early Arabic, Persian, Indian and modern western influences.

He entered a small house that doubled as a fruit shop just west of the market square and asked the proprietor for his wares. He came out of the shop carrying a leather bag with long shoulder straps and walked to the other end of the avenue where he knew a brown rented Mercedez Sedan would be waiting for him.

The vast and arid desert appeared endless in the night to the man in the sedan, with sporadic moonlight outlining the mountains of the Jabal range in the distance. Everywhere the flat surface seemed to be a dry mixture of earth and sand, a desolate, windless plain devoid of any presence, either human or animal.

As he drove, he reflected on the tool he had chosen for the night. For a while he had wavered between a sophisticated firearm and a claymore mine. The claymore is one of the most devastating anti-personnel weapons ever invented. Shaped like a disc, it leaps into the air when detonated, then sends thousands of ball bearings outwards from the perimeter of the disc at waist height. A moving sheet of these missiles will slice through hundreds of human beings. It was the fear of the claymore mines that was primarily responsible for the rare casualties suffered by the US marines in the battle for Al-Khafji during the Gulf War. But, he thought, to use a claymore mine for a simple, single target would be inefficient.

The sedan was parked now; the man walked stealthily toward the source of the light in the desert. According to his information, the target would be alone at this time. As he reached the cottage from where the light emanated, what he saw surprised him. The schedule he had obtained did not mention the three men around the cottage. There was no need to change the plan of course. The three guards would only be a minor inconvenience. He stopped, turned and made his way to a distance of about 500 metres from the cottage, crouched behind a dune and took out a pair of infra-red telescopic field glasses from his leather bag. He observed the guards for about twenty minutes to gauge whether they were moving in any set pattern. Then he put the field glasses in the bag and started walking slowly towards the rear of the cottage. Although only one of the three guards stood at the rear, he held an automatic pistol in his hand and seemed fully alert. The man paused as he neared the artificial stone track that circled the cottage, staying in the shadows, and then he bent and picked up a medium-sized pebble from the track and threw it in a wide arc so that it landed in front of the guard without giving away the direction it had come from.

The guard turned and shouted in Arabic, 'Who is there? That you Ali?' That turning motion was enough for the man to take a few rapid silent strides and come up behind the guard. He reached the guard, grabbed his left shoulder and his right wrist simultaneously, lifted his left knee into his rib cage with enormous force, heard the crack of the bone tissue, and, before the guard could scream, raised his left wrist and hit him just below the chin. The guard went limp and dropped to the ground.

The man left him there and moved to the front. He had to be careful as the other two guards were circling the cottage in turns. However, one of them was now sitting and had no weapons drawn and to him that meant he was practically unarmed. He moved on the sand, and in less than ten seconds was behind the guard, dealing him a karate chop on the base of his neck.

'My God!' The exclamation in Arabic made him turn. It was the guard who had been walking around the cottage. The guard was now standing ten feet away from him, his gun drawn. It was almost certain that he had seen his partner being struck. The man raised his hands as ordered by the guard. This was contrary to his expectations—he had calculated that the third guard would come across his unconscious colleague at the back of the cottage, which would delay him. This would in turn have given him a chance to confront the guard with his Heckler and Koch machine pistol.

'Are you carrying any arms?' the query from the guard set his mind ticking furiously.

He nodded slowly.

'Where is it?'

'In the bag on my back,' he answered softly.

'Remove your bag, and throw it at my feet. And no tricks, I am an expert marksman.'

He slowly took the leather bag off his shoulder and threw it so that it landed a couple of feet in front of the guard. Then he raised his hands above his head in a manner that brought his right hand close to his left sleeve. He choreographed the next few seconds in his mind. The guard, who had been annoyed and suspicious by his inaccurate throw, was now reassured by the prompt raising of the hands. As he bent to pick up the bag, a small blade knife was drawn in a flash from the left sleeve and hurled at the guard, the motion of the throw indistinguishable from that of drawing it out. The knife struck the guard just below the right shoulder and his grip on his pistol loosened, more from shock than pain. As he tried to steady himself, the man's foot knocked the gun out of his hand. Then he grasped the hilt of the still embedded knife and moved it diagonally towards the heart in one savage thrust. The guard opened his mouth to groan, but before any sound could escape his lips, his body convulsed and went limp.

The entire operation had taken less than four seconds.

The man pulled the blood-stained knife out, wiped it clean against the guard's jacket and eyed it for a brief moment. It was the same weapon he had used so successfully in another era. He returned it to its sheath against his left forearm and stood up. The job was still unfinished.

The next morning *The Muscat Herald* announced the assassination of Hassan-al-Wahaidi, first cousin of the reigning Omani monarch. It described how the thirty-eight-year-old royal, educated in Oxford and Princeton, was found dead in his desert retreat. Of the three men of the elite Royal Corps that protected all Omani VIPs, one was found dead and two with severe injuries. The surprising part, the *Herald* noted, was the inability of the two surviving guards to shed any light on the events of the night. The reporter, quoting anonymous administration sources, said that there was a strong possibility that the assassination was the work of a group of terrorists owing allegiance to the Allah Doves, the fundamentalist group which, led by an eighty-year-old blind cleric called Saleh Bahrudi, was demanding that the royal dynasty be deposed.

After his return from America, Al-Wahaidi had launched a severe diatribe against the Allah Doves, attributing all the problems of the Islamic nations to the fundamentalists who, he said, in his most recent interview with *Time* magazine, were power hungry wolves masquerading as clerics and priests. This outburst had evoked a vehement response from some of Bahrudi's young followers who, claiming that the West had corrupted Hassan-al-Wahaidi, promised him retribution for his sacrilegious remarks against their leader.

Yahya-al-Baloushi was a confused and distressed man when he replaced the receiver in his plush office. Being the commanding officer of the Royal Corps was in itself a nightmare, but the events of the past twenty-four hours had made earlier stressful situations look like child's play. First the king's favourite cousin, who had always accused him of being extra cautious when he would insist that he not visit his desert retreat without his six-men unit, had been assassinated. Then the autopsy so confounded the Omanis that they had to call on the resources of the CIA station head in Muscat. It was one of Austin Lancaster's men who had just identified the lethal bullets and had called him up to inform him of the results which had surprised the CIA as well. The ammunition and the weapon were most definitely of Soviet origin, Lancaster's man had said. He had claimed that even their

41

ballistics man had difficulty identifying them but was aided by a field agent who in the Eighties had seen action in eastern Europe. The field agent identified the weapon as a Sako Triace target pistol, a heavy and accurate weapon which was generally precision-made on order. The Sako Triace—used by highly selective KGB and GRU agents—used to be able to take three interchangeable barrels, with five rounds in its magazines.

Baloushi was startled at this evidence of a Russian presence in the country after the Cold War. What bothered him was the fact that though the communist block at the height of the Cold War had had a sizable presence in the Gulf, its attention had always been on Baghdad and Teheran. How had a Russian weapon used only by their now disbanded security services landed in Oman to be used against the royals confounded him.

Something different was bothering Austin Lancaster in his room at the American Embassy in Muscat. He knew for sure that the Allah Doves lacked the intelligence and the resources to carry out a near perfect assassination. His initial scepticism was reinforced by what Blake Gilroy, his ballistics expert, had told him some time back. Lancaster knew that many ex-KGB hit-men were now roaming the globe as merchants of death, offering their services for a price after the 1991 collapse of their once powerful fatherland. Unlike his Omani counterparts he also knew that the assassination of Hassan-al-Wahaidi and the assault on his bodyguards was the work of one man, and not a group of terrorists, as the Omanis were erroneously speculating.

His analysts, who had been studying detailed reports of the killing, had come to the conclusion that the type of injuries to the two surviving guards indicated that the reason they were alive and the third was dead was that the deceased man had seen the face of the assassin. And a professional assassin, more so an ex-KGB or GRU man roaming around on his turf, the identity of whom they were still no closer to finding out, was definitely going to make him lose sleep for a while.

7

CAMDEN, NEW JERSEY, AUGUST 19, 1995

The old man in the New Jersey state penitentiary cell folded
his copy of the newspaper and placed it on the steel cot. He
looked up at the ceiling of his cell, lost in deep thought, the
story of the killing in Muscat setting him thinking.

Sixty-eight-year-old Bobby Joe Carter had been sentenced
to fifty-seven months in prison by US district judge Joseph
E. McLeod for duping a New Jersey company out of an
airplane. What had the judge called him? Ah, yes, a career
criminal with a record that began in the Sixties when he
landed in Cuba after deserting the army. Carter wondered at
the sheer irony of his plight: he who had influenced the destiny
of nations, was sentenced for the light-weight charge of fraud.
The involvement of the airplane was hardly any compensation.

The Muscat story had reminded him of his days on the
ranch in Alabama, a place that had appreciated his talents. His
instinct told him that his legacy would not end with his
incarceration. Even though there was no logical explanation
for his conclusion, in his heart he knew he was right. His best
student, who had been like a son to him, was out there
somewhere. Though Carter had not heard from him in eight

44

years, he had always known that his boy was not one who could be reined in by any authority. He had always been his own master, like an exceptionally gifted horse, who no jockey could control, one who if allowed to race, could burn the track. The day Bobby Carter heard that his boy was a free man, he knew that the world was going to pay a very heavy price. Though there had been rumours for many years, and he had tried to follow up his surrogate son's movements, it was next to impossible. The boy was simply too good.

NEW DELHI

A middle-aged man in a dark grey business suit emerged from a meeting, climbed into his Maruti Esteem and asked his chauffeur to head for home. This was not the time he usually left for home but he was flushed with excitement and pride and did not want to spend the evening in his office. As the car sped towards India Gate, Asim Banerjee began thinking back to the time when he presented his brainchild *Worldwatch* every week on Doordarshan, India's national television channel. *Worldwatch* became the most popular sponsored programme on Doordarshan and Banerjee the blue-eyed boy of the channel for years to come. Of course, there had been allegations of favouritism on the part of the government but Banerjee wasn't bothered, dismissing all remarks as jealousy. Then the media scene had changed in India. Numerous private channels entered the fray and he had kept pace with the times. He had pioneered and subsequently become one of the foremost psephologists of India and his company New India Communications or NIC had continued to grow. Banerjee did not offer his advice and analysis to private individuals as a principle, but today he had made an exception in a confidential meeting called on special request. He wondered

45

how many people would have had the privilege of being requested to advise the Prime Minister of India!

M. Srinivas Reddy was seventy-five years old and rather frail. He reflected over what he had just heard. It did not augur well for him or for the organisation that he headed. He was not a particularly ambitious man. If he were forced to abdicate his position he would do so without a second thought. He was where he was only because of a strange twist of fate. Four years before, in 1991, Reddy had been packing his bags to retire permanently from the stressful life he had led in New Delhi and settle in the idyllic surroundings of his small village in southern Andhra Pradesh. There is an informal saying in Indian political circles—the chance of your getting the top job is inversely proportional to your desire for it. The quote was apt in the case of Reddy. His dreams of retirement after having been foreign minister in the Indira Gandhi Cabinet in the early Eighties never materialised. Instead, the churning that took place after the tragic assassination of Rajiv Gandhi in May 1991 changed his life. The Congress received a razor-thin majority in the general elections that year and this multilingual, scholarly and apparently unambitious Andhrite politician in semi-retirement emerged as a consensus candidate for the head of the Congress Parliamentary Party.

In the next four years, Srinivas Reddy's reputation evolved from that of a temporary figurehead, keeping the seat warm till the real aspirants for power set their houses in order, to that of a Machiavellian, a modern day Chanakya. He came to be recognised as one of the craftiest politicians India had seen. He began by trying to please everyone who had some political weight, but soon the tradition of autocracy associated with Congress party chiefs began to catch up with him. Most recently the disdain for dissent was beginning to show too, as Chandra Dev Raj—the ambitious politician from central India who had also been one of the contenders in 1991 and had been known as the No. 2 man in the Cabinet—had learnt to his discomfort. The uneasy truce between Reddy and Dev Raj had fractured after the demolition of the Babri Masjid on December 6, 1992. The fracture had then deepened into a full-scale breach as Dev Raj began to accuse Reddy of being indecisive and soft on Hindu nationalists. When his veiled attacks failed to elicit any response from the unflappable Reddy, Dev Raj went on a letter-writing spree, with the letters being more often than not leaked to the Press.

The PM on his part saw these as acts of indiscipline and petty attempts to unseat him. He retaliated by totally sidelining Dev Raj from the meetings of the Congress Working Committee. This was accompanied by public criticism of Chandra Dev Raj by leaders loyal to Reddy. Today it was being said that Dev Raj's expulsion was a forgone conclusion and his political oblivion a distinct possibility. Reddy's hold over the Congress was now unchallengeable and the party itself had a comfortable majority in the Lok Sabha. But Reddy had cause for worry: if what Asim Banerjee had told him a few minutes earlier was true, the Congress was heading for sure defeat in the elections. Not only was the prospect of defeat worrying, but its aftermath would be even worse. The Congress had never really been without power in India after 1947, if one excluded the short spells in 1977 and 1989. But those spells in the opposition had been significantly different from what would be the situation in 1996. There would be no member from the Nehru-Gandhi family to hold the party together. It was this fear of the disintegration of the party that was gnawing at Reddy's heart. The prospect of ceasing to be the Prime Minister of India did not effect him greatly, but the thought of seeing the end of a party whose life had spanned over 100 years, immortalised by men like Gandhi and Nehru, was indeed enough to make him lose his sleep.

'Whom can I turn to at this moment?' he thought. The Congress, in the present scenario, was dominated by a string of regional satraps who had been at different times prominent figures at the central level. Reddy thought about them one by one. Chandra Dev Raj was an experienced politician but he had made up his mind to reduce him to an irrelevant figure in national politics. Then there was Rajeshwar Rao Kulkarni, who had been India's defence minister for a short while, and was now the chief minister of Maharashtra. He was a shrewd but unreliable man, ambitious to the core.

The other Congress heavyweights were K. Raghavan, the wily old Malayali and G. Ramamurthy. Raghavan was greatly respected within the party and had stood solidly behind Reddy at the time of the Babri Masjid incident and during Reddy's face-offs with Dev Raj, but his relations had cooled off with Reddy after the PM had decided to replace him as Kerala chief minister. G. Ramamurthy was the supremo of the Tamil Nadu unit of the Congress and the one man on whom Reddy was banking on to wrest the state for the Congress from the domination of Dravidian parties like the DMK and the AIADMK. Apart from all these leaders, there was Hitesh Singh, Reddy's closest friend in the party and India's home minister. But Reddy did not think much of Singh's political acumen.

After a few minutes of debate, Reddy called his private secretary and told him to connect him on the hotline to the chief minister of Maharashtra.

8

ISLAMABAD, AUGUST 20, 1995

Dusk was falling in the capital of Pakistan. The commercial district of Islamabad was abuzz with cacophonic sounds of all tenors, specially motor horns. However, the noise did not affect Lt. Gen. Hussain who sat in his sound-proof office at the CFIO headquarters.

It had been more than two days since the meeting in which a major impediment to Pakistani aspirations had been discussed. Across his large table sat Brig. Nazir and Maj Gen. Waheed, the deputy commandant of the central artillery force.

'Would the agreement about the supply of M-11 missiles from China alter and aid our plans?' asked Lt. Gen. Hussain, addressing Maj. Gen. Waheed. 'If I have analysed your reports correctly, these missiles are superior to those of the Hatf series and equal to if not superior to the Prithvi and other Indian missiles.'

'Well, yes, they are, but I doubt if they could serve our purpose given the time frame under which we are working.'

What did he mean by doubt? Hussain thought with concealed annoyance. He prided himself on clear and precise

49

statements and thought that a military man's language should not be laced with uncertainty. He put it down to Waheed's Oxbridge background, places where you learn to shadowbox with language. There was another reason for Hussian's annoyance with polished and articulate English. He associated it with diplomats, who he loathed from the depth of his heart. The resentment went back a number of years when a young and idealistic Major Ghulam Hussain had been a mere military attaché stationed in Cairo. A more than enthusiastic response to an Egyptian extremist who had come to him for help in obtaining asylum had earned him a particularly adverse report from the Pakistani ambassador in Cairo which had set him back considerably in his ascendancy in the army hierarchy. Such set-backs were of course made up for by Gen. Mehmood's later appreciation of his showing in the Afghan war, but the decades old resentment and anger was still fresh in his mind. He continued to believe that he had done nothing wrong then. After all, he had only been advocating the cause of Islam, the sacred duty of every true Muslim.

'If the government in New Delhi changes in 1996 and we continue to press forward our plans, then war would be a foregone conclusion and the M-11 missiles—though in our possession but without the requisite technologies and know-how—would be worthless for operational purposes.' Maj. Gen. Waheed went on, 'That would require at least twelve to fourteen months.'

Lt. Gen. Hussain sighed when he heard this. Unlike a layperson who reads a newspaper report about a country importing jets or missiles from an established power and thinks that the armed might of the nation has increased instantly, Lt. Gen. Hussain knew that mere hardware was worthless unless accompanied with complete technical know-how, at least in the usage arena. He knew that India faced the same problem often but less in comparison to Pakistan, especially in the fields of missiles and the formation of the bomb. He softly cursed Dr. Asif Rizvi, the brain behind ISRO and DRDO and the father of the Indian space and missiles programmes. Being a Muslim how could he design and oversee the construction of weapons being made specifically for the destruction of Pakistan?

Hussain turned to Nazir, 'What do you think about the obstructions we are facing?'

'I have already made myself clear in the meeting of the K2 general command.'

'Are you sure there is no alternative to the solution offered by you that day?' pressed Hussain.

'There could be, but I had to elaborate on what, given our circumstances and compulsions, would be most feasible.'

Hussain did not press further. He knew better than to question the judgment of an officer as competent as Brig. Nazir. His thoughts gave way to the dinner bell that was ringing. That morning there had been a minor alteration made in the computerised schedule drawn for the day. At the dinner break only Maj. Gen. Waheed was to leave the office of the chief of ISI who was planning to remain closeted with Brig. Qayyum Nazir to settle some unfinished business.

'I see that you are not convinced by the course of action recommended by my report?' queried Nazir of Hussain after the two were alone in the room.

'There is nothing wrong with your report, it's just that after the damage caused by the Memons and now the uproar about Dawood Ibrahim our freedom has been severely curtailed. Something as drastic as the assassination of a prominent Indian politician, especially one being tipped to be the next prime minister, could have potentially disastrous consequences for Pakistan unless foolproof.'

51

'I have thought of that too. If no fingers are pointed towards Pakistan then the assassination would have perfect results. I deliberately omitted certain sections of the original report because it was suitable that, at this stage, the general command not know everything.'

This pleased Lt. Gen. Hussain. He was beginning to understand why Brig. Nazir was so highly rated. 'What is it that you have in mind?' he asked.

'I recommend, in fact I strongly advocate, that we take no part in what the K2 report suggests—we should contract it out.'

This stunned Hussain but he recovered soon enough. 'What! You mean a job of such importance and magnitude be given to a professional assassin?'

'Yes, that is exactly what I mean,' continued Nazir, obviously enjoying Lt. Gen. Hussain's reaction, 'Not only do we give it to a professional killer but to one who commands a top price for his skills and is not connected even remotely to Pakistan.'

'Do you have anyone particular in mind?' said Hussain, almost expecting Brig. Nazir to say yes.

'No, I could not proceed any further without clearance from you and I presume the assent of Gen. Mehmood would be required too. Also, such an exercise would require time as well as vast financial resources.'

'If I were to get clearance and the go-ahead from Gen. Mehmood and place the finances you need at your disposal, when can I expect your next report?'

'I'll need around two months,' replied Nazir. 'You know such men do not openly advertise themselves, and those in the elite category might not have their records in the files of any intelligence agencies. Even if there were a mention of them, it would take time to discover their real identities and to make contact with them.'

'But they must need to advertise somehow, how else do they get any work?'

''I am not really sure, but generally information spreads about them by word of mouth, at least in the case of those with international reputations,' answered Nazir.

'How can it be that such men do not come to the notice of the Mossad, or MI-6 and CIA?'

'I never said that they do not come to the notice of such agencies, I said that files do not exist on them. The premier world agencies are usually aware of their existence but often do not interfere. It is only when their actions come in direct conflict with the areas of interest of such agencies that they begin to take notice of them,' said Nazir.

'How would you begin your investigations?' asked Lt. Gen. Hussain.

'Oh, I have many liaison men, ranging from current to ex-agents, to government bureaucrats and even diplomats who gather just this kind of information,' said Brig. Nazir, in a matter of fact manner. He was beginning to realise that if the plan was approved by Lt. Gen. Mehmood, the next two months would be extremely taxing and tense for him. 'My sources are spread all over Asia.'

'Why only Asia?' asked Hussain.

'Because after the Cold War, Asia is the continent where there is no dearth of assassination targets, or of men offering such services.'

'I need not say that if you have to follow this course, you will have to maintain extreme discretion,' cautioned Lt. Gen. Hussain.

'I will select a small team, smaller than the one I have now, as soon as I begin work,' answered Brig. Nazir reassuringly.

'There is one more thing,' said Lt. Gen. Hussain. 'What happens if your idea does not bear the desired results? I don't need to remind you of what happened in 1984 and in 1991 when the sympathy waves generated after Indira and Rajiv Gandhi's assassinations got the Congress more seats in the Indian Parliament than they would have otherwise.'

'There are many differences between the Congress and the REP. Unlike the Congress, the REP is a one-man party. The second-rung leadership of this party is neither as politically mature nor half as charismatic as Prof. Kapre. So, in the REP, there will be no leaders who could tap this sympathy wave and generate it into votes. In addition to that, the death of Kapre may cause grief among Indians but it is unlikely to come anywhere near the sense of loss and abandonment faced by India in 1984 and 1991.' Brig. Nazir paused briefly. By now Lt. Gen. Hussain was aware of his peculiar habit of stopping bang in the middle of making an especially significant point.

'You see sir, the Nehru-Gandhi family was the closest the Indians came to having a royal family of their own. When independence sounded the death knell for royalty, Indians had no figure to revere, therefore they subconsciously adopted this family as their first family, and any member of this family at the helm of the country has always evoked messiah-like feelings amongst Indians. That is what Kapre, despite all his popularity, lacks and will never achieve. It is because of these factors that I am not apprehensive about any sympathy wave on Kapre's death and even if there are any isolated bursts they would not be enough to offset the damage caused by his death. For all you know the party may even break up.'

All through this little speech, Brig. Nazir had been extremely patient without sounding patronising. He had been prepared for a worse grilling by Lt. Gen. Hussain. He knew that his answers would be used later to satisfy Gen. Mehmood's questions. That thought reminded Nazir of a vital point. He spoke up, 'What are the chances of the briefing you give to Gen. Mehmood finding its way to the ears of Mohd. Shujaat?'

Hussain was grim as he answered, 'I would say 110 percent. Our premier trusts his son-in-law absolutely. There is no way he would not discuss such a crucial plan with him. Why? Does that bother you?' The chief of ISI looked directly at Brig. Nazir.

'Until two days ago I had only heard of Mohd. Shujaat. Of course I had seen him with Gen. Mehmood at public functions but never from close quarters. I still barely know him, but I just don't feel comfortable with the thought of such sensitive plans being revealed to him,' explained Nazir.

'You have echoed my sentiments exactly Brigadier,' said Hussain. He then became silent, deep in thought.

There was nothing particular that had caused Brig. Nazir to say what he had a few seconds back. He was basically indignant that top-secret government and military plans had to be discussed in the presence of someone whose sole credential was the fact that he was married to the premier's daughter. His years in ISI had taught him to read people and their actions. Numerous interrogation sessions and meetings with agents of friendly countries had taught him to read simple gestures. And Shujaat's behaviour and gestures in the meeting gave Nazir the impression that the premier's son-in-law did not have any integrity. He was probably faithful to Gen. Mehmood, but only because he feared him and because he was the source of all his power. Nazir had seen many such men in his career. He regarded them as worse than even soldiers of fortune. The latter at least took money from someone and then did what they had to, but men like Shujaat were not averse to dealing and negotiating with many paymasters for the same job, and then absconding. Nazir privately called such

55

men, brokers of fortune. And to place such a man on a classified committee like the general command was akin to making an unscrupulous businessman the federal bank governor.

Brig. Nazir wondered whether Lt. Gen. Hussain was aware of how disruptive a man like Shujaat could be. That he hated Shujaat was clear but that was only because he perceived him to be unintelligent and bumptious. But Nazir had always thought that a mediocre but honest man was far more desirable than a corrupt man of modest intelligence. And men like Shujaat were dangerous because years of underhand deals and shady manoeuvres would have obviously honed his cunning.

Lt. Gen. Hussain looked up finally. 'I will see what I can do about Shujaat. Actually, I had made up my mind during the last meeting of the general command that the fool would not step into my offices or conference rooms again. There is no reason for me to tolerate him day after day even if he is Gen. Mehmood's representative. If the General wants to be kept up-to-date with events here, I will volunteer to personally brief him daily.'

9

Richard Bernested, deputy director (operations) CIA, had just finished reading the communication labeled urgent from Muscat. As he sat back in his leather chair, which he had acquired recently after his back pain became more frequent, he reflected on what he had just read. The communiqué was more in the nature of a detailed factual narration with just a few paragraphs of analysis. That was surprising, thought Bernested. Austin Lancaster, besides being a stickler for details and in depth study, was one of the best analysts the agency possessed. Personally, he thought Lancaster was being wasted in a soft posting like Muscat. His opinion was based on his brief yet fruitful association with him during his stint as station head, Prague, during the peak of the Cold War. In fact, he had even casually mentioned this to Gregory Sealfont, the director appointed recently by President Clinton. Greg had promised to look into the matter, but Bernested doubted anything could be done. In 1995, there were not enough hot seats for all those who had become heroes by their exploits during the Cold War. All postings seemed too soft to veterans of the turbulent atmosphere in the Europe of the Eighties.

Bernested thought of Kevin Meyer, chief, West Asia and the Gulf whom Austin's report would have reached first. It was Meyer who should have studied it in detail and decided whether it needed to travel up. He picked up the receiver of his intercom and spoke into it, 'Tell Mr Meyer I want to see him immediately.'

Kevin Meyer was known as the 'vulture' on the ranch. There were two opinions about his nickname in the agency. One, and in all probability the true reason, was that in the past he had identified, swooped and picked on many KGB agents ready to defect. The other reason began as a joke but was now advanced seriously as an alternative to the former—his long and curved nose. Often ribbed about it, Meyer took it in good spirits. He had played a crucial role in the 1991 Operation Desert Storm and was known to have formulated the strategy of arming the Kurds again after years of lull in their struggle for an independent country. Meyer entered Bernested's room knowing the cause for his summons. The deputy director waited for him to sit and then immediately came to the point. 'Your comments on the Muscat report, Mr Meyer.' Kevin Meyer was one of the few men in the CIA headquarters who Dick Bernested did not know personally, hence the formal greeting.

'I spoke to Mr Lancaster after the report reached me, Mr Director. To me it seemed as if he was not clear on how much time and thought he wanted us to give it. He said his men were hard at work and could have something for us in the near future. As the killing was of a royal, the Omanis are more than eager to cooperate with us.' He paused, and then continued, speaking slowly. 'There is however one point on which I do not agree with Mr Lancaster. I think they are being hasty when they attribute the killing to a Russian.'

'Why, don't you think that the weapon is adequate evidence to justify that line of thinking?' asked Bernested.

'That's where I differ with Mr Lancaster, Sir. We are all aware of the make and the country of manufacture of Sako-Triaces target pistols, but they have always been readily available to assassins and killers on hire. Besides, apart from the weapon there is not a single shard of evidence to suggest that the hitman came from the old Soviet block much less of his being a Russian.'

'So what do you suggest?' asked the deputy director of the CIA.

'We should sit tight over here and if the boys in Muscat turn up with anything, then we could follow up on it. Personally, I feel they will not be able to discover anything.'

'Any particular reason for your belief?'

'None in particular, except for the profile of the deceased. See, Sheikh Wahaidi was a modern, anti-fundamentalist, influential, and popular figure of the royal family. Such men have always been targets in the Gulf. Who knows, it could have been the monarch himself who ordered it. They get very insecure over there about their relatives climbing the popularity graphs.'

'Okay Mr Meyer,' Bernested said, rising to indicate that the meeting was over. 'We will hang on till Austin can supplement this report with something more solid. If nothing turns up, then it enters the computer banks. However, if even the slightest lead turns up, I want it to be followed diligently. I hope I make myself clear?'

'Yes Sir,' said Kevin Meyer as he got up to leave the office of the deputy director and return to his section that was overflowing with work being done on the West Asia peace process.

59

Race Course Road is now the official residence of the Indian prime minister. Never specifically picked to house the most important person in India, the sprawling, colonial-style bungalow acquired the status by chance. Indira Gandhi had worked and lived at Safdarjung Road. After her assassination in 1984, her residence became a museum. Rajiv Gandhi, who succeeded her as prime minister, was then residing with her and chose to move into 7 Race Course Road.

In 1989, when Rajiv Gandhi lost the elections, the issue of VIP security was at its peak. The Special Protection Group, the elite protection force which then used to guard only incumbent prime ministers but now, due to an Act of Parliament, guards all ex-prime ministers and their families, made an earnest plea for a permanent residence to be found for the prime minister. Rajiv Gandhi, taking the suggestion in good spirit, vacated the house and moved to 10 Janpath.

The example set by him was followed and after 1989, M. Srinivas Reddy was the third prime minister to move into 7 Race Course Road. The road had now been closed to normal traffic for years.

It was the fourth time in the past week that Rajeshwar Rao Kulkarni, the chief minister of Maharashtra, was seen entering Race Course Road. Kulkarni had flown to the capital on August 20 after being urgently summoned by the prime minister. He was surprised and secretly pleased when Reddy told him what was bothering him. His initial reaction had been to laugh over the fact that Reddy was worrying about a scenario predicted by a psephologist months before the next general elections were due. He had tried to allay Reddy's fears.

That was when Srinivas Reddy arranged another confidential meeting with Asim Banerjee where the media analyst and psephologist again went over in detail what he had already explained to the prime minister. Coming from Asim Banerjee, the prediction appeared credible. Over the last four days he and the prime minister had been locked together in discussions for hours. They tried to understand why, while Reddy was being described as one of the best prime ministers India had ever had, the Congress party wasn't seeming to benefit. After several hours of discussion, they were still at a dead end.

Their apprehensions were compounded by the person who was being projected to replace them. If they had to lose, they would be better off losing to the combine of the Left parties and the Janata Dal, the party comprising mainly ex-Congressmen. Most Congressmen had social and cordial relations with Janata Dal members but the REP was a different ballgame altogether. It was an entirely different party, a different ideology, a different movement in itself. There was another reason for Kulkarni's worries since he had arrived in the capital. On August 25, the newspapers had carried reports of a joint press conference addressed by Vijay Kapre and Siddhi Narayan, the Maharashtrawadi party chief, announcing their decision to contest the elections in Maharashtra together against the Congress. The news of the electoral alliance between the MP and the REP took him completely by surprise. Narayan had also declared that after the 1996 general elections his party would align itself with the REP in parliament. It came as a rude shock because Kulkarni had been hobnobbing with several district heads of the MP to get them to defect to the Congress. The tie-up with the REP without any discordant note being struck within the MP meant that Narayan's hold over his party was yet unchallengeable and would only grow as that party's electoral chances became brighter.

Kulkarni knew that Reddy was depending on him to provide a solution to the problems the party was facing. Over the years, he had built a formidable reputation of being a wheeler-dealer in politics. But he knew his limitations. He was no magician. Today he had reassured Reddy that the MP-REP alliance did not pose any threat to the Congress in Maharashtra. One of the reasons the prime minister had turned to him was his belief that Maharashtra would be a safe bet for the party in the coming elections. Kulkarni did not want to confess how shaky his hold over his turf was becoming and run the risk of Reddy turning to Dev Raj or Raghavan. I will definitely present him with a strategy, he thought, and its success or failure can be dealt with later. He thought of his principal trouble-shooter in state as well as national politics, Bhaskar Naik.

B.K. Naik, member of parliament, millionaire industrialist, political trouble-shooter, master of dinner diplomacy, was a Kulkarni protégé. Born into a lower middle class family in Mumbai he had spent his childhood in a *chawl* in Mumbai. At the age of eighteen, Bhaskar became assistant to a prominent city contractor. For five years he had seen the morals and ideals held in such high esteem by his parents being sold for as little as fifty rupee notes. During that time, he learnt how government contracts were won, how bureaucratic delays and red tapism could be worked to one's advantage, how a tender rejected by under, deputy, and joint secretaries got accepted by the secretary and the minister.

At the end of five years young Bhaskar became an independent contractor dealing mainly with the city's municipal corporation. There was plenty of work: new buildings were sprouting up all over the city, and with his penchant for public relations and ability to bend rules here and there he started growing in the world of real estate. He got government land at subsidised prices and after clearing it of encroachers, built high-rise lucrative apartments. In due course of time he graduated from a municipal contractor to a builder, enrolled at evening college, and began studying high finance and policy making. In his early forties, Naik was now owner of three cloth mills in Parel, the industrial hub of Mumbai, besides owning a few high rises in the affluent suburb of Bandra, and possessing an undisclosed number of blue chip shares on the Bombay Stock Exchange.

His rise—though comparable to that of big bull Harshad Mehta—had its own peculiarities. While Mehta languished in jail, Bhaskar Naik entered politics. He avoided the one mistake which Mehta had paid for dearly. Realising early in life that the surest way to alienate people and to propel them to plot your downfall was to openly flaunt your wealth, he stayed away from imported cars and lavish penthouses. He lived in a comfortable flat in Colaba, and maintained close relations with friends and acquaintances in his old neighbourhood.

While expanding his business, Naik had built social contacts with many political leaders. In 1990, Kulkarni persuaded him to contest assembly elections on a Congress ticket. Despite fleeting allegations of frauds in business and rumours of underworld connections, he won, defeating Ram Nath Sawant, an old veteran of the Maharashtrawadi party who had been winning that seat since 1977. He refused Kulkarni's offer of ministership and used the time instead to grasp the rules of politics. In 1991, when general elections became imminent after the fall of the Chandrashekhar government, he was ready. He stood for parliament from South Mumbai and won rather easily. Kulkarni had then moved to New Delhi as defence minister and it was Naik's official residence where he held his political confabulations.

When Parliament was not in session, Naik would rush back to Mumbai and ensure that Kulkarni's hold over the party did not slip or loosen. It was by his singular efforts that a few months later Jogesh Bhajan, the popular scheduled caste leader from the Maharashtrawadi party, defected to the Congress with a large number of his supporters. Years before when the Kulkarni ministry had faced a rebellion over an impending revolt by MLAs from the industrial Vidarbha region over the Cabinet's decision to reduce cotton sale prices, it was Naik again who quelled the revolt. Of course there were rumours of the means he had used. It was whispered that he had opened the coffers of the Samdex group (his flagship company) and money had been used like water. Despite the numerous allegations, his reputation as a political fixer kept growing. And now it was Naik, who, as Kulkarni's emissary, was negotiating with the few dissidents in the Maharashtrawadi Party.

Kulkarni believed that if the Congress was going to lose the elections, it was better that it should start to identify allies in other political parties—those MPs who could then be persuaded to support a Congress government in return for ministerial berths and other perks. And who better than Bhaskar Naik to identify men who could prove to be the hidden aces in the pack for the Congress. Naik was even supposed to wine and dine leaders from the REP who were known to be rabid Congress haters. The chief minister decided that he would not inform Reddy that he was consulting Naik on the issue. He did not want the PM to start dealing directly with Bhaskar. The old man is a master at turning protégés against their political gurus, thought Kulkarni. He did not want Naik to turn into another Subhash Shukla.

Subhash Shukla, the Madhya Pradesh chief minister, had till recently been one of Chandra Dev Raj's staunchest followers and indeed, owed his present position to him. That was till the time the PM started working on him. Now he had distanced himself from his mentor and had declared publicly that he had full faith in the leadership of Srinivas Reddy. It was being regarded as an impressive coup by the PM.

Currently, with Dev Raj cut down to size and relations rapidly souring between Raghavan and Reddy, Kulkarni was the only leader of stature in the party who could succeed the prime minister, so there was no telling what Reddy would do to weaken him. Kulkarni believed it would be safer not to give him a chance.

10

ISLAMABAD, AUGUST 28, 1995

It was 8 AM when a black military jeep drove into the official
residence of Lt. Gen. Ghulam Hussain. Brig. Nazir got down
from the jeep and was led by the guards at the door to the
small room that Lt. Gen. Hussain used as his office. As a
principle, he did not like meeting people at his house, but this
was an emergency.

Nazir saluted him and sat down while attempting for an
instant to gauge the nature of the information he was about
to receive. He gave up when he saw the impassive expression
on Hussain's face. 'Gen. Mehmood has accepted your
solution,' began Hussain, 'but it was difficult. It seems I had
underestimated his son-in-law. He had already given the
General a detailed briefing of the last general command
meeting, his version of course, which was convincing enough
for our premier.' Nazir noticed Hussain's sarcastic emphasis
on the last word.

Suddenly, Lt. Gen. Hussain's calm front crashed and he
exploded, his face contorted with rage and his hands moved
in small convulsive jerks as he thundered, 'That son of a bitch
Shujaat, he is going to get shot by me.' For a few seconds,

Brig. Nazir wondered what would happen if this room were bugged. During Gen. Zia's rule, the homes and offices of all his military officers, down to the rank of colonel, were wired. Not only would Lt. Gen. Hussain get into severe trouble, it could cause difficulties for him too, for listening silently to the diatribe. But then he reassured himself that, as chief of ISI, Hussain's home and offices would be swept for listening devices. He also knew that a man like Lt. Gen. Hussain would prefer to live in the wilderness than serve under such conditions.

'Do you know what the bastard did?' Lt. Gen. Hussain was saying, 'just to get back at me, he described the last K2 general command meeting, and your report in particular, in such a manner to Gen. Mehmood that made it seem as if it were the work of amateurs.'

'But surely Gen. Mehmood would not take him at his word,' said Nazir haltingly.

'No, but it made my task of convincing him of the viability of our plan more difficult. For the past one week I have spent every evening at the presidential palace presenting him with expert opinions, documents, plans and solutions envisaged by us. He did eventually give his consent, but not before his bastard son-in-law's nuisance value was proved to me.'

Brig. Nazir was disconcerted by the thought that his superior could be frustrated and angered by certain conditions that may have been imposed on him by the premier. Specially worrying was the prospect of a directive to include Mohd. Shujaat in the implementation of their plan. 'What were his main objections?' he asked, looking up at Lt. Gen. Hussain who had by now left his chair and was pacing up and down the study.

'Well, apart from what that fool who married his daughter put in his head, his objections were the expected ones...' said

Gen. Hussain, looking at Nazir as if he expected him to fill in the rest of his statement. When the Brigadier stayed quiet, he continued, 'Firstly that the Pakistani connection should not be revealed. I told him that was something you would guard against. Then he had to be told how it could be done without any participation by us, and it was then that all hell broke loose. He did not like the idea of an outsider working with us, he said that it could be dangerous later on.' Brig. Nazir stiffened uneasily at this, as he knew it must have been entirely up to Lt. Gen. Hussain to give whatever arguments he wished to Gen. Mehmood, to convince him of the suitability of using an outsider.

'I convinced him by giving an exaggerated account of how successful killers on hire have already been,' Hussain relaxed a bit as he spoke. 'After I had finished, our premier was beginning to appreciate the idea in general and your efforts in particular. I must add, Brigadier, you are doing very well. I have not had the chance to judge your work earlier.'

Brig. Nazir nodded his head and said 'Thanks' in a soft voice. Taking this opportunity, he asked Hussain something that had been bothering him for the last few minutes. 'Sir, I hope Gen. Mehmood does not expect any day-to-day monitoring of this operation? Because that is not going to be possible. These kind of men do not report on the progress they make on a regular basis.'

'He did suggest it but I anticipated what you just said and explained it to him. I told him apart from the overall framework of the operation, he should not ask for more as someday, when he has to make an official statement on it, he can speak with true conviction that we knew nothing. Of course, convincing him about the need for that bastard not to be present at regular summary meetings of the project was far more difficult, but I managed it somehow.'

As soon as Brig. Nazir heard this, he let out a silent sigh of relief. His main worry had been taken care of, though God knew how Hussain had managed it. 'Then would you be briefing him or will I be expected to do that job?' he queried.

'No, neither of us would have to do it. There was one concession that I had to make to the premier on your behalf.' At this Nazir became apprehensive again. Trying to allay his fears, Lt. Gen. Hussain said, 'Really it's not much. Gen. Mehmood wanted someone from his personal staff to be part of your team, someone who would not really participate in the operation but just be there to see its execution first hand. I made it clear that it had to be an army man.' Lt. Gen. Hussain's statement did clear Nazir's mind to an extent but did not completely lift his spirits. The possibility of having some stranger as his shadow when he was going to mount the most important operation of his career was disturbing.

'There was no choice: it was either him or Shujaat. I don't think you know him personally. His name is Col. Ashraf Abbas, and he is one of the premier's defence aides,' said Lt. Gen. Hussain. 'I know him vaguely. He has had an uneventful stint in the ISI and was moved from here to the palace a week after I joined. He is a quiet, unobtrusive sort of officer, originally from central artillery and someone who won't be in your way at all. Also, I had a two-hour session with him yesterday. He seemed fairly intelligent, someone who could at times be trusted to obfuscate information being given to the palace.'

Brig. Nazir tried to relax. He did not think anyone could be worse than the General's son-in-law. The fact that Col. Abbas was a rank junior to him would in all probability make things easier for him.

'As long as you let Col. Abbas know what is going on, you are free to do whatever you wish, of course interspersed with regular meetings with me.' That was not an unreasonable demand as Brig. Nazir was well aware that if the operation failed, fingers would point at the ISI chief. Of course, he did not want to think about what would happen to him if his operation failed. Already there were murmurs of discontent; people were saying that the officer-in-charge of Project K2 was being given too much power. In a service which was obsessed with rank and hierarchy like no other country in the world, the fact that a Brigadier was in charge of a project as crucial as K2 was not being taken to kindly.

His musings were interrupted by Lt. Gen. Hussain. 'You will be introduced to Col. Abbas tomorrow evening at my CFIO office. Another thing Brigadier, when do you begin the operation formally and how?'

Nazir thought for a minute and answered, 'Sir, from our side the most important task is going to be to find a candidate who, apart from being qualified, is going to be willing to accept the contract. Once that is done and we finish negotiating with him, he would be more or less on his own, there would be nothing we could do except wait and watch.' As an afterthought, he added, 'We could offer our partner our help, though such men prefer to work alone or with their own long-term associates, if any.'

'What would be the timeframe in which such a man would operate?'

'We will have to tell him the maximum time we have, the rest would be up to him. Usually, such men are quite sensitive to the specific needs of their clients and if told to rush on a job, are willing, though, at enhanced fees.'

'When would you require the finance?' asked Gen. Hussain.

'The funds are not needed till the man is selected. Till then, I will use the K2 accounts and the in-house ISI banks.'

'Would the money from these sources not be enough?'

'Sir, if we are looking for quality, it is going to cost us a lot of money. We would use the K2 accounts, but the payments should be untraceable and seem to come from undisclosed sources. If the funds in these accounts can be withdrawn in such a manner, then I have no problems. Anyway, we can postpone thinking about how and where the payments are to be made till we find our man. Most of these men have their own preferred methods of payment, so it will not serve any purpose drawing up plans right now.'

'Lastly, when will I hear who is going to work for us and what his plans are?'

'I will draw up a shortlist of potential candidates along with my comments and submit this list to you.'

'That will be fine... Brigadier, what is the risk factor of such a man opening his mouth to discredit us at some later stage. That is one point which Gen. Mehmood was extremely worried about too.'

'Next to nil,' Nazir said immediately. 'Doing something like this would mar his reputation as an assassin in the market forever. Men like these pride themselves on their professionalism. Also, what would he gain by being on the wrong side of the ISI?'

'Does the man we hire have to know who he is going to work for? I mean, could we not set up a small organisation or a select team as a front to negotiate and coordinate with him, as we often do for many of our operations?'

'Sir, it is next to impossible to make enquiries about them without their also making enquiries about us in turn, and make no mistake, their information networks are as good as ours. They always have a fair idea of who wants to recruit them, if not the exact identity.'

'Brigadier, do not think that I am considering this as a course of action but, just out of curiosity, what if the person we use is eliminated by us after the assignment is completed?'

Brig. Nazir looked up at Gen. Hussain and chuckled. 'Sir, I was wondering when you would ask me this.'

'So what do you think?'

'Do you know the story behind Ramon Arunayake?' asked Brig. Nazir, still smiling. 'It is recommended to everybody who thinks of employing an elite killer on contract.

'Ramon Arunayake is the Buddhist monk known all over the world as the man who killed Solomon Bandaranaike, the Sri Lankan prime minister in 1959. However, it was not Arunayake who killed Bandaranaike but a young South African, James Allan, who later served in the 5th commando under Mike Hoare and John Peters. Before Allan became recognised as a mercenary in the Congo civil war in the Sixties, he was a professional assassin. The story goes that he was recruited by the extremist cabal of army officers, leading businessmen of Colombo and the head priests of the powerful Kiptoo monastery in Sri Lanka to kill Bandaranaike. It is said that Arunayake was sent with Allan simply to witness the killing. Later, he was apprehended while Allan disappeared. Afterwards Allan survived two attempts on his life though he had left Sri Lanka soon after—the nine men who formed the cabal died in mysterious circumstances within a span of three months. The army officers were killed in a particularly gruesome manner with their throats slit and their left eyes gouged out. All those who have studied the civil war in Congo know that after 1966 the 5th commando unit killed their prisoners after gouging out their left eyes. And after 1966, the unit was headed by James Allan.'

Lt. Gen. Hussain had listened in amazement. He had, of course, heard of the legendary 5th and 6th units which spearheaded the fighting in Katanga and Stanleyville in the bloodiest wars after World War II and before Vietnam. The men in the Congo then, men like Lamouline, Denard and Hoare, had been associated with the civil war from the beginning and became famous among the fighting class internationally. That is why it was possible that he had not heard of the second generation Congo mercenaries like Allan.

Brig. Nazir said, 'Sir, I am not trying to suggest that what happened to those men could happen to me or you, but there is really no need to cause someone skilled in the art of killing to have a vendetta against us.'

'I understand,' said Gen. Hussain. 'Forget that I even mentioned it, it was totally out of curiosity.'

After Brig. Nazir left, Hussain leaned back. If the operation fails, he thought, Mohd. Shujaat will not let me remain in this chair.

11

Bhaskar Naik stretched on his bed. He had been lying for more than half an hour but sleep would not come. Finally abandoning the struggle, he opened his eyes and stared at the ceiling of his modest MP accommodation in the Western Court complex. Even after coming to the national capital, Naik had not given up his preference for modest living. There was not a hotel in town he could not afford, but Bhaskar knew that hotels and clubs were good for conducting deals but living in them only attracted negative attention. Thanks to his upbringing, Naik did not need air conditioners or coolers, even in blistering heat. But he did not like the rain. It was an unnecessary nuisance in his busy routine. It was because of the incessant rain in that city that Naik had bypassed London and set up an office in Frankfurt instead.

Another of his habits from childhood was the inability to sleep more than five hours at night. In his *chawl* he had always gone to bed around 11 PM. Since the *chawl* used to come alive after 4 AM, there was no way one could carry on sleeping after that hour. The women got up early to secure a good position in the serpentine queues in front of the common municipality taps, and the men got up to get a good seat on the local train. It seemed that Naik's body clock had permanently adjusted to these timings. It caused him some difficulty when, as a successful businessman, late nights became a necessity. With great effort he stretched himself to stay awake till 2 or 3 AM but the time when he got up in the morning never changed. He could never stay in bed after 5 AM. No alarm clock was ever needed.

Now as he lay awake his thoughts were centered around his visit to his mentor at Maharashtra Sadan, the state guest house in New Delhi. Heading there he had thought that maybe Rajeshwar *ji* wanted to discuss the fallout of the alliance between the REP and the MP. Instead, he was informed of an altogether different crisis looming over the party—one of far greater magnitude. His political guru was leaving for Mumbai the next day, but would be returning the following week for two days, for a series of meetings with the prime minister. He wanted Naik to think of ways, to retrieve the situation.

Despite his disdain for a flashy lifestyle, Naik was highly susceptible to the lure of power. He had never been addicted to wealth even at the height of his business career, yet in five years he had become addicted to politics. The more he had tried to suppress this phenomenon which initially surprised him, the stronger roots it took in him. But he had kept his ambitions a closely guarded secret, even from his mentor. Political gurus, he knew, hated ambitious followers. They wanted their followers to get positions of power but without their expressly wanting it or openly enjoying it.

He began to think about what could be done to salvage the situation. There would be atleast six months before the elections were held, perhaps even eight. Maybe something could be done to set back the chances of the REP, something which would oust it from its position as a viable alternative to the Congress. In the past, public anger against the Congress had been considerable but the Congress had got votes anyway because of the lack of alternatives. Was it possible that the same could be made to happen in 1996? He was a firm believer of the fact that it was far easier to mar electoral prospects than to boost the chances of anyone, be it an individual or a political party. Naik got up from his bed and switched on a light. Putting on his slippers, he walked to the small study table and sat down. He needed to do some thinking. He picked up his pen and a small pad so that he could jot down his thoughts if required.

It was the pain shooting through his left shoulder and neck which woke him up. He glanced at the small timepiece on the desk. It was 3.45 AM. For an instant, he wondered where he was and then he realised that he had dozed off in his chair, his head resting on the desk at an awkward angle. He got up and made his way unsteadily to the small bathroom that came with the two-room flat. Returning to the study table, he picked up the pad lying on the table and looked at it to remind himself of the direction his thoughts had been taking earlier.

Naik had managed to formulate two strategies to push the REP out of the reckoning in the coming general elections. Reflecting on them again, he picked up the pen and unconsciously slipped its top into his mouth. What was beginning to bother him was how much of his plans he could disclose to Rajeshwar who would finally be reporting to the PM. The first option could be described. The second option, however, was more dangerous, and if implemented its chances of success would be inverse to the number of people involved. After a fleeting moment, Naik made up his mind. He would discuss only the first option, which he would call Plan Alpha, with his leaders. As for Plan Beta, that would be his back-up plan and a secret for now. At this moment he was not even certain if Plan Beta would be required. One thing was clear. If he was going to implement Plan Beta, he needed specialists who would have to be extremely trustworthy as well.

Naik looked at his notepad with satisfaction. He knew that with every hour, he would keep working on his plans till there was no doubt of their viability. It was the same procedure he had often followed in sorting out corporate puzzles. From his experience, he knew that answers which often seemed inadequate, impractical and crude, were the only answers; more often than not, with increased doses of time and patience being injected into them, they turned out to be strategies later hailed as brilliant and path-breaking. He got up and went to the window. It was 4.30 AM. The sky was still grey and Janpath still quiet. With its proximity to Connaught Place, silence was a prized and rare state. Naik decided that a stroll would do him good, before the hot Delhi sun rose and overshadowed everything else. Changing into a track-suit, he got out of the flat and walked down the corridor which was quiet at that hour.

Though always an early riser, Naik hadn't turned his habit of taking a morning walk into a religion. But he always indulged himself when in Delhi. That could have had something to do with the fact that walking was a much more attractive prospect in Delhi—with its open spaces and tree-lined avenues—than it was in Mumbai. Naik always took short crisp strides without going too fast, which he did not need to, as excess weight had never been a problem with him. No matter what or how much he ate, it never got converted into fat. For this he had always received compliments and envious glares from corporate acquaintances, most of whom developed paunches the day they crossed thirty. He also liked to think when he walked and did not want his energy depleted on body movements.

77

As he began his walk around the central park of Connaught Place, he was again filled with a sense of marvel for Delhi's most famous shopping landmark. Over the years its splendour had declined, but it was still grandiose enough to dazzle. He always experimented with different routes on his morning walks in Delhi, but this particular one straight down Connaught Place and back was among his favourites. At his leisurely pace it took him just over an hour to make it back to Western Court. It was 5.45 AM when he reached his flat, the delay being caused by the unscheduled stop he made at the central park to watch the pigeons.

Once back home, he focused hard on what he had been thinking. He knew that before he discussed anything with Rajeshwar *ji*, more than a bare outline would be required. He tried to prepare a routine for himself for the day. At 8 AM the Contessa would arrive to be at his service for the day. Once upon a time, he had rented cars when staying in the capital but that ended after an old friend volunteered, rather insisted, that he use one of his cars. The friend was Prakash Mittal, owner of Prakash Communications and one of Naik's best friends in his business circle. The thread that bound them together was that both were self-made men who had risen from extremely modest circumstances and had carved a niche for themselves in their chosen careers. Also, their methods had been questionable and both loved to hobnob in politics and to wine and dine the men who mattered. From being a middleman between the telecommunications department and private firms, Mittal had grown to be the president of the company which had come to be identified with dish antennas, now becoming a common feature in the country.

Naik had full intentions of including Mittal in his plans with or without Kulkarni's approval. Not only would his contacts in Delhi be crucial but he would also need the excess

78

cash that his friend had in plenty. In fact, at times he suspected that Mittal had separate accounts for payoffs, or what he called 'policy finance'. Prakash always maintained that the most powerful crutch on which industry rested was political policy made in its favour. Whoever could manufacture or restructure policy in his favour would reap the profits later attributed to financial foresight and market analysis. Naik completely endorsed his views as he himself had walked the same path in his early years, and knew that everyday men became wealthy by gaining one single contract or one overpriced tender, all because they could change the minds of the men who occupied positions entrusted with making those decisions. Despite the licence-permit quota *raj* being officially dismantled, he was aware that its momentum would stretch for at least another decade, if not more.

12

ISLAMABAD, SEPTEMBER 4, 1995

It was going to be the third time that Brig. Nazir would be meeting Col. Ashraf Abbas. In his previous two meetings, he had had to brief Abbas so as to familiarise him with the background of the operation to be launched. Col. Abbas had listened with patience, not betraying any emotion. Like most military men occupying posts of any importance, he had heard of the CFIO and Project K2, but it was the first time that he was being made privy to the functioning of the cell. The derivation of that project's name, K2, was not mysterious in the least. The double usage of the letter K signified 'Khalistan-Kashmir', the focal point of any plan to destabilise India. Abbas knew that one of the prongs on which the project had been conceived was all but ineffectual. The Punjab police, along with the resilient populace of that state, had blown to smithereens the Pakistani dream of carving out an independent state from India à la Bangladesh. He was conscious that the same result in Kashmir could sound the death-knell of military dominance in Pakistan. The truth was that the ISI needed India for its survival, more than Pakistan itself needed the ISI.

India was the lifeblood of the Inter Services Intelligence. It was on India's name that huge amounts of money were siphoned off from the treasury to undisclosed destinations. The bulk of the ISI staff worked on India directly or on mini projects connected to it. K2 was an enormous project both in terms of manpower and resources, and apart from the main project, there were several sub-projects. Hundreds of men worked day and night to compile reports on India; some were necessary, others would end up being shredded to pieces or consigned to the ISI vaults never to see light again. Research had been done on topics as diverse as the districts most susceptible to floods and which part of India would be most suitable to airdropping of propaganda leaflets. There was no telling how many hours had been spent on strategies which would make it feasible to blame every crisis on RAW, the Indian external intelligence service founded before the Bangladesh war. Not that its efforts were bearing any fruit. Despite repeated attempts to place the crisis in Sind on RAW's doorstep, not many people in Pakistan found that theory credible. Official statements alleging that the Mohajir political leaders were Indian agents had further angered the local populace of Sind and Karachi.

The vast and unaccounted sums of money had also not always reached their supposed destinations. The scandal in which Brig. Ilahi Bux Sumroo, the officer in charge of Project K2 in the Eighties, was stripped of his rank and imprisoned after a secret court martial had rocked the ISI in 1985. That was when the Khalistan movement was passing through its most active period and India was just beginning to get troubled by Kashmir. The allegations of misappropriation of funds meant for Gurbachan Singh Manochahal and Dr Sohan Singh, the self-styled chiefs of the two dreaded Panthic committees, by a disgruntled staff member of Brig. Sumroo had snowballed into one of the biggest and ugliest controversies in the army. Not only civilians, but even the military had witnessed protests and demands to make the working of the ISI more transparent. That the officer involved headed an extremely sensitive project had contributed to the uproar. Brig. Sumroo had not been heard of since then. There were rumours, not without some foundation, that he had been executed shortly after the beginning of his incarceration.

India was the source of the unlimited powers of the ISI. Hostilities between the two countries suited the ISI the most, as peaceful coexistence would necessarily involve a considerable pruning of the freedom given to the ISI.

Col. Ashraf Abbas had had a fairly satisfying career till the day he was commanded by Gen. Mehmood to be the liaison officer between him and Brig. Nazir and report on the progress of an operation which could tilt the precarious balance of power in the subcontinent. His days at the ISI had been quiet, with him working as a station officer dealing with the Pakistan artillery and compiling reports on India's strength in that field. He had been assigned to be on the staff of the General recently, when the premier had asked the ISI to get him a quiet, low profile yet diligent and active aide, familiar with the working of the ISI. Lt. Gen. Irfanullah Khaliq, the director general of the ISI before Hussain, had searched sincerely from among the officers available to him and recommended Col. Abbas to the premier. That had been a month before he was unceremoniously dumped as chief of ISI.

To the credit of Gen. Mehmood, he had not let his personal antipathy for Gen. Khaliq to cloud his vision in viewing his proposals. After a few preliminary investigations revealed that Col. Abbas did not owe any personal loyalty to Khaliq, he was moved from the ISI to the Presidential Palace which was part of the price which President Alam Khan had

had to pay to salvage his position as nominal head of Pakistan. Tipped in time by his aides that he would be ordered by the premier to vacate the palace for him, Alam Khan had tried to maintain whatever little dignity was left to him. He had preempted the move and voluntarily offered the palace to Gen. Mehmood who accepted his offer without a second thought. In addition to being a great architectural marvel, the palace in new Islamabad was also equipped with the most advanced equipment for communications and tools of surveillance. The small communications centre in the palace was modelled after Cheltenham, the legendary British communications and listening post. Despite the fact that it had not housed the president for more than two years, the palace was still called the Presidential Palace.

'Col. Abbas, I hope you now possess all the data needed to bring you up to date with this operation.' Col. Abbas looked at Brig. Nazir and nodded quietly. Brig. Nazir continued, 'I want to let you know Colonel, that once you have become part of this operation, you will be expected to contribute with your suggestions and views. I would much prefer it that way to you being only a passive spectator.' Brig. Nazir stressed on the last sentence as people often do to sound convincing about something they don't mean. Contrary to what he was saying, Nazir wanted no interference from any man associated with the palace. He would be satisfied if the Colonel remained unobtrusive.

'Thank you, Sir, I will try my level best to assist you in this operation in whatever way I can. It is my good fortune that I am getting an opportunity to work with an officer as distinguished as you, Brigadier.'

Ah! Even military men have learnt the art of flattery, thought Nazir. He hated flatterers and yes-men. He wondered whether Abbas had perfected the art while serving Gen.

83

Mehmood. Whatever it was, it was better than the Colonel sitting and nodding without saying a word. In his two earlier briefings, Abbas had hardly uttered a word, even to clarify or to press for details. His long flashes of silence had begun to puzzle Nazir. Though he disliked flatterers and people who spoke out of turn and unnecessarily, he had always encouraged his team members to be frank and forthright with him.

'As of now, there is hardly anything to report which would interest the premier. The operation is at its earliest stage,' said Nazir. Just as he was going to rise in dismissal, Col. Abbas spoke up, surprising him. 'Has the search begun?'

'Well theoretically, yes. Our agents have been out on alert. They will let us know if anything of interest comes up.'

'But Sir, does that mean the entire ISI workforce will know of this operation?'

'Obviously not,' snapped Nazir, a trifle annoyed because of the nature of the question.

By now, he had gauged that the premier would probably get his first report that day. He would have liked to reveal as little as possible because he knew any information the General got would be passed on to his son-in-law. However, that would be next to impossible. The chief of the ISI had told him clearly not to hide anything from Col. Abbas. If Col. Abbas was not provided with an accurate progress report, it would lead to Lt. Gen. Hussain being summoned by the premier, and if that happened, the entire operation could be in jeopardy. So he would have to put up with the Colonel and hope that he wouldn't get too demanding.

'You see Colonel, what happens in these kind of operations is called networking. Once you let the field agents know what they have to look out for, they work out the basic purpose behind it. But before any concrete idea takes shape in their minds, we spread the word through one of the field men that although the basic purpose is a hit, as they have already guessed, it is not going to be commissioned by the parent organisation. It could be that we are brokering a deal with one of our allies or it could be a routine data gathering exercise. These men are kept under watch for any suspicious activity or to check any loose cannon but that need seldom arises, for the cover-up gossip originates from one of the field men and it is believed readily and spreads fast. That leaves the irregulars and the part-timers. The danger from them is even less as they are approached by intermediaries. They can never figure out that the information or reports they are providing are meant for the ISI.' Brig. Nazir paused and then added in a somewhat hurt tone, 'There, I hope that allays your fears.'

'I am sorry Sir, it was never my intention to question your competence, but it is part of my job to anticipate and have the answer for questions that will most probably be fired at me by the premier.'

After Col. Abbas had left, Nazir wondered whether Abbas was really as ignorant as he was making himself out to be. After all, he had done a stint in the ISI. How could he be unaware of basic strategies and plans? It was hardly a secret that since the days of Gen. Zia, the ISI had been arranging professional hit men for friendly countries as well as private parties. He made a mental note to call for Abbas's service file to check what exactly the man had been doing in the intelligence service. He pressed the intercom switch that connected him to Maj. Azir Tariq, his most trusted team member.

13

LANGLEY, VIRGINIA, SEPTEMBER 5

Kevin 'vulture' Meyer was in an extremely agitated state of mind. The cause of his headache was the events of the last twenty-four hours. It was not that the pressures were finally beginning to get to him, as they often did to most middle-aged agency men at some stage or the other. The problem was that Meyer had always been a field man. The constant reading of reports and formulating of theoretical strategies were getting to him. He was at a loss to understand why the agency had to study files on subjects that he thought belonged rightfully to the civil servants of the state department.

After spending harrowing hours at his desk last night over the crisis in Iraq, early in the morning a report had reached him from West Asia. It was from Oman and from the office of Austin Lancaster. It had been exactly a week since the events in Oman and the meeting with Dick Bernested. He had wished fervently that Austin had not found any leads on the Al-Wahaidi killing because he was under orders from the DD operations to follow up the case, even if anything insignificant turned up. His prayers were not answered, as the report contained accounts of a few seemingly innocuous leads that had turned up.

86

Meyer knew that if the contents of this report were divulged to the DD operations, he would have to divert some resources to this case. He was torn between passing on the report to Richard Bernested and having to waste time on an insignificant killing in Oman, and devoting his attentions to Iraq where things were beginning to get serious. After endless cups of black coffee, he made his decision. For the moment he would sit on the report; after all it was his prerogative to decide which reports should reach chief of operations. Also, according to him, the idea of investigating how many foreign citizens had left Muscat within twenty-four hours of the killing of Al-Wahaidi was totally impractical and ridiculous.

CAMDEN, NEW JERSEY

For the umpteenth time, Bobby Joe Carter's thoughts drifted to his surrogate son. Carter had found himself thinking a lot about his best disciple since the last fortnight. It had been more than fifteen days since he had read of the killing in Muscat.

Thinking about his son made him reminisce about the days on the ranch. His two favourite students had revered him like a father. And then there was the Basque boy. The three had been good friends. Carter wondered where the two were and what they were doing. He was quite positive that the German would be with his son, aiding him in whatever he was doing. And he was beginning to get a fair idea of what his son was doing.

As for the Basque boy, he had to be somewhere in Spain, taking part in the struggle for which he had learnt his skills. Emilio Salinas was the son of Francisco Salinas, the chief of the ETA, the Basque outlawed nationalist organisation. Young Emilio had been sent to the US by his father to pick up the nuances of modern warfare, so he could later put them to good use in liberating the Basque homeland. Francisco Salinas knew that mere zeal and a desire for freedom were not enough to take on the might of the Spanish army. During World War II, both Salinas and Carter had participated as youngsters in the French resistance movement. So, when Francisco's son came of age, he thought of Bobby Joe, who he felt would be a better teacher than he. A few enquiries had revealed that Carter had moved to Alabama, where young Emilio had been sent.

Francisco Salinas had died in an ambush set up on one of the Basque hideouts two years after Emilio's return to Spain. From then onwards nothing had been heard of Emilio. Bobby Carter had visited Spain for a small project in Madrid in 1987 and had been told that the ETA had remained headless after his friend's death two years before. That had worried him. He feared Emilio Salinas may have lost his life too. Much later he was told that the ETA, though not as active as it used to be in the Eighties, was now being led by a man known as Julio Lopez.

Though not certain of it, Carter suspected that Julio Lopez was an alias being used by Emilio Salinas. From a Spanish contact who had once seen Lopez, he knew that Lopez was around the same age as Emilio Salinas. He wondered whether his son and the Basque were in touch. Probably not. It would be difficult, keeping in mind the fields they had chosen for themselves. Carter smiled to himself. Here he was, a 'soldier of fortune', supposedly cold and unemotional, thinking and missing those who had been his associates for only three or four years.

NASSAU, BAHAMAS

Susan Karras stood outside her condo, adjusting her field glasses, trying to make out the form of her husband who was riding the waves in a catamaran.

The small boat that rivalled for her husband's attention was within 100 yards of the shoreline when the wind abruptly shifted. She watched as her husband manoeuvred to control the dangerously swerving boat. She would have panicked had she not already seen this scene several times. She saw him fight and win against the wind everyday, sometimes twice a day. She watched him expertly lead the boat into the dock and then turned to check her dinner preparations.

Radley Karras, fifty-one and a retired commander of the US naval intelligence, smiled as he walked up to greet Susan, his wife of twenty years. 'You navy men, you can never get over the sea, can you?' mocked Susan.

'No way, it's the only thing apart from you that I could die for,' replied her husband. 'I saw you from a distance and wondered if anything was wrong.'

'Nothing, except for this fax massage from Islamabad. They never leave you alone, do they?' Radley knew that his wife was only pretending to be angry with him. He was aware of how proud she had always been of his work. He looked at the fax knowing it could only be from one person—Brig. Qayyam Nazir of the ISI. Nazir was an old friend of his. They had first met over a decade back in Afghanistan where the seeds of their friendship had been sowed. Nazir had often consulted him in the last five years after Karras took premature voluntary retirement. He wondered what had stumped Nazir this time. The fax merely mentioned that a package would soon be delivered to Radley and that it would have the details of a problem warranting advice.

As Susan watched her husband read the message and the subsequent deepening of creases on his intelligent face, she hoped that it would not be something requiring a lot of his time. After leaving naval intelligence Karras had not thought that he would be so busy. Though not in need of money, he could never say no to friends from other services in the world. His friends included highly placed people in the Mossad, ISI, MI-6, the Deuxieme Bureau and other such services allied to the CIA and NI. Susan had thought that she would be able to make up all the lost time of the previous years but that had turned out to be a futile hope. Though often disappointed, she never pestered or nagged her husband. To contend with his work for his time and attention had become a habit for her. It was something she had known she would have to do when she married him.

Though always proud of his skills, when young she had often exploded into fiery bursts of temper when separated from him. Now she rarely, if ever, lost her cool. And Radley tried to avoid taking on assignments that would take him away from his wife. When a trip became unavoidable, he would just smile sheepishly and seek her permission. She had learnt to let him go and always bore the separation with great fortitude. Once when he had gone to South America for two months, it had become too much for her and she had flown to be with their only son Jeff who was majoring in history at Chapel Hill, North Carolina. Deep down, Susan had been extremely disappointed that Jeffrey, nineteen, was academically inclined and would be taking up a sedate job as college professor. That night as she got ready for bed, the wife of one of the best intelligence officers of the US wondered what the consequences of the fax her husband had received would be. She knew that the answer would be revealed only when the promised package arrived for him. She was also aware that whatever it was, she would never find out. Susan had never asked her husband anything about his work. Whatever she had ever known was volunteered by Radley himself. He had told her that relations between the US and Islamic regimes like Pakistan had deteriorated substantially since the World Trade

Centre bombing. It was a general cooling off that was in no way connected to the fact that Pakistan was not ostensibly involved in any manner. She wondered whether the package would come through Harry Dubois, the postman who was their link with Jeff and the outside world, or, as had often happened in the past, by special courier.

14

Darkness had already fallen when Arif Rabbani left the Triple Oaks. Taking out his BMW convertible from the underground car park, he drove northwards to a flat he had been to many times. The lights were off when he got there, and there was no answer to the doorbell. Rabbani hoped the man was not out of town, but this was confirmed by the woman in the basement flat. He decided to come back in the morning. He was a bit irritated as he headed back to 42 Sloane Street, to the headquarters of the firm that belonged to his organisation and from which he had received an urgent summons while he had been drinking and gambling at the Oaks.

At thirty-five, Rabbani was quite satisfied with the way his life had turned out so far. He was half Afghan—Pushtoon to be accurate—and half Pakistani. Thirty years ago, in 1965, his father Dara-ul-Rabbani, disgusted with his hand to mouth existence in Peshawar, had taken a loan from his clansmen and migrated to England. Rabbani Sr. was a trained carpenter and mason who continued to struggle in London's East End. He had died when his son was still in high school. Slowly, young Arif had graduated from leading the neighbourhood Indian and

Pakistani boys of South Hall against English skinheads to being a part of armed robber gangs. Today, he was a respectable member of one of the prominent factions of the London underworld. He dealt in everything, from getting firms swindled to arranging assaults on professional rivals. Occasionally, he was also consulted by Maj. Mushtaq Chaudhary, the ISI liaison man in London who handled most of the information flow from western Europe.

Over the years, Rabbani had acquired a veneer of respectability. He was the sort to be found by the score in the smartest and smoothest gambling clubs of Europe with the difference that he was intelligent and had cultivated the manner of a high-level executive. He also introduced himself as chief aide to the owner of 'Sloane Securities', which though registered on the London Stock Exchange, was one of the many front companies of Roxton Miller, the undisputed boss of the London underworld. His earnings as an aide and hatchet man of Miller were enough to provide for the three-room flat, the BMW, as well as the girls.

The long drive from Maj. Chaudhary's flat to Sloane Street cooled him and he began to look forward to his meeting with him. He knew that Chaudhary would, in all probability, want information and that only meant money, maybe a lot of it for him.

The next morning Rabbani rang the bell next to Mushtaq Chaudhary's name and after a gap of about three minutes, a voice shouted 'Yes?' from behind the closed door.

'It's me,' Rabbani replied, 'Arif.'

The door opened and he ascended to the fourth floor. He greeted the Major warmly, following him to the sitting room. Once seated, he asked, 'What's with the new security consciousness?'

'Well, nothing really,' replied the Major. 'Just these RAW men keep trying to bait us whenever given a chance.'

His answer amused Arif; even in England, Pakistan's obsession with India was as strong as ever. 'I came yesterday too, but you were not there. What is it that you want?'

His coming straight to the point did not surprise Chaudhary at all. 'See, it's about a rebel group we are sponsoring in a middle-eastern state.' Arif Rabbani nodded his head in a non-commital way. 'We have helped this group for a long time and now there are rumours of a rival faction planning a coup to unseat the head of the state. That could be critical for us. If there has to be a coup, it must be led by our faction.'

'So what is the problem? Tell your group to go ahead and beat their rivals to it.'

'No, it's not that simple,' continued Chaudhary. 'Why do you think none of the rebel factions have attempted a coup so far? It's because this leader has almost impregnable security and for a coup to succeed, it would be necessary for the plotters to assassinate him first. If he remains alive, the coup would surely fail and all rebels would face execution. You know that given today's circumstances, it is out of the question to send one of our men for this assassination.'

'So?' Rabbani was getting the feeling that Chaudhary's story was a bit rehearsed.

'So the problem is we are seeking a man who can go to a hostile state and at least lead our rebels to the head of this state, if not complete the assassination himself.'

'What makes you think I could lead you to such a man?' asked Rabbani. He was not a bit convinced of the veracity of Maj. Chaudhary's story. It was more like Pakistan was directly interested is getting some political figure somewhere in the world eliminated; but he knew better than to voice his doubts.

'I am aware that London and Paris—even after the end of the Cold War—are home to such men or their contacts.'

94

What Mushtaq Chaudhary had said was quite correct. Such information did exist in London, and where better to tap it than from the underworld? 'When do you want this information?' asked Arif.

'As early as possible,' replied Chaudhary, aware that it would cost him extra money.

'I'll take one or two days. Can you wait?' On Chaudhary's assent he continued, 'How good should this man be? These days being a contract killer is as common as being a doctor or an engineer.'

'He has to be the very best, at the top in his field of work.'

'But such men are very expensive, why do you want to spend that much money for a middle-eastern state where you don't even have a direct interest?'

'The money is our headache, not yours, you just get me information about the best men. It's not my idea you see, even I follow orders,' snapped Maj. Chaudhary.

After Rabbani had left, promising to get back within forty-eight hours, Chaudhary started thinking. He had realised that his story had not convinced Rabbani. He himself was aware that the version presented to him by Islamabad was a sham. And he knew Arif was a crook, a seasoned one at that. It had been four days since the brief had come from Islamabad, marked urgent and to be given top priority. He had checked up with his counterpart in Paris, who confirmed the arrival of a similar brief in his embassy. Neither of them were fools. An important operation could only mean India.

Chaudhary was well aware that he would now be kept under watch and his activities monitored. Those would be signals enough that a major operation was to be launched in the near future.

It was a full two days before Arif Rabbani got back to Maj. Chaudhary. This time they met at a flat in Mayfair belonging

95

to a friend of Rabbani. It was Chaudhary's idea to change the venue. To Rabbani, he gave the usual excuse of RAW men on his tail. He knew that Rabbani would not understand why the ISI would watch one of its own trusted officers. Rabbani's world was different—it functioned mostly on faith.

Rabbani had four men on his list. Two were South African. They were men who had joined up as mercenaries in the early Seventies when there was still war to be found in many African and Asian countries. They had been trained by the famous James Allan.

'Aren't there any contract killers who started out as contract killers?' asked Chaudhary.

'No, that does not usually happen. Only mercenaries or renegade intelligence men take up the profession of hired killing. It's a very specialised job and requires a level of courage that you and I may never have. Such qualities get honed only in regular combat.

'Take for instance the third man I am going to tell you about—an Englishman and an ex-commando of Special Air Services. Instances of elite commando men taking to contract killing are quite frequent. In fact, we have often engaged such men to kill our rivals.'

'What kind of success has he had?' asked Chaudhary.

'Here, these are supposed to be his hits,' Rabbani said, picking up his folder and drawing out some photographs which he pushed across the table to Chaudhary.

After a few minutes Chaudhary returned the photographs to Rabbani looking sufficiently impressed. The snaps had included those of a European high-ranking diplomat in the UN, the deputy chief of the NATO forces in Belgium and a prominent industrialist based in Paris. 'His record is very impressive but we would prefer someone who has had a portion of his success in the Third World, specifically Asia.'

Arif had anticipated this so he had saved up what he thought was the most interesting option for the end. As he began talking of the fourth man, he could see Chaudhary's head moving rapidly in approval.

'Do you really have no idea of his nationality?' he asked.

'No, what happens with these men is that they possess passports and official documents of several nations. In reality, they could be citizens of some third country. For example, in the case of the first two men, they may not be from South Africa at all, but since it is indicated that their early years were spent there, we reckon that they must be South Africans.' He paused, glad that Chaudhary was finally showing signs of real interest.

'However,' he continued, 'in this case, I could not turn up anything to relate him to a particular country. Some contacts revealed that he may be European, while others indicated him to be an Arab. Most likely he is neither. There is another thing you should know.' Chaudhary craned his neck forward. 'It was the hardest to obtain information about this man, and whoever spoke about him did so with great deference. I am not trying to detract from the ability of the other three men I told you about but this itself should tell you something about his reputation.'

Had it been any other person dealing with him, Chaudhary would have thought that such lavish praise being heaped on one person could mean that Rabbani was acting as his agent for a commission. But his past dalliances with him had taught him that howsoever unscrupulous he might be, when it came to jobs done for a price, he was extremely reliable. So he could rest assured that Rabbani was only telling him what he himself believed.

'I am very impressed with your work. Now I want you to do something more. I want whatever you have just told me in writing, and I want you to do it yourself. It would be better if it is in the form of a small brief or report that has to be read by someone who has not heard whatever you have just told me. I will pay you extra for it.'

After the meeting, Chaudhary took a taxi back to his flat. He had spent 10,000 pounds so far on Rabbani and would pay him another 2,000 when he got the written report. Not for a minute did he think that Rabbani was charging too much, rather he was flush with the excitement of hitting upon the right man. From his perspective the decision to deal with Rabbani had been totally sound. As soon as he got the report from him the next morning, he would arrange for it to be sent to Islamabad, or he may even be asked to bring it over personally. The chances of that happening though were slim. But if his report pleased the top brass in Pakistan, as he was certain it would, he was bound to be called to Islamabad. Chaudhary was comfortable in London, yet always welcomed a short trip to his homeland. It made his chest swell a little more with pride.

15

'Really there was no need to inform me of these preliminary developments. You could have come to me after the summaries had been prepared.' It was not that Lt. Gen. Hussain had not taken kindly to an urgent session requested by Brig. Nazir, but he believed in absolute delegation of work.

'That is exactly why I requested this meeting,' replied Nazir. 'If what has turned up is true, we won't need to search any further.'

'First of all, I want you to evaluate the sector from which this information has arrived. Who is the officer?'

'It came from our man in London, a Maj. Chaudhary not known to me personally but an old contact of one of my deputies, Maj. Tariq Azim, who has told me a lot about Maj. Chaudhary. It seems that he has been in London for quite some time and has been doing quite well. He had played quite an important role in arranging our meetings with Anton Balasingham, the LTTE ideologue two years ago.'

'From where did he turn up this report?'

'He acquired it from an independent source on payment, but one who would not be aware at all of the purpose behind the requisitioning of this information.'

99

'Have any other sectors turned up probables?'

'There have been some reports filed from eastern Europe, most likely to be ex-KGB men, and a few from the ASEAN region.'

'But you are obviously interested in what this Maj. Chaudhary has sent from London.'

'Yes. He has talked of four men but has added his own comments on one of them. And from whatever little could be learnt from it, there does seem to be a distinct chance that this man may be exactly what we want. He has also asked for our permission to make a few more enquiries about this man. Let me add, what caught my eye was the fact that this man has done most of his work in Asia.'

'What about the men from the ASEAN countries? Have you checked them out?'

'Only made basic enquiries. These men belong mostly to the region of the Golden Triangle and it's my guess that they have generally worked for drug lords; that wouldn't suit us at all as our operation requires more skill than what local drug-wars call for. As we have seen in Afghanistan, half of them are addicts themselves.'

'Okay, go ahead with this man, but keep your other channels open too so we have alternatives. As soon as something definite comes up, you can summon Maj. Chaudhary here and we will discuss it with him before we approach this man.' With that Lt. Gen. Hussain got up from his chair.

When he had arrived at his residence, Nazir had been informed that the General was expected for an important meeting at the palace shortly. From their men assigned to President Alam Khan, he had heard that the president also had an evening appointment at the palace. Brig. Nazir was sure that Gen. Mehmood was going to discuss the strike called jointly by the PPP and Nusrut Beg's parties, which was expected to paralyse the country completely.

He made his way to his office in the CFIO headquarters and immediately called for his chief aide Maj. Azim Tariq. As Tariq made his way to the office, Nazir suddenly recalled something and groaned in misery. He remembered that now he would have to report whatever progress had been made to Col. Abbas. 'I want you to send a message to Maj. Chaudhary in London immediately, it should be green-lighted,' he told Azim. Green lighting meant that Maj. Chaudhary was being given the go ahead signal but with orders to speed it up and to exercise even more caution that he would be expected to ordinarily. 'Also, I had directed you to produce Col. Abbas' service files—why have I not received them till now? I don't want to divulge any fresh information to him till I know more about him.'

Azim Tariq shrugged helplessly. 'I had relayed your orders immediately to personnel, but there are going to be problems in getting his service files.' At this, Nazir looked surprised so Tariq went on, 'First of all, he was, or is, on the staff of the premier and all army officers deputed to the palace have their file transferred to a different section in personnel department. Secondly, we want to obtain his record without a written endorsement by Lt. Gen. Hussain.' That was true, as Lt. Gen. Hussain would probably regard such a request as an unnecessary attempt to irritate the premier. 'But rest assured, I will get you his service record soon, only it will take some more time, as some rules will have to be bent.'

'I don't care how many laws you break or rules you bend, I want to check out his background. Go and burgle the palace if you have to,' bellowed Brig. Nazir.

'Yes Sir. You will get what you want before next weekend.'

NASSAU, BAHAMAS

Radley Karras knew that his wife's garrulous behaviour over the last two days was a sham. He knew that despite his assurances, she was still skeptical of his forthcoming trip. It had been four days since the arrival of the package mentioned by Brig. Nazir. Even though he had been expecting that his help would be asked for, the package had confounded him. This was the first time that Nazir had revealed the blueprint of an entire operation to Karras. Karras's presence in Islamabad would be required for a few days as well. He had never been asked to help with something as critical as this.

He wondered if Nazir had taken clearance from his superiors to divulge details and to ask for his help or was proceeding on his own accord. He sensed that it was the latter. Anybody else would have been surprised to hear what Nazir had told him. In a way it had surprised him too. Absolute trust was implicit in the dealings between Nazir and Karras. Till recently, Karras had received invaluable tips from Nazir which had helped the US in thwarting many a terrorist strike. A few years ago it had been due to Nazir's cooperation that the CIA had managed to locate the Lockerbie bombing suspects in Libya. Over the years, Nazir had built up contacts with most of the Islamic fundamentalist organisations active in the world. The one common thread that ran through all of them—be it the Allah Doves of Oman or the Hezbollah of Palestine—was a deep-rooted hatred for America. These men were always on the lookout for an opportunity to injure America in whatever way they could. Thanks to the network, the ISI, and Nazir in particular, the US had been able to preempt many attacks.

It was known in New Delhi that one reason why the US could not alienate Pakistan entirely was that Pakistan was a bridge between the US and the more hostile Islamic nations. But to what level the cooperation between the intelligence men of the two countries extended was not clear, so the Americans could not go beyond mild criticism of Pakistan even in the face of mounting evidence of their involvement in terrorist activities in India.

From what Radley could make out, Nazir wanted him to help choose a man for a particular operation. He was not aware what method he was expected to use. Normally, all of Nazir's messages were perspicuous. To gain any more insight, it was clear that he would have to go to Pakistan. He was relieved that it was not something which would put him in a bind. In this case he knew that the operation being planned by the Pakistanis would in no way adversely affect his nation. It might indeed work to his country's advantage. He would have to pull in a lot of his contacts if he was going to be of any use to Nazir. His mind was made up about one thing. He was not going to stay away from his wife for more than a week or at the most, ten days. Nazir would have to make best use of his presence during that period. He turned towards Susan. 'I will have to go to Pakistan for a few days soon.'

'I had already realised as much. When, and for how many days?' Her tone was resigned.

'I don't know when I have to leave yet, but I won't be gone for long.'

'I guess it's futile to ask if I could come along?'

'You could, but I would prefer that you don't.' His answer was as politely voiced as her question. He knew she would not press him for more details. She had never been the pestering kind, even in his days of active service.

LONDON, SEPTEMBER 14

Despite Rabbani's repeated assurances, Chaudhary looked uncomfortable. That morning the reply had reached him. Not only had Islamabad approved and lauded his efforts, the communication had been green-lighted. They were giving him the go-ahead to investigate the fourth man. Immediately after that, Chaudhary had tried to get in touch with Rabbani.

Islamabad had made it clear that before they seriously considered him, they needed more than a bare outline about him.

It had taken Chaudhary almost half a day to contact Rabbani. What he had in mind was a small private meeting at either his or Rabbani's flat. That had not gone down well with Rabbani who had insisted that they meet at a restaurant. Rabbani had booked a table at the Baker and Oven in Wembley and the meal was the kind he had learnt to enjoy—enormous portions of English roast and vegetables, washed down with two bottles of champagne. Rabbani had insisted on the champagne as he had wanted a celebration. He had apparently executed a job flawlessly and had been praised and lavishly rewarded by his boss, Miller. He was in good spirits.

What had been bothering his guest was that the restaurant was packed, and worse, a lot of the customers seemed to know Rabbani. Some of them were Asians which had disconcerted him more. Coupled with this was the knowledge that he himself was being watched. He had wondered how Rabbani would explain his socialising with an important official of the Pakistan High Commission. He suspected that Rabbani had called him there to impress his friends and co-workers. He voiced his concern after a while to Rabbani who, with his customary nonchalance, tried to get him to relax. He urged him to concentrate on the food instead. Another reason for Rabbani's good mood, Chaudhary thought, could be that he had realised that his work had pleased the ISI and more work commissioned by Maj. Chaudhary could only mean more money. Working for Chaudhary also satisfied his patriotic urges. Since the time the Soviets had invaded Afghanistan, Rabbani had looked upon Pakistan as his country. The fact that before Rabbani Sr. had migrated to England he had been a resident of Peshawar, added to that feeling.

Chaudhary had made it known to him that he was only interested in the fourth man, and that they would need more details on him. 'What we require now is anything you can find out about this man and how he can be recruited. I trust you have the means to get me that information?'

'I don't know, I will definitely try, but in these matters, as you probe deeper, it becomes more and more difficult...'

'...But you will manage, I know,' interjected Chaudhary in an attempt to boost Rabbani's ego.

'I trust I will. People eventually cough up information but their price keeps rising.'

'Don't bother about the money, you can bill the tongue-loosening charges to me.'

'Of course, but there's another thing that has to be kept in mind.'

'What's that?'

'I will have to beef up my security. I don't want any professional killer chasing me or asking too many questions.'

'And that obviously warrants more money doesn't it?'

At this, Rabbani grinned sheepishly. Chaudhary had guessed that, secure with the fact that his client's needs were urgent, Rabbani would certainly play some games. But he was in no mood to bargain with him. So far he had paid him 12,000 pounds and was willing to pay whatever was asked. It was not his own money, he was drawing it from the designated service account at the embassy.

After assuring Rabbani of unlimited funds and eliciting a promise that he would contact him at the earliest, Chaudhary made his way to his flat in north London. He was beginning to get the feeling that he would soon be part of a large plan, one that could change his destiny along with the nation's. Because of this his irritation at the blatant display of greed by Rabbani evaporated, and he went to sleep almost immediately.

16

The three men standing on the banks of the Rio Tormes gazed quietly at the smoke that was rising over the town of Salamanca. 'I feel quite sad that we had to do this,' said the man called Miguel Sierra.

'It did not gladden me either. Remember I studied in that place for a while,' replied Salvatore Carillo.

They both then turned to the third man, their leader. He had a faraway look in his eyes. Carillo addressed him. 'Eh Julio, you never told us which university you went to.'

'My university, yes I did go to a university, but my education was different from yours as my college excelled in a particular subject.'

'What was that?' pressed Sierra, who had done an honours course in fine arts.

'Forget it,' replied Julio. 'What matters today is that we are in the same place and doing the same things with the same tools.' So saying he raised the automatic Scorpio machine pistol which all of them carried. At that both Carillo and Sierra also raised their firearms.

Julio Lopez, the current chief of the Euskadi ta Azkata Suna, was always reluctant to talk about his past. That was because he felt that the past belonged to Emilio Salinas and he did not wish to communicate with Salinas at all. Sierra and Carillo, his two most trusted lieutenants and friends, knew this and never pressed him. Besides, it had been twelve years since he had left his university or college, whatever it could be called. Today, he had more urgent things to look into than reminisce about his past. He had been a young man of twenty-three when he left the academy. The ETA had then been much stronger. The thought that his organisation was considerably weaker than it had been during the days of Francisco Salinas always disconcerted him. There had been times in the Eighties when the ETA men could roam about openly in towns like Bilbao, Guernica and San Sebastian. That had changed now. They had been forced to take to the mountains and the dense woods that surround the Basque countryside.

He was well aware that the Basques had become weary of the struggle for an independent nation. That was one reason why the ETA was facing recruitment problems as well. Lopez did not blame his people for losing faith in the ETA. He knew that, the world over, insurgent organisations like his own were grappling with dipping popularity and advancing armies.

But he was hopeful that the bad patch his organisation had hit was temporary and things would change for the better. He knew that if the organisation remained in the news the cadres would return in droves. For that purpose, he had to take tough decisions like bombing the University of Salamanca. Even though they had taken care to ensure that there would be no casualties he still felt a twinge of remorse. It had taken a lot of planning and daring apart from the large amount of Samtex-H to bring down the Gen. Franco block of the university. He watched smoke rise from Bourbon Square where the University of Salamanca stood, isolated in the darkness, devoid of its most magnificent structure, the Gen. Franco Memorial Block, named after the Spanish dictator.

Julio knew that the university was a visible soft target, a target of the sort often used as a last resort by revolutionaries the world over. He had never had problems defining the ETA warriors as revolutionaries. The rest of Spain referred to them as terrorists but he believed that 'one man's terrorist is another's freedom fighter'. He fervently hoped that coming generations of Basque children would read about them in their history books and perceive them in that light. He had drawn a whole list of targets. He wanted the Spanish government to start worrying about his organisation again the way it used to in the past. But it seemed that the movement was beginning to get hijacked by men with political leanings. He hated such men, men who had ambitions of winning elections and raising matters of Basque pride in Madrid after being a part of the power structure.

One such man was Col. Ramon Arrieta, mayor of San Sebastian, the hometown and birthplace of both Emilio Salinas and Julio Lopez. Col. Arrieta was a Basque by birth, a decorated officer of the Spanish army who had led the force that hunted and eventually caused the death of Francisco Salinas. Before standing for elections in San Sebastian, Arrieta had resigned from the army. It was an ominous sign of the changing times that the man who caused the death of one of the most beloved leaders of the ETA was today the mayor of a prominent Basque town.

Soon after becoming mayor, Col. Arrieta had issued an appeal to the ETA to lay down arms and join the mainstream. He had arranged a meeting with Julio to try and persuade him to surrender in return for guaranteed amnesty. He wanted Julio to aid him in repairing links with Madrid. In return, Col. Arrieta had narrowly escaped getting killed by Lopez and his men who came disguised as representatives of the International Red Cross, in whose presence the meeting was to have taken place. A dazed Arrieta had been unable to understand why a genuine attempt at reconciliation had been spurned. It had been a while since Salinas' death, so that was an unlikely reason. He had always been aware that many ETA men held him directly responsible for the death of their chief and had sworn revenge, which he had dismissed as empty rhetoric from a group fast losing its footing. Till date Arrieta did not know that Julio Lopez was Emilio Salinas, the only son and heir of Francisco Salinas, presumed killed in the same raid that killed his father.

Very few people outside the top brass of the ETA knew that Salinas and Lopez were the same person. Most people, like Arrieta, thought Emilio had died with his father. Francisco Salinas, his son Emilio and a small band of men had been caught unawares in a local chief's village on the outskirts of Bilbao. Salinas Sr. and the five men with him had managed to persuade an extremely reluctant Emilio to run away, as a fierce gun battle raged with the army group led by Col. Ramon Arrieta. Salinas and his men had pleaded with the young man that for the sake of the ETA's future, he would have to stay alive. Francisco was aware that, as the raid had resulted from information divulged by a traitor, the army would know the exact number of men they were facing. However, Salinas reasoned that the presence of a local Basque youth who had sought an interview with him to join the ETA was not known to the army or Col. Arrieta. When the gun battle began, the local lad volunteered to stay and help. The minute he was shot dead after getting caught in the hail of bullets, Salinas had carried out the unpleasant chore of spraying his face with bullets. To his body were added certain objects that would later identify him as the son of the chief.

After three hours of searching, Col. Arrieta and his men had found seven bodies, two of which were quite naturally taken to be those of the chief and his son. For the next year Emilio had gone underground. A few changes in his appearance helped him accomplish the rest of the mission. He had soon realised how wise his father's decision had been, for after Francisco Salinas' death, the ETA had been scattered and managed only to regroup around Emilio Salinas.

For a while he had remained hidden by families of sympathisers and the remaining ETA men. It was not that his past scared him, because he had been suitably toughened by his stay outside the country, it was that his father's death was not bearing fruit. Francisco Salinas had died so the ETA and a Basque nation should live, and now, ten years after the fateful day in Bilbao, the organisation was at its weakest. Julio Lopez wanted nothing to do with Emilio Salinas till the time his organisation became what it used to be under Salinas Sr. His feelings towards Col. Arrieta were but natural for a young man who had seen death at close range. The fact that Arrieta had now become a respected political and public figure had added insult to injury. The failure of repeated plans to kill him were doing nothing to assuage the desire for vengeance. Meanwhile, Arrieta was using the attempts on his life after offers of clemency and peace to whip up disgust amongst the Basques for the ETA. The military man-turned-mayor was still not aware of the reason for such seemingly irrational behaviour from Julio Lopez.

Julio knew that he had to get Col. Arrieta in the near future. The failed attempts had cost the ETA dear in terms of public goodwill. Every attempt drove the people further from his organisation. He reckoned that if Arrieta were killed, the Basques would forget his death soon enough. Then the ETA could consider a non-violent solution. But Col. Ramon

Arrieta's death was non-negotiable. Till he lived, Julio would continue to spurn offers of talks across the table, and if that meant annoying the majority of his people, so be it.

The Basques were essentially a peace-loving race. Sections wishing to ingratiate themselves with the Spanish mainstream felt that such acts further weakened their case for a gradual and peaceful solution. The younger lot could not understand the ire of the ETA as most had not been born when the worst atrocities had been committed on the Basques. And it is a cardinal rule of human nature that what has not been faced by someone, will not move them either.

Sitting in the wooded hills and gazing at the blazing university, Julio Lopez wondered if the assassination of the mayor of San Sebastian was actually beyond his men. It was a fact that the Colonel was now heavily guarded. Over the years as the heat being faced by the ETA had increased, time spent in the intensive training of his men had been compromised. For men constantly on the run, it was next to impossible to practice the skills of destruction. Maybe he needed a specialist to achieve what he and his men had failed to do. Europe and even Asia, he knew, were crawling with men who offered their services for money. Men who had perfected killing to an art. Such men, he knew, had only professional motives and their vision would not be clouded by feelings of hate and vengeance. The one hitch was that a man based outside Spain, if requisitioned, would demand a lot of money. Suddenly he thought of someone who could be the panacea to his troubles. Yes, why had he not thought of him earlier? He had heard murmurs that his old friend from the Camper school had become a professional killer. If only contact could be established with him, Julio was sure that he would be able to convince him to come to Spain. At least he would be able to guide him and his men.

It had been years since they had lost touch. The last he had heard from him was when his old friend had been a part of a respected and feared intelligence service. He pondered for a few minutes on what course of action to follow. He had no idea under what name his friend was known or what part of the world he had made his turf. Then he recalled the rumours he had heard and hoped there was some truth to them. It was said that he could be reached in London. That presented a problem. There was no way he would be able to leave the organisation headless even for a few days. Added to that would be the risk of leaving the country. He would have to send somebody else to London and that somebody would have to be Raoul Gonzalez. Raoul was a new recruit. He had been educated in England but had chosen to return to Spain to serve the organisation his father Luis Gonzalez had served with distinction. Luis Gonzalez had been with Francisco Salinas at the time of the fatal ambush. Being relatively new and having arrived in Spain after years abroad, Raoul was not known to the authorities. It would be easier for him to leave Spain. He also had the advantage of knowing London. Raoul could manage the job, he was sure.

17

In the complex London underworld, there is a category of men who are known as operators. They were originally known as arrangers due to the nature of the tasks performed by them. Around the late seventeenth century, the London underworld was dominated by two groups known as the enforcers and the crushers. The enforcers were the men retained by the criminal war-lords who punished errant people on direct command of their masters. The crushers, on the other hand, were the predecessors of what are today called hit-men. They were the freelance artists who could be hired by any gang-lord. In fact, in times of excess demand, rival gangs would often even bid for their services. The operators acted as the agents or information banks for the enforcers and the crushers.

Occasionally, the operators would be rounded up for questioning by the authorities. This could spell trouble for both the men whose agents they were and those who were their customers. Though by and large reliable, they were not able to withstand interrogation like hostage families of the Sicilian mafia could.

113

The London operators had links with assassins, safe crackers, men who specialised in ambushes, explosion handlers. Most of them were aligned to one professional group or the other. A few even worked for more than one group. There were some operators who were not aligned to anyone but were primarily information banks and acted as links to the best in the business. Hugo Stone was one such operator.

By making discreet enquiries, Arif Rabbani had discovered that Stone was the expert on professional assassins. It was said of Hugo Stone that he knew so many assassins and hit-men that it was a wonder he was still alive. Because Maj. Chaudhary had asked for more information on the assassin, Rabbani decided to contact Stone. After introducing himself over the phone as an aide to Roxton Miller, Rabbani invited him for dinner at the Highland Manor. Hugo Stone turned out to be a small bespectacled man who looked more like an academician, than an operator. The Manor was an expensive, old-style English restaurant. From his reaction, Rabbani felt that either his guest was not accustomed to such places or he had recently fallen into bad times. That suited him fine as his purpose was to impress upon Stone that he intended to reward him handsomely for his labours. He wanted to make sure that Stone would treat this deal on a top priority basis.

Without wasting time in spinning tales about the purpose of the meeting, Arif questioned Stone about the man Maj. Chaudhary was interested in. 'I am sorry, but offhand it is extremely difficult for me to place a person who would correspond to this description,' replied the professor look-alike.

'I just want you to know that any effort you make shall be compensated with sums you can't imagine.'

'That is all right, but consider what you have placed before me. All I know is that this man is a top-level contract killer and has some link with this city.'

'I would not have come to you if I knew what this link was,' replied Rabbani politely, though he was exasperated. Either the person who had given him Hugo Stone's name had exaggerated grossly or the man was just playing games to increase his price.

'I think you overestimate the resources of my kind of people,' said Stone. 'Our work is to tell you how to engage and reach these people.' By these people he meant the former crushers.

Rabbani thought for a moment and shifted to an approach that Maj. Chaudhary often used with him. 'You are not saying that someone who operates internationally and beyond the territorial limits of London is beyond you?'

'No,' countered Stone, unwittingly swallowing the bait. 'I am only trying to tell you that the background information you have supplied is inadequate.'

'That's another reason I came to you, Mr Stone. I knew that this would require a little research, and who better than the best operator in the city?'

'Well... it would involve following leads on all activities suspiciously resembling fronts.'

'But it can be done,' interjected Rabbani.

'Yes, then I have to further follow up these fronts, and check where and since when this man has been operating. Also, what kind of contracts have been undertaken, and the success rate...'

'And...' said Rabbani, trying to coax him further.

'Then the question is what do I compare these records with, in order to check whether he's your man. You have told me nothing.'

Rabbani had intentionally not told Stone what he thought was the crucial identifying feature. He had postponed it till he was reasonably sure that Stone would agree to the job. 'Just remember that he is supposed to have entered the scene about five years back, and most of his kills have been in Asia.'

'Yes, that would be a great help,' nodded Stone slowly.

An assassin may have been operating for years incognito both in terms of his identity as well as standing. But he begins to climb the rungs of his world when his reputation starts spreading. This is usually related to the status of his victims and numerous other factors like the manner of the kill and the method of escape. Of course all through this, if his identity remains unknown except to a select few, it adds greatly to his stature. The reputation spreads by way of whispers and information, generally true but conveniently tagged to be rumours. It was these rumours that Arif Rabbani had picked up during his initial investigations.

'I am severely constrained by time,' said Rabbani.

'Well I cannot even give you a deadline because I have never faced a demand as daunting as this.'

On a hunch, Rabbani offered an incentive he thought would greatly speed up Hugo Stone, his pleas for time notwithstanding. 'Every day you save would gain you 1000 pounds in addition to the general terms of payment,' he said and noted with satisfaction that, from the look on Stone's face, the ploy seemed to have worked.

LONDON, SEPTEMBER 22, 1995

Rabbani was furious. For two days he'd been forced to go into hiding because of the stupidity of one of his gang members. O'Reilly, one of his protégés, had got into a fist-fight with certain well-placed members of a rival gang. Unfortunately, one of the men injured happened to be the boss' nephew. O'Reilly had cleverly disappeared, and the Andrew Weinburg

116

clan had then taken out a contract on Rabbani, who was widely known as O'Reilly's mentor, was forced to go underground. The last thing on his mind was Choudhary on the job he'd been asked to do.

18

For the fourth time in the last hour there was a soft knock at the door of the resting room of Triple Oaks. Rabbani froze. He slowly drew out the Smith and Wesson revolver he carried in a shoulder holster, and crouched beside the door. The gun had been a recent acquisition. Before the scrap with the 'German boys' into which he had needlessly been dragged, he used to only carry a very small locally made pistol.

'Mr Rabbani,' the voice from outside became louder.

Arif recognised it as the voice of Henry, the young bartender at the Oaks. 'Ya,' he grunted in a low tone. Two more short but crisp knocks followed. At this, he relaxed. He had arranged with Henry that if he were forced by hostile strangers to reveal his whereabouts, he would give three short knocks. Two knocks indicated that there was no danger.

While negotiations between the chiefs of the Miller and the Weinburg clans were in progress, there was negligible chance of his being hit as long as he lay low. But if the eventuality arose, Arif Rabbani intended to go down fighting. In which case, he would not have relied solely on the Smith and Wesson—he had, in his room, a small carton of Belgian-

118

made hand grenades and a miniature special version of the Kalashnikov automatic rifle. The carton contained six hand grenades and the rifle was accompanied by three full magazines. All these lay in a velvet bag under the couch of the resting room. 'What is it, Henry?' he barked from inside, deciding against opening the door.

'There's a call for you, Mr Rabbani. Shall I transfer it to the line in the rest room?'

'Who is it?'

'It's a Keith Hall, he says it's urgent.'

'Yes, get him on the line immediately,' replied Rabbani, his voice quivering in anticipation. Keith Hall was the personal bodyguard of his boss, Roxton Miller. Keith must be calling to let me know of the latest developments, he thought, as he picked up the phone and waited for Keith's familiar voice to come through.

'Arif, are you there?' Hall's voice sounded relaxed, thought Rabbani. After a few minutes he replaced the receiver with a sense of relief. Keith had called to let him know that the 20,000 pounds contract on his head put out by the Weinburg gang had just been lifted fifteen minutes ago.

Roxton Miller, Joe Miller and the top brass of their clan were the only people who had known of Arif Rabbani's whereabouts as he lay underground at the Oaks. This was necessary, as they would have to get in touch with him whatever the course of the negotiations with the Weinburgs. The contract could have been lifted either with the Miller gang promising a pecuniary compensation to the Weinburgs, or possibly an undertaking that they would trace and deliver O'Reilly to them. In some cases, there could have been a chance of an attack being carried out on the subject of the contract, even after the lifting of the contract. If that happened, full-scale war would be on the cards. As Rabbani set off from the Oaks, he was aware that his first destination had to be the abode of Roxton Miller where he had to thank him and re-pledge his loyalty. The London underworld, though not based on personal man-to-man relationships as in the case of the Italians, still relied on some degree of personal loyalty. Once Rabbani had done the needful, he would contact Maj. Chaudhary to complete his assignment.

Five hours later, Rabbani was sitting opposite Stone, watching in amusement at the way the small-built man was able to put away his drinks. He had gulped down two large ones in less than thirty minutes and was beginning his third. All of a sudden he put down his glass and addressed him. 'Look Mr Rabbani, what I am going to reveal to you today is extremely confidential. If it reaches ears it should not reach, then your life and my reputation would be in serious jeopardy.'

'I appreciate that, you have my word.'

'I have your man, or at least I think it is him.' Stone fumbled in his coat pocket and brought out a piece of paper. 'Memorise this name, and then tear it up.'

Rabbani obeyed and then asked, 'Does he go under this name?'

'No, but this is someone who you have to reach to be able to get in touch with your man.'

'Where can he be reached?'

'Well, there is an easy part and a tough part in the answer to that question.'

'Tell me the easy one first,' said Arif.

'I was going to. He is a resident of London, that is confirmed, but what he is and where he is cannot be said with any precision.'

'What?' said an aghast Rabbani, 'that is almost as good as nothing!'

'No, it is not,' rebuked Stone, 'and you know it, Mr Rabbani. You now possess a name, and it is a name that is in proper use, it's not an alias or anything. Trace it, or better still, if you are making these enquiries on someone else's behalf, tell your clients to trace it.'

'Is he an agent or a manager?'

'That I am not sure of, but yes, without him it's practically impossible to reach your man. Can I tell you something I've learned from experience?'

'Please proceed,' urged Arif.

'Usually I have observed that the final decision to take up a job rests with the professional himself. Who you contact him through may be a party to that decision but it is unlikely that the contact can take a decision and give you an answer on behalf of the assassin.'

'Have you been able to learn anything else about him?' asked Rabbani as he poured Stone his fourth drink. He himself was still sipping his second small Scotch.

'He is one of the best men in his field, as well as the most feared.'

'Feared? Why?'

'He is feared because of his ruthlessness, his dedication to his profession.'

'Are they not all ruthless?' interrupted Rabbani.

'Well to a certain extent but this one takes the cake. During his early years, a contract he took up was also awarded to another of his tribe. What your man did was he raced his rival to the job, beat him to it, killed him on the same day as his target and also killed the party that had employed his rival.'

Rabbani shuddered. 'Then he can't be as professional as he is reported to be.'

'On the contrary, he is a thorough professional. The people who had employed the other assassin were the rival group of his clients, so he just claimed a price for them as well as from his clients who most gladly paid.'

'How do you know all this Mr Stone?'

'This is my job, Sir, I make my living from it. Who would know all this if not I? Didn't you say I was the best in the city the last time we met?'

'Yes of course you are,' replied Arif, beginning to note the effects of the Scotch on Hugo Stone. Thankfully, he had the information he needed. 'One last question. How have you found out this name?'

'That, I am sorry, I cannot reveal. It's like asking you how you became the right hand man of Roxton Miller, or how you survived the contract put on your head last week.'

This retort from Stone stung Rabbani. He thought for a second. What if he got this oaf eliminated and pocketed the money he had taken from Maj. Chaudhary for him?

'Don't think I am drunk and not in my senses,' said Stone, interrupting Rabbani's little fantasy. 'If I don't tell you, it's for your own good, Mr Rabbani. Any mistake, and you die. In my world, no contracts exist, no warnings are given, one wrong question and you could end up with a bullet in your throat.'

Rabbani didn't mind if he had lost respect, at least he was alive to hear this man's taunts. 'Thanks for your work Sir,' he said, withdrawing an envelope from his jacket and handing it over. Hugo Stone looked inside and pocketed it with a satisfied look. Arif signalled to the waiter attending them, paid the cheque and then left the Manor. He would contact Chaudhary. The Major could trace the man himself or wait for a few days if he wanted it to be done by him. He would need a few days to trace that bastard O'Reilly. Miller had told him that his gang had had to submit to a few demands of the Weinburg group. Certain concessions had been given to them that would remain in force unless O'Reilly was found and handed over to them. Rabbani had promised his chief that he would personally find O'Reilly and deliver him to Andrew

Weinburg, to free his chief from Weinburg's debt. Joe Miller had further aggravated the situation by giving a detailed account of how aggressive and dismissive Andrew Weinburg had been during their meeting. Rabbani attributed that to the influence Mike Orlean and Jon Malet, Joe's best friends in the gang, had over the younger Miller. They hated his guts and it was a wonder they had not persuaded the Millers to get him killed themselves.

As dusk merged into darkness, Maj. Chaudhary was deep in thought. Just an hour back, Arif Rabbani had left his flat after giving him an update of what had transpired with Hugo Stone. Chaudhary had told Rabbani that in case his services were required again, he would be contacted. The Major was wondering whether he ought to try and find the man Rabbani had named or whether he should report the latest events to Pakistan.

After much weighing of his options, he decided upon the latter course of action. It was clear that he was on the right course. Why ruin it by taking a step that might not go down well with the authorities in Pakistan? And a response from Islamabad would not take more than a couple of days.

SEPTEMBER 25, 1995

Chaudhary was glad he had not gone ahead on his own. He read for the third time, the communiqué that had come in coded form from Islamabad. It showered generous praise on him, which was followed by the next set of instructions.

His superiors in Pakistan had ordered Chaudhary to try and ascertain whether Rabbani's man existed in London. If he did, then his whereabouts and business were to be determined by the Major. However, there was a catch. Islamabad made it clear that neither Chaudhary nor any ISI contact were to get involved. That would mean another meeting with Arif Rabbani. This precaution again confirmed Maj. Chaudhary's suspicion that what he was doing was definitely connected with India.

At the very moment that Chaudhry was thinking of him, Rabbani was celebrating his latest success at a small restaurant called the The Asian Queen at Leicester Square. Barring its name, there was nothing royal about the restaurant. At that hour the Queen was reverberating with the hysterical cacophony of heavy metal music. There was a distinct odour of marijuana. It was a seedy joint in which it was difficult to see people because of the layers of heavy smoke. The gyrating bodies belonged mostly to lower middle class Indians and Pakistanis. The Asian Queen was the only link that Rabbani had kept alive with his community.

The cause for celebration had been the speed with which Rabbani had found O'Reilly. It had taken him less than twenty-four hours to trace the Irish thug in a small village in Surrey some thirty miles from London. He had immediately shared this information with Andrew Weinburg. By now he was sure O'Reilly would have left this world, after being made to endure the suffering he had inflicted on young Deiter Weinburg, the nephew of Andrew Weinburg.

19

ISLAMABAD, SEPTEMBER 28

Brig. Qayyum Nazir was sitting hunched at his desk at the CFIO headquarters when his intercom buzzed. 'Yes, put him through at once, yes, through the buzz net line.' The buzz net line was the line that was entirely secure. No records of any calls made or received on this line were maintained. Initially this facility was available only to the ISI chief, but with the passage of time it had been extended to certain officers in ultra sensitive posts such as the in-charge of Project K2. The call had come from the newest addition to Islamabad, The Royal International. It was from Radley Karras to inform Nazir of his arrival in Pakistan. Brig. Nazir had no intention of announcing Karras' arrival to anyone. Left on his own, he could have considered sharing this with Lt. Gen. Hussain, but since this might in turn mean having to report it to Col. Ashraf Abbas, he was willing to keep this to himself even at the risk of incurring Lt. Gen. Hussain's wrath.

Karras had been told to take certain precautions like registering himself under a different name, and to act like a tourist. With the experience that Karras had at his disposal, this and more would hardly be a problem for him.

The last brief that had arrived from London was to be shared with Karras. He had already discussed the contents of Maj. Chaudhary's report with Maj. Azim Tariq. Brig. Nazir had known from the beginning that his team would encounter such a situation sooner or later. For this reason he had invited Radley Karras to Pakistan. Maj. Chaudhary had filed the name given to him by Hugh Stone, after which he had confirmed that there was indeed a man of that name in London. In fact, there were around twenty-six men of that name in London. After a hectic day of investigations by both Maj. Chaudhary and his contact, they had short-listed the men to eleven probables. Any more eliminations would have meant venturing into the arena of blind conjecture. The fact was that no other ISI sector had turned up anything that was half as suitable. This was the problem that Radley Karras, retired commander of the US Naval Intelligence, was expected to solve.

'How are you my dear friend?' said Karras, as Nazir entered his suite and embraced him.

'I am very grateful to you Radley, that you have come from so far,' replied Brig. Nazir, visibly touched.

'That's no problem, provided I am of some help to you.'

After enquiring about the wellbeing of each other's families, the two intelligence men became quiet for a few minutes as if preparing to move on to more serious issues. 'What shall I get you, Saint?' Karras asked Nazir. He had first called him Saint in Afghanistan when Nazir had been the only officer in a crowd of American and Pakistani intelligence men who drank no alcohol.

'The usual.' By that Nazir meant orange juice. With Nazir sipping his juice and Karras his own drink they began.

'I see that you are embarking on a most ambitious plan. As I feel that you have made up your mind to go ahead, I shall not try to get you to reconsider it.' Karras paused and then began again, as Nazir remained silent. 'But I just want to let you know that you will have to face several odds in such an operation. My own country has once or twice in the past attempted similar operations and not with happy results. In your case, the odds begin from the first step itself. The target or the intended victim, I mean, is not a rival intelligence man or a dangerous tycoon, he is a man widely tipped to become the next prime minister of India.' Brig. Nazir was not discouraged by what Karras was saying. He knew that he would present a totally objective and clear picture to Nazir. That was one reason why he had called him—to ensure that someone completely unbiased could evaluate the plan.

Karras continued. 'Then comes the probability of your name getting dragged into it. With the kind of relations Pakistan has had with India, you invariably end up getting blamed for whatever happens.

'But we intend to use a professional, a non-Pakistani this time,' interjected Nazir.

'That is truly a wise move. The good thing about a professional assassin is that even if he messes up in the end, it will not reflect on you. If he is really competent, he will try to get his man later. Secondly, how he escapes is not going to be a worry for you. Such men normally have their own escape routes and methods. If he succeeds, chances are you will never hear from him again.'

'I know this. It's precisely for these very reasons that I have convinced Lt. Gen. Hussain that we need an outsider for this operation. Anyway, what are the other problems?'

'Well, money is certainly one of them. A good man is going to be more expensive than you can imagine, and in all probability he would expect payment in western currency.'

'The money shall be taken care of.'

At this, Karras smiled to himself. It was the same story with all these countries. Half their populations were starving, disease stalked every corner, many lived in slums, there was no education... Yet men like Brig. Nazir could be so nonchalant about a sum that could possibly run into millions of dollars. While Pakistan was wasting money in trying to promote terrorism in India, India was in turn using its precious resourses in developing everything from patriot missiles to AWACS and their own version of the stealth bomber.

'The dead end that we have reached is how do we make contact with this man.' Karras' eyebrows moved enquiringly. For the next one hour, Brig. Nazir narrated to Karras the progress made by Maj. Chaudhary in London. It was apparent that Karras was impressed.

'So you have eleven people, all of whom seem to be associated with a top grade professional assassin. And you want me to help you narrow down this list.'

'I know Radley, that it is not easy,' said Nazir.

'It's not very hard either,' said Karras in a tone which was calm and confident but not arrogant or mocking. 'In fact I am quite amazed at how an original number of twenty-six has been pruned to eleven in the first place.'

'You mean the answer to our search could be in the men we have eliminated?'

'I do not know, I hope not,' said Karras in a noncommittal manner. 'However, do not bother about what is done. I suggest we trust that your London associate knows what he is doing. First deal with the list you have. If this does not turn up something, then we will think of the other fifteen.' Karras waited for his assurance to Nazir to take effect, and then continued, 'I need a few hours alone to think about your problem. We will meet tomorrow. I am sure your puzzle will not appear so convoluted after a good night's rest.'

As Brig. Nazir got up to leave, he turned to Karras, 'What are your plans apart from this?'

'Well, first I shall try and send a message to my wife and then I will try to convince the staff of this hotel that I am indeed a harmless tourist.' As soon as Nazir left, Karras picked up the phone to the reception desk and began to dial.

As Brig. Nazir made his way out of The Royal International he looked back with satisfaction at his meeting with Karras. He knew that Radley would definitely have a way out by the next day. They would have to decide what to do next and then inform London. For a moment, he wondered who Maj. Chaudhary's contact in London was. Then he checked himself, remembering Karras' advice. He had come to the hotel in his personal vehicle. As he pressed the accelerator and began to pull out onto the road, he groaned in irritation. He would have to brief Col. Abbas about Maj. Chaudhary's progress tomorrow. There was no way he could postpone doing this by another day. At that instance, Nazir was flooded with anger at his most trusted junior Maj. Tariq. It was close to a fortnight since he had promised to get hold of Col. Abbas' service record.

He was sure that Azim was trying his best, but that was not enough. In the kind of service they were in and the work they did, there was no grading for effort. If you failed to get the desired results, you were as good as a hopeless bureaucrat. And the ISI was in no way similar to the bureaucracy. Men like Brig. Nazir and Lt. Gen. Hussain thought of it as a service that was superior even to the army. And within the ISI, the best that could happen to you was the CFIO. That was the place to be not only because it was a sensitive department that satisfied your patriotic callings, but also because it brought with it numerous perks. You were whispered about in social gatherings, and you received reverential looks. The promotions were quicker and the monetary emoluments were also several notches higher. The latter was in order to keep the CFIO men immune to poaching from any other covert service, particularly India. It also had professional benefits that an officer would not otherwise be entitled to, such as the facilities of your own satellite links, the buzz net line, etc. but there was one string attached—a slip up in CFIO was dealt with in a much quicker and tougher manner, as had happened in the case of Brig. Sumroo, Brig. Nazir's predecessor. Sumroo had not been given even a routine court martial.

'Excuses and nothing else I get, even from you Azim,' bellowed Brig. Nazir into the mouthpiece when he reached his residence. 'First it was one week, now you ask me to wait another week, what is happening to your level of competence? Have you forgotten you are working in the CFIO?' It was clear that Nazir was not listening to whatever defence Maj. Tariq was attempting. 'No, it's time you admitted that this task is beyond you,' he shouted and then stopped, apparently now listening to something that the harried Major was saying. 'All right, but get here within fifteen minutes. A second more and you are out of the CFIO, leave alone K2.'

Exactly thirteen minutes later, Maj. Azim Tariq reached his angry superior's residence.

20

Brig. Nazir was watching a tennis match. It had been half an hour since he had arrived at Karras' suite. Karras had silently waved him in, pointing towards a seat. It seemed that he was in the midst of some serious thinking and did not want to be interrupted. As Karras paced the length of his room, Nazir watched him patiently. No one could have said this was the same man who a day before had given Maj. Tariq only fifteen minutes to save his career.

There were two primary reasons for the Brigadier concealing Karras' presence in Pakistan from everyone. First, in a military state one could never tell what would be held against you, and who would cause your downfall. The exposure of Brig. Sumroo had been engineered by one of his most trusted lieutenants. Despite all his faith in Maj. Tariq he could still have been a palace man keeping an eye on Nazir. Besides, many would have given their right hand to be in Brig. Nazir's place. The charges that could be brought against him could vary from common breach of trust to high treason. The second cause was the average Pakistani's rabid attitude towards westerners, Americans in particular. Nazir was not sure whether any

131

officer's ego would tolerate taking help from an American intelligence man. He himself, he believed, possessed enough objectivity to rise above these petty feelings. He needed Karras' opinion and expertise if that would lead to success. He saw Karras as an exceptionally brilliant man with great integrity. This opinion had nothing to do with the Asian tendency to look up to the West, but a view based on solid facts.

One important character trait that distinguished Brig. Qayyum Nazir from an average ISI functionary was an ability to correctly evaluate the limitations of his service. He was the last person to get carried away with the hallowed image of the ISI, so carefully crafted by the military masters of the army. According to him, what the people of Pakistan thought about the ISI was one thing, and what the truth was, was another. Letting oneself believe in the invincibility of the service would do more harm than good. He was well aware that his organisation had never handled an assassination of the level he had planned. He was also aware that American intelligence had great experience with professional assassins. The actual contacts and record of the American intelligence, particularly the CIA, was not hidden from other covert services in the world. What kept them quiet was the unassailable position of the US post the Cold War era.

'You will have to begin with a very close observation of the men in question,' said Karras. 'Watch them at their homes, at places of work and in public gatherings. Clues are bound to turn up.'

'What are we going to be looking for in the first place?' replied a worried Nazir, as the enormity of the task began to now dawn upon him.

'Anything that points to a break in the chain—the chain being an ordinary lifestyle.'

'What if our man likes to keep a low profile?'

'You are confusing life with lifestyle. What I mean is, you are bound to get a hint about his work. Look, try and pin your men to their supposed professions. If their work seems to be unexplained or vague in comparison with the others, you could be very close.'

'Rad, is there any particular field in which an agent or a manager of a professional killer is likely to be engaged?'

'From what I have seen in my time, no. Such an individual could have any sideshow under the sun. And for you, it could be a costly error to pay more attention to any one in particular, or think one of the eleven to be more likely than the others. Because if you entertain such an assumption, you will pass that feeling to the men in the field and their impartial observations will get affected.'

'Do you think we should take a look at the details of their bank accounts? Would that help?'

'I suppose so, but I am doubtful whether such information would be available. I mean, I do not doubt your men but honestly this could be beyond them.'

'Ah, that's where you are mistaken my friend. We now have a few sources even in the Swiss banking industry.'

This came as a surprise to the American. The ISI, it seemed, had grown. 'Really? You can persuade them to break their code of silence?'

'Well, we can definitely try, and if they are handling funds from Islamic countries, chances are they will.'

'That would be a great help; try it, but do not pin all your hopes on it. Remember, the important thing is a break in the chain: some place, somewhere, a visit outside the country, contact with people outside the western sphere, an association with someone who frequently travels abroad.'

'Another thing: everyone has a past, and pasts can be dug up. One of the most prominent clues can be his past, or to be precise, a lack of it.'

'A lack of it?' repeated the Brigadier.

'Yes, in such a trade you are dealing with men who do not want details of their pasts out in the open. But however much the effort to clean a record, there is always some trace left. A trace, if not of the past, the attempt to erase it. I would call that a significant break in the chain of an ordinary life.'

'Yes of course, you are absolutely right! I should have thought of it earlier,' exclaimed Brig. Nazir in a state of excitement. He looked up at Karras, 'I have always wondered though, why this obsession with trying to veil one's origin? Today you can alter your appearance quite easily.'

'You are right, surgery can change faces, but are you aware that the newest forensic software can tell you what changes have been made, so it is as good as having one's picture splashed all over the world? What good would an altered appearance be then?' As Nazir nodded in agreement, Karras went on, 'Also, there are certain traits which cannot be altered at all, or not without a great deal of effort. You must be aware of the problems that are encountered by those who try to alter their fingerprints. The results are as good as negligible.

'The moot point is that if your past is known it's an unnecessary peril. There are features like dental work, fingerprints, gene patterns, DNA charts that can be looked at. If the hired killer or his associate are from the armed forces or are renegade intelligence men, it becomes all the more important that their pasts are well and truly buried before they embark on their new careers.'

'Tell me, why do so many intelligence personnel cross the fence and hire themselves out as assassins? Are our services not challenging enough, or are their hearts not involved in serving their nations?'

Karras paused for a couple of minutes and, rubbing his forehead with his forefinger, spoke. 'None of those. Our services are more challenging than ever, and your average renegade ex-CIA or ex-ISI man is just as patriotic as you or me.'

'Patriotic? I do not understand,' interrupted Nazir.

'It's usually a combination of more than one reason. Firstly, such men are usually extremely good at their work. Please understand me, it's not as if they become good by experience and training. It's this natural ability and aptitude that makes them different from the other good operatives. And this ability is often quickly noted by their superiors, men like you and me, who begin to use them for more and more dangerous missions. It's us who get the promotions, and to make sure that our men put their heart and soul in the field, we let them know how good they are. Again, make no mistake, not to genuinely praise them, but to ensure that they remain involved. Soon they begin to believe in their greatness. This happens again because of two factors. First, the more missions they complete and survive, and the more they are praised, the more they become convinced about their own invincibility. At this point, if they have to face any sort of reprimand which they perceive to be not in conforming with their status, they turn. It's actually a slap to their superiors and political bosses, a rebellion, an intention to show the world what has been unleashed on them by insensitive handling. And thirdly, of course as their self-esteem gets enhanced, so does the resistance against authority and a desire to be free, to be their own masters.'

'But there are cases of people like James Allan, who switched from being a professional killer to a professional soldier.'

'Those cases are exceptions. In the days of Allan and company there was war to be found quite easily, so men like him could satisfy their genius on the battlefield. If you look at the Eighties and Nineties you will realise what I mean. The

135

famed Carlos, before he became known as Carlos, was an officer in the intelligence section of the Venezuelan army.

'Really, it is indeed a strange world.'

'Oh yes it is, and not half as glamorous as projected in the books and the movies. It's only a few who make a name for themselves, if you can call it that. Most realise their folly, sometimes with terrible consequences.'

'What do you mean by terrible consequences?' queried the Pakistani military man.

'Well, about twelve years ago my immediate junior was an Italian–American called Roberto Fiore. Fiore, after a small reprimand from our director, decided that the department needed him more than he needed the department. After a failed attempt at setting up his own private investigative agency, he decided he would be most comfortable amongst his own countrymen. He offered his services as a freelancer to the two Italian families that dominated Chicago then. Four days later he was found dead in a deserted warehouse. Poor Roberto had been taken to be a government plant by both the groups and was killed jointly by their hit-men. That incident deterred at least a whole line of US intelligence operatives who were planning to leave the agency and start on their own.'

'How good was he according to you?'

'He was very good, no doubt about that, only he was caught off guard. You see Saint, it's not always that our departments leave the field men unaided and alone in hostile territory. That happens only when an emergency pull-out occurs. In the world Fiore entered, there was no back up and he was new, no tips, no informers, no emergency signals, and he could not even last a week. You would not believe, the same man once survived for eighteen days in East Berlin, dodging the Stasi and the KGB after losing contact with his usual liaisons in that city, with his cover almost blown.'

'Phew!' said Nazir, shaking his head.

'Incidentally Saint, the director then was Ronald Mcintyre. I once introduced you to him at a reception in Riyadh.'

'I remember him, very tall and burly man, dark black hair, was it not?'

'Yes, he's still quite tough, retired now, has his own ranch, and oh, the hair is almost gone.'

21

It had been more than a month now. Bhaskar Naik had nearly finalised Plan Alpha. He had discussed it with Prakash Mittal and had also explained the details to Kulkarni. The chief minister liked it immensely. In fact, he had got so excited after hearing it, he wanted it employed against some of his own party men too. That of course was not the urgent need. In the time that had elapsed, the Congress had suffered additional setbacks. The prime minister's patience had finally given way and he had expelled Chandra Dev Raj from the party. The reason given was indiscipline and anti-party activities. Along with Dev Raj, also expelled was Atma Ram Pradhan, another veteran leader of reasonable standing.

Pradhan belonged to Uttar Pradesh where the Congress had once reigned supreme, but was now only a marginal player. The state was dominated by the Janata Dal-Samajwadi Party combination that jostled violently for space with the REP that was making rapid inroads into the state. Pradhan had once been the chief minister of the state and had represented the hill districts of the state in the Parliament for years. Reduced to being an unimportant leader, he had been in a sulk in recent times. With nothing to lose, he had been voicing support for Dev Raj, insisting that the leader from central India was needlessly being ignored. He had been sharing the dais with Dev Raj at a small rally that had been called by the latter when anti-Reddy and anti-Kulkarni slogans were raised. As the workers present had insisted that the two leaders on the dais were the real Congress, Dev Raj had, on the spur of the moment, announced the formation of a new party. He had also announced that Pradhan would be its president. The party had been named Congress (N), with the N standing for Nationalist.

Expectedly, both Dev Raj and Pradhan had been expelled from the party for a period of six years. With this, divisions in the Congress had increased. Though the Central Working Committee, full of Reddy's men, had endorsed the expulsions, many senior leaders had criticised the split. The line was the same: that the split, though not large, would certainly mar the already bleak electoral prospects of the party. The pressure on Kulkarni, and thereby Naik, was even greater that it had been thirty days before.

In such circumstances, the scenario predicted by Asim Banerjee was appearing more and more likely. In the intervening period, Naik had been shuttling between Bombay and Delhi. He had been clear on one point with Kulkarni: the schedule according to which he intended the plan to unfold would have to be followed strictly. Any undue haste would result in further harm to them.

Prakash Mittal had been assisting Naik throughout this period. On occasion they had been joined by Prakash's son Rajan who had been roped in by his father. In the beginning, Naik had reservations about this, but his friend had reassured him. Prakash Mittal claimed that while he had risen the hard way, his talented son had watched and assisted his father. He

139

claimed that Rajan possessed wisdom beyond his years. Naik had dropped his objections after a while. He knew Bombay but Mittal knew Delhi and he needed Mittal's expertise. In addition, he wanted to involve the least number of people. It was preferable that Mittal got his son along rather than strangers over whom he would have little control.

Rajan Mittal had not actually struggled as his father liked to believe. He had watched his father struggle. That was the end of it. He had stepped into college and stepped out when the senior Mittal was striking gold. He had not taken the shift from a two-room barsati in Karol Bagh to a mansion in Greater Kailash with stability. The next few years of his life had been spent in discotheques and bars and discovering women. He had not quite understood that the girls came only for the money he spent every night and for the experience of riding in his Mitsubishi Pajero. His father had not changed but he had no time to monitor his son. It was a constant party for the younger Mittal. Wealth was making him self-destruct.

At that stage, a temporary setback restored his sanity. He had been out dancing at Ghungroo, Delhi's well-known disco, when he saw what he thought was the most beautiful face ever. Being accustomed to the persuasive power of his wealth he had asked her to dance. She had agreed, but reluctantly. The problem had arisen when Rajan had attempted to extend their meeting from the floor of the disco to the rooms of the hotel. She had refused. He had taken it as an invitation to become more forceful. When the verbal tiff degenerated into his pounding her face with a small club he carried, the police entered the picture. The following morning the matter was taken up by the Press. The girl was the daughter of a retired bureaucrat. Her family promised vengeance.

Prakash Mittal immediately arranged for his son to be let out on bail. Then he called a meeting with the girl's father.

After listening to his threats and abuses, he began to talk business with the man. The compromise involved his paying for the girl's trip to the US, both for reconstructive surgery and subsequent stay abroad. Her parents on their part withdrew the case and stopped talking to the papers. In addition to all this the magistrate had taken a sum of two lakh rupees to grant bail to Rajan. Prakash had personally gone to the jail to receive him. Throughout the journey from the jail, he didn't say a word. The minute they reached the office, he had given vent to his feelings. He thrashed his son. He didn't accuse him of loose morals or harming his prestige but repeatedly questioned his foolishness.

'You think I have slogged all my life for this?' he thundered, again slapping his son. 'And for what, for a girl? You want women, do you? The next time your libido starts galloping just let me know, I will arrange for ten women and all at home.' He taunted and ridiculed his son for many hours. That effort had salvaged Rajan's life. He turned a new leaf. He was still hot-blooded and impulsive, but he stopped making petty mistakes. Now he let out steam in business. He was not above hobnobbing with the denizens of the underworld, from local strongmen to experienced sharpshooters. It was rumoured that the dreaded Bunty Yadav was his friend, and he was said to have intervened in the fratricidal feuds that dotted the gangster-infested belt of Delhi–Ghaziabad and Noida.

22

The man emerged from his black Maruti Esteem. Slowly he walked towards the small market. It was late afternoon and he needed to eat. He looked at the two Chinese restaurants standing side-by-side and then chose the one that he'd patronised many years back.

Who said that everything had to evolve, he thought after he'd ordered. If one wished, nothing had to change. The restaurant had not changed, their menu cards had not changed; he thought he even remembered some of the waiters. His soup arrived, and he began eating. As he ate, he became conscious of a pair of eyes staring in his direction. He turned to look.

There were four of them. Two young boys, probably with their girlfriends. It was the boys who were looking at him. Their gaze seemed hostile. He shook his head, smiled to himself and turned to his soup. It was obvious that the girls had commented on him, thus infuriating their partners. It was amusing the way young men let themselves be manipulated, he thought.

Aware that the two couples were looking at him, he turned his attention to the spring rolls. He was not particularly fond of them. In fact, he was not fond of food at all. Had not been for so long. To be precise, from the time he had become vegetarian. It had been a good step in a way. It had released him from the bondage of food. He remembered how, as a teenager, he had loved non-vegetarian food. Even today when he ran into old friends, they would gasp with disbelief that he had turned vegetarian. He did not remember the exact date he had given up meat though normally he was a genius with dates. But he remembered the year. That had been the last year.

The last year he had enjoyed life. The last time he had a desire to live, when he had enjoyed the sun, when he had slept at night. After that, there had been no taste in food, no pleasure in sleep, no desire to enjoy the chirping of birds in the morning. Nothing was the same after that year.

After that particular year gone through the motions of life zombie-like, like a robot making programmed moves. He did not like the way he had become but he knew he was helpless to an extent. That was why he had not made a particularly strong attempt to counter the pain. The pain gave his life some semblance of a normal life. He paid the bill, left a generous tip and walked out.

Rajan Mittal strode confidently into his cabin in Prakash Chambers, the corporate headquarters of Prakash Mittal's companies which occupied one full floor of Nirmal Towers on Barakhamba Road. Rajan had just had lunch at the United Coffee House in Connaught Place with an old client-turned-friend. As he settled into his leather chair, he thought about his schedule for the rest of the day. In the evening, he had to meet Bhaskar Naik with his father. It was time to set Plan

Alpha into motion. Its success would depend heavily on his contacts working out: his father was leaving the execution of the plan totally in his hands. It would be his men they would use. After Naik okayed it, one final report would have to be given to Kulkarni. Kulkarni was constantly demanding reports despite the fact that he trusted Naik with his life. The reason Naik had given to the Mittals was that Kulkarni wanted to ensure that no limits were crossed. According to Naik, even a small hitch could, instead of boosting the party's prospects, harm them further. Rajan was quite impatient with the tight control that was being imposed by Naik in Kulkarni's name. He suspected Kulkarni was less interested than Naik himself in receiving all information.

When Rajan had raised the issue with his father, Prakash had calmed him and attempted to explain that whatever role they were going to play in the plan was courtesy Naik. He had given them a golden opportunity that they could not afford to squander on issues like Rajan's ego. He had told his son of the opportunities that would be open to them if the plan went the distance and succeeded. He had explained that once wealth had been acquired, what remained was power. Power was the ultimate aphrodisiac, according to Prakash. After a long discussion with his father, Rajan had agreed to be patient and accommodating towards Naik.

He, unlike his father, did not admire Naik. He found fault with his pace and style which were too slow and too placid for his liking. He prided himself on living on the edge and still delivering the goods with efficiency. He did not believe in the slow fixing techniques of wining and dining. He belonged to a generation that revered money instead of god. He had grown up in a time when bullets made of solid and efficient steel were cheaper than food. So where was the need to build relationships with people? It was far simpler to buy them and their loyalty. And for those who could not be bought, there was always the efficient steel.

In college, Rajan had, apart from studying the fairer sex, also dabbled in politics. He had never had the time to contest elections but had supported candidates. It was the first-hand experience of those heady days that had made him addicted to politics.

His father was right, this was the first time he was getting a chance to get into the big league of political fixing. He hoped his contacts would not fail him when he needed them the most. The man he would be banking on very heavily in the coming days was an old friend. He hoped Rajesh Rathee had not lost any of his sharpness.

The black Esteem turned into the parking lot of Lodhi Gardens. He had been driving towards home when he had remembered something which had made him advance his walk by a couple of hours. As he began his walk, he was no longer smiling. He was now beginning to get annoyed with himself. He was aware that he was slipping far too much. It was out of the ordinary. He had decided to watch himself for another day and then decide on his course of action. Now it was time to burn the spring rolls and exercise his heart. What had made him take his walk earlier than usual was the thought of the two women who had followed him yesterday. He had tried his level best to ignore them but had finally given up. His senses were simply too trained to block out the awareness of being watched.

Five minutes into the walk and he was still unable to switch off from the present. That had rarely happened. It was all due to those blasted women. He cursed them softly. He would have to get in touch with his consortium and put his mind to work now. His whole schedule was getting disturbed.

His thoughts grew quieter, the turmoil settled as he approached the small squat stone benches near the first bend. Yes he was now entering the past, the metaphysical recesses of his soul would soon take over, and he would be under his own spell. It had to be a man under a spell to whom two square stone benches could mean anything.

Exactly an hour later, he got back into his car and headed for home. He had ultimately managed to drift, but his body was not aching as much as it normally did. The hot water bottle would not be required today, of that he was sure. As he turned into his gate, he found himself remembering David. What a pair David and he had made—friends, philosophers and guides to each other. Supporting each other, understanding each other's hurt, not trying to demean each other with platitudes and words of sympathy that never lessened the pain. Yes they were a pair, leaving an imprint on time, on the world, in their own way.

23

CHANDIGARH, OCTOBER 3, 1995

The capital of the states of Punjab and Haryana is an exceptionally beautiful city—an aberration in the crowd of unplanned Indian concrete jungles. It has a distinctly serene air to it, possibly a reason why it is often dismissed as a city for retired people. The Punjab and Haryana high court is part of the city's French architect, Le Corbusier's glorious vision. It occupies one end of a huge rectangle with the opposite end bounded by the state secretariat. On the side of the secretariat is the assembly, both buildings designed so as to appear like large ships.

The roof of the high courts, with its consistent crests and troughs of concrete, is constructed so as to appear as waves. The huge gap between the two ends of the complex was originally designed to accommodate a large pool so that, looked at from a suitable vantage point, it would appear like a ship gliding through the sea. Unfortunately the grand vision of the Frenchman seems to have been frustrated by the reality of official neglect.

It was lunch hour and small groups of lawyers sat in the gentle autumn sun chatting and gossiping. Rajesh Singh Rathee sat with his cronies, all conversing in chaste Haryanvi. They were busy commenting on the vital statistics of a new lady lawyer. Their risqué remarks were interrupted by Rathee's clerk. He whispered in Rathee's ear and Rathee excused himself and got up. Bhupinder Hooda, Rathee's lunch mate and courtroom rival, yelled after him, 'Are you in so much of a hurry to make contact with the new lawyer?' Rathee ignored the friendly taunt and hurried to his chamber.

Five minutes later he replaced the receiver. He had some important cases coming up and he did not want to leave them in the hands of his two juniors and his clerk. The problem was that it was no ordinary person who wanted him in Delhi. It was Rajan Mittal. Rathee knew that Rajan could not be refused casually. Also, if Mittal wanted him in Delhi, he must have an important reason for it. Rathee was the same age as Rajan Mittal. He had known Rajan since their college days in Delhi. Rathee used to live in a rented tenement in Outram Lines in the vicinity of the university and Mittal had often spent nights with him. In fact, Rathee's room had been a second home for Rajan. The young Rajan had been generous with money, often bailing out Rathee with his rental liabilites. Rathee had in turn shown Rajan a side of life he had never been exposed to.

Once Rathee had started practising, Rajan came to him often for advice on quasi-legal matters. Rathee was aware that Rajan flirted with interests that were not quite above board and liked the feeling of living on the edge. Rathee yelled for his clerk, and told the man to arrange for his tickets to Delhi. He would catch the Shatabdi Express that linked Chandigarh to Delhi.

ISLAMABAD

Brig. Nazir was extremely excited. He had received an urgent message from Maj. Tariq ten minutes ago. Tariq had informed him that he had managed to get hold of Col. Abbas' entire data file before and during his service. He was heading straight for Nazir's residence. Nazir had decided that this file was something that required his total attention, so he would pore over it at length sitting at home and not at the CFIO headquarters. Maj. Tariq had not even opened the file. The minute he had got hold of it, he had contacted his superior. Nazir's heart beat rapidly with anticipation. He fervently hoped that he would find something to link the colonel with the premier's son-in-law, any small reference that could justify the niggling doubts that he felt every time he spoke to him.

Nazir went to his front gate as he heard the screech of Azim's jeep. Tariq entered without greeting his superior, laid the file on Nazir's desk in his study and waited with bated breath. Nazir slowly picked up the file and started flipping the pages. Maj. Tariq watched him without a word. 'Nothing really odd in his service record. Let's look at his pre-service record.' After twenty minutes he sat down without a word on his chair. Tariq tried to guess what Brig. Nazir was thinking. Then Nazir spoke. 'My God Azim, what have you done, what have I done!'

'I do not understand Sir, what is it?'

'Do you realise your delay could have put both our careers, and our lives, on line?' Azim stared at him, worry lines now beginning to crease his brow.

'Do you know where Col. Abbas was born and spent his early years? In Mallo Majra—I think the village is called Shah Khan Kucha now. Gen. Mehmood's life was once saved by his faithful batman, when his vehicle had almost blown up while he was on an official inspection tour. The General and his staff had taken refuge in the nearest village. There the village chief's house had been his abode for next twenty days till he recovered his health. Our premier was so indebted, he took the chief's son with him to the city and brought him up like

149

his own son. The village, my good major, was Mallo Majra and the boy was our very own Mohd. Shujaat.'

'Oh God! I do not believe this!' exclaimed the major.

'We both have to believe this Azim. I do not think we need a link stronger than this!'

'Sir, when was the last time you briefed Col. Abbas?' Tariq asked hesitantly.

'Ask when I have not briefed him! Shujaat is sure to be aware of my latest move. He even knows of my coming moves.'

'Well, whatever you are planning is for the glory of Pakistan. What will he gain by interfering in it?'

'What you are saying makes sense with a normal man. Mohd. Shujaat is not normal. He will do anything to disgrace me. Pakistan's glory means nothing to him,' Brig. Nazir said, shaking his head. 'Although I have interacted with Shujaat only once, it was enough to judge him. I saw him for the parasite that he is; a manipulator of the lowest kind. Such men are not the kind who will let this opportunity go. He will only look at what he will get out of it—revenge for being removed from the CFIO meetings—and see it through, regardless of who else it affects.'

'So what is it that can now be done to salvage the situation? Our plans cannot be abandoned without jeopardising the eventual success of K2 itself.'

'Yes, I know that. The plan has to go on as before. As if I did not have enough worries, I now have that bastard to contend with as well.'

'Why do we not just eliminate Shujaat as well? Let us pay our hit-man double and first get rid of Shujaat.'

The trick worked. Tariq had said it to ease the tension, and Nazir started laughing. 'Would not work either. Our man will be insulted by a target as insipid as Shujaat. I think there is only one serious option that can be examined. I have to confront Col. Abbas with this information. I have to demand from him the extent of information that has been passed on to Shujaat.'

'You think he will be honest with you?'

'I do not know Azim, I have no time for subtleties now. I have got to take the shortest and the straightest way out.'

'I do not know, Sir. If he owes his success to Shujaat in any way, I am not sure whether a confrontation would help.'

'It's the only way. I will give Col. Abbas the glory of the country on the one hand and his loyalty to Shujaat on the other. He will have to choose. If he really is an army man, I have no doubt he will make the right choice.'

Maj. Tariq walked out of Brig. Nazir's residence a worried man. He was not as convinced as his superior that Col. Abbas would be able to forsake whatever loyalty he had towards Shujaat. He knew from personal experience that old loyalties took years to build and years to destroy. They could not be wiped out in a flash. If there was any substantial link between the families of Shujaat and that of Col. Abbas, the Brigadier was in for serious trouble. Azim had often imagined himself heading the ISI one day or at least being in Nazir's position, but that was in the past. Today he was glad that he was only a lowly Major and not Lt. Gen. Hussain or Brig. Nazir. It was good to be free, thought Azim to himself.

Plus he had to also think of his own interests. He had bent several regulations and used a lot of old contacts to get Abbas' data file. If Abbas was so powerful, he could also be in trouble for daring to check the data record. That was also one reason why he was not very enthusiastic about Brig. Nazir using the direct approach with him. That would for one involve telling Abbas how the information had been obtained. For a moment Azim cursed himself for not choosing cricket as a career. He had after all once played for the same club as Rashid Latif and Mushtaq Ahmad.

Meanwhile, Brig. Nazir was desperately trying to clear his mind. Today was Radley Karras' last day in Pakistan and Nazir was to meet him for a final briefing. Maj. Chaudhary had sent more information from London that would have to be painstakingly sifted by Karras. After that, he would have to either write to Karras or contact him via satellite channels for his advice. Nazir knew that to request Karras to extend his stay in Pakistan would be abusing their friendship. It was enough that the man had come from as far as the Bahamas. He would have to make do with whatever advice Radley gave him now. Once they zeroed in on the contact in London, the rest could be managed.

Karras noticed Nazir's agitation when they met that evening at the hotel. But when he was told the reason why, Karras was dismissive. Nazir was getting too focused on peripheral problems, Karras felt. Nazir tried to argue that Mohd. Shujaat was in no manner a peripheral problem. But Karras would have none of it. Finally, he said that Shujaat could be taken care of later. Right now, they had more pressing concerns. Nazir showed him all the latest correspondence he had received from London.

'This man you have in London, what is his name?'

'Chaudhary, Maj. Mustaq Chaudhary,' replied the Brigadier.

'He is good, very good. He is quite systematic and extremely thorough with his enquiries. If you become the premier of your country consider this man for the chief of ISI.'

'I'm probably not going to even make General, Rad,' said a nervous Nazir.

'No Saint, in your country you never know. Anyone could be president tomorrow, even you.' Like most Americans,

Karras was hugely proud of his country's unshakable democratic credentials. Being an intelligence man, he understood why Pakistan kept lapsing back to dictatorship. But because he understood the basic dynamics of that country, he was sympathetic rather than contemptuous. 'Okay, let's get down to business, Saint, shall we? Your man in London has now narrowed down the list of men to three. You will now have to approach all of them.

'Is it safe to just walk up to them and ask their partner's or their boss' working price?

'Of course not, you cannot just walk up to them. You take formal appointments first after introducing yourself. The two wrong men will balk at the thought of an alien country's intelligence man seeking appointments with them. Our man, the real contact, will be very composed. Actually he will probably be a little worried, but he will not show it. He will be aware that you may well have an attractive assignment for him. So he will sound very crisp, formal and businesslike. The other two will be all confusion. With the other two, don't take it beyond the appointment. Apologise profusely, tell them you mistook them for someone else, which is anyway true, let them yell at you if they want and then just leave quietly. Trust me, they'll probably be too scared to even mention the meeting to anyone, leave alone report it to the authorities.'

'And with the third man, the real contact?'

'Yes, the third man. You have to be careful with him. Treat him as you would a business executive. Do not fool around with him. Make sure you convey to him that you are serious. If he decides otherwise, he will not entertain you for even a moment.'

'We will do that no doubt, but how can we convince him of our bona fides and our seriousness?'

'Well, if you think or get the impression that you are not being taken seriously, weave the discussion towards the various intelligence services of the world.' Karras paused as Nazir listened intently. 'Bring in Mossad and then say that its elite Shalom brigade did a lot of good work in the Gulf War.'

'Fine, anything you say, but what does that mean?'

'That doesn't matter. It will serve your purpose, trust me.'

'That's okay but I would feel a little foolish uttering words that do not mean a thing to me. At least tell me what this Shalom brigade is.'

'I am telling you, you and your men are better off not knowing about the Shalom brigade.'

'Rad, you are making me very anxious. What is it, some unit like our CFIO or an execution squad?'

'Okay, I will tell you this much: ten men of this force can thrash all the irregulars you have in Kashmir, and that too within a matter of hours. Any more questions, Saint?'

'No, I think I have heard enough.' Nazir was a little shaken by the reference to Kashmir.

'That's good, I thought you would understand. Now just relax and concentrate on what you have to do.'

For the next two hours Radley Karras explained the logistics of the approach. Later that night, after Karras had left the country, Nazir reflected on what the American had told him. He knew what the Mossad was capable of; but what he had heard from Karras had chilled him. What if, in the future, India's RAW and Mossad started collaborating? Decades of hard work would go down the drain. To guard against that eventuality, he *had* to succeed now. To add to his worries was a news report he had seen an hour before. It mentioned that Avadh Shukla had just returned to India after a long friendship tour to Israel. Shukla was the second in command after Prof. Kapre and the man who would most certainly be foreign minister in an REP government at New Delhi.

154

24

ISLAMABAD, OCTOBER 3, 1995

The minute his wife fell asleep, Shujaat got up from the bed and walked to his dressing room. The wing assigned to the premier's daughter and her husband was slightly cut off from the main palace. Mohd. Shujaat opened the console next to the chest of drawers and dialled a number from his secure line. No secure lines were allowed from the presidential palace but Shujaat had managed to circumvent this order. If Gen. Mehmood had one chink in his armour, it was his attitude towards his son-in-law. He trusted him implicitly and could not refuse his requests. Over the years, Shujaat had become used to getting his way with the premier. His ego had taken a massive beating when he had been barred from attending the meetings of the K2 general command, he had even sworn vengeance against Lt. Gen. Hussain. As he replaced the receiver after getting the most recent update, his mood lightened a little. His chance was coming.

The only hitch was the price attached to his getting vengeance against Lt. Gen. Hussain. It could be the glory of Pakistan itself. He thought for a moment. Could he let this opportunity slip and postpone his revenge? No, he decided, the country could wait, not he. He would make sure that the ISI had a new chief within the next few months. And this time he would ensure that the service was headed by someone who would respect him.

His last move had been a masterstroke. He had managed to place a mole near the officer-in-charge of K2. Now he had two or three informants in that section. He knew he had the resources to influence the outcome of Brig. Nazir's grand plan and ensure Hussain's humiliation. The altered scenario, he was sure, would not affect the position of his father-in-law. Shujaat counted his father-in-law among the few people he respected. According to him, Gen. Mehmood had made only one error. That was appointing someone as arrogant as Lt. Gen. Hussain to the second-most important position in Pakistan. And now he had taken it upon himself to make sure that error was rectified. He was not bothered too much about K2 and its allied projects. If K2 ended, some new project could always be started. Anything for the ISI to play with. He was not too concerned with destabilising India.

India, by his yardstick, was an extremely soft state and could never threaten his country. The time for that had long passed. They had let go of chances in 1947, 1965, even 1971. Whatever had been achieved by India in 1971, according to Shujaat, was out of sheer luck. And in a way they had done Pakistan a favour, for which his country should have been thankful. East Pakistan was a mistake from the start. It was an unnecessary burden, an appendix-like addition to the main body. Pakistan should have been concentrating on better and more purposeful things, rather than spending millions of dollars on a neighbour which was itself in decay. So the opportunity to settle scores with India was not as priceless as an opportunity to settle scores with Lt. Gen. Ghulam Hussain.

He now had information of even the minutest details of Nazir's plans. Including Radley Karras' visit. He smiled to himself, thinking how secure Brig. Nazir was probably feeling in the knowledge that his secret meetings with the American were not known to anyone. The knowledge of Nazir's attempts to collaborate with Karras was of special benefit to Shujaat. For now, he need not complain to the premier in order to put a spoke in the plans. He could proceed without the premier's clearance and later on justify it as having needed to act immediately. For that, he would use his own loyal staff. He had over the years built up his own team of men. These men considered his word to be gospel and their numbers cut across all the services and the Pakistani bureaucracy. These men would die for him, without expecting any reward whatsoever.

25

Radley Karras always had a problem passing time in planes. For years he had envied passengers who could just pull back their seats and fall asleep or those who would spend time reading books. He was unable to do either. All he could do was think. He had missed his connecting flight from Frankfurt to New York which had meant a delay of six hours. As he lay back in his seat on the Lufthansa flight, he couldn't help but think of his last meeting with Nazir, particularly the reference to the Shalom brigade of the Mossad. There had really been no reason for him to tell Nazir what he had. His original intention had been to limit himself to nothing more than tactical advice. But now he had made sure that the contract would be taken. He was feeling a twinge of guilt for breaking his own unwritten code. He was again interfering in matters falling within the domain of active service. He did not want the REP to come to power in India. The United States did not want it, the CIA did not want it, his own naval intelligence did not want it.

Saddam Hussein was enough for them. It would be too much for his country to have to cope with a Prof. Kapre now.

158

The REP had the bomb on its agenda, they had Diego Garcia on the agenda, Agni and a lot more dangerous plans that his friend, the Saint, could neither imagine nor understand. Of course, the REP advocated closer ties with his country but Karras knew that with such policies, India would inevitably clash with the US. His friends in the CIA had told him three years back that a man called Kapre was soon going to take over and that he was going to be bad news for the States. Yet they could not touch him directly. But now it was the ISI that would. And he had in his own way made sure that they could. He smiled as he thought how Nazir had been shocked by the information he had given him about the Mossad.

It had all begun three years ago. Sam Langford, the regional head of Citibank had been killed in Riyadh after a prestigious project with some local businessmen had gone awry. His colleagues in the CIA had told him that the Americans had worked extremely hard to sniff out the trail of Langford's killers. The trail had led them to a Jordanian double agent who had access to the Mossad.

The rumours doing the rounds of Mossad were that another Carlos was in the making, one that was more accurate than the Jackal immortalised by Forsyth and less arrogant than Carlos. But the Israeli service, much to the annoyance of their American counterparts, had left the matter alone, believing the killings to be a few lucky hits by local fundamentalists or freelance anarchists acting on behalf of the warring feudal families of the oil-rich sheikhdoms. After that Karras had heard whispers distinctly suggestive of a renegade Mossad man, someone who had served in the Shalom brigade once. But they were all rumours, nothing more.

His instincts now told him that there could not be two expert assassins operating in the Middle East and Asia. It had to be the same person that had killed Langford. There were

159

very few good contract men left now. By his own estimates there was Robert Lee, who operated primarily in the Golden Triangle. There was Alberto Numez who was working for both the law and the mob in South America, and there was the ex-Mossad man. Europe, thankfully, was being spared. Only the Soviets and eastern European freelancers roamed there, unlike the Seventies and Eighties when Ursa Gomez and Illich Ramirez Sanchez had both plied their trade with a vengeance in Europe and had on occasions crossed the seas to come to the US. One of these visits had cost Karras his most respected superior, William Ford, then deputy chief of naval intelligence. It was Ford who had been responsible for the resounding success achieved by Britain in the Falklands war. Men chosen by Ford and trained by Karras had been responsible for Noreiaga's downfall in Panama. Ford had been found dead in his home, the result of a contract brought out on him, allegedly by Vassily Kirichenko, then chief of the KGB and a proclaimed lifelong enemy of Ford.

It was this and similar information that had always been sent to Karras in the Bahamas. His friends living on the mainland, some still in service and others retired but better informed, knew that Rad loved getting regular updates.

Karras had full faith in the abilities of the man from the Mossad, but he did not have the same confidence about Nazir and his men. The service was full of internecine feuds and personal rivalries. He was not sure that Nazir would be able to keep his end clear. In fact Karras was betting on the fact that if the Pakistani plan ran into hot weather it would be because of treachery from within the ISI. Such instances had occurred in the CIA and ONI as well during the Cold War. A successful step had meant a climb of three to four rungs and correspondingly a failure had ensured retirement at the same position. For career intelligence men, the stakes were poised extremely delicately. And if the American intelligence was not immune to this malady, he was sure the Pakistanis weren't either.

SOMEWHERE IN THE ASIAN CONTINENT, OCTOBER 6, 1995

The man moved towards the special room. He was supposed to check it during this time of the night: it was a rule that he followed. The room at first glance was fairly ordinary. Built into the east wall beyond and above the oblong table was a console of audiovisual components that included projectors. Through the technology of a remote controlled miniature disc on the roof, the sophisticated unit was capable of picking up satellite and shortwave transmissions from all over the globe. The mechanism was so built that its waves did not interfere with the normal transmissions of the host country and its official satellite links.

He sat down in front of the table to watch. He knew he had to wait for twenty minutes. If what he was looking for was to happen, it would happen within that time. He waited patiently. After about ten minutes a small red light glowed on the fourth lateral. A carousel of slide photographs had been inserted and was ready for operation. The man got up and ran to the second lateral in the signals. Now the slides would be accompanied by decoded messages describing what the slides were. He pushed a few more switches. There was a whining sound. The first slide lit up. It was a man in civilian clothes. He looked at it with interest and then checked the digital decoder. He read it with part interest, part amusement. What was the world coming to? The next slide came on. It showed yet another man. He again checked the digital decoder. He rubbed his forehead again. This was becoming more and more interesting. He remained at the screen for the next few minutes. Then he switched off the electronic panels and left the room.

He had been presented with the preliminary information. The decision was up to him. He had to think for a day and then he would communicate his decision via the same satellite link. The final terms, as always, would be negotiated by him only.

ISLAMABAD, OCTOBER 7, 1995

Brig. Nazir and Maj. Tariq sat in the CFIO chief's office at the headquarters. 'You're still not convinced that we can trust him even now?' queried the worried Brigadier of his most trusted lieutenent.

'Sir, I had told you earlier also, it's all a perception of loyalty. I just think that he owes more to Shujaat than he can owe to anyone else, or even to the country. Apart from that you have probably done the right thing. There will be no hitch, I hope, yet we should still be careful. The time has come for you to stop briefing the Colonel accurately. Let him prove his loyalty. Let him report what Shujaat is up to for a change. After that we will treat him like one of the boys.'

Nazir remained silent. It was one thing to not give Col. Abbas the full picture, to leave out small details, but to deliberately mislead him…that would be very risky. How would Gen. Mehmood react if he ever found out, and what would Lt. Gen. Hussain say? The ISI head would probably understand. But the premier was another matter. The other option was no less risky. Brief Abbas fully and risk Shujaat's chance of using the information to his detriment. Both Lt. Gen. Hussain, his own and several other heads would surely roll.

Maj. Tariq looked with concern as his superior repeatedly rubbed his forehead. He did not interrupt the Brigadier. He

162

was aware that the coming weeks would see Nazir in similar moods. He himself was beginning to succumb to the tension. But Nazir was beginning to rely on him increasingly, so he had to remain calm. Nazir and Maj. Tariq were waiting for a communication from Maj. Chaudhary in London who had conveyed to them that he may have already made contact with the right man. The day after Karras had left, Brig. Nazir had decided that they would not contact the man in London directly; they would go through Maj. Chaudhary again. Once the assassin's aide agreed and gave some indication of his partner's willingness, they would take over.

The intercom on Nazir's desk buzzed. The Brigadier picked up the receiver and muttered a few words into it. He then turned to Tariq. 'Maj. Chaudhary has sent a detailed message from London and it is being faxed to this office.' Azim got up and went to the fax machine installed in one corner of the office. After a few minutes the four sheets were handed over to the Brigadier who carefully went through the contents.

'Chaudhary found our man.'

'He did?' said a visibly relieved Maj. Tariq.

'Yes, he managed to reach him, though with great difficulty. According to Ray Darrel, that is his name, his partner will consider taking up our offer.'

'They are still at the considering stage, Sir?'

'So this Darrel claims, but Maj. Chaudhary has added that it seemed to him that Darrel was convinced of our intentions.'

'Then what is going to be the next development?'

'Well, Darrel asked Chaudhary a lot of questions and then took his contact numbers from him. After that he told him to leave with the standard interview line—don't contact us, we will contact you. So what do you make of this report?'

'It certainly sounds promising, but were no terms regarding the payment or any related requirements discussed?'

'I told you, this man has to first discuss it with his partner, then he will inform Chaudhary of the decision. Only if they are interested will the details be discussed. At that stage only, will we meet the man and brief him about the target.'

'Sir, did Maj. Chaudhary have to use the magic words to convince this Darrel?' After Karras had surprised Nazir, the Brigadier had told Tariq what had been said about the Israeli strike force.

'Yes, he's mentioned it in the report. He had to, and it had the desired effect. It was after this that he talked business with Chaudhary.'

'So we can do nothing but wait?'

'I'm afraid so, that's all we can do at present. We have no clue where Darrel's partner is, in which part of the world, how much time Darrel will need before he can get in touch with this man. Whether he will be able to trace him at all. What if the man is in the midst of a mission, what if he is not in the mood to take on a fresh mission? I tell you, our line must be prey to the maximum number of imponderables.'

'Sir, what if there is no partner at all? I mean could not this Darrel be the killer himself?'

At this Nazir started laughing. 'It seems all you majors think alike.' The remark was not made in contempt but was laced with genuine humour. 'Do you know Chaudhary commented on the same possibility in his report. But at the same time he says that Darrel looks like a retired gentleman.'

Both men remained quiet for the next few minutes, aware that the final countdown had begun.

'Azim, I think the time has come for Maj. Chaudhary to be included in the inner circle. He is already aware of the plan. It would be better to summon him to Pakistan for a few days and brief him. So far he has acquitted himself in an exemplary manner. You will have to make arrangements for his meeting with me.'

164

'That shall be done Sir.'

'Of course it will have to be after Darrel gets in touch with him. And another thing, I want the watch on the Indian High Commission to be intensified. Make sure that there are no stray incidences of either torturing or beating up of any Indian staffers. That would just lead to unnecessary alarm across the border which we should avoid. Everything should be totally smooth for the next few days.'

Tariq nodded in agreement. 'I will pass the word to all the station CFIO headquarters so that all the station chiefs can keep their men in check.' Pakistan had hundreds of CFIO stations all over the country. These stations were staffed by squads of six to eight men, all commanded by one station head. These station men kept a watch and monitored the activities of all Indians in the country as well as the Hindus settled in Pakistan. Special targets of these squads were also the Mohajirs or the Pakistanis that had originally come from India. Pakistani families who would otherwise be above suspicion, but had relatives in India were also on the watch lists. 'Do we also put our men in India on extra alert?' asked Tariq.

'No, not yet, we will do that after this man begins his assignment officially. He will have to visit India in advance to understand the logistics of that country. At that time, or just before, we will put all our Indian agents and freelancers on full alert. No point in making them anxious right now.'

26

NEW DELHI, OCTOBER 7, 1995

Rajan Mittal turned his car into the driveway that was choked with vehicles. The light blue signboard at the gate said 'District Courts, Tis Hazari'. As his Toyota Crown Royal Saloon struggled for parking space, Rajan wished he had brought the smaller Maruti 800. He had heard about the Delhi's district courts but this was the first time he was seeing it for himself. The place was literally crawling with people.

Finally he managed to squeeze his Toyota into a small gap and got out of the car. From his pocket he pulled out a slip of paper. The address scrawled on it—Chamber No. 550, Western Wing, Tis Hazari—was one his friend Rajesh had given him. Rajan had told him what he was looking for, and a few days after he'd returned to Chandigarh, Rajesh had been able to deliver.

Having asked for directions from the parking attendant, Mittal trudged on. He was taken aback by the sheer size of the building. It extended at least over a kilometre lengthwise from end to end. He reached the rear of the building. The area looked more like an old Delhi bazaar. Between thousands of men in black seated on rickety tables and chairs, there were policemen, fruit vendors, *chhole bature wallahs* and others.

He had now come to a gate that led to what appeared like a thousand dingy lanes. It reminded him of his ancestral home in central Delhi's Karol Bagh. There were rows of small rooms, all numbered and carrying the names of their occupants. He heard a screeching sound and looked up. Hanging from an electric wire was a monkey. In fact there were many of them. He smiled to himself. What a contrast this place presented from the lawyer's offices he had seen in even the smaller country towns of the US!

He reached number 550 and looked at the signboard. It said 'Prithpal Singh Rathee, BA, LLB, Advocate'. Rajan looked inside nervously. A man was seated behind a small table. He looked up. 'Come in, come in, Rajesh had called up from Chandigarh today.' Rajan introduced himself to the lawyer, handing him his card. 'What will you have? Tea, coffee, or something cold?'

'Nothing, don't bother.'

'No, no, how can that be, you have come here for the first time, at least you must have coffee,' said the lawyer, clapping his hands a couple of times. A young boy appeared. The lawyer handed him a ten-rupee note. 'He is my *munshi*, you know, clerk. He is new, I am still in the process of training him.'

Rajan nodded and then spoke. 'Did Rajesh tell you why I have come?'

'No, he didn't want to mention it on the phone but he did say that it is something very important.'

'Yes, it is. I am looking for this man. I think you can help me find him.' He passed him a small slip of paper.

Rathee's eyes flickered with interest at the name on the sheet. 'Did Rajesh tell you why I would be able to help you?'

'I did not ask him. I don't question his judgement on most matters, I just told him what I wanted and he referred me to you.'

'Do I arrange a meeting with him or do I just tell you of his whereabouts?' asked the lawyer. Rajan remained silent. He needed a few minutes to think. By then the boy had returned with two plastic cups of steaming coffee. Mittal took his cup with skepticism. A few sips and he changed his mind about the coffee altogether.

Rathee laughed, sensing his change of heart. 'Everything is good here, but you have to experience it. Don't be deceived by the environment. This place grows on you. You see all these lawyers? Do you think they are here because they need to earn a living? In fact most of them cannot do without this place. If you give them the option of shifting to the other courts in the city, they will refuse. You see Tis Hazari is a place that has its own charm. After a while you get addicted to it.'

Mittal listened with rapt attention. He had been extremely put off by the chaos in the complex when he had arrived. But now he was being entertained by riveting anecdotes by the lawyer. He spoke in a mixture of rustic Haryanvi and everyday Hindi, which added to the impact of the jokes. Rajan had picked up a smattering of the language, another vestige of his college days.

After about a quarter of an hour, he was ready with his answer. He informed the lawyer that he did not need to meet the man right now and would be satisfied with knowing his whereabouts.

'Then Rajan *ji*, I cannot divulge to you his whereabouts right now.'

'Why not?' Mittal asked, startled.

'A man like him could have many enemies. When you have to see him, you can contact me, and I will tell you where you can find him.'

'You don't trust me do you? It seems that Rajesh did not tell you how far we go back.' Rajan's tone was angry as well as injured.

'Rajesh told me everything and he would understand what I am saying. It does not have anything to do with trust or honour. It is purely a matter of taking precautions. Let us assume that I tell you this man's whereabouts, and again assume that you pass this information to the wrong people, then who will suffer? And Sir, please don't take offence to what I am saying, I am only talking of possibilities. When you wish to see him, let me know.'

Later, as he cooled his heels in a traffic jam alongside the Inter State Bus Terminus, Rajan cursed both the Rathees. When his temper cooled, he began to wonder at the irony of the situation. He had gone to a lawyer to be able to contact the best sharpshooter in the western Uttar Pradesh underworld. A lawyer was guiding him to a man sought after by the police departments of seven states. It appeared as though lawyers were going to be an integral part of both Plan Alpha and Plan Beta.

In the meeting with Naik the previous evening, it had been decided that preparations had to be made for both the plans simultaneously. It would be too risky to put off planning for Plan Beta till it was required. Naik had cautioned the Mittals that Plan Alpha might not be enough due to the rapidity with which the political situation was deteriorating. Naik had also given a last opportunity to the Mittals to reconsider their role in the entire plan after weighing the pros and cons.

Prakash Mittal and his son had had no second thoughts. Their reasoning was simple: they were so closely identified with the Congress in Delhi that any change in government would be mortally dangerous for them. They would go the whole hog, they had assured Naik. Despite noticing the irony of the link between lawyers and denizens of the underworld, Rajan had not even momentarily been bothered by what his father and he himself were getting enmeshed in. The difference according to him was that they, unlike lawyers, were not the keepers and guardians of society's conscience. Lawyers were, like doctors, under a moral obligation to serve society, he felt. But they were only businessmen. They were there only to make money.

SOMEWHERE IN THE ASIAN CONTINENT

As he sat in the room that often decided his destiny, he made his decision. He would go ahead with the project. He would convey his decision the next morning. It was past midnight already and he was doubtful about the signal coming in now. After all it had only come last night. In all their years of working together, assignments had never come on consecutive days.

Exactly at that moment, the red light glowed on the panel. He ran to the control switches and made the slide illuminator functional, also switching on the decoder. The first slide came on. The man in it was not known to him. It was the message that surprised him. After a good six years, he was hearing of the ETA. The second message came across. Yes it was from his old friend Emilio. They wanted his help. He was filled with admiration for Emilio and his men. He had not kept any contact with them, yet they had managed to find him. It was the same story all over the world. Insurgency groups everywhere were on the run. Even the group he had once instructed was in trouble. He decided he would send a response to London immediately. David would not be prepared, but this could not wait. He went to the panel and started pulling many small levers. The message would go in the form of a signal to the satellite in the eastern hemisphere of the world. From there it would be relayed to London where it would be received in a similar room by David.

Now he would have to work out a timetable for both the projects. He would have to meet with both the parties after David worked out the basic formalities. With Emilio's man, David would have to check when the ETA would need his service. As far as money was concerned, he doubted whether the ETA and Emilio would be able to afford him. But that did not matter. He would not charge his friend anything.

27

Maj. Chaudhary was hunched over his typewriter, typing furiously. He always typed his reports on his old Remington 984. He had not been lured by computers; he felt very uncomfortable around the machines. The Major was very excited and pleased with himself. This was going to be the final report he would send to Islamabad. His part was almost over. The evening before he had been contacted by the man called Darrel. Darrel had conveyed to the Major that his partner would take up the Pakistani project, of course at an extremely steep price. Mushtaq had not been granted the authority to negotiate the price. That would be taken care of by his superiors in Pakistan. Darrel had also conveyed that his partner would like a meeting with the Major's bosses in Pakistan.

The meeting had to be arranged within the next few days. It was this demand that was worrying Chaudhary and which he was incorporating into his report. He doubted whether the ISI top brass would be available at such short notice. As he gave the finishing touches to his report, he wondered whether he would be summoned to Islamabad. After all, it was his hard work that was responsible for tracing the man. It was also amply clear that he could no longer be kept in the dark about the true purpose of the plan. No stories about commissioning an assassination for some friendly country would convince him. It had to be India.

ISLAMABAD

Agent Gabriel sat in his room, his heart thumping with excitement. In the past, he had passed on many secrets to RAW but the present one was bigger than the lot. He had been on the Indians' payroll for more than three years now, and no longer suffered from any nervousness. He knew that he was the biggest catch RAW had in Pakistan. It had all begun three years ago in Islamabad itself. He had first been spotted by a sharp-eyed, relatively junior attaché at the Indian embassy. Three weeks later, he had been approached tentatively. The terms had been finalised at a function where a lecture was being delivered. The lecture focused on the similarities between Islam and Christianity. It was here that his Indian recruiter had named him Gabriel. Since then it had been a full-time job for him. He had passed on numerous nuggets of information, had blown the cover of hundreds of Pakistani agents in India, pre-empted many bomb blasts, almost led the Indians to the Memons, supplied the photographs of the Karachi hide-outs of Yakub Memon and Dawood Ibrahim and several other Indian criminals being sheltered in Pakistan.

Now he had crucial information for the Indians: the most ambitious operation launched in the many years since the inception of Project K2. In fact, thanks to him, the Indians were aware of K2, though for his sake they pretended ignorance. But this time they were in for a pleasant surprise. The plan to assassinate Prof. Kapre would give them great leverage against Pakistan in the international community. If they could apprehend the intended killer, it would be the icing on the cake. Gabriel was aware of the damage this could do to his country. He was aware how important Kapre's death was for Pakistan. But he was helpless.

People betray the land of their fathers for many reasons: resentment, ideology, lack of prospects, hatred of a superior, and of course the honey trap. Gabriel was a true mercenary. He was more than satisfied with the way his career had progressed. What troubled him was the fixed income. He wanted free cash, and he wanted to be able to spend it. Payments from his Indian bosses were accumulating in the Cayman Islands in the Caribbean. For three years he had waited for that one big bit of information that would make it worthwhile for him to flee Pakistan. That one huge payment after which he could leave the country and finally enjoy his earnings. It seemed that this was his chance. He was dead sure that the Indians would pay whatever was demanded for this bit of information. There was also no danger of them abandoning him. He was much too valuable for them. Besides, they had no idea that he was planning to quit for good.

He was aware that even the ISI had men placed in both RAW and the IB. As was his norm, he would convey the information only to the man who had recruited him, even though he had been transferred to London. It would involve a circuitous route, Islamabad to London and London to New Delhi, but there was no other option. This was the only safe way. If the information fell into the wrong hands, not only would it be rendered useless, but there would also be the danger of his cover being blown. And there was no way Gabriel was going to risk being exposed.

From a study of other spies, Gabriel had learnt that the ultimate test of a good spy was how long he could remain undetected. His heroes were Kim Philby and Guy Burgess. In recent times Aldrich Ames had been very successful. Ames, a CIA officer, had been a spy for the KGB—the highest paid spy in the world—for nine years. He had sold the identity of countless US agents before getting caught in 1994. Gabriel would not let that happen to him. And he wouldn't commit suicide or anything of that kind. He wanted to enjoy his hard-earned money.

ISLAMABAD, OCTOBER 10, 1995

'Well Major, this message from Chaudhary in London clears up the whole thing. We have our man now.' Brig. Nazir sounded extremely relieved.

Tariq however was not relaxing. He knew that within a few hours, the Brigadier would most probably find something else to worry about. 'What is going to be our next step then?' he asked his superior.

'It seems that this man is in a hurry to meet us and finalise the contract. He is ready to come to Pakistan whenever we are ready, but the earlier the better.'

'Can we meet him here or would neutral territory be better Sir?'

'No, no, let him come here. I am sending word to Chaudhary that we are prepared to receive this man and also that Chaudhary should reach Pakistan immediately.'

'What about Abbas, Sir?'

'Henceforth he is with us, but to prevent Shujaat from doing anything destructive, he plans to keep feeding him with unclear information.' What Brig. Nazir did not tell Tariq was that Abbas had informed him that, apart from him, Shujaat had other loyals in the K2 general command. Their identities were not known to the Colonel. Secondly, he had told Nazir

175

that Shujaat was aware of Radley Karras' visit to Pakistan. Both these bits of information had convinced Nazir that Col. Abbas had indeed turned in his favour.

To cover his own tracks, the Brigadier was going to meet Lt. Gen. Hussain in the evening. Nazir had decided that he would explain to Hussain the circumstances and the logic behind Karras' visit to their country so that when Shujaat informed Gen. Mehmood, and the premier in turned questioned Lt. Gen. Hussain, the ISI chief would not be taken by surprise.

Maj. Azim Tariq walked through the long and winding corridors from the wing that housed the CFIO headquarters to the one that was home to the ISI communications centre. He was supposed to send an urgent message to Mushtaq Chaudhary in London. As he walked, his thoughts again went to Col. Abbas. He was still not convinced of his loyalty. If he had the authority, he would have walked up to Lt. Gen. Hussain and told him everything. After that the whole risk would have shifted on to the shoulders of the chief of ISI. Though generally full of admiration for Brig. Nazir, Tariq was critical of his boss as far as the affair with Col. Abbas went. He genuinely believed that Nazir was making a mistake in trusting him.

He reached the communications centre and walked up to the electronic experts. After a few minutes the intelligence decoder was summoned. This man would encrypt the message to be sent to London in such a way that if it were interrupted by any electronic surveillance station between the tracks of London and Islamabad, it would become worthless. On being interrupted by even the same electronic frequency but signals different from those of the Pakistani High Commission, the encrypted message in the form of electronic signals would literally fade. In addition, the special technology was guaranteed to ensure that the location of the station from where the signals emanated would not be revealed. The general region would, of course, show up in the infiltrating satellite's data but the precise location would not be pointed out. Also, the break in the link would be reflected in the communications centre in Islamabad so it would be able to re-flash the signal in a different encrypted mode.

SOMEWHERE IN THE ASIAN CONTINENT

The man who Maj. Chaudhary had worked so hard to trace was sitting on the floor, cleaning his tools. He sat like a child in his play pen—an assortment of things lay around him. In front of him was the stiletto that he carried primarily for luck. Actually it was an extremely small blade knife, so small and compact that it fitted snugly into the small pouch strapped to his left arm. The small leather pouch that he had himself designed. The knife was many years old, a relic of a bygone era. He always carried it, but had rarely used it. The last time he had needed it was in Oman. Also in front of him lay cartons of Claymore mines and small pouches of Semtex. The carton and pouches had been delivered specially to him all the way from the Gulf.

He turned his attention to the guns. There was a small treasure that lay there—from Heckler and Koch machine pistols to the Czech Scorpions. He wasn't particularly fond of automatic pistols. They were too quick, too machine-like. What he liked was the personal touch of a Walther P-38. He had used the Walther on several occasions. The official pistol for the German forces throughout World War II, the Walther P-38 was a robust and straightforward 9 mm automatic based on a reliable recoil system of operation and reasonably easy to make. He had purchased it six years ago while on a mission in Dusseldorf. The features that impressed him were its reliability, easy maintenance and the weapon's tolerance of minor variations in ammunition.

177

The stiletto knife was not the only tool that he carried for luck. There was a Beretta military pistol that he carried strapped to his right leg. He loved the Beretta for its light weight and its small barrel size.

The Beretta that he carried was a special custom-built model. Its length was even less than the normal six inches of the standard gun. Normally a handy gun, this piece was even more so because of the additional inch and a half lopped off. With a few technical variations executed by Willy Moore, the weapons expert in Alabama, the small Italian arm had retained its range and accuracy. Unlike the Walther, he had never used the Italian pistol for a kill. He kept it mainly for his own protection and luck. Apart from these standard arms, for kills he only used custom-made arms like the Russian Sako Triaces. Again, the last time he had used a Sako was in Oman. He only used the Sako Triaces when the targets were easy and immobile and had no surrounding guards that needed to be taken out. Thinking of the Russian weapon reminded him of a phone call he would have to make the next day. The last Sako he had possessed now rested off the Muscat waterfront. He had to place an order for a few more. And he needed it before the Pakistani assignment got underway and also before he left for Spain.

The Russian target pistol had first been introduced to him in Alabama by Willy Moore. Moore, he thought, was an absolute genius with small arms and might have been on par with the two great pioneers, John Browning and Samuel Colt themselves. After his stint in America, he had seen the same weapon being used in the jungles of Sri Lanka. He had been surprised to see the Tamil militants of the LTTE use the heavy Russian pistol. As he finished cleaning the guns, he tried to recall whether he had ever used modern technology for a mission. Perhaps the only time had been in Mecca two years

178

ago. The target had been the designated chief of a quasi-religious sect based in Sudan. The man had been on a pilgrimage to the holy city under a heavy escort of Saudi government forces. It had been virtually impossible to breach the security cordon. That was when he had used a computer-guided bazooka, controlled from a terminal three miles away from the site. The target had been obliterated along with the special tent and the whole Saudi squad stationed just outside the campsites of the Great Mosque. On all other occasions, he had taken out targets with his own hands.

28

LONDON, OCTOBER 11, 1995

Mohan Bhargava was the designated assistant cultural attaché at the Indian High Commission to the UK. He was also a RAW officer. He had now been in London for over a year, before which he had spent more than four years in Pakistan. The Islamic nation had been a tough and stimulating assignment. There had been the occasional harassment by the Pakistani police, but by and large he had done well. He had been directly responsible for the most impressive coup RAW had made in the last few years.

Gabriel was the name Bhargava had given to the Pakistani—the most valuable asset India had in that country. Till date Gabriel dealt only with him, his handler. When informed of his transfer to London, the Pakistani had flatly refused to transmit information to any other Indian official. He had made it clear that he had faith only in his handler. So for the last one year, all of Gabriel's important messages had been routed to New Delhi via London. Somehow the Pakistani always managed to reach him in London. Bhargava had received Gabriel's phone call twenty-four hours earlier, informing him that extremely sensitive information was on the way. And this morning the message had arrived from Islamabad. Gabriel had been right. It was a scoop.

The plan to assassinate India's future prime minister was worth its weight in gold. Just what his country's representatives at the UN would welcome. As Bhargava walked to the high commission building off Aldwych, his mind was abuzz. He would have to go to India immediately. This was not the kind of information that could be relayed safely from a distance. It called for a personal briefing. A face-to-face meeting with Rajnish Mishra, the Director of RAW, would have to be arranged. Bhargava was sure that Mishra would then call him for a second meeting, this time in the presence of Anand Kishore, director of IB and Hitesh Singh, the Union home minister of India. Bhargava was aware that once the home minister took it seriously, it would in all probability lead to the convening of the internal security council, the eight-member apex body whose remaining members would be Ponnuswamy Ramalingam, the defence minister, Jagdish Thakur the external affairs minister, and the three service chiefs. The prime minister would, of course, be an invitee.

29

LONDON, OCTOBER 11, 1995

Maj. Chaudhary read the communiqué from Islamabad for the third time in fifteen minutes. His hands were trembling with excitement. He was wanted urgently in Pakistan. Lt. Gen. Hussain wanted an audience with him. This could only mean he was being inducted into the big league. The project could not move ahead without his active involvement. They now wanted to tell him what it was all about. Chaudhary was familiar with the entire process. Medium-level operatives were always given narrow outlines within which to work. When they came up with gold, an induction would take place, with certain riders attached.

If his suspicions about the plan were correct, then his days outside Pakistan were numbered. Once initiated into a plan as critical as he imagined this one to be, there would be only one course of action. They would recall him to Pakistan, probably post him at the headquarters or some other allied station. Even here in London, he was sure that an eye had been kept on him. He had on several occasions in the last few days known that he was being tailed. When he first suspected this, he had employed the usual techniques of pausing at shop windows, suddenly turning back, and so on. Lack of faith in its own operatives was a known failing of the ISI.

The men who had tailed him had not realised that they had been spotted by their alert quarry. It was only the 'watchers' who avoided detection for long periods of time: that elite team of MI-5 agents who on their own turf at least are reckoned by all the western services to be the best tailers in the world. If Chaudhary wished, he could on several occasions have given his tailers the slip, but that would have unnecessarily made the top brass in Pakistan suspicious. So, for the sake of his long-term goals, he put up with the indignity. Even as recently as this morning, he had noticed a tail. The tail had ended right at his apartment complex. As he had ascended the stairs the men had signalled for their vehicles. Once inside his flat, he had rushed to grab his long-distance field glasses. He saw that the tailers were Englishmen, and not Asians as he had presumed.

That further confirmed his belief that his service was on to something hot. The fact that Britons were being recruited meant that large sums of money were being spent. And to spend large sums of money to ensure that a Major didn't divulge what he had learned meant that the information he had acquired was extremely valuable.

He made a call to his travel agent, booking the earliest available Emirates flight to Pakistan. He would need to inform Islamabad when he would be arriving and explain that there might be a slight delay in getting a reservation because it was a busy season. Even minor delays might be looked upon with suspicion in the ISI.

The woman kept her cleaning machine aside and walked to the cluttered desk. As always she gave a cursory glance to the files that were kept on it. Then she took out the key that she

183

had been given and opened the first drawer on the right side of the desk. This was something she did once a week. She rummaged through the drawer hurriedly. The man to whom the office belonged could be back any time. He had been called for a meeting by his superior. Before he returned, she had to be out of the room. At the bottom of the drawer lay a cream envelope with the word 'important' imprinted on it in bold letters. The envelope was open. She took out the papers and spread them evenly on the desk. She dug into her apron pocket and took out her special Minolta camera. Photographing each sheet twice, she returned the envelope to its position. Then retrieving her cleaning machine from the corner, she walked out of the room. Those papers had seemed important. She would take the day off and, after contacting the man she worked for, go and deliver the film roll.

When the phone rang at Maj. Chaudhary's flat, he expected the call to be from either his travel agent or the airlines office. They had promised that they would work on getting him on an earlier flight home. He listened for about five minutes. The call was from Gracy Burns, the minor tap they had in the Indian High Commission. Burns was only a cleaning lady and had till date figured on the lowest rungs of the ISI informants. In fact, she was so insignificant that the last review report from the headquarters had strongly recommended discontinuation of her services. At that stage, it had been Chaudhary who had stuck his neck out and resisted the move. His argument had been a simple analysis of costs. According to him, the few pounds they paid the woman every week was worth it. There was always the possibility that Burns would turn up something big some day. Today Burns had called up to inform him that during her routine rounds she had come upon some papers. She would be arriving shortly to deliver the rolls of the photographs she had taken. The cost would be the usual thirty pounds.

Burns was a middle-aged woman with reasonable intellect but little formal academic training. She worked as a cleaner in several apartment complexes, which is how Maj. Mushtaq Chaudhary had become acquainted with her. She liked the handsome Pakistani who often tipped her generously. Chaudhary had always kept his eye open for people the ISI could use in the future. Soon enough, his perseverance had paid dividends. He had spotted an advertisement by the Indian High Commission for cleaners and other helpers. He had requested Burns to apply. And she had got through the detailed screening process. After that it had taken her six months to be allowed to work in the cultural section of the High Commission. Maj. Chaudhary had then given her names of Indian officers whom she had to keep an eye on and whose offices could yield valuable information.

He had also supplied her with special tools—miniature cameras, skeleton keys and bolt sharpeners or tiny sound detecting electronic devices that could be magnetically attached to the metal parts of a door. When a door with this gadget was shut, it could pick out any sound from a long distance and thereby warn the person on the other side of the door. As Maj. Chaudhary was pressed for time, he asked her to come to his residence. Never before had she directly brought him anything. They had followed a more roundabout procedure of exchanging information. For over two years she had diligently followed the routine drawn up for her by her Pakistani benefactor:

She would lunch at Hyde Park and then place the empty carton of her usual helping of mustard salad, with the film rolls inside, in a nearby dustbin. This would be retrieved some minutes later by a young deputy of Maj. Chaudhary who would be waiting nearby.

After Burns had left, Chaudhary began work on the electronic enlarger that he had had one of his deputies bring

185

over. The special film would be simultaneously developed and enlarged in less than an hour.

A series of beeps indicated that the machine had completed its work. The first thing his eyes caught was his own name. That immediately told him of the enormity of what Gracy Burns had stumbled on. He nervously scanned the photographs of all the six sheets. He could not believe his eyes. It was the entire blueprint of the operation for which he himself had been working for more than a month. So it was Prof. Kapre of the REP who was to be assassinated!

He felt a sudden fury build up within him. All the hard work, all the preparations, practically wiped out. He wondered who could have tipped off the Indians. His first suspicion was directed towards Arif Rabbani. But he soon dismissed it. The Afghan could not have known the details of the plan. For that reason, even Hugo Stone could be discounted. So his end in London was clear. The leak had been from Pakistan, probably from Islamabad. He ran to the phone. In all the excitement he had forgotten to ask Gracy Burns whose office she had picked up the envelope from. When he heared the name Maj. Chaudhary was aghast. It was Mohan Bhargava, the brightest RAW operative stationed in London. In addition, Bhargava was a man familiar to many in the ISI. Though he was a reasonably young officer, of the rank of assistant cultural attaché, he had already made a name for himself. Chaudhary was aware that before being posted to London, Bhargava had spent time in Pakistan. In fact Mohan Bhargava had been one of the people specially mentioned to Burns by Chaudhary. The Major was aware that Bhargava had been a nuisance even in Pakistan. It had been rumoured that he had picked up certain prize catches for RAW. And he had done it cleanly, without allowing the ISI to place the blame on him.

The ISI had wanted Bhargava out of Pakistan. Finally, they had got their chance when a Pakistani spy was caught in New Delhi. This man had intentionally named, as his handler, an official in the Pakistani High Commission of roughly the same rank as Bhargava in Pakistan. Expulsion of the Pakistani official by the Indian authorities had followed. After that the Pakistanis had retaliated by expelling Bhargava. Now the day's events had proved beyond doubt that Bhargava had cultivated people in the top levels of the ISI. He would have to relay this news to Pakistan as soon as possible. What effect this would have on the operation, he could not even imagine.

The message to Bhargava was signed by 'Gabriel'. All RAW field agents had a real name and a code name. Chaudhary knew these code names were generally derived from Indian mythology. Many years ago when he had been a captain, he had had the chance to be present at the interrogation of an Indian official who had been caught red-handed. That man's code name had been Garuda. He had also heard rumours that Mohan Bhargava, during his stay in Pakistan, had been known as Agni. For the next few minutes Chaudhary fantasised about getting his hands on the index of these codes and the real identities of all the RAW agents. He wondered where the index would be—probably in the home ministry in North or South block. What he didn't know was that the Fifth Veda, or the index of codes, was kept in a special cellular vault in the CGO complex in New Delhi.

If the information had reached Bhargava, Chaudhary thought, chances were high that it had not yet reached India. He knew Bhargava would want to personally relay a matter of such importance to his bosses in New Delhi. If Gabriel could be apprehended, the credit for it would go to Maj. Chaudhary. So not only was he playing a crucial role in the operation, he was also preventing the plan from going awry by catching a traitor. The combined success would propel him to the rank of Colonel, he was sure. Until now Chaudhary hadn't thought beyond serving his nation. The glory of the nation was reward enough for him. But if he could checkmate the treachery of Gabriel, the reward was definitely an attractive end in itself.

30

Nazir, who was not normally given to violent bursts of temper, slammed the vase on the table. The expensive crystal smashed to pieces. Twenty-four hours had passed since he had got the news from Maj. Chaudhary in London. He had then ordered the Major to stay put in London and check what Mohan Bhargava was up to. He agreed with Chaudhary's theory that Bhargava would in all probability rush to India to reveal the plot to his superiors. And today Chaudhary had called to confirm their worst fear. The Indian intelligence officer was booked on a British Airways flight to New Delhi. The actual target of Brig. Nazir's temper was not the Indians but Gabriel, whoever he was. He wanted to stop all activities and concentrate only on smoking the traitor out. But he knew that, right now, his priority would have to be to stop Bhargava from communicating what he had learnt.

There was another problem he had on his hands. The assassin was scheduled to visit Islamabad in three days. Now they would have to postpone his visit till Bhargava was taken care of. Also irritating him was Maj. Chaudhary's suggestion that Gabriel was probably an officer who was privy to all the

189

details of Project K2, not just the latest plan. Tariq was one such possibility. Brig Nazir had relied on Tariq more than he had on anyone else for a long period now. Even the remote possibility of Tariq being the traitor was revolting. He knew that keeping Azim out from the future progress of the plan would cripple him to a great extent. Of course, there was the attractive option of believing that the traitor could be one of Shujaat's plants elsewhere in the CFIO. Yet, as a responsible officer in a position of great importance it was his duty to investigate all possibilities.

He decided to call for Azim's data file and scan his entire service record. He picked up his private line and dialed several numbers in the next fifteen minutes.

When he was done, he sat back and waited. There was a lot more to do but he needed to relax for a while and gather his wits about him. After tackling the issue of Azim and Gabriel, he had to plan how to stop Bhargava. Nazir loathed the man. But in his heart, he also feared and respected him. Well not exactly the man, but his talent. Two years ago, it had been his idea to manipulate the expulsion of their man in New Delhi so that they could do the same to Bhargava. Brig. Nazir was sure that the Indian officer had a great future. If he lived.

His mind was still on RAW and Bhargava when a member of his personal staff got him the relevant file. Nazir spread the file on the desk and started scanning it carefully for any small incident that would expose a link with Bhargava. An addiction to drugs, wine, women, anything that could contribute to his most trusted man becoming a spy. Before he entered the army, his birth, his upbringing, for traces of a tough childhood or any destabilising influence during his early years. There was nothing. Azim was the only child of a college teacher. He was born in Karachi and had spent his childhood years there. He had had a comfortable childhood, and gone to the best schools.

Young Tariq had been a good student and an avid sportsman and in his teens he had played club cricket and excelled in it. If he had continued, he could have entered the Pakistani national team. Yet Azim Tariq had chosen the army.

Nazir again scanned Tariq's day-to-day record after he joined the army and the ISI. It was all clean. He shut the data file with a sigh of relief. There was nothing that could connect the Major to any Indian. No secret rendezvous, no excessive spending beyond his income, no job dissatisfaction. He made up his mind to tell Tariq about the latest setback and seek his advice on how to eliminate Bhargava. If Azim was Gabriel, he would not let the handler die. Brig. Nazir was aware of the delicate and special relationship that developed between an agent and his handler after a period of time. But before he spoke to Major Tariq, he had to inform London. This was so that Maj. Chaudhary could in turn contact Ray Darrel and inform him that there was a slight alteration in the schedule.

One hour later, Nazir had Maj. Tariq sitting in front of him. The Brigadier had told him what had happened and was studying his reaction intently. Azim seemed genuinely upset. His first response was that they ought to eliminate Mohan Bhargava immediately. That removed whatever vestiges of doubt that remained in Nazir's mind. Of course he did not reveal that Tariq had also been under suspicion.

'I think we should first get Bhargava, then go after Gabriel, whoever he is.'

'Do you think we can get Bhargava in London before he reaches India?'

'I believe we can get him in any part of the world, such is the reach of our operations now, but...'

'But what?' asked Brig. Nazir.

'But this Sir, that the ideal course of action would be to hit Bhargava in a way that it seems like an accident. Otherwise there will be alarm bells ringing in RAW.'

191

'Hmm, I agree with you.'

'So, if it is made to seem like an accident, it's better we get him in India. In fact, we should get him immediately after he sets foot in India. The Indian police are far easier to fool than the British bobbies.'

At this Nazir became quiet. He again marvelled at his junior's clear and precise analysis. It was because of these very qualities that he had become so dependent on Azim. He then spoke up. 'We can get him in India before he reaches his headquarters. A motor accident on the way would be ideal. Yes, I'll get to work on it.'

'Can that be managed at such short notice?' asked an obviously impressed Tariq. 'Yes, you'll be surprised at what all can be managed. I have many Varuns to extinguish their Agni.'

'What about informing Darrel and his associate—they have to be told as well,' advised Tariq.

'Yes, I've told Maj. Chaudhary to handle that.'

After Tariq had left, Nazir tried to analyse his reactions. He was quite sure now that Azim was not Gabriel. He got up too. He had an appointment with Lt. Gen. Hussain. The ISI chief had thrown a fit when informed of the existence of Gabriel. The meeting had been fixed to explore the possibility of a link between Gabriel and Shujaat.

SOMEWHERE IN THE ASIAN CONTINENT

The man sat reading a magazine. It was called *Soldier of Fortune* and it was better known as a lifeline for mercenaries. Assassins and professional fighters placed ads in it. He remembered that in the beginning the magazine had even carried his contact number. Now of course he did not need to do that. He was far too big for such methods of approach. He was scanning it for a different purpose. He wanted to check if any new arms dealers had placed ads in it.

As a precaution, he liked to use the services of different arms dealers. He never met them personally. The orders were always by post, the shipments couriered to neutral ports and the money paid in banks across the world. Out of the many he had interacted with over the years, he had found the team of Alan Sanders–Brad Leithauser the best. Their arms were good, the shipments prompt and there were no over-curious meddlers involved. Adnan Khashoggi on the contrary, was not very good. According to him, the man was too much of a high flier. That kept him from concentrating on his work. Khashoggi was too busy flashing his connections with the Sultan of Brunei. He recalled with amusement how, a year back, he had almost taken a contract on the richest man in the world, the Sultan.

The red light on his international phone flashed and he ran to attend to it. It was his associate telling him to go to the panel that they used for communicating from London. He went to the room and began following the standard procedure. After five minutes he stood back, a trifle irritated. The Pakistanis had sent an SOS that he should postpone his visit to Islamabad. This was annoying. It would alter his plan for Spain as well. For a moment he considered refusing the assignment. Then he decided against it. He wanted to work in India, at least once. His only association with India so far had been an indirect one: he had trained the LTTE men involved in the murder of EPRLF leader Padmanabha, who was then visiting India. The actual killing had been done by the Tamils themselves. He had only planned it for them, sitting in their hideout in the Vavuniya jungles.

NEW DELHI

It was 8 P.M., the appointed hour. Prithpal Singh Rathee arrived exactly on time at the Greater Kailash mansion belonging to Prakash Mittal. He was met at the entrance by the father and son. The Mittals looked at the run down Fiat that Rathee had driven in and offered to take one of their cars. 'No, this car is perfect, it is untraceable and would be apt for this journey.'

'What, I hope it is not a stolen vehicle?' asked an aghast Prakash Mittal.

'No, it's not stolen, it was one of the vehicles lying in the district court premises for auction. I have borrowed it for one night from the *malkhana* in-charge.' The reassured duo sat alongside him in the car and they sped off. The car moved further down Greater Kailash, passing Hemkunt Colony, towards Chiragh Enclave. At Chirag Delhi Marg it got caught in a sea of traffic. After spending an excruciating twenty minutes at the traffic lights, Rathee finally turned left. During this period he had left the wheel in the hands of the younger Mittal and had run to the phone booth by the roadside. The Mittals presumed it was to inform his friend of their delay.

For an old and run-down Fiat, the car was not doing badly. The lawyer pressed the pedal with all his might. As they passed Nehru Place and then moved towards Kalkaji, the car stopped again. Rajan leaned forward. There was no traffic light in sight. It was quite odd. 'Why have you stopped here?' The lawyer gestured towards the right. In the distance they could see the dome of the Kalkaji temple. Rathee folded his hands and bent his head in the direction of the temple. He then chanted an inaudible prayer. After five minutes, he gunned the engine to life again. 'Sorry about that delay, but it is a ritual.'

'What is a ritual? That every time you pass a temple you have to stop and pray?' said an irritated Rajan.

'No, I don't stop whenever I see any temple,' said the lawyer patiently. 'I grew up in these parts and every evening I would visit the Kalkaji temple. So, whenever I pass this way, I at least stop and pay my respects from a distance.'

'You were born in Kalkaji village?' Rathee nodded. 'And where do you stay now?'

'Now I am putting up in Defence Colony,' replied Rathee.

'You must have a flat there,' said Prakash Mittal.

'Well, actually I have two houses there, one I use for rental purposes and the other I use as my residence.' Both the Mittals were surprised. Rathee didn't seem that successful a lawyer to them. It was quite clear that he supplemented his income with capers such as the present one. It seemed that Rajan's friend from Chandigarh had sent them to the right person.

A few minutes later, their car got caught in traffic again. This time the reason was the crowded Okhla railway station. From there Rathee took a right turn towards National Highway 2 and Mathura Road. They passed the Kalkaji bus depot and a stretch of the Okhla industrial area. About two kilometres down, the lawyer turned left onto a narrow dirt track. Both the Mittals wondered where they were headed. It was now 9.15 PM. 'Where are we going, to some village?' asked Rajan.

'Have patience my friend, you will soon see,' responded their unruffled host. They kept along the dirt road, which was bumpy and poorly lit. Rathee stopped the car as several large concrete structures came into view.

'Where are we?' asked an amazed Prakash Mittal. Their surroundings seemed to be straight out of a scene from a movie. One of those dark and dangerous factory sites where the villain and his men lure the hero for a final showdown.

'Welcome to the Jasola sewage disposal works,' Rathee said. As the three men moved further on foot, the stench of sewage hit them. Holding their noses they followed the lawyer who led them to a cluster of semi-pucca hutments about 1000 meters from the large sewage tanks.

The lawyer told them to wait outside while he entered one of the hutments. He returned with another man, slim and of slight built. He had a cold face and appeared to be in his late thirties. He had a crew cut and his scalp almost gleamed through the stubble. Rathee introduced the father and son duo to him, saying, 'You can call him Thanedar, all his friends call him that.'

The man looked at the Mittals for a few seconds and then spoke in a UP accent. 'Prithi has told me you want my services. Do you have the details?'

'Yes, do we begin here?' asked Rajan.

'No, we go inside, you two and me, Prithi will wait in the other room,' he gestured to Rathee who moved to another hutment a few meters away.

They entered the hutment the man had emerged from. Rajan Mittal looked with amazement at the bare room. In one corner lay a small set of wires and an electronic device that he was sure was a wireless set. The Delhi-UP underworld had indeed gone hi-tech.

31

'We may or may not need your services,' Prakash Mittal began, looking at the man called Thanedar.

The man looked stolidly at them. 'If you are not sure, why have you come to me? First make up your mind and then we will talk.'

'We want to give you time to prepare if we decide to go ahead.'

At this the man looked offended. 'How much time do you think I need? I was bumping off people when you were playing in half pants.'

Rajan pursed his lips, about to respond but he felt his father's restraining hand on his arm. 'Here, take a look at this,' he said, handing a photograph to the man. It was from a newspaper and the man looked at it with disinterest.

'So?'

'So, what do you think of him?'

'Think? What should I think? I am not a politician. I hear he is probably the next prime minister of the country, that is all,' he shrugged, returning the newspaper cutting.

'It is him we need you for,' Prakash Mittal said slowly.

197

'What!' he exclaimed. 'Are you joking?'

'We are very serious.' said Rajan in a deadpan voice. The man grew silent. He was now looking at the Mittals with new respect. 'Can you take him, or is he too big for you?' persisted Rajan.

'The biggest till now, but I can do it,' the man replied softly.

'Remember, it is still tentative, we are yet to decide.'

'When will you make up your minds? Elections are due and his security will intensify.'

'Maybe a fortnight or maximum one month, and we will let you know.'

'You will have to let me know in advance. Apart from the preparations, I will have to cut down on my routine assignments.'

'We will let you know soon enough but you will have to work absolutely alone.'

'What!' The man looked tense. 'Even for the planning?'

'Yes that is exactly what we mean. Of course money is no problem.'

'When do I hear from you?'

'We will tell Rathee when we want to see you. We assume he always knows of your whereabouts.'

'Yes he does, you can contact him,' the sharpshooter replied.

As the Mittals left, the assassin began to wonder at his own reputation. He had never been approached for a killing of this scale. He had grown up in Meerut. His father and elder brother were both junior engineers in the local administration. The Mittals were not aware that he had been an aspirant for the civil services. He had spent many nights in the hostels that dotted Delhi University's north campus. That was how the

Rathees, Rajesh and Prithpal, knew him. Thanedar had begun as apprentice to the notorious Mahender Fauji gang. His skill with a *katta*, or country-made pistol, had soon been noticed by Fauji. He had steadily risen through the ranks. After Fauji's death, he had gone independent. The money had flowed from the Bombay underworld. He had of late been working for the Chhota Rajan gang, pitting his wits against the D company, as Dawood Ibrahim's men were now known in Bombay.

His identity was known to the local Delhi police. Yet he managed to evade arrest. That was as a result of his equation with the many Haryanvi and UP men in the force. In fact, he had been arrested only once. Even on that occasion he had not been taken to jail but had managed to get himself freed while at the police station. Legend had it that his exploits had made the police station house officer offer him his seat. Since then, the name of Thanedar had stuck with him.

Thanedar thought about the person the Mittals wanted him to kill. He enjoyed the protection of a local REP leader. Would it be proper for him to offer his services for such a job? After half an hour he got up, the dilemma fully resolved. He would do it. He was, after all, a professional. As far as protection was concerned, he would seek out the local leaders of some other political party. It was not too difficult for underworld men to obtain political patronage in the chaotic political scenario. One had to sit still and they came flocking to you. It was men of his ilk who provided back up for the capturing of voting stations and the stamping of fake ballot-papers.

The Jasola sewage works had been his lair for the last few days. He would be moving out soon. He was required to go to the city for an assignment. His next abode would be the Tibetan colony opposite the Inter State Bus Terminus.

As he looked at himself in the large mirror, he was aware that he looked good. Satyaki Das was in his late forties, boyishly handsome, with greying hair carefully styled at Habib's according to the latest fashion. He had just graduated from JJ Valaya to suits from Horn's in England. The shoes were Gucci and the mandatory Mont Blanc gleamed in his breast pocket. If one attributed his success in the field of journalism to the force of his personal appearance only, he would have been offended. Born an orphan, he had started a press after the 1971 war with Pakistan, turning out handbills commemorating the Indian victory and the liberation of Bangladesh. Impressed with his devotion, the then Congress chief minister of Bengal managed to get him a low-interest loan to start a full-fledged magazine of his own. Today he was the owner of *The Weekly*, a semi-investigative magazine. Das' method was simple: Feed the public with scoops regularly, backing them up with authentic pictures. His track record was impressive. It was *The Weekly* that broke the story that had cost one of Maharashtra's chief ministers his job. It was Satyaki's people who first reported with photographic evidence that the regime was allowing the Americans refuelling facilities during the Gulf War. His list of exposés was endless. Satyaki now owned three magazines and two medium-sized newspapers, his subjects ranging from love stories for teenagers to outright sleaze. He was a multi-millionaire.

The money had brought him a spacious mansion in Vasant Vihar, three cottages converted into his own leisure palace in Mussoorie and a fleet of cars ranging from a Benz SLK to a Lexus Harrier. In his long journey from the streets of Calcutta to the bars of the Delhi Gymkhana club, he had married a former Miss India and had two sons who now studied in

England. Apart from all this he was a devoted Congressman and had been so for a long time. After all it was the benevolence and largesse of a Congress chief minister that had changed his destiny.

As he prepared to leave for the headquarters of his group, his housekeeper walked in and announced the arrival of visitors who were insisting on seeing him. For a minute he was tempted to yell at the petrified woman but stopped himself. 'Take them to the small drawing room, I'll join them in a few minutes.' The relieved woman turned to convey the message. Das wondered who it could be so early in the morning. He had issued standing instructions to the gateman not to admit any visitors at this time of day. It had to be somebody capable of browbeating the gurkha. He made final adjustments to the knot of his tie, checked his hair and put on his spectacles. Though he did not require glasses he liked to wear them; he thought they lent a touch of seriousness.

Seated on his Italian sofa now, facing his two old friends Prakash Mittal and Bhaskar Naik, he frowned. 'Right, I have understood the situation. But what can I, or for that matter you, do to change it?'

'Read this, just the first two summary pages.' Naik handed him a few sheets of paper stapled together. After ten minutes Das closed the cover of the file and handed it back to Naik. His face was impassive. He remained silent, knowing that either Mittal or Naik would break the silence. He was right.

'All right, so what do you think, can it work?' asked the MP from Bombay.

Satyaki pursed his lips. 'Depends.'

'On what?'

'On several factors beyond your control, in fact beyond anyone's control.'

'But it has a good chance, you have to admit?'

'Again, it depends.'

'What is this "depends" that you keep repeating. Give it straight to us, we have come to you after all for both your advice as well as your participation.' Mittal was losing patience at what he perceived to be a put-on air of intellectual superiority by Satyaki.

'Okay, first and foremost, nobody, I repeat nobody, can control the mind of the public out there, specially the upper middle classes at whom you are aiming this,' he gestured at the file in Naik's hands. 'Influence, yes we can influence them, but control no, they will only believe what they want to. In fact, that is the whole trick of publications like mine. To recognise what they are thinking and to push them into believing that what they have been feeling is shared by many other people.'

'There seems to be a very thin line between this control and influence you are talking about.'

'There is a hell of a lot of difference, Bhaskar. For instance, today my readers believe that Prof. Kapre is going to be the next prime minister of this country.'

'And?' encouraged Naik.

'And, it is that much more difficult to make them believe that the man they have already subconsciously accepted as their prime minister is not fit to hold any public position, let alone the top job in the country.'

'What would be a good story today according to you?'

'Let me think. We'll probably do a story on the likely Cabinet if Kapre wins, or how much Srinivas Reddy has marred the electoral chances of our party.'

'Nevertheless, we feel the people would want to read about the activities of their Mr Clean. You know the middle classes are amazingly sensitive to corruption.'

'Yes, they will read it all right, then curse my magazine, call it a stunt managed by our party and vote for him in heavier numbers.'

'Why are you so pessimistic about this? What you did to that chief minister began with less, if I remember.' Now it was Naik who was getting irritated.

'Yes, but that case was different. We all know who was interested in his fall.' Das looked into Naik's eyes when he said this, making sure that no names were taken in front of Mittal. They both knew that Mittal would work it out anyway.

'A person in a similar position is behind us even in this matter,' said Naik softly.

'So the establishment would back the story fully?'

Mittal and Naik could understand Das' reluctance. Unlike them, Satyaki's business was too mainstream and visible to be effected by a change in government. He had nothing to gain by preventing the REP from coming to power.

'Yes, we assure you of that. Of course, every newspaper will pick this up the minute you break it.'

'Then why not get a national newspaper to break it in the first place?' He was still not convinced.

'Come on Satyaki, you know very well where the big three bend in their political affiliations. Once you break it, then what will drive them will be pure competition.'

'What is the reason behind this operation? I mean, don't you think sitting in Opposition for a couple of years would benefit our party and its leaders?'

'Try telling that to the top brass,' Naik said in a challenging tone.

'Them I can understand, but the two of you, you are businessmen first, politicians later, what is your interest in it? I know you, you are not the men to take this active an interest only on orders.' Mittal and Naik first looked at each other, then at Das. He was very astute. He was indicating to them that he would do what they wanted but not without being told the entire story. They would have to level with him. Das looked at them. 'The party is not the only reason, is it? There is another reason, probably many reasons.'

'Yes,' Naik answered slowly.

'I thought you would have made enough money by now.' Satyaki's tone was not taunting or offending, just matter of fact.

Both Mittal and Naik shook their heads.

'It is not the money or the business? Then what is it? If I am going to be the detonator of this bomb, I need to know of all the wires running through it.'

For the next two hours the three men remained seated in the drawing room, as two spoke in turn and one man listened first in shock, then amazement and finally with a sense of disgust. When Naik finished, Das was exhausted. Exhausted with the burden of all he had been told. In his mind, he was now more reluctant than before to be part of the operation. But during the course of the last two hours, he had been told that he had never really had a choice. His old friends had brought certain material to ensure his cooperation.

The material consisted of audio cassettes of conversations on the phone, photographs and even a video tape. Satyaki had always loved his beautiful and famous wife. It was just that he could not control his roving eye. And a man in his position got too many tempting offers to resist. So he gave in off and on. His two friends were now conveying to him their intention of using all the resources at their disposal to force his participation. They also assured him that they had copies of everything and would hand them over to him on the day *The Weekly* hit the stands with their story. 'So, when do you want it to appear in *The Weekly*? he asked. 'It will require heavy preparation,' he added as discouragement.

'Don't worry, we have some loose ends to tie up. As soon as we are done, we'll let you know. You will be supplied all the data, the names of those who are to be interviewed, as well as the names of certain others who are to be named in the story.'

'What! There are others also? This is getting more complicated. Who are these others? More REP leaders?'

'Here, these are the names,' Naik said, handing him a slip of paper. Das looked at the names in dismay. The story would be too big to handle in one issue. He'd have to do a series of articles.

'Why them?'

'To lend credibility to the story, my friend,' said Naik.

'But their political careers will surely be destroyed, while Kapre may still recover.'

'They are finished anyway. Besides, they have to be sacrificed for the larger benefit of the party.'

'But a loss to their reputation could affect what chances the party has. It does have some support.'

'You forget, they are no longer in the party.'

Das shook his head. 'As you wish. It's your plan, your responsibility, just remember. If I am sued, you pick up my legal fees.'

32

One of Brig. Nazir's Varuns sat smirking in his office. This particular man was a medium-level operative in the communications section of RAW. He had been on the Pakistani payroll for the past six months or so, during which time there had been nothing of interest. The reason why he was in a good mood now was that at last he had been given a chance to prove his worth to his recruiters. It had not been any direct work on his part though. His girlfriend had intercepted the message from London. She was the private secretary to the Director, Rajnish Mishra, and what she had found out was that the man in London had told his chief that he had not noticed any suspicious activity and would not require any armed escort from the airport.

The RAW man did not try and figure out why this information was wanted. Owing to his place in the hierarchy, he had got used to accepting orders without the slightest trace of curiosity. The complex bureaucracies of the developing nations were wonderful in destroying any initiative. All that mattered to this particular man was that he was getting paid for doing very little.

In his own office, Director R, as the chief of RAW was known, was a very worried man. He didn't quite agree with Mohan Bhargava's argument that all was fine and no pre-emptive action was needed. From the tone of the letter that had arrived from London, Mishra had understood the import of the message. For Agni to leave his post when a high-level LTTE sympathisers' conference was on in London implied that the news that Bhargava had to convey was top priority. In addition to that, Rajnish Mishra knew Bhargava's methods and style too well. A raw and new Bhargava had learnt the ropes working with Mishra in Colombo and Moscow among other postings. Mishra was sure that Mohan had not communicated his correct flight schedule to his chief. The lack of this information would hamper the agency's effort to protect Bhargava after his landing in the country. But Agni was an extremely wary man; he trusted no one. He had often tried to convince Mishra that it was obvious that there were Pakistani, Chinese and American spies in RAW.

Director R was the only man besides Bhargava himself who was aware of the existence and identity of Gabriel. Had Bhargava had his own way, he would not have shared this information with the chief of RAW. Yet, he had been forced to do so because of security considerations. Prudence warranted that at least one other person be aware of the important agents recruited abroad. Mishra knew that Gabriel's identity would shock the Pakistanis and the entire ISI if they were to ever discover it. At the sustained and forceful pleading of Mohan Bhargava, Mishra had broken a rigid convention: he had erased the details about Gabriel from the Fifth Veda, the sacred book of RAW.

The gold covered book was in fact a diary which contained comprehensive information about all assets, both domestic and overseas, of RAW. It also contained the true and fictional names of all Indian agents of the research and intelligence wing. In short, the Fifth Veda was a virtual treasure trove for any country hostile to India. The purpose behind the book was that in the eventuality of the death or an unforeseen event involving the director or the agents, there should not be a blackout of information. The rationale behind calling the book the Fifth Veda was in itself simple. The intermixing of ancient, mythical and spiritual ideas into modern espionage techniques is a worldwide phenomenon. Among the Anglo Saxon countries, names like 'Saint', 'Angel' and 'Priest' were the most common nicknames given to outstanding officers. It was said that the modern day warriors did this to assuage their deepest fears. It was like invoking ancestral spirits.

The reason why a computerised index of these extra-sensitive identities was not maintained, was because of the Aldrich Ames case. RAW had closely monitored the US's experience in the Ames fracas. Having gained access to one particular document, the CIA mole had been able to sell to the Russians, the identities of spies who had remained hidden for decades. It was believed that, had the information on the identities of American agents been spread over more than one index, the damage Ames had done could have been considerably reduced.

Rajnish Mishra belonged to the old generation of Indian police service officers—the tough men and the dogged deskmen, the intellectual giants and pen pushers, but no computer wizards. Mishra had a mortal fear of computers because he had seen, via his computer-wiz son, how no information stored on a computer, no matter how well protected, was safe from the prying eyes of another computer wiz-kid. Mishra preferred the good old method of hand writing his information. He had stuck to his guns although the systems department had scoffed at his fears. But since Rajnish Mishra headed RAW, he got away with this eccentricity.

And his caution had indeed borne fruit. Brig. Nazir's Varun in the communications section of RAW had hacked into the main computer terminals several times in an effort to find the names of the Indian assets in Pakistan.

33

ISLAMABAD, OCTOBER 18, 1995

Brig. Nazir looked bleary eyed at his luminescent wall clock. It was two hours past the stipulated time. The hands showed a quarter past four. He was tense. The confirmation was now overdue for more than an hour. Earlier, he had thought of inviting Maj. Tariq to wait out the long evening at his house. But the chains of military protocol had held him back. However if the confirmation came through, he would definitely invite the young Major for a celebration. After all, young Tariq had saved the day for him. A few hours earlier, the Brigadier had reached a dead end as his contacts in RAW had failed to deliver. Mohan Bhargava's schedule had turned out to be a complete dud.

On checking with Major Chaudhary in London, he had inferred that the wily Agni had kept even his service chief in the dark about his travel plans. Maj. Chaudhary had a rough estimate of the time when Bhargava could have boarded his flight at Heathrow. He had not been able to get the exact hour because his liaison man at the airport had an unexpected change in shift at the airport. Mushtaq Chaudhary's contact at the Indian High Commission in London had also failed to come up with the travel plans. At 5 PM, the Brigadier was in panic. He knew that not only was the best chance they had in years to eliminate Agni passing them by, the new plan to resurrect Project K2 was also going to die with a whimper.

If Agni blew the lid off the latest ISI salvo in India, the security around Prof. Kapre would definitely be beefed up. Any increased security presence had the potential to alter the plans of an assassin, however accomplished the man might be. It was absolutely imperative to get Agni out of the way. Not only was K2 at a critical stage, there was also an opportunity to orphan Gabriel. Brig. Nazir felt Gabriel could have had only one person from the Indian side handling him. It was an established principle of international espionage that the higher the position of the mole, the less the number of handlers. It was clear that Mohan Bhargava was the main handler. Psychologically, the loss of the main handler would be an extremely unnerving experience for the asset.

The Brigadier had faced a similar situation during the Bangladesh war. As a young captain stationed in Dhaka, he had cultivated an Indian colonel of the much vaunted light infantry headquartered at Calcutta. The Indian Colonel had extended invaluable nuggets of information to the young Pakistani Captain. An exultant Nazir had been the cause of the destruction of three units of the Mukti Vahini but the Indian had been careless and had been found out. As war clouds had loomed, a hurried court martial and a quick execution had followed. Young Nazir had felt personally bereaved. So he knew that without Agni, Gabriel would most probably be shattered. And a man in that condition would be prone to errors. One small slip, and Nazir could get to him. The telephone rang three times before Nazir even heard it. With trembling hands he lifted the receiver and brought it to his ear. 'Yes,' he forced himself to say.

211

'Sir, we got him!' Tariq exclaimed in joy.

'Are you sure?'

'Our man in UNI has confirmed it.'

The Brigadier let out a deep sigh. He knew that news confirmed from the United News of India was as accurate as it could get. 'I want to see you now.'

'Yes Sir.'

In fifteen minutes, Azim's jeep screeched to a halt on the uneven gravel and the bell chimed. Tariq saluted the Brigadier, his face flushed with pride.

'How and when?' queried Nazir.

'The body was identified. UNI prepared a report calling him a cultural attaché.'

'Of course, what else,' said Nazir.

'They're treating it as a motor accident.'

'Good,' said Nazir, now satisfied. 'Come, it's time for a small celebration.' Tariq followed his superior to an inner room where next to a bare wall stood a finely polished cabinet. Brig. Nazir opened one of the racks and took out a bottle of whisky. Johnny Walker, Blue Label. Tariq was impressed. He knew his senior never drank alcohol. Nazir set the bottle on the table and poured a drink for Tariq. For himelf he rang for orange juice. 'I have had this bottle for four years. Always wanted to have it on a special occasion.'

'Yes, I think Agni's death is an extremely special and triumphant moment for Pakistan.'

'Our victory has only begun. This is going to be followed by the destruction of Gabriel and the sure success of, first this operation, and then the realisation of K2.'

'I think the elimination of Agri is an omen,' said Nazir. 'It's time we named this operation. Any suggestions?' he asked a beaming Tariq.

Tariq remained silent for a few minutes, his lips pursed in thought. 'It has to be a symbolic name, one that indicates the importance of the operation to the eventual success of Project K2,' added the Brigadier.

'How about Karakoram, Sir?' asked Tariq softly.

'Karakoram? You mean the mountain range on the western end of Pakistan?'

'Yes Sir, the same range. Its has great significance for Pakistan. It is, after all, the winter snows from these mountains that provide the waters for the mighty Indus. It's also home to the second highest peak in the world Godwin Austen, better known to surveyors across the world as K2.'

'All right, Azim. Operation Karakoram it is going to be.'

The words were celebratory, yet Nazir's face was grim. Maj. Tariq inferred, correctly, that the present crisis had made the Brigadier lose his smile temporarily. He knew that his superior would rest with ease only when the spectre of the REP was taken care of. The two army men sipped their drinks in silence. Nazir poured another one for Tariq. 'How far is Gabriel now?' he said to himself, although it was clear that Tariq was expected to respond.

Privately, the Major knew that Gabriel could still remain anonymous, but for the benefit of his superior he said, 'Quite close, if he panics.'

'What would you do to flush him out now?' Nazir asked between sips.

'Well, make sure every ISI operative knows that Bhargava is dead, and hope that Gabriel panics and makes a mistake.'

'That is precisely what is going to happen; plus, I am going to spread the rumour that Agni left clear clues about the identity of Gabriel.'

'Yes, that will scare him even more.'

'Well, we'll worry about him tomorrow. For now Azim, you did well.'

'Thank you Sir, although I think Rachel Harris deserves the praise more.'

Two years ago Tariq had befriended Rachel Harris, a tourist in Lahore. Rachel had been lost and Tariq had helped her out. The two had kept in touch. Harris had moved from the freight and cargo section of Lufthansa to the ticketing department of British Airways. Four-and-a-half hours ago, a frantic Azim had called Rachel in Manchester. She, in turn had pulled out her contacts and confirmed the flight schedule of one Mohan Bhargava. The Pakistanis had contacted their agents in India to complete the elimination of one of RAW's best operatives.

In another darkened room in the Pakistani capital, the subject of Major Tariq's and Brig. Nazir's conversation was pacing the floor. Gabriel had learnt of Bhargava's death and was worried. At this stage of his life he did not want to be found out. After a few minutes he walked to his refrigerator and took out a cold bottle of water. Draining it in one long gulp, he continued his pacing. He was aware that Pakistan would be desperate to find out the identity of her single most dangerous traitor. Well, he was not going to give the ISI or the army the pleasure. He would lie low for awhile. It would be some time before any Indian requests would come to him. The Indians would be rattled too, with their best operative gone.

34

Rajnish Mishra grieved silently. He had just returned to his office from the cremation at Nigambodh Ghat. Bhargava's wife had been stoic but Mohan's parents had wept throughout. Mishra remembered Bhargava as a young man full of fire and enthusiasm on his first posting in Colombo, under his direct command. He had been quick to learn how to temper guts with guile, to reconcile courage with subtlety. Bhargava had risen fast. The upper echelons as well as the field agents of RAW admired him and his colleagues respected him. From Colombo it had been Moscow, and from Moscow, the rough streets of Islamabad.

The Pakistani sojourn had brought out the best in Bhargava. He had outshone all his predecessors. An entire ring of informers had been cultivated. The pictures of the building that had sheltered the Memons had been his handiwork, the same pictures that had later been on the front page of all the Indian newspapers. They had been able to snap the Qandahar-Muzzafarabad-Srinagar drug route because of him. But the RAW chief knew what had been Bhargava's biggest contribution. It had been the setting up of Gabriel, the agent

215

that was worth his weight in gold and more for India. In spite of several attempts, Mohan had not revealed how he had managed to ensnare Gabriel. In fact, Bhargava had been extremely protective of Gabriel. For more than four years the Indian authorities had enjoyed the consistent and accurate information that Gabriel supplied. Quietly reminiscing about Bhargava, a pensive Mishra wondered what had prompted him to head for India. For a moment, Mishra wondered whether it was the secret that Agni had been on his way to reveal that had led to his death. His own team had reached the same conclusion. Bhargava's death was no accident. It had been a superbly executed and meticulously planned murder. And now, it was Mohan's obsession with secrecy that stood in the path of working out who was behind it.

Surendra Nigam, the local DCP, was extremely agitated, as he had been ever since the 'accident' the previous night. It had seemed innocuous enough at first. A visiting Indian officer, probably on vacation, dies in a car accident on the way home from the airport. Then the calls had begun. First from his immediate superior, the additional commissioner, then the call from the prime minister's office. He had been told to keep in close touch with Rajnish Mishra. Mishra, as Nigam was well aware, was the chief of RAW. Within the Indian police service, Mishra enjoyed the reputation of being an exacting and demanding superior. It was this facet of Mishra's personality that worried Nigam. He quite enjoyed his job as a relatively senior Indian police officer. That cases remained unsolved was just a minor problem, a statistic that could easily be thrust under the vast carpet that the Indian bureaucracy often used. Nigam was not looking forward to the next few days. Days when he would actually be required to rough it out.

As a youngster, Nigam had been obsessed with the armed forces. As an adolescent, he had imbibed a fascination for the army from an older cousin. From reading commando comics, he had graduated to writing his own war stories, building mechanical warplanes and being a virtual authority on the armed forces. To sit for the National Defence Academy examination was his aim, and to serve the country, his goal. It was then that his mother had stepped in. An extremely ambitious lady, Mrs Nigam was an English teacher at a local school. She had detected the academic potential in her son and slowly began to brainwash him. A young and energetic Surendra had gradually evolved into a focused bookworm. Mrs Nigam's pressure resulted in Surendra clearing the joint entrance examination and enrolling in the Indian Institute of Technology, Delhi, for a course in mechanical engineering. After five years, Surendra had graduated with the most valuable degree in India but at heart he was a bored man, bereft of energy and creativity.

A confused and irritated Surendra rebelled. He refused to join the corporate rat race. After a hiatus, he had sat for the civil service entrance examination and joined the Indian Police Service. He loved the power, the uniform and the lack of responsibility. Although a straight and honest officer, he had fallen prey to chronic lethargy, the symptom of a man in a profession he hadn't wanted. His once brilliant brain lay dormant for want of activity.

OCTOBER 19, 1995

Satyaki Das took off his expensive sunglasses on entering his plush office. He looked around satisfied, as, for the umpteenth time, his eyes confirmed for him his success. He settled himself on his custom-made leather chair, lit up a Havana cigar and began sifting through his daily correspondence. He looked up, aware that his cabin door had been opened soundlessly and someone had entered his inner sanctum.

He saw who the visitor was and his face broke into a smile. It was Reena Bhalla, his personal secretary. She possessed a voluptuous body which Satyaki found a pleasure to behold. Actually, he had done more than just behold. As she smiled at him, he rose, walked across to the black opaque door and locked it from inside. He then turned and looked at her.

Reena was dressed in a lovely transparent salwaar kameez. The kameez was low cut, exposing her generous cleavage. He moved to her, brought her close and lowered his head in her bust. Reena uttered a soft guttural moan. She then moved her fingers towards his waist. Satyaki was in the throes of desire yet aware that it was going to be a big day, so he dispensed with the foreplay. He led her to the large sofa at one end of the room and lowered himself on her. Minutes later, his urge satisfied, he got up and asked her to check if their tabloid had hit the streets. Reena rose and walked out, now very much the professional.

A few minutes later Satyaki's intercom buzzed. He spoke into it for a minute and replaced the receiver. Arun Malhotra, his other secretary, walked in and sat down with his steno pad and pilot pen. Satyaki began dictating rapidly. By the end of the hour he would have dictated responses to letters plus shot off many letters of his own. Letters to celebrities thanking them for interviews, letters to his editorial staff congratulating them on particular stories, letters of gratitude to various corporate sponsors and so on.

At ten minutes to eleven, he stopped. He told Arun to bring the letters in for his signature within the next half hour. At eleven thirty, he had a meeting with his old friends, Bhaskar Naik and Prakash Mittal. They had called him up the previous night, wishing to finalise the plan agreed upon four days ago. A harassed Das had pleaded a day full of prior appointments in a bid to escape from the painful chore of being party to their nefarious plan. They had been insistent, secure in the knowledge that he could not refuse them, and he had reluctantly complied.

Half an hour, he had stressed, was all he could spare. More than enough, the two politicos had responded. However, Satyaki knew the meeting with Naik and Mittal could extend to even two hours. And it would be a stormy two hours. He wanted some time to himself to reflect, to recharge his tolerance batteries. His mind was made up. He would do the bare minimum, and for the rest plead fear of defamation as well as action by the Press Council of India. He lit another Havana, buzzed for his customary glass of chocolate milk at the hour, and shut his eyes to calm himself down.

Bhaskar Naik and Prakash Mittal arrived at Satyaki Das' office five minutes before the agreed time. They smiled at Reena, a happy smile at seeing a beautiful woman, and walked in to see Satyaki. At exactly ten minutes past twelve, Kumar Shankar walked in and was told to wait outside. He accepted the offer of hot coffee and began a wait that ended only when two men he recognised walked out of Das' office at a quarter past one. Reena went in to inform Satyaki that his editor was waiting for him and came out five minutes later. She told Shankar that Satyaki wanted to have a discussion with him over lunch, if the editor did not have any prior appointment.

Shankar had one appointment at half past one with his deputy director, to discuss a story. He communicated his willingness for lunch to Reena and went to the board line operator to cancel the meeting with Sudip Gupta. After ten minutes Satyaki came out of his office and they walked out, heading for their common favourite, the National Dhaba at Connaught Place, for lunch. Shankar could tell that his boss was not in a very good mood.

35

Ray Darrel awoke with a start. He flipped the light switch and the next instant the small bedroom was flooded with light. The nightmare had been the same. The same unchanged icy expanse of nothingness, the dull atmosphere split by the sound of rifle cracks. Their wielders taking perverse pleasure in discharging the heavy snub-nosed pellets into moving targets. Darrel's longing for a distant land had left him years ago. The humiliation, the charges, the names—it had sickened him. It had left a part of his soul inert, numb. First the persecution from an alien race and then from his own people. The experience convinced him that the system, the establishment distinguished between no one. The powers that were didn't really approve of freedom and happiness. They just took varying forms. If it was Nazism in Auschwitz and Treblinka, it was Bolshevism in Siberia and Murmansk. It would later evolve into pure unadulterated corruption and misuse of hierarchy in Jerusalem.

The meek would never inherit the world. Darrel had begun to believe that the biblical quote was a sham, a mirage to keep the meek happy. That faraway hope, that distant

220

flicker, that someday, somehow with unlikely providence or miraculous intervention, their time would come. The reality was the opposite. The meek were just sinking deeper into a morass of nothingness. But men like him had chosen to defy tradition. They had rebelled. They would not wait for divine justice, they created their own heavens and hells. To Darrel, the Left and the communists were an impersonation of man's fall from grace, a descent from Eden to Earth. A descent initially guided by noble thoughts but degenerating into a lustful quest as low as for any common commodity. He moved out of bed, rubbing his eyes with one hand and walked to a small cabinet. He opened it, took out a bottle of brandy and took a generous swig. The bitter spirit running down his throat soothed his frayed nerves.

Nerves! That was also a recent development. There had been times, or an era, he thought, when he had been commended for his calm nerves. He had learnt an invaluable lesson, that nerves, or a lack of them, were more voluntary than men chose to believe. It was akin to a psychological thriller where the demon always turned out to be a physical manifestation of a man's mind.

Darrel felt relieved, a relief borne out of a realisation that the nightmare was over. Possibly for two, three, four nights. It was a mysterious sensation that swept over him, a strange mental relief in confluence with a physical tiredness. He debated whether to have another swig and then decided against it. Instead, he dragged himself to his book cabinet. The fresh reddish-brown polish gleamed on the wooden cabinet. The first two rows had been neatly segregated into small sections capable of holding four to five thick volumes. The racks had alphabets pasted on them in black. He raised his left hand, searched the rack marked J, and pulled out *Jane's Collected Small Arms Encyclopedia*.

221

He read pages he was already familiar with and then stopped at a page he seemed to have missed earlier. It listed the irregular small arms manufactured and possessed by individual rebels and insurgent groups. His attention was attracted by a few paragraphs on the burgeoning small arms bazaar on the North West Frontier of Afghanistan and Pakistan, the cause being his partner's forthcoming visit to Pakistan. In his career, Darrel had seen pens that discharged one lethal slug, lighters that expelled eight small pellets in one go, enough to immobilise a man. He was now reading for the first time of a wristwatch discharging the function of a fire arm. In the past, in a different era, Darrel and his friends had often hidden cyanide-tipped pins in watches, but this was the first time he had heard about a wristwatch that could expel up to three slugs for a distance of ten metres and at a reasonable velocity.

The snub-nosed miniature slug the magazine listed was coated with gelatine, laced with a rare carbon compound manufactured locally. Once it entered the human body, the slug—its gelatine and carbon compound reacting with the increased temperature inside the human body—would explode, causing gaping internal injuries. The injuries permeating the muscles and the nervous system, preventing immediate bleeding, would give enough time to the wielder of the weapon to get away. The ingenuity did not end there. The maker had thought of the post-death scenario. If retrieved during the course of an autopsy, the remaining solid part of the slug would look almost identical to the pellet of an air pistol commonly used for sport and amateur target practice.

Darrel did not believe all the specifications of weapons, unless listed by *Jane's* or a publication of comparable repute. But in the case of the lethal wristwatch, he was skeptical even after referring to *Jane's*. He looked at the close-up of the watch.

It looked like a perfectly normal quartz watch. Like one of those cheap Rolex imitations. He looked at his own faithful Seiko. The watch informed him that it was 4 AM. He calculated the time difference in the subcontinent. His pocket diary gave him the number of Rizwan uz-Zaman. He got up and walked to the directory to look for the international dialling code for Peshawar. There was only one way of finding out if the watch slug was as accurate and efficient as described. Zaman could find the weapon, if it existed, and if it was available.

There was always the chance that a particularly ingenious weapon was created for a particular mission and discontinued once the mission got over or was abandoned. He hoped that was not the case with the watch slug. If such a creation existed, his partner deserved it. It would be a blend of one peak of creativity with another.

PESHAWAR

It took only two rings to wake Zaman. Like all men of the frontier, he slept light. In fact, to him sleep was the scourge of men in general. At least men with pride, men who led a dignified life. For such men, more often than not, made enemies. They also lived in environments immune to standard social dictates: a minor insult could invite death, and the time for contemplative and preventive action was never more than a few seconds. In such an environment, the faster one awoke from slumber, the harder it would be for vengeful adversaries to get to them.

Rizwan was a Pashtun by birth. In addition to being the second-in-command of his clan, he doubled up as an arms expert, at least in the irregular arms market. He led a simple life, but had amassed enough wealth to last the next generation as well. The strife in neighbouring Afghanistan had

223

made him a rich man. Before that, his fame had spread only by word of mouth. He had specialised in wares used for public assassinations. Camera guns and fountain pen slugs had been his speciality. His wares had reached all corners of the world, from the Vavuniya jungles of north-east Sri Lanka to the mountains of Bolivia.

In addition to regular clients such as the Taliban and the LTTE, Rizwan also serviced niche clients like Ray Darrel. The dollar payments not only swelled his coffers but also gave him access to the meetings called by the more glamorous and powerful arms dealers. These men would never manufacture irregular strong arms because it wasn't commercially viable but had to contend with requests for the same once in a while. They would then turn to men like Zaman and others in similar businesses.

Rizwan had met Darrel only twice—once when he had been called to London for negotiations and to have the procedure of payment and other formalities chalked out, and the second time, when Darrel had visited Peshawar to see for himself the expertise of Rizwan uz-Zaman. From the two meetings and subsequent requests for arms, the clever Pushto had worked out that Darrel had been requisitioning weapons for irregular mercenary purposes, in all probability, assassinations. He had also worked out with little difficulty that Darrel was not the eventual wielder of his weapons. The dour and partially handicapped man, according to Rizwan, did not have it in him to take a life. Zaman had been consumed with curiosity about the identity and any attendant information on Darrel's collaborator or partner. Of course, the arms dealer was not aware that the security agencies of half the world were also trying to answer the same question.

Today, as he disconnected the transnational call, he again sat up with raging curiosity. It had been Darrel. The man had

224

requested him to find out about a gun in the form of a wristwatch that had recently been advertised in *Jane's*. Zaman had promised his cooperation and an early response to the caller from London. He had not revealed the small detail that he, Rizwan uz-Zaman, himself was the creator of that beautiful piece of weaponry. To reveal that detail would limit the cost potential of the art piece in case the Londoner opted to buy it. He would take the stand that another manufacturer of the huge arms bazaar was marketing the watch. The cost price of the timepiece varied from 800 to 1200 dollars, depending on specific variations demanded. In the case of Darrel, Rizwan was aware he could manage at least 5000 dollars, even more, depending on the need and the time-frame of the request.

He would even consider designing a better version than the one he had shown to the correspondent from *Jane's*, of course at a much higher cost. There was a lot that could still be done with the watch gun to improve its accuracy. The metal component could be made lighter and the slug stronger, subject again to the restriction that it should not cause any external bleeding for at least a few minutes after impact. In addition, he was working on incorporating a range-enhancing component for the watch-gun. At present, the range was six metres. Rizwan was aware that *Jane's* had listed the range to be about ten metres. He had deliberately quoted the range to be in excess of twelve metres to the correspondent. The correspondent, while writing the story, had on his own account lopped off about three metres to account for exaggeration.

Zaman was working to increase the range to at least eleven metres. To achieve the modification, he was trying methods such as reducing the gelatine component to increasing the dial width of the watch. The ideal course he knew was to increase the range to about nine metres, retaining the accuracy till six metres.

SOMEWHERE IN THE ASIAN CONTINENT

He neatly folded the pile of newspapers lying in front of him. Once the identity of the target was revealed, he always gathered information on the person. As he had done before, the newspapers were his first stop. They always offered the first glimpse into the personality of the hunted. And their reports would be objective. The reconnaissance could follow later to add to the first base of information. So far, the Pakistani assignment seemed easy enough, but then he had reached a professional level where all hits seemed simple.

36

NEW DELHI, OCTOBER 20, 1995

He rose at 5.30 AM and walked across to the alarm clock. The digital alarm clock radio was set for 6.00 AM. He switched it off. He had long since won the competition with alarm clocks. It was pitch dark outside. He padded to the bathroom, splashed cold water on his face till the focus returned to his eyes. A sweatshirt and a pair of track pants had been neatly folded on the table next to his bed. Once out in the gentle autumn, he debated whether to walk the entire distance or to drive a part of it. He decided against the walk, as valuable time would be wasted. He would park the car at some convenient middle point and walk the short distance.

The papers had given Pandara Park as the residential address of the professor. He vaguely knew of it as an old, quiet and peaceful government colony of New Delhi. He had heard of it when he had studied in Delhi. Many of his classmates at school had come from there. It took him about twenty minutes to walk to Pandara Park from where he had found parking. The numbering of the houses was clearly marked on signboards that had been freshly painted.

He took several rounds of the central park where a lone youngster waited for the rest of his team to show up for a game of cricket. Prof. Kapre's was the corner house; armed guards stood at the front gate and another posse of paramilitary guards were stationed in a makeshift tent outside. On his third round of the park, one of the uniformed men walked up to him and asked him —more out of curiosity than caution—if he was new to the locality. The man took out a card from his sweatshirt pocket and showed it to the guard. It was a press card displaying his accreditation with the *Financial Express*, London, in bold letters. The card had been obtained for him by his partner in England more than two years ago. As promised, it had given him access to many places. The small plastic card—the same size as any common driving licence—had a depression in its centre where another small piece of plastic, the size of a microchip, could be fitted. This chip was meant to carry the name of the holder. He possessed at least four identification chips. The present chip identified him as an Indian. The other chips identified him as an English national, an American correspondent and a Swiss correspondent.

The enthusiastic guard was told that the foreign paper had commissioned a story on the occupant of the house, and that he would be returning in a day or two with photographers. The guard returned to his post impressed and hopeful of a picture in a 'phoren' publication.

He resumed his walk around the park. By now, the lone cricketer had been joined by his friends and a serious match seemed to be in progress. As he walked, his mind was awash with various scenarios. He had heard of the daunting security arrangements in the subcontinent. Professor's Kapre's house was in a lot of four houses. If he used a remote controlled bazooka, as had been used in Mecca, the other houses and their occupants would surely be reduced to dust. Mecca had been different. His target's posse of 400 tribesmen and guards had occupied the neighbouring tents. Those men had borne the brunt of the attack and no innocent people had been killed.

He hated killing people who were not connected to the victim. He wouldn't be too concerned about the guards of Prof. Kapre, for their jobs and lives were intertwined with the man they were sworn to protect. It was the innocent for whom he had always watched out for. Since that one dark night on the streets of Tokyo when the uninvolved had fallen victim, along with Nobuhiro Sahoto, the executive chairman of the Mitsubishi Motor Company, he had tried to ensure that bystanders did not fall as well. The fact that in the Sahoto case the bystanders had consisted of a mother and two children had added to his guilt. The image of the small bodies riddled with bullets had often troubled him. Nightmares had been frequent, and sleep hard to come by.

His mind leaped from the streets of Tokyo to the lanes of Pandara Park as a squeal of delight reached his ears. He looked around and saw a young girl chasing a balloon right in front of him. The girl was followed by the mother who looked amused and angry at the same time. She ran to the girl and picked her up along with the balloon. He smiled at the lady, she smiled back apologetically and then went inside a house where a doting man stood on the balcony. His mind again flashed the image of the Sahoto killing. Newspaper reports the next day had given the children's ages as nine and six.

He walked on, towards the main road. Explosives were no longer an option if he was going to get the professor at his house. It would kill too many people. He didn't want the number of casualties to be as high as they had been in the case of the Rajiv Gandhi assassination. Prabhakaran's men had slaughtered eighteen other human beings in addition to the former Indian Prime Minister. Even otherwise, suicide killings had always disgusted him. It was, according to him, an easy option. The real triumph lay in reading about your work in the newspapers the following morning. He had worked often for political terrorists, many times at lesser prices. He knew that if they didn't get a professional assassin to do it for them, they would attempt it themselves with near catastrophic consequences.

It was the political assassin who had given the professionals a bad name. The politicos had killed innocent bystanders in high multiples of their actual targets. One of the few creative and intelligent assassinations had been that of JFK in Dallas. The men behind the President's death had wisely hired a professional and then crafted an amazing drama around Lee Harvey Oswald and Jack Ruby. Like many in the assassination trade, he also knew that the Kennedy killing had originated in the United States itself. The identity of the planners of Kennedy's death was known to hundreds, if not thousands of people both in and outside the US. However, few people knew that Robert Kennedy had, four days before his death, come into possession of a file labeled 'True Killers of the President'. An old FBI contact had passed it on to him. Before Robert Kennedy could do anything about it, he had been killed as well. Within three days, a similar fate befell the FBI contact Michael Davies. Few members of that caucus were now alive. He knew at least two, whose arms had been twisted by Mossad operatives for benefits ranging from cash contributions to lobbying in the Congress and the White House for Israel.

JFK's killer had died only in 1989, in a nondescript village in the Swiss Alps after a comfortable retirement that began in 1963 itself. The man had been talked about in whispers at the Camper school, his actual identity never revealed. The exception had been two young men by the names of David Steiner and Jack Singer who had travelled all the way to

Saxeburg to pay homage and to seek the blessings of the most famous and elusive assassin of the century.

OCTOBER 20, 1995

Surendra Nigam was in a pensive mood as he waited in the small annexe attached to the room of Director R. It had been two days since orders had first come to coordinate with the RAW director. Although Mishra's reputation preceded him, Nigam had spent the last two days in a relatively calm frame of mind. He still had some faith left in his own ability. The ability that had taken him to the hallowed portals of the Indian Institute of Technology and then brought him success in the tedious civil services entrance examination. The tendency to maintain status quo had taken possession of his soul, yet he knew that this was the predilection of every Indian administrator and police officer. He just prayed to his lord that his brilliance was lying dormant somewhere within him.

'You can go in Sir,' the perpetually nervous peon came and informed him. Nigam strode in confidently and was received by one of the last of the great Indian police service officers.

'Welcome, young man.'

'Thank you, Sir.'

'Take your seat, and let's get cracking.' Small talk was bound to be rare in such environs. 'Are you aware of your brief, and why you are sitting here?' enquired Mishra of the younger man.

'It's about the death of Mr Bhargava, Sir.' Surendra's voice was low and steady.

'Yes, the point is that Mohan's death has left us with several unsolved puzzles, puzzles which I am hoping you may unravel.'

Surendra looked his distinguished superior in the eyes. There seemed to be genuine hope there. Not the usual look

231

of defeat and resignation he had seen on many occasions on the faces of his superiors.

'Do you know why you, and not someone from the Central Bureau or the Intelligence Bureau, are sitting here?'

Nigam shook his head.

'Because I was once in your position as a young officer, when investigations were carried out over our heads and it used to hurt. So, before an investigative team could be assembled, I thought I would check out the background of the area officer. There are no great cases behind you Nigam, but you do have a most impressive academic record. It's that brilliance that I am hoping to harness.'

Nigam was a trifle surprised. In his few years of service, this was the first time he was hearing anything even remotely inspirational. He nodded his head and muttered a low 'I shall do my best, Sir.'

'Good, I hope you can help me. If you succeed, you shall also be rendering a great service to the nation.'

Nigam's mind now began to race at top speed. He had guessed that Mohan Bhargava had been no cultural attaché, but a highly placed RAW official. Now with the way Mishra was talking, it seemed that Mohan Bhargava could have been much more significant than an ordinary intelligence officer enjoying the perks of a foreign posting.

'What did your preliminary examination of the accident site reveal?'

'Well, it seems that the taxi in which Mr Bhargava was travelling was entirely faultless. The blame seems to be on the vehicle that rammed it.'

'What kind of vehicle?' interrupted Mishra.

'Definitely a truck. We found pieces of rope and scattered cargo, the usual plastic crates.'

'Hmm, well, let me inform you that this accident was no ordinary hit-and-run case but murder.' Mishra paused, waiting to see the effect of what he had said on Nigam. When the shock subsided, he spoke again, 'Don't worry, it's not anything that your investigation missed. We know this because of another source.'

Nigam let this sink in slowly. The real magnitude of Bhargava's accident was beginning to hit him now. He had been worried before coming to the RAW headquarters. He now felt relieved. At least he was getting a chance to prove his mettle.

'Now I want to impress upon you that the Mohan Bhargava case is to be investigated and solved under the utmost secrecy. Maintain the lie that it was an ordinary accident. Including you, not more than six officers are aware of the true circumstances of his death. I could have requested for you to be temporarily deputed to RAW but that would unnecessarily raise questions. So, you stay where you are and report to me. I have arranged that your normal duties will not interfere with this investigation.'

Nigam listened in silence. He was becoming aware that this was probably the last chance for him to snap out of the defeated and cynical mode that he had slipped into.

37

NEW DELHI, OCTOBER 26, 1995

'We will sue them for defamation.'

'Hang on, let us first see the exact contents of this so-called confession.'

Both men were furious. The former, K. Shekhar Rao, was the spokesperson of the REP and the latter, Devender Yadav, the quiet and low profile general secretary of the party. In the last five years, the REP had won many fanatical followers in the southern states of India. Rao belonged to Andhra Pradesh, the same state as Srinivas Reddy, the incumbent prime minister. The REP had yet to achieve any electoral successes in this state; however, it had many followers in certain isolated pockets.

The two men were irate. Sitting in the press room of the party headquarters at Ashoka Road, it was part of their routine to sift through the various political and semi-political magazines and formulate responses to reports relevant to the party. They had just received a copy of the *The Weekly* edited by that playboy caricature of a journalist. The lead story was titled 'Indian Political Class—On The Take?' The story had detailed the arrest of a key member of a money-laundering ring. The group was based in Delhi and had connections in

Mumbai. Certain diaries had been found that led the police in the direction of two important politicians. The investigating officer had claimed that the initials VK stood for Kapre and CDR stood for Chandra Dev Raj.

As Chandra Dev Raj had fallen out of favour with Prime Minister Reddy, the accusation was yet to evoke any major reaction in the headquarters of the party from which he had been recently expelled. Krishan Suresh, the coordinator of the Congress press cell, had seen the copy of the *The Weekly*. He went over the article slowly and deliberately. He knew that Dev Raj had made millions from his long stint in power in Madhya Pradesh, yet he wasn't sure of the authenticity of the story. Suresh also knew Satyaki Das. He had met the journalist at social gatherings a few times. What struck him as odd was that Das was not one to make powerful political enemies. On the contrary, he was the kind to cultivate people like Dev Raj. Unless a patron who was even more powerful than Dev Raj had assured Das of his support. Such a patron could only be one of two men, Suresh thought. The prime minister, for instance, had never ceased to amaze Suresh.

He had personally met Reddy when the latter was in the process of leaving the Capital after a listless stint as the Congress foreign minister. The man had been a physical wreck with one very weak foot in the grave. That unsure, doddering man had now transformed into a Machiavelli, playing with the political destinies of his party mates. Suresh knew that Srinivas Reddy hated Dev Raj, more so because of Dev Raj's proximity to the group that had been close to Rajiv Gandhi. Relations had never been exactly cordial between the Prime Minister and this group. They had worsened after the letter-writing episodes.

The Prime Minister could certainly be behind this attempt to tarnish whatever remained of Dev Raj's reputation. The second suspect was Rajeshwar Kulkarni, the chief minister of Maharashtra and the de facto number two in the Congress. In fact, the story in the *The Weekly* seemed to be just the kind to appeal to Kulkarni. Suresh knew that Kulkarni was rather pleased that Dev Raj had been sidelined. If in the next elections the Congress could hold on to power, Kulkarni could emerge as the frontrunner. Suresh was not very sure of the scenario, yet he was certain that the Maratha chieftain saw it that way. It was more his kind of scheme than Reddy's; or perhaps it had been planted in Kulkarni's mind and then approved by the prime minister.

Sitting in the REP office, Rao and Yadav knew it was crucial that the party carefully craft its strategy in the coming days. It was a fact that Indians were becoming sensitive to corruption and moral turpitude. The two REP strategists clearly remembered the role played by the Bofors scandal in unseating Rajiv Gandhi. The REP was very close to capturing power at the Centre. But for the leader of the party—which had used the current government's corruption as an election slogan—to be tarred with the same brush might hurt the REP's prospects.

When the phone rang, Yadav picked up the staid MTNL instrument, paused for a second and turned to Rao with a pained look on his face. 'It's the Press, they want the party's reaction to the *Weekly* scoop. As they cannot reach the professor, they have come to the party headquarters.'

Rao thought for a moment before he spoke. 'Tell them to wait, I will be with them in a few minutes.' As the official spokesperson, Rao was well aware that it was crucial for him to maintain his poise before the Press. If the fourth estate detected any signs of nervousness, he knew that they would not hesitate to move in for the kill. He was aware that his party was yet to climb the popularity charts with individual pressmen. Although the editors of the big three were behind the REP, he knew that ordinary pressmen were not entirely at ease with certain of his party's views.

Rao walked to the washroom, combed his thinning hair and cleaned his rimless glasses. He then went to the press conference room. On his entry the assembled crowd of journalists burst into uproar. There were at least fifty of them, including reporters from the big three. Rao refrained from sitting down and instead walked into the crowd of reporters. As questions were fired at him and light bulbs flashed, he formulated a common answer to the cacophony of voices. 'Where is Kapre at the moment?' 'Is this the morality that the REP preached about?' 'Is it true that Kapre has been forced to resign as the chief of the party?' 'Who will lead the REP in the next elections?'

'Look,' Rao began, 'I can understand your anxiety, however, let me say that we are yet to completely go through the allegations. We will first read them carefully and then respond formally and officially.'

'What is Prof. Kapre's reaction to this?'

'I am yet to speak to Kapre *ji*, he is at this moment on the road to Pune, it is difficult to contact him.'

'Does the REP see power slipping from it now that its real face stands exposed?'

Rao turned at the provocative question. It had come from a girl he recognised—Sulekha Bhatt, one of Asim Banerjee's favourite reporters.

'No. I don't think Satyaki Das is the nation's conscience keeper.'

'Has Prof. Kapre resigned as the party head?'

'I told you the party leaders are yet to meet and discuss the allegations in the *Weekly*.'

'Any informal comments on the allegations?' This came from a *Times* reporter, one of the REP's strongest supporters.

'Well, all I can say is you all know Prof. Kapre and what he stands for, and you also know Satyaki Das and his brand of investigative journalism. You make your choice and the country will make its own.' With the punchline firmly in the party's favour, Rao walked out of the pressroom and the doors were shut.

In the evening, Reddy, along with Kulkarni and Hitesh Singh, watched the seven o'clock news which showed the press conference. Reddy turned to Kulkarni, 'This Rao handled the press well.'

'Yes, he is a seasoned spokesperson,' the admission was made grudgingly by the architect of the whole drama.

'They don't seem to be worried,' Hitesh Singh remarked.

'Wait for a couple of days, such events trigger panic slowly but surely. Let the damage sink in, then they will start running for cover.'

'Well, do let me know, the two of you, when you feel it is the right time, I can't stall J.S. Kahlon forever,' the Prime Minister said, referring to the officer who had taken charge as the chief election commissioner of India a year back.

Kahlon, thought to be independent in action, was hardly so. He had been a staunch Congress supporter all his life. His faith in the party had got him the sought after constitutional post. He had been waiting for the prime minister to give a press statement regarding the tentative schedule of the coming general elections. He had already visited Srinivas Reddy twice in the last month. The Prime Minister was worried that Kahlon might be forced to announce a schedule that would not work to his party's advantage.

38

Surendra Nigam sat in silence, the only sound in the room coming from the old ceiling fan. He was hunched in his chair, looking like he were asleep. In fact, the deputy commissioner's mind was working furiously. Nothing new had turned up since his meeting with Director R over a week ago. He kept wondering if the key to Mohan Bhargava's death lay in London. He had been given access to all Bhargava's service papers. The record of the deceased RAW man was unblemished. Bhargava had been a superb officer. He had been in London for over two years and had made only three visits to India during those two years.

Who could have wanted Bhargava dead? What had Bhargava unearthed that was so important as to warrant a personal trip? And why the secrecy, why the stubborn refusal to divulge the flight schedule and other details? Unless he suspected people within his own organisation, those who could have interfered with the mission, whatever it may have been.

Nigam got up from his worn out leather chair and walked to the window of his room. He was feeling a little better. The

239

good old brain was not yet dead, in spite of his mother's consistent attempts to kill it. It had retained a propensity for clear thinking. He again focused his mind on the problem at hand. If Bhargava wanted to keep his itinerary secret, then it was possible that he may have taken certain precautions in London. However, the ace intelligence officer had made one glaring error. He had made the mistake of travelling by British Airways. The British airlines with its procedures was absolutely out of his control. All it would have taken was a simple phone call to the booking office. Nigam walked to his desk and punched the soft pad of the electric bell.

'Send Avdesh to me, right away,' he barked at the peon. After about three minutes, Avdesh Kaushik, the superintendent under whose jurisdiction the international airport fell, came in. Without waiting for the junior officer to sit, Nigam began giving him instructions. 'I want you to check with the head office of British Airways if anyone called to find out when Bhargava was flying. Kaushik nodded and walked out. In times of urgency, they dispensed with niceties. Nigam's hunch was growing. And if Bhargava's itinerary had been found out in London itself, perhaps it meant that the message had been relayed to New Delhi and a fast but efficient plan for execution had been formulated.

ISLAMABAD

A few thousand miles away from Surendra Nigam, the actual architects of Mohan Bhargava's death sat discussing business with the most notorious executioner in the world. They sat in the super deluxe room of the same hotel that had played host to Radley Karras a few weeks back. The two ISI officers sat opposite a man they knew simply as Jack Singer. He wore dark glasses, t-shirt and slacks. The glasses were sleek, with small frames just barely covering Singer's eyes. Nazir looked around the room. He noted the open windows and curtains. It didn't seem as though this Singer apprehended any danger to himself. He seemed composed. They had been sitting there for over five minutes. Except for a request to be seated, the man had not said a word.

Nazir looked at Maj. Tariq who remained quiet. The Brigadier cleared his throat and began. 'Can you do it?'

The man called Singer looked at them through his dark glasses. His voice was soft, and he spoke in slightly accented English, 'If I couldn't, would I be here?'

'When can it be done?'

'I normally take from twenty-four hours to a week, depending on the circumstances. If there is any urgency, it can be handled.'

'We want him dead before December 31.' They looked at him, expecting a response. He said nothing. The quiet in the room made Nazir feel uncomfortable. To break the silence he asked, 'Can it be done easily?' and regretted it the minute he said it.

'There is no one, howsoever well protected, who is safe from an assassin's bullet.' The voice remained soft, the tone indulgent.

'Anyone?' That was Tariq.

'Yes, even your Gen. Mehmod is not safe.' The voice was again expressionless. At their premier's name being taken, Nazir felt some annoyance. He didn't know how good this Singer was but he could easily vouch for the man's arrogance.

'Name your price.'

'Ten million,' he looked at them intently through his dark glasses. Nazir looked at the Major first, then at him, and said nothing. 'In US dollars, plus expenses, seventy-five percent to be paid upfront before the execution, the remaining after.'

Tariq's lips moved in shock, as his breath escaped in the form of a sharp whistle.

'Where is the proof that you won't run away with the money?' Nazir was getting angry. Despite Karras' warning, he was beginning to lose his cool at what he perceived to be a less than professional show of attitude.

'There is no proof or guarantee; I *could* run with your money.'

Tariq pursed his lips. He fervently hoped that the Brigadier would not take the bait. They were sitting with a hard-headed murderer who would give them no assurance about anything. One either believed him or took one's business elsewhere.

Brig. Nazir unfortunately took the bait—hook, line and sinker. 'You wouldn't take on the might of an entire organisation?' It was a challenge.

The man called Singer said nothing but his face broke into a smile. Tariq couldn't help noticing how much gentler the man's face looked when he smiled. 'Why do you think I am free to discuss business with inefficient officers like you? Obviously you and your ilk have come up as second best against me, or else I would have departed from this earth years ago.'

Nazir's face twitched for a few seconds, then it returned to its normal expression. That minute he remembered Karras' instructions about maintaining his composure.

Karras had told him that such men worked more for the satisfaction of their egos than for the lure of the lucre. And he had unwittingly taken on the man's ego. He looked at Singer and smiled, knowing that the sharp assassin would understand that Nazir had noticed his own mistake.

Singer took the hint and said, 'If I fail, then except for the expenses, I will refund your entire money.'

'What if the first attempt is unsuccessful?' Tariq interjected, worried whether two attempts meant two packets of ten million each.

'There is never a second attempt. Either I succeed the first time, or I never succeed.'

'Have you ever gone in for a second attempt, maybe because of factors outside your control?' persisted Tariq.

'Never. And I take millions to ensure that no factors remain outside my control.'

'When do you begin your preparations?'

'The day I receive seventy-five percent of ten million.'

'And your expenses?'

'I will contact you after the hit with a total of the expenses. Then you disburse it with the remaining twenty-five percent.'

'What if we need to contact you to know of the progress or the date of the likely hit?' The thought of one man holding the lifeline of Project K2 was now beginning to worry the Brigadier.

'You will not be able to contact me. If you decide to call off the contract then you contact the man you contacted to reach me. If you do that, I will stop immediately. Of course I will then keep fifty percent of 10 million dollars, plus the expenses that I would have incurred till that moment.'

'Is there no way for us to be able to monitor, or at least know, how far you may be from your goal?' As he said this, Nazir's voice was deliberately deferential. At least that is what the Major thought.

'Look, I don't have any time for games. If you want to keep track of my movements because you have questions about my credibility or to increase your general knowledge, then I am not the right person.' With that the man called Singer rose and indicated that the audience he had granted to Nazir and Tariq was over.

Nazir rose and said, 'Please don't get me wrong. All right, consider the contract on. When and where do we transfer the money?'

The man remained standing. 'My associate in London will let you know within a week.' With that he opened the door of the room.

Now it was Tariq's turn to lose his temper. 'What protection do you have against us if we chose to kill you now?'

Singer smiled broadly and with a sweep of his left hand took off his sunglasses. His eyes were a clear blue and were, the Pakistanis thought, probably lenses worn to mask their true colour. However, what was strange about them was that they seemed to be absolutely emotionless. 'Do you see that black diary lying next to the lamp?'

'Yes,' Nazir nodded, wondering what kind of protection a piece of stationery could provide to anyone.

'That is a sound sensitive explosive. Even a silencer-supressed crack of a bullet would cause it to explode. Within thirty seconds this entire block would be rubble, and you along with me would be ground to dust.'

'What if I didn't use a gun?' Tariq pressed.

'A gun is the only way you can get the better of me. In physical combat you would have to wait for me to fall asleep or better yet, be unconscious.' There was no derision in his voice. All the statements were made in a deadpan tone.

Tariq twitched with irritation. As he braced himself to respond, he felt the restraining hand of Nazir. After a second, both men walked out of the room. Singer walked to the bedside and picked up his diary of addresses and flicked its pages amusedly. Islamabad or Muscat, the clients were the same bunch of fools everywhere. He paused at a page, made a mental note of a number, and then slowly walked to the corner of the room to where a dark charcoal grey briefcase lay. He put the briefcase on his lap, slowly turned the combination lock and opened it. Once opened, the briefcase looked like an old-fashioned jukebox. He felt for the safety

244

code button and then pressed it. With a silent motion, the soft leather of the top of the case parted to reveal a small digital object. He took the dialling computer in his hand and dialled a number on the customised satellite phone. After five minutes, he replaced the dialling computer in its resting place and packed the satellite phone that was constructed to look like a briefcase on the outside.

The camouflage of the marvelous piece of machinery was not restricted to the outside. The interior of the case was specially designed to look like an old jukebox and to function like a compact disc with the capacity of twin decks. All this effort had been made to conceal the satellite phone from the prying eyes of airport x-ray machines. The dialling computer looked like a remote control. The person who had designed and finetuned this music box was James Bradley. Bradley was, in addition to being the designer of the ingenious satellite phone, the chief designer in Rapiscon International Corporation, the conglomerate that builds the x-ray and scanning machines used at international airports all over the world. Bradley was also a former consultant to the Israeli intelligence agency, Mossad. Among his best friends was a fellow Jew called David Steiner.

James Bradley had only once breached the confidentiality clause of his lucrative contract with Rapiscon International. That had happened when he designed a satellite phone prototype that could elude even the most advanced detection machines used at international airports. To repay a blood debt to a childhood friend, Bradley had made a phone that looked like a music box and escaped all detection machines. Of course, that was not the only precaution that the user of that phone undertook. Every time Jack Singer walked into an international airport with the music box he also took papers that identified him as one of the senior sales representatives of the Toshiba Music Corporation.

Out of all the Japanese companies engaged in the designing of music boxes and compact disc boxes, Toshiba's research was at the forefront. The Vice-President, Research of Toshiba Music Corporation, Chicoro Mifune, had lost his life on the streets of Baghdad to an assassin's bullet. The irony amused the wielder of the Toshiba music box.

Only once had the music box been opened. That had happened at Terminal 3 of Heathrow airport when the security staff had stopped him. He had, of course, complied calmly. The beauty of the dialling computer/remote control designed by Bradley was not only that it doubled up in functions but was also synchronised with several Toshiba music systems. The security staff at Heathrow even tried the remote system on the decks lying at the duty free shops. The excellent piece of gadgetry worked everywhere. It would only turn into a dialling computer with a reach of thousands of miles after a four-digit code was punched into the machine. According to Jack Singer and David Steiner, James Bradley deserved a Nobel Prize for engineering.

One of Bradley's assistants at Rapiscon had, by chance, found out about the music box. This gentleman, a mousy looking Briton called Thomas Hargreaves, had attempted to blackmail Bradley. After six days of his collection of the first installment of 5000 pounds, Hargreaves' body had been found floating in the Thames at the edge of the Houses of Parliament in London.

39

Superintendent of Police Avdesh Kaushik got into his rundown second hand Fiat and started the rickety engine. When it grunted in rebellion he pressed the accelerator and sped towards the office of his superior, Surendra Nigam. His heart was pounding with excitement. Within twenty minutes he had reached his office. Nigam was busy on the phone. After a few minutes he replaced the receiver and looked at him expectantly. 'I suppose you have hit a dead end?' he said cynically.

'On the contrary, you won't believe what I learnt Sir.' The excitement was palpable in Kaushik's voice.

'Sit down and begin.'

'I started with the ground staff of British Airways at IGI airport. The passenger lists are accessible to anyone. Sitting in this office, you can call their office in London and get the name of a passenger.'

'Hmm!' nodded a pensive Nigam. 'Is that why you are so thrilled?'

An unfazed Kaushik carried on. 'On a hunch I made enquiries regarding the computer terminals of the airlines recording any such oral queries.'

247

Nigam's brow was knitted. 'How can an oral query be recorded by a computer?'

'It's very easy, Sir, let me explain how it is done,' continued an excited Kaushik. 'I have been told that British Airways has a particular software through which any check of this kind is recorded in the main terminal.'

'And?'

'Not only does their system record such a query but it also marks the name of the passenger for whom such a query is made.'

Surendra Nigam stood up from his desk and walked to the window of his room. His mind was racing. He reached for his pack of Wills Navy Cut cigarettes. He lit up and puffed leisurely to slow himself down. After a minute he spoke. 'Did the airlines agree to part with such sensitive information?' His voice was loaded with disbelief, as though it were too much to expect such a lucky break.

'They were reluctant initially but a few words from the customs officer-in-charge of their section made them cooperate.'

'And?'

'On October 17, the Manchester office of British Airways confirmed to a caller that one Mohan Bhargava was on the flight to New Delhi.'

'Who was this person who took the call?'

'An English woman in the ticketing department of British Airways.'

'I trust you have her name?'

'I am sorry Sir, but here my luck ran out. The Delhi office said that they don't have the name in the first place, and added for good measure that they would not part with that information. I am sure though that they knew the name, else how would they be able to say that it was a lady officer?'

'It is clear that this issue requires the intervention of higher authorities. You have done well, Avdesh, you can go now. In case I need any more follow up, I will let you know.'

Two hours later, Nigam repeated the conversation to Rajnish Mishra.

'I will speak to Govind Menon who can have a word with Lord Holmes,' Mishra said, referring to his batchmate from the academy who had risen to the position of foreign secretary. 'I will arrange for you to go to London after Menon has done the groundwork. It may be possible to unearth some clue there.'

ISLAMABAD, OCTOBER 30

It was pre-dawn in the Pakistani capital. The man known as Gabriel sat in his room alone. He was habitually a late riser, but since the death of Agni, sleep had been playing hide-and-seek with him. It had been more than ten days since the savage end of his handler. He had heard whispers that Mohan Bhargava had left certain clues about the identity of the spy. He had refused to take those rumours seriously. He knew that the distribution of such nuggets of information was a ruse to smoke him out. If at all Agni had confided in Rajnish Mishra, then Mishra would be aware of the acute danger that surrounded him now. He had once met the Indian intelligence chief at a joint dinner that had been hosted by the Indo-Pak and Bangladesh cultural delegations at a United Nations seminar.

That seminar had been four years ago, when the Indian had not ascended to the position of Director. Gabriel had formed an extremely high opinion of Rajnish Mishra. He knew that Mishra would not act in a way that could remotely endanger his position. He wondered for a moment if he should contact Mishra. But he dismissed the thought quickly. Too much was at stake for him.

He rose from his chair as the pre-dawn darkness metamorphosed into the orangish glow of morning. As he thought about himself being the single-most dangerous spy that his country had seen, an icy chill descended upon him. Slowly, he began to carry out his daily ablutions while his mind raced ahead to the future of Pakistan and Operation Karakoram in particular. He now had clear information about the plan to eliminate the future prime minister of India.

Gabriel knew that the success of Operation Karakoram would be beneficial to Pakistan but detrimental to him as well as certain others in the Pakistani power establishment. It would end up strengthening the hands of Gen. Mehmood. In general, Gabriel was a supporter of the General but the hawkish line of the ISI bothered him. The organisation's repression of the common Pakistani was increasing every day.

Gabriel knew that to topple Asad Mehmood, it was crucial that K2 and the vital Operation Karakoram should fail. In addition, it was imperative that as many people as possible be aware of the failure of the grandiose operation. Already cynical whispers about Brig. Nazir's brainchild had begun.

NEW DELHI

Satyaki Das watched with pleasure as Reena removed his belt. Though it was only 9 AM in the morning, the media baron had decided that his secretary should begin the day with personal services. As Reena led him to their regular sofa, her boss indicated that he wanted a variation today. Now he watched the fully clothed Reena open his trousers and slip her delicate fingers inside his crotch. His breathing became quicker as she stroked his throbbing organ. She then drew his manhood out of the warm confines of his undershorts. Das continued to look at her, the sight of her deep in concentration exciting him further. She smoothly took his organ in her hand and drew it to her lips. His low moans began to fill the sound proof room as Reena's tongue flicked down the length of his shaft. Gradually she took it within her lips and began to suck it. Satyaki moaned louder as he felt Reena's teeth make contact with him.

Satyaki continued to sway in ecstasy for the next five minutes as Reena's impatient tongue wove sinuous patterns on his organ. He touched her head to indicate to her that he was nearing release. Reena released him and turned to look at him as he rushed to the attached bathroom. She heard the sound of the flush and a moment later Das walked back into the room. 'All right, let's begin our day,' he said, indicating that it was time to commence the professional services.

As Satyaki took his seat and began arranging the list of phone calls to be made, he was disturbed by a knock. He looked up in irritation to find Arun Malhotra's head peeping in. Das gave his secretary a questioning look. In response, Arun moved from the door and the forms of Bhaskar Naik and Prakash Mittal took his place. Satyaki rose to welcome the two visitors. It was Naik who spoke first. 'We have come to thank you for the excellent exposé you carried four days ago.'

Das grimaced as he thought of the chain of events the story in his magazine had set. The ruling party led by Rajeshwar Kulkarni, Bhasker Naik, and Jagdish Thakur had demanded the immediate prosecution of Prof. Vijay Kapre on charges of gross corruption. The REP had defended its chief with an unexpected show of fury and cohesiveness. The day after the story, A. Shukla had given a long interview to one of the big three, in which he declared the story of foreign currency kickbacks as completely fictitious. He had added for good measure that the owner of *The Weekly* was a known lackey of the Congress.

The unexpected reaction from within the Congress—in particular the group oweing allegiance to the late Prime Minister—had unsettled Reddy. Satyaki had, in fact, received urgent summons from the Gandhi faction within hours of the Shukla interview. He had listened in horror as the leader of this group had questioned his sources for the hawala story. The leader had been particularly upset over the inclusion of Chandra Dev Raj in the so-called exposé and had wanted to know whether the Prime Minister's Office had been behind the story. Satyaki had vehemently denied the charge. He had, however, rued his fall in the eyes of the single-most powerful leader of the Congress Party. Das was well aware that Srinivas Reddy had become Prime Minister only because the leader had declined the post. He also knew that even today it would take the leader five minutes to unseat Reddy and install someone else as Prime Minister.

After this unhappy meeting, Satyaki had been summoned by Prime Minister Reddy who had lauded the brilliant journalism of *The Weekly* and had hinted that there was to be no let up on the accusations against Prof. Kapre and a few of his own partymen, in particular Chandra Dev Raj. Also included in the story, on the explicit instructions of Naik and Mittal, were Sureshan Nair and Srikanth Rathore—loyalists of Dev Raj.

Satyaki Das was in deep distress, caught as he was between the conflicting commands of the Prime Minister's men and the leader who was the soul of the party that Das had come to love. To further add to his woes was the position taken by two of the national dailies. Their editors had termed the story as a weak attempt to derail the victory lap of the REP. Prof. Kapre's stand had been unexpected. Confronted by demands to withdraw from the prime ministerial race, the tough professor had stated that he would abide by the wishes of his party. Kulkarni had been sure that the REP would have asked Prof. Kapre to withdraw as the prime ministerial candidate, but remain the party chief. But the entire party had rallied around their leader: there had not been a single voice of dissent when it was stated that their leader was innocent till proven guilty and would continue to remain their prime ministerial candidate till he was convicted of any criminal offence.

40

'Papa, papa, your omelette is getting cold!'

Rajnish Mishra started. His mind had been on Mohan Bhargava, Surender Nigam and British Airways. 'Okay, okay, I'm eating it. No college today?'

'There's a strike today.'

'Oh!' Mishra looked up at his nineteen-year-old daughter. He had two children—Naina and a twenty-five year old son, Ashish. Both were exceptionally brilliant. In addition, they had both inherited their mother's good looks.

Atreyee Mishra had been and continued to be a beautiful woman. At forty-four, she was almost twelve years younger than Mishra. She had been a princess of one of the minor ruling houses of Assam in 1970 when she had fallen in love with the dashing police officer posted in Dispur. A short romance and a long opposition later from both families, the couple finally got married.

Atreyee was an immensely popular hostess in the social circuit of the capital city of India. The women envied her and the men fantasised about her. She had always laughed at the attentions of other men and had remained completely faithful to her loving husband.

Bringing up two children had given her little time to pursue her own interests, except a daily regimen of exercise. It was only after her son had left for the Unites States, that she had found the time to indulge in several hobbies.

She exercised at the Delhi Gymkhana Club gym and was actuely conscious of the male attention she attracted. Naina would tell her mother that she ought to accompany her and her friends to a disco once in a while, to jolt their father into acknowledging the fact that with age, his wife had become more lovely, but also more lonely. Naina would also tease her father that if he continued his uni-dimensional existence, he would lose his wife to a younger man, but Mishra just laughed it all off. It was this nonchalance and complete lack of insecurity that had begun bothering Atreyee.

Naina's playful remarks about younger men were having a diabolical effect on her. Of late, Atreyee had begun grappling with thoughts of a sexual tryst with a stranger. It was just the whiff of a fantasy that was taking hold in her mind, and she was attempting to fight it. However, her return to swimming in the heated pool of the Gymkhana a week before had further watered the seed of fantasy. As she had stepped out of the changing rooms towards a pool after nearly twenty years, she had become aware of two boys in their early twenties following her with their eyes. It was not the leering that had bothered Atreyee but the delicious warmth that had spread through her body as their eyes had undressed her. She knew she was slipping.

NEW DELHI, NOVEMBER 5, 1995

The backlanes of the Tibetans refugee colony beyond Rajghat housed over 30000 people. Several small shanties doubled up as eateries and while most students came to the colony for the momos, there were several who came searching for illicit drugs. Although the elders of the colony disapproved, the younger generation continued to ply their trade. In the last few years, the refugee colony had provided shelter to some wanted men of the underworld of Delhi and western Uttar Pradesh. The police kept away as the Indian government was extremely sensitive to the feelings of the displaced community. The younger boys also banded with the local warlords as these gangsters acted as both suppliers and buyers of narcotics. Therefore, it was only natural that once in a while the druglords and the hitmen be provided with shelter, for which they contributed handsomely.

Thanedar sat alone in a spacious room which was bare except for a small fan and a bulb. Confirmation from the Mittals had come five days ago. Their instructions were to eliminate the REP supremo at the earliest. He sat with a road map of the city spread before him. Thanedar had decided that he would kill Kapre at his residence and flee from there. He knew from his sources in the REP that, every Friday evening, the REP chief met party workers at his Pandara Park residence. He had also been informed that when the crowd exceeded the limited capacity of his drawing room, the party chief held the durbar in the open courtyard outside his residence.

His sources had also informed him that when elderly citizens from his home state of Maharashtra visited Kapre, the respectful professor often escorted them till the road to their waiting vehicles. It was this that the hitman from Meerut was pinning his hopes on. He was now trying to chalk out an escape route for himself from Pandara Park. Thanedar knew that it was futile to attempt to flee the city after a crime of this magnitude. He planned to stay on in Delhi for at least two months after the hit. Accommodation would be no problem for him as the Mittals had agreed to his price of Rs thirty-five lakhs. They would pay his old friend Prithpal Rathee, who would in turn ensure that the money remained safe. As his finger traced a route from Pandara Park to Defence Colony, he became aware of a buzz in his mind. He knew that the buzz meant doubts were germinating in his brain. This was going to be his biggest hit till date and he was worried.

Thanedar knew that after killing Kapre he would be unable to operate in the bad lands of his home state. The story of his success would eventually find its way to all men of authority amongst his clan. He may not get cornered but the risk would remain. He had, therefore, decided to sneak into Nepal and to move to Bangladesh from Kathmandu. He knew from friends who had followed the same escape route that the Bangladesh authorities would be cooperative. The eventual plan was to fly to South East Asia from Dhaka. Thanedar had heard of certain Bombay gangsters moving to Thailand and Malaysia as the internecine feuding in the Indian commercial capital had made operations unprofitable.

The weapon would be the trusted AK-47. A favourite gun of Punjab and Kashmir terrorists, the Russian automatic rifle was easily available in Delhi and Uttar Pradesh. In fact, Thanedar had already placed an order for it with Siraj Iqbal. The old dhaba owner from Chandni Chowk was a well-known conduit of small and medium-sized arms. The weapons were always in good condition and untraceable having been directly imported from Muzzafarabad in POK. For extra protection, he had also decided to carry his silencer equipped Webley Scot .32 bore revolver. Thanedar was a staunch fan of the now antique English revolver. He laughed at his friends from the UP underworld who called the sleek revolver a weapon fit for a woman. He had had it for over six years since he had looted it from a rich landlord in the farming town of Pilibhit. The beautiful English revolver had never failed the rustic gangster and he had developed a strong bond with it.

AIRSPACE, NOVEMBER 6

Surendra Nigam adjusted his watch to London time as the stewardess announced that the flight would touch down in the British capital within half an hour. After his meeting with Rajnish, things had moved fast. The RAW chief had personally met with Menon and requested him to pull a few strings with Lord Holmes. The condition that had been imposed by that government was that the Indian police officer would be accompanied by Scotland Yard officers who would handle the actual questioning. Nigam would be required to brief his English colleagues who would attempt to extract information from the communications and records department of the British Airlines.

Nigam had informed an old family friend of his father of his arrival, and the Sikh emigrant, who had been settled in London for over thirty years, had promised to be there at the airport to receive him. When Nigam walked out of Heathrow, he recognised the portly Sardar Jasmeet Singh Sethi. As Sethi came forward to hug him, Nigam looked around to see if anyone else had come to receive him. Finding no one, he busied himself with loading his luggage in Mr Sethi's Vauxhall Omega.

'What is this latest hawala scam?' queried Sethi, referring to the controversy that had fizzled out within five days of its coming to light.

'Nothing but a political stunt,' replied Nigam. He was a staunch rightist, having reacted sharply to his dominant mother's leanings towards the Congress and the Nehru-Gandhi family.

'You don't think this Kapre took money then?' said Jasmeet Sethi.

'Look at all the leaders accused—Chandra Dev Raj, Nair, Vijay Kapre—all sworn enemies of the Prime Minister. It's a set up uncle. And where's the proof? Just one little diary with initials in it and figures written next to the initials.'

'Are they going to be prosecuted?'

'Well, the Central Bureau of Investigation is questioning them but I expect very little to come out of it. All of them have in any case been granted anticipatory bail by our judiciary, so I don't think any magical confessions will be forthcoming.'

At this the Sikh smiled. To hear a highly placed police officer talk so cynically about the Indian establishment made him feel justified for having left the land of his birth. 'What about this Kapre's chances in the election?'

'No harm done. Whatever Asim Banerjee and his reporters may say, I am sure that the REP will get more seats than it was previously expected to get. The people are not foolish uncle, they smell a stunt when they see it.' Nigam had intentionally referred to Asim Banerjee as he was conscious of the reach of the news company of the old Congress acolyte. Asim Banerjee and his team of newspersons were the only media group apart from Satyaki Das who were predicting a much reduced REP tally in the elections. The print media was uniformly sticking to its prediction of an REP government and the ascension of Prof. Vijay Kapre as the Prime Minister of India.

'By the way, please wear your seat belt or else it's fifty pounds fine.'

Nigam absentmindedly strapped on the seat belt and began admiring the greenery of the suburbs of London as the Omega continued its journey to Ickenham, the western London suburb where the Sethis lived. After half-an-hour, Mr

Sethi pulled into the driveway of 18, Breakspear Road South. Nigam got out of the car and admired the picturesque location of his host's residence and commented as much.

'It was your aunty's choice, she had always dreamed of these kind of surroundings.' After they had entered the house and Mr Sethi had switched on the heating, he asked Nigam if he wanted any breakfast.

'No uncle, I had a meal only an hour back in the plane.'

After Sethi had shown him his room, he asked once again if Nigam wanted any refreshments. 'Nothing as yet, but if you could tell me how to dial central London?'

He was led downstairs to the drawing room where his host demonstrated how to use the phone and the relevant city codes. Nigam then waited for his host to leave the room after which he dialled the numbers given to him by Rajnish Mishra. At the third ring, a female voice answered 'Scotland Yard' in a clear, crisp voice.

'May I speak to Inspector G.E. Taylor?'

'Please hold the line.'

There was a musical tone as Nigam waited. Then a sonorous voice answered, 'Taylor here.'

Nigam proceeded to explain the situation.

'Can you come over to my office at 4 PM?'

'I'll be there,' said Nigam and replaced the receiver.

41

Marvelling at the technological wonder of the London underground, Nigam walked down the stairs to the platform at the West Ruislip station. His host had dropped him at the station and had also presented him with a miniature map of the London underground. He had advised Nigam to stick to the central line and disembark at the Holborn. At the Holborn station, the Indian officer was to take the Piccadilly line for Picadilly Circus.

The Picadilly Circus station was reached in barely five minutes. Once at the Piccadilly Circus station, Nigam took the escalator that took him to the ground level and then tried to remember the directions that had been given to him by Inspector Taylor. He followed the landmarks and paused in front of the obscure building that was flanked by the Standard Chartered Bank on one side and the Chase Manhattan on the other. The entire street was full of bank offices. Being an infrequent traveller Nigam did not know that London, like New York, was the headquarters of the world banking industry.

He went down the narrow alley that led to the entrance of Scotland Yard. The door on the first floor was labelled 'No entry'. Nigam climbed on and reached the second floor. As he pushed the thick glass door, he found himself in a small reception area. The blue plaque read 'Scotland Yard Division for International Liaison'. He asked for Inspector Taylor. Taylor emerged after about five minutes. The British inspector was a large and square man, as wide as he was tall. He was prominently red, with his hair, moustache and also his cheeks almost crimson.

Once inside his office he said, 'I have already conducted the background investigation. Your request, though a little unusual, is quite logical and I assure you that we have followed it to its conclusion. What I am going to tell you is confidential and sensitive, diplomatically also.' A confounded Nigam wondered how to react. He decided to remain silent and let Inspector Taylor carry on. 'I don't know how you found out about the Manchester link but it is confirmed that a leak did happen. One of the employees of British Airways did divulge information to a caller. I can't tell you the name of the employee and I would also request you not to attempt to trace this person.'

'I assure you that I have no such intention, Mr Taylor.' Nigam tried to sound earnest. He blinked as he saw Taylor search his eyes, to verify if he meant what he said.

'For your purpose, I assume it would suffice if I told you the location of that call?' Taylor asked.

'Definitely, it is the most important lead that we could get.'

'The call was made from Islamabad.'

Taylor waited as he saw the expression of the obviously flabbergasted Indian change. 'Is there anything else, Inspector, that you can let me know?'

'Yes, here is the pin code of that area in Islamabad.' Taylor handed Nigam a small slip of paper with a six-digit sequence of numbers written on it. 'I am afraid you will have to find out the rest on your own.' Nigam took the hint that Taylor and the British knew the exact identity of the caller but would not reveal anything further due to restrictions of official secrecy. 'I can further assure you that our British Airways employee, though negligent, had no inkling of the tragic consequences of her cooperation with this caller. We have already checked out her story and she is no spy.'

Nigam sat stunned for a few minutes. It was clear that he was in the centre of an exploding international conspiracy. Inspector Taylor interrupted his reverie. 'I must let you know that someone wishes to meet with you, a meeting, I again request, that should be treated as confidential.'

Nigam nodded.

The inspector picked up the intercom lying on the side table and spoke quietly into the receiver. After three minutes, a short Englishman in a white shirt and khakhi trousers with a matching jacket walked in.

'I am Ronald Greystoke, undersecretary, foreign office, he said, shaking Nigam's hand.' Greystoke was about fifty and had a tanned face with bright blue eyes that bore a disappointed expression. After the informal introduction, both Greystoke and Nigam sat down and Inspector Taylor left the room.

'Mohan Bhargava was a friend, a close friend in fact,' began Greystoke.

Nigam replied, 'His death is a great loss to my country.'

'Yes, I know, I have had a detailed meeting with Lord Holmes. However, I knew Mohan on a personal level. We were introduced to each other in Islamabad.'

'You have served in Pakistan?'

'Not exactly. I was only visiting. It was there that I first met Mohan. Then when he was posted here, we got to know each other better.'

Nigam began to wonder whether this was only a condolence meeting.

'Yesterday I spoke to Mishra. We have met in the past, through Mohan. He told me the exact nature of Mohan's death, and after Lord Holmes and I discussed this matter in detail, I decided I must personally express my condolences to the first representative of the Indian government who arrives in London.'

Nigam stayed quiet, wondering what Greystoke was arriving at. 'Please accept my sincere condolences and convey them to Mohan's family too. Mohan and Mushtaq Chaudhary were my two closest friends from the Asian community in London.' At the mention of the second name, Nigam looked up at the undersecretary's face. The English civil servant wore no expression at all. He got up and walked towards the door, where he paused. 'Notwithstanding the nature of your duties, do make it a point to explore this great city of ours.' Leaving a surprised Nigam, Ronald Greystoke walked out of Inspector Taylor's room.

At half past five, Nigam walked to the tube station. His mind was in a whirl after his conversations with Taylor and Greystoke. It was obvious that he had been given clues. It was also clear that they knew a lot more than they had conveyed. He needed to get in touch with Mishra. Who was Mushtaq Chaudhary? Why had the undersecretary brought up his name? Why had a senior British officer not summoned Nigam to his own office?

'The next station is West Ruislip,' a mechanised voice informed Nigam. As he emerged from the station, a cold blast of air hit his face. In his excitement, he had forgotten to ask his host to pick him up from the station. He clutched at his leather jacket as the London winter cold assaulted him. He walked as fast as his freezing legs would carry him towards

Breakspear Road. The intense cold prevented his mind from indulging in any kind of analysis. After ten minutes of fast jogging, Nigam reached the Sethis' residence. His hosts were surprised to see him. Seeing his cold face, they fussed over him, rebuking him for not telling them to pick him up from the station. Dinner was a steaming cup of tomato soup followed by fried chicken and toast with cheese. Nigam ate fast and furiously. After he had finished, he asked his host if he could make a call to India.

NEW DELHI, NOVEMBER 9

The persistent ringing of the phone woke Rajnish Mishra. He picked up the receiver and whispered to the caller to call again after five minutes. After replacing the receiver, Director R tiptoed out of his room so as not to wake up his wife. He went to the study, punched the digits that connected him to the communications centre at the CGO complex and instructed the assistant on duty to place his residential lines on scrambler. He then waited with the cordless in his hand, wondering what it was that could have prompted Nigam to call him at 1.45 in the morning.

As the chief of RAW waited for his call, his wife tossed and turned in her bed. Atreyee Mishra was awake and grappling with the fantasies that were seducing her mind. The picture of the teenager who had been exercising alongside her at the Gymkhana kept appearing in her mind repeatedly. He had been nearly six feet tall with well-sculpted biceps and a trim waist. In addition, his eyes had never left her as she had jogged on the treadmill. She had been thinking of him for the last two hours that she had been in bed. As her husband lay next to her, she had been careful to be quiet and not sigh or breathe fast.

Aware that Rajnish had gone to his study and would not be back for at least half an hour, she goaded her mind to accelerate her fantasy. As she began to think about the boy, his body covering hers, her legs began to spread on their own. Her breathing became fast and loud, as her mind took in the invisible thrusts inside her. Her body began to react to the smooth commands of the mind. She began touching her thighs and imagining young and strong legs separating them. Her fingers then moved to the essence of her warmth, only to realise in shock that the welcoming spurt had already begun. Within minutes, Atreyee realised that she was close to having an orgasm. She decided to let go and began moving to the imaginary thrusts of her tormentor. After a little while, a satiated Atreyee got up and went to the bathroom.

As she examined herself in the full-length mirror, she relished her appearance with a mixture of pleasure and embarrassment. She slipped out of her nightdress and examined her body. Her curves were so smooth that for a moment she forgot her age. She looked at her full breasts with their upright nipples. Her waist was slim and tapered into wide buttocks. She made up her mind. Her husband neither had the time nor the inclination to arouse her any more. Her days of abstinence were definitely over. If she needed sex, she would now go and aggressively seek it rather than grow old having erotic dreams.

In his study, blissfully unaware of his wife's mental infidelity, Rajnish Mishra sat brooding over the news from London. Nigam had informed him of the developments and had sought further instructions. Mishra had ordered him to await word from him in the morning. Not only had Nigam pinpointed the exact location in Islamabad from where the call had been made but he had also found out that the area was the commercial district of the Pakistani capital where the headquarters of ISI were rumoured to be based.

266

Nigam had also made enquiries from the Indian High Commission in London and found that Mushtaq Chaudhary, after spending six months in London, had been very recently summoned to Pakistan. Not only had the Pakistani officer left London a few days before the death of Bhargava but he had not returned to London since. The post that he had occupied in the Pakistan High Commission was lying vacant. It was clear that Mohan Bhargava had uncovered some Pakistani plot and had been murdered to prevent him from sounding the alarm. That the murder had taken place in the capital city of India was of course a matter of great shame for all self-respecting Indian intelligence officers. The chief of RAW made up his mind. He would order Nigam to stay on in London for the next few days. The Indian officer could further investigate Mushtaq Chaudhary from Indian sources in the Pakistani establishment. Surveillence of all known assets of Pakistan would also be stepped up all over India. Mishra fervently hoped that the domestic intelligence agency, the IB, would cooperate. He was deeply disappointed over its constant attempts to sideline RAW and to operate on its own. He hoped it would rise to the challenge and complement RAW, so that some fruitful work could be done. Mishra made a mental note to call up Anand Kishore, chief of IB, first thing in the morning. Though a political appointee, Kishore was regarded as a fairly competent officer and the chief of RAW hoped that for once IB would be able to rise over petty feuding within its cadres.

42

As Friday morning dawned, Rajnish Mishra began planning his schedule for the day. His daughter was a little surprised to see her father all dressed and ready for work at a time when he usually would have been reading the newspaper. Naina had a hurried breakfast and rushed out of their Rabindra Nagar residence to her bus stop a few meters away. The two security guards in plainclothes ran after her. Though Naina detested the security, she bore with it because of an understanding of the sensitive nature of her father's post.

At exactly 8.30, Mishra walked to his waiting Ambassador and his chauffeur drove towards the CGO complex adjoining the Jawaharlal Nehru stadium. Within six minutes, he was in the lift heading for the top floor that housed the office of the chief of RAW. At about the same time, Atreyee Mishra entered the gymnasium at the Delhi Gymkhana club. As she began her warm-up exercises, her eyes searched for the young boy who she had seen the day before. If she saw him, she said to herself, then she would go through with this. A little part of her hoped that she would not see him; that her insanity would pass. After fifteen minutes, she began jogging on the treadmill, relieved that there were no men at all in the gym. As she began to jog faster, she failed to notice the man who began to run on the neighbouring treadmill.

The man was of medium height, possibly an inch below six feet but somehow he gave the impression of being taller. He was fairer than the average Indian and his brown eyes had an intensity about them. His body was not too muscled but had the look of an active life. The man began jogging furiously. As he jogged, he thought about his stategy for his upcoming job in another country and his midnight flight to London. His nerves were steady but his heart was pounding as it always did before an important meeting. As he looked at the monitor of his treadmill he spotted, out of the corner of his eye, a conveyor belt slipping dangerously to the left, leaving a large gaping portion of metal board exposed underneath. He immediately looked to his left to warn the person jogging on the treadmill. The loud music prevented his voice from reaching the lady. He stopped his own treadmill, jumped off it and as he raised his hand to stop the adjoining machine, the belt shifted a little more.

As a result of the jerk, the lady slipped, her left leg almost smashing against the metal board. Fortunately, the man caught hold of her in time. A shocked Atreyee limped away from the machine with a few cuts on her right leg a little above the knee. 'Are you okay, ma'am?' asked the stranger as Atreyee sat down on one of the benches. The coach was on leave but his young attendant came running. He apologised profusely to the lady whom he knew to be the wife of a senior officer and a former member of the managing committee of the club. She waved him aside with a nod. 'Ma'am, I think you should go home,' the stranger suggested in a soft voice. She turned to look at him. He was in his late twenties, maybe early thirties and he looked extremely concerned.

269

Atreyee noticed that his brown eyes were focused on the red patch on her track pants where a little pool of blood had dried up. 'Call my driver,' she told the attendant. As he rushed out, she realised that because her intentions had been less than honourable in the morning, she had sent her driver away. The plan had been to strike a conversation with the young boy and then see how the situation developed. 'God, I sent my driver away,' she exclaimed out of both pain and disappointment.

'I'll drop you, if it's okay,' he volunteered.

'No, no, I live close by; I'll call for my driver, he will be here in no time,' she insisted.

'Look ma'am, even I stay close by and I am on vacation, so it's no problem, I will drop you.' Then he helped her up and led her to his car. As they turned left towards Tughlak Road, he said, 'That accident could have been dangerous, you should complain to the sports committee, ma'am.'

'I will, thank you,' she replied, and then smiled. 'My name is Atreyee, Mrs Atreyee Mishra, not ma'am.'

He smiled back at her.

'Where do you stay?' she asked, as they reached the Aurangzeb Road roundabout.

'Prithviraj Road. No, Mrs Mishra, I am not royalty, just a financial consultant and the inheritor of a large amount of wealth.'

'Oh,' she responded, directing him towards Khan Market and then added, 'please call me Atreyee, I am old, but not that old either.'

He smiled again and pointed out his house as they took the turn towards Lodhi Gardens and sped towards Rabindra Nagar. 'You, I presume, belong to the modern rulers of India, the IAS?' It was a harmless question, asked in half jest.

'You're pretty close, my husband is Rajnish Mishra, the director of RAW,' she said as the Esteem stopped in front of her house. 'Thank you so much.'

'No problem at all. And, by the way, my name is Karan.'

'You saved my leg today Karan,' Atreyee said as she got out of the car.

'The pleasure was all mine, Atreyee, I got lucky and met one of the most beautiful women I've ever seen.' And, leaving a stunned Atreyee behind, the man drove off.

At 11.15 AM Atreyee returned from the CGHS dispensary on Dr. Zakir Hussain Marg, her surface wound on the knee cleaned and sanitised. The servant told her that there was a message from her daughter, that she would reach home only by 6 PM as there was a festival on in her college. She sighed with resignation and sat down on the sofa, thinking of her escape at the gym. She thought of the man called Karan. The young fellow had looked shy and introverted, yet his parting remark had stunned her. Was it a young man's attempt at flattery or had he genuinely meant what he had said? She got up and went into the kitchen to take her mind off the man. At 12.30 PM she looked at herself in the mirror, all dressed to leave. She had spent the last forty-five minutes bathing, perfuming and dressing herself. She adjusted her saree for the nth time hoping that it accentuated her naturally curvaceous body. She had chosen a red sheer chiffon with a matching blouse. She held aside her pallav to verify that the cut of her blouse was deep enough to expose a large part of her shapely cleavage. Satisfied with her efforts, she picked up her shawl, covered herself and informed the servant that she was going to the club for a session of bridge. Outside, she waved the guards and the chauffeur aside. 'I am only going to the club,' she said, and got into her Maruti 800.

He acted like a gentleman and the least I can do is to thank him personally, she thought as her car pulled in at the driveway of the house he had pointed out earlier. She wondered if he would be home, and if he was, what if he turned out to be

271

married? Then the shawl will remain, and I will walk out in ten minutes, she thought. A young Nepalese servant boy opened the door. She asked for Karan. He led her to a tastefully decorated living room. After a few minutes, the man walked in. If he was surprised to see her he didn't show it. 'Well, aren't you surprised to see me?' she smiled.

'After I saved your beautiful leg today, the least you could do was thank me personally.' Atreyee realised that he knew her desires better than she did. She also noticed that his slow lingering gaze travelled all the way from her face down her body, and back again.

'What will you have Atreyee?'

'Coffee should be fine, I must apologise for barging in at lunch time.' She didn't sound sorry in the least and hoped that he noticed it.

'Do you want lunch? I am not hungry so I was planning to give my fellow the afternoon off.'

'I am not hungry either, so that's fine.'

'I will make coffee for us,' he said, getting up.

'Wait, why don't I join you?' As she said this, Atreyee realised a slight lilt had crept into her voice. Her body was burning and she wanted the verbal foreplay to end fast.

'Sure, come along.' She left her shawl on the sofa and followed him to the kitchen.

As he began beating the coffee, she raised herself onto the marble slab next to the sink. 'I hope this can take my weight.'

'You are slim and light, it will handle you.' He began increasing the pace of the beating. She crossed her legs so that her saree hitched up a little, exposing her ankles. She watched as he paused, his eyes lingering on her shapely ankles. The water began boiling. As he turned for the sugar, the spoon he had been holding fell. Atreyee got off and bent to pick it up. She was fully aware that he was looking into her low cut blouse and that her breasts were clearly visible. Without a word she looked at him, aware of the throbbing and hardening between his legs. She moved towards the door of the kitchen as he followed her. In the living room, she sat on the low-slung diwan as he brought his coffee cup towards her and raised a mock toast. 'To a beautiful lady.' She smiled. 'You think I am beautiful? Are you flattering an old and out-of-shape middle-aged woman?'

He sat next to her on the diwan. She felt his hot breath as he whispered to her, 'I am telling this middle-aged woman that she is the sexiest woman this widely travelled man has ever seen.' Her face turned red. She wavered for a moment but made no attempt to put any distance between them. His face was now inches away from hers. Before she knew it, he had her in his arms, embracing her roughly. His lips seared hers, prising them open, pressing until he found her tongue, then moving her down on the diwan.

With difficulty, she raised her head a little. 'Karan,' she said in a husky tone, 'do you know what you are doing? You don't even know me.'

'This is what I've wanted to do since this morning when I first saw you. And as for knowing you, let's get to know each other now.'

She debated for a few seconds. It was now or never. This was her last chance. She was after all a respectable married woman with two grown up children. She breathed deeply. 'Yes,' she said slowly, snaking her arms around his neck. Her mouth found his lips and began reciprocating his hungry thrusts.

As the kiss deepened, he lowered himself alongside her on the diwan. His hand touched her waist and savagely tugged the saree off. The fingers of his other hand struggled with the buttons of her blouse. In a minute, the blouse joined the crumpled saree in a heap on the floor. His fingers moved across her back, groping over her backbone until they reached the outline of her petticoat. As the other hand lowered the petticoat, she began to moan, losing her inhibitions to the wonderful touch of this man. Her hand moved till it found his crotch. 'Please, oh, please,' she whispered.

He shifted, rose to a sitting position, picked her up effortlessly, and crossed a corridor to a bedroom with all the curtains drawn. He lowered her onto the bed and locked the door. Without a word, he undressed completely. He could feel her gaze longingly at his fit and young body. As he turned to face her, she closed her eyes, her breath now coming in low moans. He joined her on the double bed and slowly moved her petticoat all the way down her thighs, knees and feet. Her long hair spread across the pillows in disarray. He looked into Atreyee's large eyes and her slightly parted lips. 'You are beautiful,' he said. She closed her eyes.

He lay alongside her and began kissing her mouth. Her lips parted immediately and she returned his kisses hungrily. With deft fingers he stroked her naked shoulders, her neck and ears. She moved closer to him and surprised him by her sudden gesture of clasping his erection and stroking it slowly. He then shifted and moved above her. He caressed her breasts and with his strong legs lifted her knees and spread them apart. Then he lowered himself and slowly thrust into her, slowly and slowly, and deeper and deeper. As she gasped in pleasure, he began moving back and forth, steadying into a rhythm which was appropriate for her. After a few minutes, her rounded hips began to rise and fall with a frequency that matched her moans. As he increased the pace and force of his thrusts, her fingers dug into his shoulders and she began to explode into a volley of pleasure and convulsions.

Just when she thought that it had ended, he slid down his torso between her thighs and kissed her navel. His tongue flicked in and out. As Atreyee gasped, his head moved lower. His lips pulled at the soft folds of her skin. She was too stunned to react as his tongue began to probe the crevices and then he parted her folds to thrust his fingers inside. He then flickered his tongue over her clitoris. As he continued, she forgot her shock and lost all restraint. She moved her hips in an undulating manner, faster and faster, oblivious to anything but the pleasure of her body. The thrill built up and climaxed into her screaming. He moved again and without giving her a chance to end the sequence, kneeled beside her, goading her to return what he had done for her.

Atreyee hesitated for a moment. She had not performed oral sex in years and the erect organ throbbing inches from her face paralysed her for a few seconds. Then she gave in, lifted her head, and her lips closed around the shaft. He emitted a low sound. He had her head in his fingers, moving as she licked and sucked him intensely. She continued till he indicated to her to stop. She wrapped her legs tightly around his waist and abandoned herself to ecstasy as he finally lost control and came.

It was close to 5.30 in the evening when she returned to her residence. Devesh, the household retainer, ran up to her as she entered. 'Saab has called four-five times in the last twenty minutes, please call him back.' She panicked. Could it be that he had tried to trace her at the club? With trembling fingers she dialled his private line and waited. He picked up on the second ring. 'Atreyee, where have you been all day?'

'I was at the Gymkhana, the session went on longer than usual.'

'Are you women so out of it that nothing moves you?' Rajnish sounded more irritated than angry.

'What has happened?'

'There has been an assassination attempt on Kapre.'

'Kapre!' she repeated with disbelief, 'Professor Kapre?'

'Yes, Professor Vijay Krishna Kapre, the chief of the REP.' Her husband sounded worried and angry at the same time.

'Is he out of danger?' she asked anxiously. Although a Congress voter, she did not wish the charismatic Kapre any harm.

'What's wrong with you, I said attempt, didn't I?' Rajnish was almost yelling. 'The assassin missed him, but only just, three of his security guards died though.'

'And the killer, they got him?'

'He crashed his car two hundred meters from the residence of Kapre, but Kapre's foolish guards pumped him with bullets when he was injured and unarmed. Why do you think I am in this mood? The man is dead now and of no assistance to anyone. Where is Naina, back home?'

'No, she said she would be late.'

'My God, this girl has longer hours than the intelligence chief of this country. Now you please stay indoors. We are expecting some kind of backlash. I will be in touch later,' the line went dead.

At 7 Race Course Road, a deeply disturbed Reddy stood lambasting Rajeshwar Kulkarni and Bhaskar Naik. 'This is what you have to show after all your assurances? A botched attempt that has probably added to his voters tally by now?' Kulkarni stood quietly, angrily glancing at his protégé Bhaskar Naik every few minutes. 'Maybe I should have relied on some Delhi police inspectors or constables to have done the job for me. You spend months, make me consent to criminal conspiracies and then can't even guarantee the success of these schemes. What if this comes out in the open? Will you save me from a prison sentence at my age? Imagine the headlines, "Prime Minister of India implicated in plot to kill his successor"!'

'Nothing will come out, Reddy *ji*,' Kulkarni interjected gently. 'That man is dead.'

'That was the work of Inspector Murthy who I put in the team that guards Kapre, so don't try and take credit for it.'

More than six months ago, Hitesh Singh, the home minister of India and a close friend of Reddy, had placed Inspector T. Murthy in charge of the posse of security guards that guarded Kapre. The move had been made at the behest of Reddy. Murthy had been attached to Reddy in the early Eighties when Reddy had served as foreign minister under Indira Gandhi. Although the sharp inspector had had no knowledge of the participation of any of the Congress bosses in the attempt on Kapre, his excellent instincts had directed him to ensure that his team gunned down the assassin. The team, stunned by the coldblooded murder of their three comrades, had readily responded to the prodding of their commandant. In hindsight, it had turned out that his instincts had protected the prime minister of India.

SOMEWHERE IN AIRSPACE, NOVEMBER 11

He watched the BBC World Service report on the failed attempt on the life of Professor Kapre with amusement. These amateurs give everyone a bad name, he thought. He knew that his decision to complete the Spanish assignment was the right one, as he would have to postpone the Indian project by ten to fifteen days. He knew from newspaper reports that the Indians would go into overdrive and overreact to everything. There would be loud proclamations of the failings of the entire security set up, the security of political leaders would be beefed up, while in reality the poor souls would remain as unprotected as before. The man had fired at Kapre with an AK-47. The amateur did not even choose the appropriate weapon. As he slowly shook his head, the stewardess passed him. This was the third time in two hours she had passed this

277

goodlooking man and seen him talk to himself and smile. Either he was a great thinker or slightly imbalanced. A mixture probably, she thought.

His mind drifted to the encounter of a different variety that he had indulged in the previous day. Not usually wont to taking advantage of situations like that, his easy yield to temptation made him wonder. Am I getting too soft or was it just a primal need? It had been a bit of both, along with an instinctive decision to make an investment after learning the identity of the person. He was confident that he would not need any information from the asset that he had acquired yesterday but it didn't hurt to build up potential resources for an emergency. He then stretched on his seat and let his mind dwell on the remarkable beauty of the asset.

43

Thousands of miles to the west, Brig. Qayyum Nazir, Maj. Azim Tariq and Maj. Mushtaq Chaudhary were equally unhappy with the failed attempt on Prof. Kapre. 'If he had tried, at least he should have succeeded. That would have saved our money. Now the security of the accursed professor will surely be enhanced and our man's chances will recede.'

'Who do you think was behind this attempt?' Tariq asked, looking at his tense superior.

'Probably an Indian conspiracy, someone in the corridors of power in New Delhi I bet.'

'Do you mean the incumbent prime minister?' ventured Maj. Chaudhary who was now attending every meeting at the invitation of Brig. Nazir.

'No, the old man is pretty ruthless but I don't think he has the heart to order an assassination. But someone in the ruling party is bound to be involved. After all, the professor's security was breached. That took a lot of planning. Is it not clear yet what saved Kapre from the nineteen bullets that were fired?'

'No,' Nazir shook his head. Our people at UNI are working on it. We will get the complete picture in some hours.'

'When will this Singer contact us?' Maj. Chaudhary had got over his initial hesitation and was now an active participant in all discussions.

'After we deposit seven-and-a-half million dollars in his bank account.'

'We have till the fifteenth of this month to make the deposit,' Tariq reminded Brig. Nazir.

'I know, I know, we would have done it today. But the development in New Delhi alters things a bit. I have to discuss it with Lt. Gen. Hussain, who in turn will need fresh clearance from Gen. Mehmod.'

'Do you anticipate any problems, Sir?' pressed Tariq.

'I don't know, honestly. I can understand Lt. Gen. Hussain and the premier's doubts but what choice does Pakistan have?' Nazir was genuinely worried. He had invested a lot of time and effort in the operation to let it be abandoned by a stroke of ill luck.

The same thought had struck Maj. Chaudhary. He had sweated for hours in London, had played ball with a crook like Arif Rabbani for the sake of this operation. To see it fall apart before his eyes would be very disappointing. Both the majors were well aware that if the operation fell through or was not executed successfully, Brig. Qayyum Nazir would not survive the purge that would result. The Brigadier also knew that his enemies like Mohd. Shujaat and several other military leaders were waiting in the shadows to see him make one false move.

'I hope Shujaat does not brief the premier before Lt. Gen. Hussain,' Tariq said in a voice filled with hope. 'He has not been in Pakistan for the last three days. Col. Abbas has informed me that Mohd. Shujaat has gone to Canada on official business, ostensibly sent by the premier for some sensitive diplomatic manoeuvering.'

Later in the day, when Brig. Nazir returned to the CFIO headquaters, he was a worried man. His meeting with Lt. Gen. Hussain had not gone off smoothly. The normally supportive Lt. Gen. Hussain had been full of doubt about the wisdom of dispensing millions of dollars in attempting to assassinate one of the most protected men in India. Hussain had suggested postponing the operation until things cooled off in New Delhi and complacency set in again. Nazir had reasoned with him using all his persuasive skills. He had impressed upon the ISI chief that their man was a professional, while the attempt had been made by a local gangster. He had claimed that no matter how high the odds, Pakistan had to take the risk of derailing the REP's sure march to power in New Delhi. At the end of the meeting, Lt. Gen. Hussain had been noncommittal. He had promised Nazir that he would try his best to persuade the premier to let the operation continue as planned.

As Brig. Nazir and Maj. Tariq had been extremely worried, Maj. Chaudhary had not informed them of the latest bit of information that he had received from London. Maj. Ahmad Usmani, his colleague at the high commission in London, had informed him of heightened intelligence activity by the Indians over the last one week. There was nothing to link this activity with the Pakistani operation, yet it was something that should have been investigated in the normal course. Nigam's tenacious and slightly indiscreet follow up had left traces that had been picked up by Maj. Usmani and his boys in London. Usmani, the second-in-command to Maj. Chaudhary, had been overseeing Pakistani activities in London. As ordered by Nazir, he had also been sending daily reports to the ISI office in Pakistan. He could feel and anticipate that some critical operation was about to be launched by Pakistan.

It was this bit of crucial information that Maj. Chaudhary suppressed from Brig. Nazir, not realising the immense significance of this information. Nazir had seemed so worried that Chaudhary did not have the heart to worry him more by informing him of the developments in London. In any case, he thought, the information did not seem all that important.

MADRID, NOVEMBER 12, 1995

The taxi was a Mercedez Benz and the famed car was eating up the miles rapidly as it sped towards San Sebastian. Singer was the lone passenger and he was resting with his eyes shut and his head on the backrest. Although apparently asleep, Singer's mind ticked along at a furious pace. He knew that if anyone needed his special skills for survival, it was the ETA. His mind repeatedly played out the plan that was to be followed. He· knew that he was banking heavily on the information that had been handed to him by Elliot Inglesias. Elliot, the son of a British-Jewish father and a Spanish mother had been a comrade of Singer in the past. He had also left in disgrace and chosen to pick up the threads of his life. He had found favour in Madrid, and then moved to picturesque Donostia-San Sebastian as a security consultant to the deputy prime minister of Spain. Inglesias did not owe anything to Singer except a common phase that had culminated in disgrace. That in itself was an unbreakable bond between the two. Elliot had not needed to pull any strings to obtain the hourly schedule of Ramon Arrieta, mayor of San Sebastian. The schedule had been a weekly one, so Singer was aware of the activities of the mayor from November 11 to 18.

Singer opened his eyes and studied the schedule again. The mayor would begin his day with a lecture at the Moneo's Cubes, which housed the Kursaal congressional palace and auditorium. At 12 noon, the mayor was to reach the San Telmo Museum, where there was a convention on the culture capitals of Europe. The convention was to go on till 4.30 in the evening and after that the mayor was to leave for his residence for a short rest. At half past seven in the evening, the mayor would attend a prayer convention at Santa Maria Basilica, the main church of the city located on the south slope of Mount Urgull, the hilly precipice that had once served as the fortress citadel of the old city of San Sebastian. The church would be an apt place to perform a work of art, thought Singer.

Once in his hotel room, he slept for four hours, awaking with a heightened sense of anticipation. He padded to the door of the room. There was a message informing him of a courier awaiting him. He picked up the phone and dialled the bell captain. Within ten minutes, the bell captain had brought the package for him. 'You are a musician?' he enquired in halting English. 'Yes, I play for an orchestra.' The captain nodded and left. The Palermo Philharmonica was playing that week at the Santa Maria Basilica. Singer unzipped the guitar case. The cardboard fell apart leaving intact a leather covering which required a digital unlocking mechanism. He fiddled with its combination and it came off.

He then took out the beautiful Hawaiian guitar that had been sent to him from Barcelona, via road by his old friend, Roy Deitrich. He picked up the metal clip and began to play a soulful tune.

44

BILBAO, SPAIN, NOVEMBER 14, 1995

'Do you think he will be able to pull it off?' asked a worried Raoul Gonzalez.

'Yes, I know him. He won't fail us.' Julio Lopez aka Emilio Salinas attempted to instill confidence in the skeptical minds of his men.

'But he should have at least contacted us. We could have activated our information network for him,' Raoul persisted.

'He has never required anyone else's information.'

'We don't even know if he is in Spain.' There was annoyance in their voices as the local news showed the mayor of San Sebastian arriving at Moneo's Cubes to deliver a lecture at the congressional palace.

'All I know is that he will do it within days. You will know when you see it on the news.'

'What makes you so confident, Julio?' Lopez's ranks and frontline lieutenants had not taken too kindly to his requisitioning an outsider for a job that they all wanted.

'First-hand experience my friends,' Lopez continued to be patient with his men. 'I have seen him in action. Never in my life have I come across a man who is such a combination of physical conditioning and mental finesse.'

His officers had reason to doubt, he thought. After all, they had not seen his friend in action. They had no knowledge of the ease with which the man they spoke of so lightly had eliminated Anderson Coltrane, the favourite cousin of Prince Charles, better known by his title of Lord Magor. Lopez of course knew that the Scottish baron living in style in Sharjah had been guarded by a posse of former SAS commandos. He had been found blown to bits with four of his guards also killed in a clinical and efficient manner. The Sharjah Police, and later Scotland Yard, had drawn a blank on any leads. The man who had done it had charged his recruiters one million pounds. The money had changed hands in London where the sole surviving relative of Lord Magor, Sir Kenneth Coltrane, had succeeded his deceased cousin as the fifteenth Lord Magor of Essex.

The executor of Lord Magor sat in the small café on the northern slope of Mount Urgull. It was late afternoon and he had plenty of time to kill. After downing his third cup of coffee, he left the café and walked to the small woods of Urgull. In his left hand was his guitar. Once sure that he was alone in the small glade, he placed the guitar on his knees and began tightening the fourth string. It was ruining the rhythm. With three gentle tugs, the wooden cavity in the hollow guitar opened to reveal black metal pipes and barrels. He kept the carcass of the guitar on the side and began fiddling with the metallic pipes expertly. After ten minutes, the metallic tubes had taken the shape of a Parker Hale 85, one of the deadliest sniper rifles known to mankind. He then separated the detachable bipod and kept it on one side with the palm stop rail. He knew that the ordinary range of the Parker Hale averaged around 900 to 950 metres. But, as with all his other tools, he had carried out certain modifications and the Parker Hale could now accurately deliver to around 1700 metres. He knew the spot that he had chosen to strum his guitar was only 1200 meters from the courtyard of the Santa Maria Basilica.

To a man as talented as him, several modes of execution would have been open. On this occasion, he had chosen to use the relatively simpler method of sniper fire in order to save himself the mental hard work. He knew that the operation in India would require his grey cells to work at optimum. The amateur had spoilt it all. Kapre could still definitely be killed, but the time that the planning would involve had increased manifold. To familiarise himself with the Indian modus of protecting their VIPs, he had devoured all available material on previous assassinations.

He was aware that Indians would crowd their leaders, sanitise entire traffic routes, frisk all possible visitors, but when it came to actual levels of alertness, they had miles to go before they could even come close to the calibre of the American secret service or the British prime ministerial bodyguards. He was also aware that the elite commando group known as the SPG would not be guarding Kapre, as this group only protected the current and former prime ministers. In contrast to the planning required to kill Kapre, the murder of Col. Ramon Arrieta was much easier. He knew that Julio Lopez and his men had failed on more than one occasion. But that failure had been more out of a heightened sense of anxiety rather than any actual problem of logistics. After cleaning the Parker Hale carefully, checking and rechecking its front adjustable sight and the fold down rear calibrated sight, he set it back inside the guitar. Three quarters of an hour remained before the mayor of San Sebastian would approach the most famous church in all of Spain. Few, of course, knew that the day's events would make the Santa Maria Basilica even more famous than it had ever been in history.

Even as the most accomplished assassin of the decade sat awaiting his quarry, his close associate in distant London received a package from Peshawar. Ray Darrel had transferred ten thousand pounds to the frontier man who had posted him the entire blueprint of the latest watch slug. Although his associate had not mentioned it to him, Darrel felt that such a weapon could come in handy. The delighted Afghan had even volunteered to send a prototype to Darrel, but Darrel had politely declined. He had his doubts about the actual functionality of such a weapon, unless it was designed and tested by an expert. Now that he had the blueprint, he would send it to Marshal Owen, the finest gun designer in London and possibly Western Europe. Owen had often provided his services for MI-5 and MI-6, and had made up a personal fortune only by carrying out modifications in guns owned by private wealthy citizens who then retained such pieces as artifacts.

As Darrel studied the design, the man for whom he had acquired the wristwatch slug strummed his guitar. The tune of the strings merged with the quiet chirping of birds as dusk fell over the Basque country. At around 7.15 PM, he stopped playing and walked two hundred meters down the northern slope. He stopped when he reached a glade covered by thick brush. The clusters of the shrubs were thick and only someone who had spent two hours cutting a square patch in the centre of the undergrowth would attempt to pierce the thick and thorny undergrowth. The square patch was large enough for a man to stand and remain unobserved to anyone passing by. He moved to the patch and set down his guitar. One side of the brush undergrowth had a narrow clearing that overlooked the main courtyard of the Basilica. He took out the Parker Hale and carefully began taking aim. From the special telescopic sights, he could make out a crowd of people entering the Basilica.

He took out the large photograph of mayor Arrieta from his belt pouch. This was a recent photograph, only two months old, and had been obtained by him from a picture book of the Basque country that had been published by a Basque trust based in London. He looked carefully at the picture, and then searched for the stern face in the crowd of people. He peered intently into the enhanced sights of the Parker Hale. In a minute, he saw the hooked nose and the steel grey cropped hair of the mayor. He then took out the special bullets and loaded them into the Parker Hale. The men in the courtyard, oblivious of the danger, made their way towards the giant columns that formed the entrance of the Basilica. He winced as he realised that one of Arrieta's bodyguards was blocking the path of the bullet. He was annoyed only because it would mean using more than one of his valuable bullets. The special ammunition was strong enough to pierce Arrieta after exiting the body of his guard but that would involve the risk of the bullet deviating from its original trajectory. A deviant bullet could enter the body of the mayor from the side and the impact would make Arrieta sink to the floor. He could not risk not getting a clean second shot at Arrieta.

He thought for less than a minute, pursed his lips and, taking careful aim, fired. Ronaldo Carrero, special security guard to the mayor, sank wordlessly to the floor as a stinging missile decapitated his right leg. A concerned Arrieta looked on in confusion as the other bodyguards yelled to him to drop to the floor. In less than twenty seconds, the mayor became incapable of reacting to any human voices as his cranium was shattered by an explosion. As his guards and followers looked on in stunned disbelief, the man who had delivered the deathblow, sure of his success, removed the Parker Hale and slung it back inside the guitar. He exited the underbrush and walked rapidly to the car he had parked on the road adjoining the mountain.

He took the wheel of the rented Mercedez and drove to downtown San Sebastian. Future records would indicate that the authorities reacted to the killing by sealing all exit points from San Sebastian. The embargo continued for three days. No one thought it fit to check any of the cars that entered the city. A thorough search of the vehicles entering San Sebastian would have yielded their man. But the man in question had made his plans after a careful study of human behaviour in similar situations. After four days of the killing, he was on a plane to Paris and the Parker Hale lay buried in the garbage shaft of a local hotel. The gun had been dismantled expertly and even its discovery would have been reported as the recovery of a few metal pipes and rods.

NEW DELHI, NOVEMBER 18, 1995

'Who was it?'

'Kahlon, who else? He wants an appointment to discuss the election announcement.'

The Prime Minister looked worried. He sat with his one true friend, Hitesh Singh, the home minister of India who was his contemporary in both age and time spent in politics. 'Do you think your rivals in the party are pushing him?' Although Hitesh Singh was not hostile to any particular faction his loyalties lay with Reddy. 'Could be. It is clear that they want me out of power. If the Congress loses the elections, it would be a small price for my rivals. They reckon that they are even now completely marginalised, so they don't mind waiting for another couple of years.'

'Hmm,' nodded Singh. He was quiet for a few minutes. It was clear that he wanted to say something to Reddy but was contemplating how to phrase it.

'I know you have come to lecture me, Hitesh. Go ahead, I will hear you today.'

Hitesh Singh smiled weakly, happy that his old friend knew him well enough to be able to read his mind. 'Yes, you guessed correctly, Srinivas. Before I start my lecture, I want you to know that in the end, whatever you choose, I am by your side.' Singh paused as a visibly touched Reddy nodded. 'Think of the Sixties, when you became chief minister of Andhra Pradesh against all odds and I was elevated to the top post in Uttar Pradesh in similar circumstances. Both of us were intellectuals, party thinkers but we didn't possess the mass base that Chandra Dev Raj, or even Raghavan possessed. Yet, Indira *ji* gave us those posts. You were chief minister for three years, and I remained chief minister for five years. You are aware that in the last ten years or so, our two states have not had a single chief minister remaining in the saddle for more than two years.'

'Those were different times, when loyalty and respect dominated politics.'

'Exactly the point I am making, Srinivas. Because of our style, we had difficulty in getting elected to our legislative assemblies. Yet we became chief ministers. Do you remember May 1991, when Rajiv was killed? You had been packing your bags and I was already in retirement in Allahabad. I called to congratulate you when I heard that your name was doing the rounds to succeed Rajiv as the Congress parliamentary chief. Remember what you told me?' Hitesh Singh paused as he saw a faraway look in Reddy's eyes. 'You said that you wished to do some writing in Andhra. That was nearly five years ago, Srinivas. As Prime Minister, you have done well. You gave India its first qualified finance minister in the form of an economist. You supervised our march from economic poverty to rapid development. Together, we survived several attempts to dislodge us, both in Parliament and outside it. What I am saying is that we are from a different generation. We have had our time in the sun and a good time it has been. Let us retire

290

gracefully. Let us not be trapped by the petty ideology of thugs like Kulkarni and Naik.'

Srinivas Reddy listened attentively but didn't say a word. He looked at Singh, silently urging him to carry on. 'Call for elections, Srinivas, call for them before they are due, and the discerning amongst our nation may still vote you back. Stall for time and you run the risk of being identified with quasi-criminal elements like Rajeshwar Kulkarni and his cohorts. What has happened with Dev Raj and the others cannot be undone but let us check our steps before we lose our way completely. Let us retire and let history judge us when we are gone. It's a win-win situation for you. If you win, you would have pulled the greatest upset in Indian electoral history; lose, and you will be rid of this crown of thorns.'

Srinivas Reddy was quiet as he reflected on what his closest friend in the Indian polity had said. 'Hitesh, you have verbalised the conflict that has been raging within me for the last few months. You are right, it's time for us to move aside. I only worry about elements like Kapre. Where will his extremism take this country?'

'India is strong enough to survive him. Let the other leaders worry about him now.'

An hour after Hitesh Singh left, the Prime Minister of India granted an appointment to chief election commissioner Kahlon so that an announcement for the general elections could be made. He also called up Satyaki Das and told him to let up on the hate campaign that the beleaguered Das was running against the REP and Kapre. In his own office, a harassed Das heaved a long sigh of relief. Reddy also sent stern messages to Rajeshwar Kulkarni, Bhaskar Naik and Prakash Mittal that no attempt was to be made either on the life of Vijay Kapre nor were any schemes to be hatched to derail the likely march of that party to power.

The next morning, chief election commissioner Kahlon met with his two colleagues. Around noon, he called a press conference to announce that the 1996 general elections would be held in the first week of February. The announcement shook all the political parties, including the REP. The REP thought the Congress had panicked a little, as it was burdened with the weight of expectations. Its strategists went into a huddle to chalk out a fast campaign trail for Prof. Kapre. The election announcement also surprised Kulkarni and Naik. Both the Maratha leaders were facing heavy odds in their home state and they decided to give first priority to securing Bombay. In his office, Satyaki Das debated whether to expose the truths that he knew about Bhaskar Naik and Prakash Mittal. For the first time in his life he felt a surge of patriotism. He shuddered every time he thought of the true agenda of the two businessmen-politicians who were widely respected in the country.

Das was aware that if he got on the wrong side of Naik and Mittal, he would risk losing all that was precious to him. His wealth, his fame, his very life. In the end, the businessman in him won over the patriot. I will wait till the elections, he thought. If Naik and Mittal are on the winning side, I will threaten them with disclosure to the Congress leadership. If they lose, then I will settle for a lesser indemnity.

ISLAMABAD, NOVEMBER 19, 1995

'It's close now,' said an excited Maj. Tariq as he put the copy of *Dawn* on the table. The Pakistani daily carried on its front page a story of the coming elections in India.

'Yes, the countdown has begun,' added Mushtaq Chaudhary. They both sat waiting at the CFIO headquarters. Brig. Nazir was expected to be back any minute from Lt. Gen. Hussain's office. He had called them earlier in the morning

292

to let them know that Hussain had summoned him to inform him of the decision on Operation Karakoram.

'What do you think will be the decision?' asked a nervous Major Chaudhary.

'I don't know,' said Tariq, who did not want to indulge in any guesswork before Chaudhary, aware that if the operation did not fare as it was projected to, loyalties would shift in no time. Major Tariq had read with great interest the news report about the Indian elections. The paper had reported that the Indian political parties had been taken by surprise and were desperately chalking out their election schedules.

He knew that campaigning would take Kapre to remote corners of India. Jack Singer was clearly of Caucasian descent and would stick out like a sore thumb. His anxious thoughts were interrupted by the opening of the shutters that announced the arrival of the chief of CFIO, Brig. Qayyum Nazir. The Brigadier entered the room quickly and walked to his table. Both Tariq and Chaudhary stood up to greet him, their faces betraying their excitement and anticipation. 'Sit down boys,' Nazir said. Then he turned to Tariq. 'Azim, please make immediate arrangements to transfer seven-and-a-half million dollars into the account specified by Singer.' Major Tariq's face broadened into a smile. 'And Major Chaudhary, I want daily reports from London on my table. Please cover any unexpected activity in Europe too.' Nazir had a huge smile on his face.

'Operation Karakoram is underway then?' began Chaudhary.

'Yes, but no celebrations please, we have work to do. Speaking of Europe though, do you think that this killing in Spain was done by our man Singer?' As Tariq's and Chaudhary's brows furrowed in surprise, Nazir added, 'I don't know, but a perfect assassination although in another continent, seems to be a good omen for the success of Operation Karakoram.'

45

ZURICH, NOVEMBER 20, 1995

Marie Stossel turned her head as she cleaned the filing cabinet of her superior officer. As the general clerk for the transfer section, she had had occasion to deal with Krantz earlier. She knew his eye for detail. Every morning before Krantz arrived at his office on the fourth floor of the Hoffman & Handel Bank, she cleared his filing cabinet and arranged any papers that may have arrived for him during the previous night. Her searching eyes noticed the single sheet on the fax machine. She gave it a cursory glance before placing it on Krantz's desk in the tray marked 'urgent'. Her eyes had noticed the number 081911014360 printed on it. She knew nothing about that account number except that the owner of that account was an important client who dealt with Krantz personally. In the past, she had received similar faxes. The security attached to the account intrigued her, but she was experienced enough to realise that the selling point of the Swiss banking industry was its obsession with obeying the instructions of their wealthy patrons.

An hour after Stossel had arranged his papers, Walther Krantz arrived at his office. One look at the tray marked 'urgent' and he knew what to do. Herr Darrel and the mysterious Roscoe Craig were at it again. After invigorating himself with a cup of hot black coffee, Krantz began work on his computer. As the security code was accepted, he waited to see the source of the funds. The amount of seven-and-a-half million dollars did not surprise him. What surprised him was the source. He looked intently at the screen of his computer. The name of the transferor bank flashed. It was the Bank of Pakistan, Rawalpindi branch. He shook his head in surprise. The Middle East he could understand but Pakistan was new to him. He tried to think of the country. All that registered was that it was ruled by some military dictator masquerading as president. He wondered what venture Darrel or Roscoe Craig could have opened in Pakistan. That country had not been in the news lately. There were no reports of any joint venture having been signed or any substantial foreign investment having been made there.

Roscoe Craig remained the most mysterious account that he had handled in the seventeen years of service he had put in with the bank. Most of the clients who operated three zero accounts began with an obsession for secrecy but usually ended up revealing their true identities within two years. The Darrel and Craig account was now close to five years old, yet he had no clue to the identity of the two men, if there were two men at all. Krantz had met Herr Darrel twice when the account had been opened. He had indicated that he had a partner called Roscoe Craig but Krantz had never met, spoken or even seen a signature of Roscoe Craig. After four-and-a-half years, he was close to believing that Craig was an assumed name of Herr Darrel who in turn was one of the men involved in Walter Simpson and Associates. With a sigh of resignation Krantz got ready to send a confirmation of the receipt of the transfer to Ray Darrel in London. On an impulse, he picked up a directory of London companies to look up Walter Simpson and Associates. After two minutes, he replaced the directory with a snort of exasperation. The directory indicated the presence of 134 corporate entities by that name in London. Most appeared to be trading or stock broking firms in the banking capital of the developed world. It would be impossible to guess which one Darrel belonged to.

NASSAU, BAHAMAS

Radley Karras, former commander of naval intelligence, sat on the steps overlooking the unusually calm sea. Spread before Karras in a heap were several newspapers. The former intelligence officer was thinking of the recent events in Spain. The assassination of the Basque mayor of San Sebastian had surprised him a little. From friends stationed in Paris and Madrid, he knew that the ETA had long ceased to possess the skill to take out a target as protected as Arrieta had been. The accounts of the assassination in San Sebastian were unanimous in one respect: all analysts agreed that the assassination was carried out by a professional and that there was little chance of the killer being apprehended. Karras knew that the forty-eight hours following a murder were always crucial. If no leads could be uncovered in that time, chances were that the killer would not be caught.

Ranging from the Kennedy killing to more recent ones in Oman and Riyadh, Karras had seen the same pattern emerge. An assassination of an extremely well-protected person, a clean getaway, the total lack of any clues. It all indicated the hand of a professional. He wondered if San Sebastian had been visited by the same person that the Pakistanis would be hiring. Karras wondered how the US had reacted to the Spaniard's assassination. In his days of service, the CIA as well as the ONI had little or no respect for the ETA. The general consensus was that the Basques, like the Kurds, were inherently incapable of mounting a successful war for independence. Though ferociously brave and recklessly daring, they lacked in guile and cunning.

The entire American intelligence community believed that Fransisco Salinas and his son had died together. They had heard of one Julio Lopez but could not connect him to Salinas Sr. in any way. The common belief was that the ETA needed the Salinas charisma to be revived. Years ago Karras had seen a detailed dossier on the entire Salinas family. The intelligence report had mentioned that the inspirational Fransisco Salinas had a dynamic son who had learnt his craft in the US. Karras knew that insurgents from all over the world sent their cadres to the ranch in Alabama. Yet the ranch had failed to produce any outstanding graduate in the last decade or so. An old, out-of-shape Bobby Carter, before his death in October, had raved about a 'Jack and David' who he believed were shaking the world. The prison authorities had dismissed his ravings but Karras had known the connection that Carter had with Camper and his deadly school. He wondered whether Jack and David were actually out there changing the history of the world, without the world ever realising their silken touch.

Could Jack or David be related to Israel and the Mossad? Karras knew that the man the Pakistanis and Nazir were seeking was of Israeli origin. The bit about the Shalom Brigade that he had told Brig. Nazir had been told to him by Ben Tauber. Ben, short for Ben Hur, was an old friend of Karras' who had served in the Mossad for many years. Son of a Holocaust survivor, Tauber had been named after the legendary hero that had catapulted Charlton Heston to superstardom. During one of their uninhibited discussions in Washington DC, Tauber had told Karras that his professional service had made a critical error of judgement. They had failed to retain in their fold a man who had once single-handedly disarmed the famous Carlos and his band of six in Paris in the Eighties. This had been after 1975 when Carlos had shot dead two officers of the French Surete and had escaped from questioning.

In the late Eighties, Carlos and his men had camped again in Paris to sabotage the meeting of NATO foreign ministers when one of their gang members had a run-in with an old foe from Mossad. Instead of exiting silently from the scene, this man had stupidly attempted to assault the Mossad operative who had supposedly fled the scene. Two hours later, the Israeli operative had tailed the Carlos henchman and had raided their hideout in suburban Paris. He had single-handedly decimated Carlos' gang, and would have apprehended Carlos too if the French Dieuxeme Bureau had not chosen that very moment to stage a search and seizure operation on Carlos' hideout on a complaint from suspicious neighbours.

According to Ben Tauber, the Mossad had failed to retain a talented man. Karras had been close to persuading Tauber to reveal his identity when Tauber had received an urgent call from Jerusalem. Years after that discussion with Tauber, Karras had heard rumours that had emanated from the Middle East about the growing reputation of an assassin on hire. His instincts had told him that this man could be that former Mossad operative, as the rumours had indicated that the Mossad had not shown any sign of pursuing the source of those rumours. Karras of course knew that the main reason that the Mossad had let this mysterious assassin be was that he had never crossed their sphere of work. And the Israeli secret service was known to let assassins alone even if they were in striking distance as long as they did not harm or hinder the strategic interests of the Mossad. Being in retirement, Karras had no idea how the Israelis felt about India, or the REP and its leader Prof. Kapre.

Karras wondered whether he could trace old Ben. He knew that Tauber was from Tel Aviv. After retiring from Mossad, that's probably where he would have settled. He also knew that Tauber's two sons were American citizens and were based somewhere in California. Would the junior Taubers reveal the whereabouts of their father to him? He knew that there were several hundred men in Palestine and Lebanon who would consider it an honour to kill Tauber. It was certain that Tauber would have an unlisted address. Although killings of reprisal by the Palestinians were rare in the Israeli capital, prominent former Mossad officers were expected to take precautions. Karras knew that the single most protected man in Israel, more protected than even the prime minister, was the famous Merlin Kramer, the man revered as making the Mossad the most feared and respected intelligence service in the world. Rumour had it that Kramer was guarded round the clock by a commando force capable of invading a small nation or decimating an entire division of an army.

BILBAO

The entire group sat in a semicircle celebrating the death of Col. Ramon Arrieta. For most of the Basque population harbouring dreams of an independent nation it was cause for jubilation. More than being the death of one man, it was a symbol. An event that could provide the spark for the rejuvenation of the tottering ETA. As all the Basque towns of Salmanaca, Bilbao and San Sebastian celebrated, the man called Julio Lopez was given a quiet burial. In his stead emerged Emilio Salinas, son and heir of Fransisco Salinas, the inspiration that ETA needed. Emilio Salinas and his men chose to react carefully to the assassination of Arrieta. Fully aware that they would be suspected as being the brains behind the killing they shot two local informers and placed papers on their bodies identifing them as Julio Lopez and Miguel Carrillo. An already shaken Spanish media reported it as an internecine organisational feud.

In a span of six days, the two main problems of the ETA had been resolved. The towering figure of Col. Arrieta that had gradually begun eating into the ETA's support base had disappeared and the manhunt for Julio Lopez was called off. Emilio Salinas and his trusted lieutenants planned to fan out through the Basque countryside to take immediate advantage of the wave of Basque nationalism. Although the public believed that Lopez and his men had pulled off the impossible in killing Arrieta, knowledgeable insiders knew otherwise. ETA insiders were sure that the assassination was executed by a professional.

Although Singer did not receive anything from the cash-strapped ETA, his reputation grew. In time the information, or the total lack of it, would give rise to several theories about the man responsible for the Arrieta assassination. Such theories would then be refined and percolate to the top echelons of various intelligence agencies of the world. As one of the suspects, Jack Singer's name would do the rounds. Eventually, all the theories would die down as no identity papers existed on Singer. It was believed that the organisation said to have utilised him in his early days had destroyed all the papers linking him to it. But if Bobby Joe Carter had been alive, he would have seen clearly the hand of his foster son in the killing of Col. Arrieta.

NEW DELHI

Rajnish Mishra seethed with anger at the humiliation that he had suffered. He had just returned from a meeting with the

Prime Minister of India. After his cathartic conversation with his home minister, Srinivas Reddy had begun devoting all his energies to the serious business of governing the country, including reviewing the security of India. He gave a piece of his mind to all the pivotal agencies responsible for the lapse in security. The first victim of the purge was the commissioner of police of the national capital, Raj Mohan Tiwari. He was transferred to the insignificant post of director, training and was replaced by Shekhar Rao, a senior career officer from Reddy's home state. Both the chief of the IB and Mishra escaped being axed by the calming influence exerted on the Prime Minister by Hitesh Singh. He convinced Reddy that too many transfers would indicate that the Congress was panicking.

Nevertheless, the Prime Minister severely reprimanded both Anand Kishore and Rajnish Mishra. He insisted that the top priority of both agencies was to ensure that Vijay Kapre remained unhurt till the conclusion of the general elections. It was this rebuke that was bothering Mishra. The seemingly effortless killing of a well-known local European leader further depressed the director of RAW. If a man as well protected as Arrieta could be killed, what guarantee could the Indian security apparatus take for the safety of Kapre? The only light at the end of the tunnel was DCP Nigam and his investigation. Mishra had made up his mind to re-establish communication with agent Gabriel after the return of the DCP from London. He knew that in doing so he would severely compromise the safety of the Pakistani but he had no option. He had decided to offer Gabriel double his usual fee for any information that could lead to the deciphering of the mysterious death of Mohan Bhargava.

Mishra was meanwhile completely oblivious to what was germinating in his own backyard.

46

NEW DELHI, 1972

He looked around him in a daze. The stream of people walking in and offering their condolences did nothing to awaken his numbed senses. He was eleven and in severe shock. One of his father's friend's wives sat next to him and tried to make him eat. It was futile. He had refused to eat since he had heard of the death of his father. He couldn't understand how this had happened. He remembered how terrified he'd been during the 1971 war when he had realised that his father was in the thick of battle.

His relations with his mother being as they were, Jai had had to stay over with his father's friends. The boy had somehow endured those days in 1971, listening out for any conversation on the war. He had gone to school every day, and recoiled in fright as excited classmates had recounted the number of casualties in the war. But his father had came back home. The little boy had pleaded with his father to leave the air force. J.B. Singh had agreed. He had put in his papers and had joined the Tatas as a commercial pilot. On the morning of October 6, 1972, a routine flight from Delhi to Bombay for some Tata executives had been scheduled. Singh had left home promising his son that he would be back in the evening with gifts for him.

At 6 PM young Jai was told that the plane had crashed, and that there were no survivors.

Jai's parents had divorced when he was very young. Squadron Leader Singh had met Joann Singer in 1958 in London when, as a young flight lieutenant, he was undergoing a course in advanced flying. It had been love at first sight for the dashing Indian Air Force officer and the beautiful English club dancer. In 1959 he had returned to India. Four months later, the English girl had followed him. Within a week they were married.

In 1961, they had a son who was named Jack Jai Karan Singh. The family led a happy existence till 1966 when J.B. Singh had returned earlier than usual from work one day and found Joann in bed with a young diplomat serving in the British High Commission in New Delhi. Joann admitted that she had been cheating on her husband for more than a year. She had begged forgiveness and cited boredom for her straying. A broken J.B. had not known what to say and had retreated into a shell. Joann had known that the marriage was over and she had suggested divorce by mutual consent.

A shattered J.B. had attempted to pick up the pieces of his life with his little son. Joann had left, promising to take their son to London for two months every summer but had failed to write even a single letter. It had been difficult for the boy as he had clear memories of his mother that did not dim even with time. He had become shy, introverted and withdrawn. A hapless J.B. had changed schools repeatedly to find the ideal environment for his son. The taunts of playmates and friends had made life more difficult for little Jai. The boy had started hating going outdoors, even to school. By the time the boy was ten, he finally began to adjust to his school. But then war broke out and the home that J.B. had painstakingly constructed for his son was shattered. His son was now obsessively attached to his father and terrified at the prospect of losing him. When in 1972 the Squadron Leader died in an air crash, his friends wondered what to do with his already traumatised son. Wing Commander Prakash Khurana somehow traced Joann Singer in England and wrote to her, informing her of the death of her ex-husband and pleaded with her to take responsibility of the young boy. A twice-married Joann wrote back refusing. Old enough to understand that his mother did not want him but not old enough to comprehend the difficulties that Joann Singer was facing, the boy was flooded with hatred for all womankind.

After 1972, some of J.B. Singh's friends had taken upon themselves the responsibility of supporting the son of their deceased friend. Till the boy finished his schooling, he moved from one family to another, from one town to another. Since young Jai Karan had no attachment to anything in life, he focused all his energies on academics and books. He developed into a brilliant student who ranked amongst the top students in every school that he attended. For class XI and XII, Wing Commander Khurana and his friends took the decision to put him in a hostel so that Jai Karan could complete his education without any disturbance and interruptions. Their efforts paid off and Jai Karan had graduated out of school ranking first in the entire state.

Although the prestigious St. Stephen's College had admitted him, he had chosen to study at St. Xavier's in Bombay. Jai had wanted to get away from the painful memories that Delhi held for him. In his second year of college, he had met Priya. She was one batch junior to him and had chased him with the single-mindedness of a tigress. Although still shy, Jai was now aware of the effect his looks had on women. Just under six feet in height, he had inherited his mother's blue-grey eyes. He was fair, but the Indian sun had tanned him. Priya Menon was dusky, tall and a charmer to the core. She was one girl who every boy in college had fancied at some point or the other. There had been only one who ignored her. On enquiry, she learnt that his name was Jai Karan Singh.

She had chased him for close to six months till he had relented and accepted her as a friend. After that, she wove her natural web of charm over him, into which an unsuspecting Jai had fallen. They had dated for more than a year before Priya had begun showing the first signs of boredom. Jai was a natural introvert who could not fit into her vast circle of friends. The day he finished his final year examinations, Priya informed him that she had begun seeing someone else. A stunned Jai had asked the reason. 'We are incompatible, that's all,' Priya had replied nonchalantly. Jai had found a job and worked for exactly one month—enough time to buy a one-way ticket to London.

By the time he emerged at Heathrow, the twenty-one-year-old Jai Karan Singh had changed into a different person. In the place of a boy was a deadened man. At the first lodging that he took in a cheap inn at Hammersmith, he gave his name as Jack Singer. His routine would begin at 5 AM in the morning. He would walk to the nearest tube station, head for central London and wash cars in a huge underground car park at upmarket Marble Arch. At 9 AM he would head for a café at Soho and work till the afternoon as a waiter. At three in the afternoon, he would head for the rich suburb of Hampstead where he gave private tuitions to primary school children. Some of the women he met while giving these tuitions had taken a fancy to the handsome tutor and sought sexual favours from him.

Every evening he worked out at a local gymnasium. He had no desire to be ogled at by women but he pumped iron to dull his mind. He reckoned that a dulled brain would not feel the pain that wracked his insides. However, those hours of exercise and part-time labour did not heal his mind and soul but turned his body into a block of muscle. Within six months, Jack Singer had raised enough money to fly to the promised land, the United States of America.

One woman had chosen to repay his sexual favours with generosity of a different kind. Of Jewish origin, she gave Jack references of some of her relatives in the US who could help him out.

In the time that he had spent in London, Jai had not made any effort to find Joann Singer. Nor did he know what his goal in life was. He only wanted to find some way to dull his senses. He tried to think of what he wanted his future to be like but every time he shut his eyes a swirling mist of blackness engulfed him. He realised that he was as clueless about his life as he had been when he had first landed in London. Then he felt inside his shirt and touched the little locket that held the picture of Squadron Leader Jai Bhawani Singh. His father had been a soldier. He would be a soldier too, like him.

But he was no patriot. He had never felt at home anywhere. He would be a soldier for hire. Tough as he was, Jack Singer was aware that he was a novice as far as training in weapons, explosives and combat skills was concerned. He knew that there were training centres in the United States, usually falling within one of these three categories: first would be the franchisee or commercial establishment that offered training to law enforcement agencies or security firms. The second category was the paramilitary and survivalist organisation that offered training in the use of small arms, map reading and survival under extreme circumstances. He was interested in the third category—the pure mercenary training camp, the only goal of which would be to offer the knowledge and skills necessary to be a soldier for hire. He had heard of the Merc School in Dolomite, Alabama and its owner, Frank Camper. He had heard that Camper was a thorough professional who did not waste any time on trivialities like ideology.

The next day, Jack Singer left London and headed for New York City. The relatives that Claire Shepherd had talked about in Hampstead turned out to be only one distant nephew. David Steiner, about the same age as him, ran a small grocery store in Queens. Without any questions, he took in Jack Singer and allowed him to share his studio apartment. It seemed to Singer that his host neither ate nor drank but only worked.

47

David Steiner had been in New York for two years. He was a Jew of German descent who had been born in the Siberian town of Ekaterinburg in the Soviet Union. This town's claim to fame, or rather notoriety, was that it was where the last Czar of Russia, Nicholas II, and his family had been murdered by the Bolsheviks.

David's parents had seen his birth as a true blessing from God. His mother, Theresa, had had two miscarriages and she and her husband, Benjamin, had decided that this would be their last try.

The Steiners never spoke to David about the past but the sharp boy had imbibed it all, listening to his parents talk at night—the loss of their homes, their families, Auschwitz. Benjamin and Theresa had been prisoners in the same concentration camp. When they were freed in 1945, they stepped out, hoping to build a new life together.

Unfortunately, it seemed that fate had only willed tragedy for the Steiner family. Through years of hard work, Benjamin Steiner had reached the level of shift supervisor in the gold mines of Sverdlovask. His pay was better and as they watched

308

David creep towards adolescence, they began to smile after years. Young David was also happy to see his parents beginning to get over their long periods of sadness.

But in 1968, Benjamin caught a few Russian commissars participating in the smuggling of gold from the mines. The cornered commissars offered Benjamin Steiner a share in the profits and tried to buy him with the vision of his being able to reach Israel one day. The honest Jew refused and promised the Russian rogues that he would let the authorities know. Within two days, a KGB detachment awoke Steiner and his wife at midnight at their modest town apartment. Benjamin thought that the secret police needed him to supply information about the smugglers. He was beside himself with shock when the arresting officer informed him that he and his wife were accused of treason. They arrested them on the charge of robbing the country of its mineral wealth. A hapless David was allowed to accompany his parents to the cold prison camp of Lubyanka, a few hundred miles from Sverdlovask.

For three days, the boy watched his father dodge bullets as the camp guards played with him till they finally shot an exhausted Benjamin Steiner dead. A day before, the middle-aged Theresa Steiner had been brutally raped in full view of her husband and son. The authorities decided to release the boy and he was sent to a school for orphans at Sverdlovask. Watching his father and mother being killed like animals in front of him had made David mature beyond his years. He learnt quickly to lie and manipulate his way out of trouble. He was also determined to leave the land that had brought nothing but misery to his parents. Within five years, David Steiner was helping the same smugglers who had killed his parents. Not only did he learn the tricks of the trade but he also saved enough money to bribe the mining guards and learnt of a way to leave the Soviet Union forever.

The same communist party leader who had issued orders for the arrest of his parents arranged for the exceptionally brilliant David Steiner to reach Moscow and work for the CPSU. He reached Moscow, took a vow to renounce his religion and pretended to be a dedicated student of Communism. Within one year, he was on a plane to London as part of a group of students sent on an exchange programme to Oxford for two weeks. Four days into the programme, David Steiner disappeared and surfaced under another name and another identity. As Ray Darrel, he worked for years in London and in Manchester. From 1974 to 1980, he worked hard to make enough money to be able to leave continental Europe forever. His goal was to settle in Israel but he knew that he would have to first reach the US and educate himself to be a figure worthy of respect in the sacred land of the Jews.

In 1980, he managed to board a ship to New York where he reverted to his original name of David Steiner. While other young men of his age spent their energies in chasing girls, David Steiner spent all his extra time reading. He joined a local Jewish fruit-seller as an assistant and impressed him with his sincerity. The man noticed that the young boy would arrive at the Manhattan shop earlier than every other employee and would leave late at night after counting the stock and clearing the mess. David's boss did not know that one reason why Steiner worked so hard and slept so little was because he was afraid to sleep. Sleep brought nightmares of that cold evening in Sverdlovask when the boorish prison guards had disrobed his mother and his hysterical father had tried to cover the young boy's eyes. If that nightmare did not visit him, the other one took over, where a tired Benjamin Steiner ran like a cornered dog in the icy desert, as the cracks of rifle fire boomed in the ears of the little boy who watched helplessly.

By early 1982, David had saved enough money to set up his own little shop in a relatively cheaper suburb of Queens. And it was later that year that David would play host to another guest with a traumatic past, the enigmatic Jack Singer. Within days of Singer moving into Steiner's house, the two became good friends. Sleep would not come easy to either of them and they would walk along the Eastern river talking of their respective family histories. Both shared every single detail of their lives and narrated the facts and circumstances that had deadened their souls and had made them impervious to emotion of any kind.

After staying with Steiner for two months, Jack Singer informed him of his wish to enroll at the Camper school for mercenary training. A directionless Steiner was also taken in by the idea. Both headed to Dolomite, Alabama to enroll at the Ranch. The admission committee immediately agreed to enroll the brawny Singer but was reluctant to grant admission to the rather weak looking Steiner. One instructor at the Ranch, who specialised in mental conditioning, Bobby Joe Carter, pleaded David Steiner's case with the committee. When asked what he saw in the Jew, Carter replied, 'His eyes: they are so full of fire, if we don't harness it, someone else will.' As Carter had been an old associate of Camper and had trained hundreds, the committee couldn't refuse him. From 1982 to 1984 Jack Singer and David Steiner trained at the Ranch, goaded and guided by Bobby Joe Carter.

A friendless Carter began to treat Singer like his own son. In the disciplined environs of the mercenary school, Singer and Steiner became close friends with an idealistic Spanish revolutionary, Emilio Salinas. Salinas was at the Ranch for a mission. On him rode the hopes of an entire people. The three, completely different from each other but united by the common thread of difficult pasts bonded well. As far as training went, Jack Singer excelled in all disciplines. Whether it was with small arms, sophisticated arms, hand-to-hand combat or even psychological toughness, his reputation aquired legendary proportions at the Ranch. David Steiner was not far behind the two. Carter called them the three S's: Singer, Steiner and Salinas. Singer and Steiner trained harder than anyone else on the Ranch to overcome personal pain that was deeply embedded in their hearts. A normally withdrawn Singer barely reciprocated the fatherly warmth of Carter but neverthess respected the old teacher.

Towards the end of 1984, Carter introduced Steiner to a man known as Ben Hur Tauber. Tauber was a middle ranking officer in the Mossad, the dreaded Israeli intelligence service. Carter convinced Tauber that if the Mossad recruited Steiner, it would have acquired a potential prize operative. Tauber offered Steiner a ticket to Tel Aviv for a routine screening and discussion on the kind of work that Steiner wanted to do for the service. Steiner agreed to visit Israel but insisted that his friend be allowed to accompany him. Ben Tauber arranged for travel documents for both David Steiner and Jack Singer. In Tel Aviv, Steiner was interviewed and his family history checked out. Convinced that Steiner was a staunch Jew who had a fierce sense of loyalty towards the state of Israel, they placed him with the covert intelligence gathering arm of the Mossad. On special request, his first posting was Moscow.

Before Steiner left Tel Aviv for Moscow, he asked his best friend what he wanted to do in life. 'I just want to fight, no matter where or for whom, but I cannot return to a normal life.' Steiner put in a word to Ben Tauber, who pleaded Jack Singer's case with the Mossad director personally. Although not a Jew by birth, Singer was a man of extraordinary talent and the two years at the Ranch had converted him into a fighting machine. The director relented and placed Singer in one of the peripheral fighting units of the Mossad. After its wars with its Arab neighbours, the Mossad ran several rogue commando units that excelled in operations of sabotage and destabilisation. Singer saw fierce fighting in Lebanon where the Mossad units operated behind enemy lines to disrupt the supplies of several guerilla bodies, aiding the militant wings of Yasser Arafat's PLO. As a fighter Singer was par excellence, and in 1985 he fought his way alone out of Beirut, surrounded as he was by over sixty enemy soldiers. He would also be a part of daring raids carried out on Gaza town, deep into Palestinian territory. What surprised Tauber and the other Mossad officers was the complete lack of nerves that Singer exhibited.

Although he was not reckless, he had a certain disregard for danger. From the confines of Beirut to the streets of Tripoli, Jack Singer showed how expertly he could wield his weapons. Within two years he was made a member of the elite Shalom Brigade, an elite fighting force that the Mossad had never publicly acknowledged. The Shalom Brigade's prowess was so advanced that six members of the unit were known to have pushed back an entire force of 120 regular Egyptian army men. As a part of the Shalom brigade, Singer saw action in the dangerous Baaka valley and several other places where the strongest of nerves could crack. He emerged out of all his operations a lesser human and more of a robotic killing machine. It was during a short break in Paris in 1988, that Jack Singer had a run in with Carlos' gang and Carlos himself, an encounter which Tauber was to narrate years later to Radley Karras in Washington DC.

The rise of both Steiner and Singer was simultaneous in the top echelons of the Mossad. While Singer became known in Mossad circles as a killing machine, Steiner acquired a reputation as one of the most ruthless field agents operating

313

for the Mossad. After a brilliant one year tenure, Steiner was transferred to the extremely crucial station of Muscat. His superiors were, of course, not aware of the scores that Steiner had settled while in Moscow. He had arranged the assassination of Valery Andrev, a high ranking member of the Politburo. Not many in Moscow knew that in the late Sixties, the same Andrev, then only a local commissar, had been the ring leader of a gold smuggling operation in Siberia. From the proceeds of this operation, Andrev had bought off contacts and had risen rapidly in the ranks of the CPSU. Valery Andrev had also sent, among others, a Jewish couple by the name of Steiner to their deaths.

The need for retribution was not Steiner's alone. In a way, every successful kill was, for Jack Singer, avengement for what he had been through.

At the end of 1988, when Steiner and Singer met after a long time in Tel Aviv, they did not have to discuss with each other their experiences. One look into each other's eyes and they knew that the world had begun to pay for what had been inflicted on them. Both friends were happy that they were at last in an environment which suited them and amongst people who understood their need for violence. It was this belief that was to be betrayed in the near future for both Steiner and Singer and which eventually led to the irreversible degeneration of both men.

It all began with the kidnapping of the daughter of Raymond Rosenthal, Steiner's colleague in Muscat. There were no ransom demands made for the twenty-four hours following the girl's disappearance. In those twenty-four hours, Steiner threw in all the resources he possessed to trace little Evy, the daughter of a low-rung operative. He managed to trace the kidnappers to a deserted warehouse on the Muscat waterfront. He made a plan for the immediate storming of the

314

warehouse and the release of Evy Rosenthal by force. The authorities in Tel Aviv, however, refused permission. It was March 1989 and an extremely high profile Israel–PLO conference was to take place soon in Washington DC. The Israeli leadership did not want Israelis to be painted as trigger-happy arsonists without first exhausting the option of negotiations with the Arab kidnappers. The negotiations had barely begun when the kidnappers, in an attempt to convince the Israelis that they held Evy Rosenthal, sent them the little finger of the left hand of the child. Raymond was delirious with grief.

It was at this point that Steiner's patience snapped. He decided to storm the warehouse alone. He had landed in Muscat that morning on a reconaissance mission for the Shalom Brigade. Singer insisted on accompanying Steiner in the operation. The determined duo entered the warehouse at midnight and succeeded in rescueing Evy Rosenthal. They also left in their wake the bodies of eight Arab terrorists. Steiner received a wound in his right leg that crippled him for life. The next day's headlines read 'Vigilante Israel ends negotiations'. An embarrassed Israeli political leadership announced exemplary action against both Steiner and Singer, particularly Singer, as he was not even supposed to be part of the storming team. A worried Tauber, who had recruited the mercurial duo, argued fervently on their behalf. Other than being aware of their talents, he had some idea of their troubled pasts and worried where the duo would seek re-employment. The hawkish leadership of the Mossad decided to spare Steiner because he was a Jew but announced its decision to sack Jack Singer.

An upset Steiner put in his papers the day Jack Singer's Shalom stripes were taken away. In May 1989, David Steiner and Jack Singer, the new outcasts of Israel, left their temporary home forever. As newly relieved agents of the Mossad, their movements were watched. Within three weeks, the trail ran cold. Nothing was heard from the two; Tauber gave up as well, after all stations reported a dead end. Tauber of course knew that together, Steiner and Singer would be lethal. He wondered from time to time where the golden boys of his service had disappeared. He even had his men watch the Camper school in the hope that the two would return there. It was all to no avail and within one year, an overburdened Tauber forgot about David Steiner and Jack Singer.

48

Rajnish Mishra was all attention as Surendra Nigam summarised the results of his London sojourn. Painstakingly, he explained each step to him, the evidence that revealed Pakistan's involvement and the potential consequences. An impressed Mishra had no time to either compliment Nigam or to laud his efforts. 'What have you been able to find out about this Maj. Chaudhary?'

'Other than the fact that he was the most active ISI operative in Europe in the last three months, not much Sir.'

'Why do you call him the most active operative?'

'Simply because most of the ISI men in Europe treat these postings as leisure vacations, as do operatives from RAW and IB.' Nigam paused for a moment to see the director's reaction to his candid assessment. Mishra nodded, encouraging him to continue. 'Frankly, Europe is not where the action is for our boys. Almost all the time is spent meeting with exiles and political rebels of each other's countries. We knew that an important LTTE meeting took place in the last two months. Yet, Maj. Chaudhary did not cover this meeting at all.'

317

'And how did he spend his time in London?'

'Our spotters have reported that he spent a lot of time in the company of an Afghani gangster. This man, a half Pakistani, half Pashtun called Arif Rabbani, is a Londoner for all practical purposes and is supposed to be an active member of the Roxton Miller gang. What is more, he has in the past doled out information to our operatives also, of course for a price.'

'Hmm, the perfect mercenary then, who works for both sides.'

'Clearly,' nodded Nigam.

'Do you think the Pakistanis used him to get Bhargava watched?'

'No Sir. At first, even I thought of the possibility but then I thought that in a place like London, why would the Pakistanis need outsiders to watch Bhargava?'

'Then what could be the reason? Is Rabbani a hitman?'

'I ran a background check on Rabbani. Though he is known to have killed in self-defence, he is not your quintessential assassin. Besides, Sir, Mr Bhargava was killed in India. There is no evidence of Arif Rabbani being in India during that period.'

'This is the problem with Agni's death. We keep getting clues but no concrete proof of why he was killed. I mean, the Pakistanis have often delighted in bashing our operatives but they have never committed murder.' A puzzled Mishra looked at Nigam but the police officer remained quiet. The director of RAW had not revealed anything about Gabriel to Nigam yet. Mishra wondered about the present whereabouts of Gabriel. He knew that there was a post box in Islamabad that could be used in an emergency to reach the spy. Despite the risks involved, he felt it was time to contact Gabriel. It appeared to be the only way they would unravel the mystery of Mohan Bhargava's tragic death.

318

'Sir, I was thinking, wasn't Mr Bhargava killed to prevent him from meeting you?'

Mishra nodded.

'But why was he not provided security and why was there no reception party for him?'

'Well, that's the way Bhargava operated. He was absolutely unpredictable and that's what made him so brilliant. I am sure he changed his flight reservation several times before he finally boarded the one that brought him to Delhi.'

'But what could be so important that he had to come all the way from London? RAW possesses secure enough telephone lines.' Mishra stared at Nigam who was quick to clarify. 'I am only doing some loud thinking. I don't want to know any information that is classified, Sir.'

'Your remark makes sense. The only explanation I can offer is the one weakness that Mohan Bhargava had. A tendency to build up suspense. It is that one weakness for which he lost his life and which has caused us to reach a dead end.'

Two hours after Nigam had begun the briefing, a tired Mishra indicated that he should leave. Although theoretically Nigam's investigations had been exhaustive, unfortunately they were no closer to knowing why Mohan Bhargava had been killed. India had solid proof of Pakistani involvement but that had become a regular feature since the late Eighties. The Pakistanis would deny it and the Americans would demand more evidence. Again his mind drifted to that post box in Islamabad. More than a month had passed since the death of Agni, reasoned Mishra. He knew that Gabriel was still alive, as a man of his importance could not be killed without his death being reported in the Press. It was time he reestablished contact with him. Mishra knew that Gabriel's services did not come cheap. Even a normal communication with Gabriel cost RAW big money. But the information that India's secret weapon in Pakistan supplied had always been worth it.

After Nigam had left, Rajnish Mishra sent urgent instructions through his OSD to the communications section of RAW. He wanted a letter to be sent via special courier to the Indian High Commission in London where the markings that identified it as having originated from India could be erased by an expert. Then it would be posted from London so that any investigation by the receiver would indicate its origin to be London. Although Mishra had never used this process before, he had full knowledge of the precautions to be taken. Bhargava and Mishra had together formulated the entire procedure for a condition similar to the one that had arisen now. The innocuous letter would be received from its designated post box in Islamabad by Gabriel who would then take the initiative to get in touch with New Delhi.

As Mishra drew plans to use the last weapon he possessed, Nigam brooded over his dal and chapattis. His domineering mother looked at her son with annoyance. She had entertained dreams of her only son settling in the US after an MBA and here he was wasting his youth on the problems of the government of India. As the tasteless dal cooked by her grew cold, she decided it was time to begin nagging her errant son. 'If you don't want to eat, at least look at those photos that Mrs Sikka has sent.' Surendra ignored her. 'At least look at this picture. Her father has his own factories and they have a few imported cars also.' Nigam continued to ignore her. 'If you are not going to talk to me, I am going to bed, Surendra,' she declared as she rose from the dinner table. 'This boy has ruined my old age,' she said to no one in particular.

The minute his mother had retired to her bedroom, Nigam grabbed his plate and went into the kitchen. Having stayed in hostels, he was self-sufficient as far as cooking was concerned. He warmed the dal, added garnish and spices to it and scrambled an egg for himself. After ten minutes he returned to the dining table to have his dinner in peace without having to bother about the pictures of prospective brides that his mother kept selecting for him. As he ate, he thought of the entire Bhargava case, from the day that Mishra had first summoned him till his meeting with him a few hours earlier. What had they missed? Obviously Bhargava knew something that the Pakistanis hadn't wanted leaked. What could it be? A blueprint for war, an offensive that Pakistan was planning, a new missile that Pakistan would be testing? He finished his dinner, rinsed his plate and then looked around the house for something sweet. His search led him to a three-day old burfee that was close to spoiling.

He curled up in the drawing room with an *India Today* for company. The magazine had some film actress on the cover whom he could not identify. He remembered seeing promos of her last movie in which she had seduced the entire nation by heaving her bust in a skimpy outfit. After ten minutes he kept the magazine aside. He knew that his mind was on the verge of deducing something that could shed some light on mystery of Bhargava's death. Should he sleep on it, he wondered, or should he push his brain harder? He remembered his days at IIT Delhi. He had often wrestled with problems and if a stubborn problem presented no solution, he would just sleep on it. The next morning after a hearty breakfast, the solution would usually present itself. Surendra decided he would adopt the same approach. He finished his burfee and retired for the night.

While Surendra dreamt of heaving busts and his IIT days and Rajnish Mishra spent another sleepless night at the RAW headquarters, Atreyee Mishra cried in guilt for the hundredth time. It had been more than two weeks since she had had sex with a stranger. Her tears of guilt did not stem from a sense that she had done anything immoral, but from having enjoyed herself so much. She hoped she would never meet the stranger ever again because she knew that if she did, she would crave another session to quench her physical thirst.

LONDON, NOVEMBER 27, 1995

It had been ten days since he had pulled off Arrieta's assassination. Today was the last day of his rest before he left for his next assignment. He sat discussing the logistics of his assignment with his partner and friend, David Steiner. 'The money has reached Zurich, you know that don't you?'

'Yes, I know, but my mind is elsewhere at present.'

'I can see that.'

'Do you think this Indian leader will present a problem?'

Singer shook his head. 'Not a problem, just a slight change in plans. This bumbling assassin tried to get him at his residence. That is what I was planning as well. I had done a recce of the area.'

'What level of security?' questioned David.

'Primitive: sentries at the gate, little group stationed in a tent close by, nothing that can actually prevent an assassin,' he smiled.

'Have you managed a blueprint of his revised security yet?' asked Darrel.

'No, as of now I am not even sure if I need anything more than what I already have seen at the site. There is a sharp weakness in the target's location itself.'

'But can this weakness not be sealed?' persisted his close friend.

'It can be to some extent, but nothing that an exact awareness of the target's schedule will not expose again.'

'And you know this schedule minute by minute as usual?'

He smiled at his friend. 'Not yet but I have a source that will reveal it.' He turned the discussion to the weapons of his trade, not wanting to discuss his latest asset with David, the man with whom he could normally talk to about anything.

'What are you planning to use, sniper's rifle?'

'I don't know. I could, but you know I do not like to carry out two successive kills in the same manner. Don't want any patterns emerging.'

'Does it matter who is chasing us now? No one even knows that we exist.'

'I would not be too sure; perhaps it is only that nobody minds that we exist. After all, we haven't crossed any one's paths yet. Maybe if we got the US President, they would sit up and take notice.'

'How difficult is it to get a US President? I mean, after Kennedy, they have become come quite careful, haven't they?'

'No,' he shook his head, 'it still remains as easy as it was then. Too much of bravado, secret service this and secret service that. The actual killing would still be a joke if anyone attempted it seriously.'

'You mean that, don't you?' David knew that his partner never said something unless he meant it.

'Of course I could do it, but it would have to be the last assignment then. I can do it at a month's notice if I get 50 million or more in US dollars.'

'We already have enough.'

'Yes we do, but after the US President, we would need to change our faces, our bodies, our fingerprints, everything. Too much of a hassle.'

'How was Pakistan?' questioned David.

'The same as always, same bunch of doubting fools, same volley of questions.'

'What?' David was amused. 'Did they threaten to kill you?'
His partner nodded.

'And what did you say to them?' He was now smiling broadly.

'I showed them this.' He took out his address book. 'Told them it was a sound sensitive explosive that would go off even if they used a silencer.'

'My God! And they believed it?'

'Yes, and they were military boys.'

'I had thought that these Pakistanis would be bold.'

'You know, people are bold till it comes to losing their lives. We retain our nerves because we don't fear death. Rather, I wait for it, every day silently goading it to come and get me.'

'Yes, I know what you mean.'

David limped to the cabinet where he had some drawings that he wanted to show to his friend and partner. Singer got up from the floor where he was resting to check if his hot water bottle was ready. David and Singer knew from their past experiences that death rarely ever obliged those who sought it. Death was a stubborn guest which believed in surprising unsuspecting people who had no wish to meet it.

As the two men retired for the night in the expensive and luxurious flat in central London, it was only a few minutes to dawn in New Delhi, thousands of miles to the east.

NEW DELHI

Surendra Nigam woke up, hoping that a fresh brain would give him the solution he so badly sought. Nigam knew that if this one case could be cracked, his mind would forever be free of the inertia that had gripped it. He lay awake in his bed. In the darkness he stared at the outline of the stationary ceiling fan. He turned to look at the clock that lay at his bedside.

It was half past four, one hour before his mother rose for the day and began listening to the devotional songs that played on All India Radio. He had woken up hours before his normal time. He realised that he had been dreaming of the puzzle that was challenging his brain. He stirred his mind to run through the exact sequence of events that had taken place. Mohan Bhargava had informed Director R that he was coming to New Delhi on an unscheduled visit and would require an urgent appointment with him. He had also hinted that what he had to tell his director could not be told over the phone, and also that a meeting of the cabinet committee for security would be needed. So obviously what he had to tell the director was of national importance. It was important enough for him to leave his post when the crucial LTTE meeting in London was approaching. Nigam knew that after the assassination of Rajiv Gandhi, the LTTE was second only to the ISI on the hate list of the Indian intelligence agencies.

He also knew that Bhargava had landed at Indira Gandhi Airport where there had not been any reception committee because he had not revealed his flight plans to anyone in India. Yet, word had got out and the information had been leaked to the neighboring country which had supposedly arranged for Bhargava's death. What had Bhargava known that could have ruined a Pakistani operation? And the method of killing— a brutal accident, where the body of the victim had been badly mangled but had not burned because of the wet weather that night. Could it be possible that Bhargava may have been carrying on his person a blueprint of an operation or minutes of a meeting? Could the method of killing have been designed to destroy that manuscript or a transcript that the perpetrators had known about?

If the car had not burned it was possible that some evidence may be found. He knew that only Director R would know where the remains of the ill-fated vehicle were or whether any search had been carried out in the mangled mass of metal and flesh. He was aware that Bhargava had died on October 17, and that more than a month had passed. It was reasonable to assume that several investigators had already examined the metallic carcass and had not found anything. Yet a niggling doubt tugged at his heart. In crucial investigations it was often the glossing over of a single small piece that held the key to the mystery. Could it be possible that the mangled mass had not been examined beyond extricating the last remains of the unfortunate Bhargava for his last journey?

He rose from his bed and paced up and down, looking at the clock every three minutes. Director R had given him his residence telephone number for emergencies but Nigam was hesitant. He would wait for the clock to strike at least 6 A.M. before he would dare wake up the chief of RAW.

Unknown to Nigam, Mishra was awake, waiting for the night to end so that he could rush to the familiar environs of his office. He knew that the communications section had carried out his instructions during the night. In fact, an hour ago, Mishra had been informed that one of the RAW agents had already boarded the SAS flight that was to halt at London on its way to Copenhagen. Within hours the package would reach London and be ready to commence its onward journey to Islamabad.

At exactly six, Mishra's private number rang. As he was in the bathroom, it was picked up by a sleepy Atreyee Mishra who called out to her husband. 'Some Nigam on the line. Don't your guys ever sleep?' Mishra walked to the phone, his brow furrowed in concentration. What could be so important that could not wait till 10 AM?

49

NEW DELHI, NOVEMBER 29, 1995

He had his Press card dangling around his neck on a chain in case he was stopped and questioned. The card identified him as Ames H. Morton. If any verification were to be carried out and the numbers of the concerned publication dialled, they would verify that an Ames H. Morton was actually on the rolls. Not only that but Mr Morton would of course not be reachable, as he was travelling somewhere in Southeast Asia for a story. The little nip in the air did not bother him as he walked slowly around Pandara Park. As compared to his first visit, the security presence was more visible. There were men toting automatic weapons on both the parallel roads that bounded the little colony. As he paused to tie a shoe lace he noticed that the narrow service lane behind Kapre's house also had security men guarding it.

The road dividers were manned by constables of the Delhi police. He also noticed that there were several policemen stationed at gaps of fifty yards throughout the length of Pandara Road and Zakir Hussain Marg. He finished untying and retying his shoe lace and began a new round of the central park. The dividers had little gaps, enabling the crowd of morning walkers

327

to pass through without any discomfort. As he walked, his eyes took in all the buildings in the neighborhood. All the residential houses were at ground level or had one additional floor. His eyes turned to the conspicuous multistoreyed apartment block that stood perpendicular to the lane where Kapre resided. This building was home to several bureaucrats.

He began his walk out of Pandara Park, his mind moving at its usual breakneck speed. The newspapers had already reported that the general elections had been announced by the Election Commission, and were scheduled to commence in February. He also knew that Kapre was the REP's sole crowd-puller and would need to indulge in sustained campaigning and electioneering outside Delhi, specially in the northern state of Uttar Pradesh that sent eighty-five MPs to the Lok Sabha. As he walked to his temporary home, he thought that since the REP was very strong in Delhi, its chief would not spend much time in the Indian capital. The REP campaign managers would be sure to plan an extensive itinerary, as the REP had lost precious time in tackling allegations of corruption against it in the recent past.

It was clear that he had to get Kapre before he left Delhi on his campaign trail. As his footsteps quickened, his mind began to cover all his past feats, searching for an appropriate tool for his project. He thought of Lord Magor, of Muscat, of the streets of Tokyo and several others. For a few minutes, his mind lingered on the Parker Hale that he had used in Spain a few days ago. But to use the same weapon again on a successive kill would mean admitting that the logistics of the present project had confounded him. He had to admit that the number of security men had surprised him. He had not expected an Opposition leader to have been provided with such an enhanced security cover prior to elections by a government that was anticipating defeat.

Meanwhile, an exhausted Nigam sat slumped in a broken armchair. He was in the official junkyard of RAW, in the huge basements of the CGO complex on Lodhi Road. Since obtaining the green signal from the director, Nigam had literally taken apart the junkyard where the scrap that remained of Mohan Bhargava's last ride had been stored. Already two searches had been carried out but nothing remained that could indicate anything to the frustrated Nigam. He was not even sure what he was searching for. All he knew was that there had to be something which could shed some light on the near perfect murder. Nigam was now supervising the last attempt with his own men, with Avdesh Kaushik personally leading the search. He knew that time was running out for every member of the investigating team. It would be only a few days before the director would have to report the status of the investigation to the cabinet committee for security.

At his last meeting with the director, Mishra had let slip the fact that the political bosses had become increasingly impatient with the way RAW was devoting its time and energies. Nigam knew that RAW was amongst the most autonomous services in the country and its director was answerable only to the prime minister. The prime minister, on most occasions, chose to seek progress reports only from the principal secretary in the prime minister's office or the cabinet secretary, the de facto chief of the Indian Administrative Service. Nigam was aware that since the abortive assassination attempt on Prof. Kapre, Prime Minister Reddy had directed that all energies should be expended on protecting the REP chief. In fact, the director had mentioned that the cabinet secretary had shown his disapproval of the time that was being devoted to unravel the death of Bhargava, who the cabinet secretary had called 'only a middle-rung RAW staffer'. The cabinet secretary, of course, had no idea of Bhargava's contributions to the country.

Close to midnight, Atreyee Mishra tiptoed into her house. One look around told her that her husband was still not back from work. Her daughter, she knew, was staying over at a cousin's place after a birthday party. She walked to her room and silently began to slip into her nightclothes. She lay down, not because she was tired but to ruminate in comfort about her dinner meeting with him—a dinner date made when they had bumped into each other at the gym. They had met at the Oberoi and she had been acutely embarrassed because of their first encounter at his home. He had talked about himself, his work, his travels and a few of his women as well. The sheer honesty of his confessions had inspired her to lose her inhibitions. She had begun talking about her life, her meeting and marriage with her husband, her children, her loneliness. How her husband was extremely tense since the attempt on the life of the man widely tipped to become the next prime minister, and the demands being put on RAW to protect Kapre now and through his campaign tour. Atreyee had found herself telling him about her likes, dislikes, her insecurities, her family background, the unspoken strange tension between her and her husband despite the deep love that she had for him.

As she had no vehicle, he had offered to take her home. Instead of the short journey, she had instead been treated to a long drive in his comfortable Esteem, as they had continued talking. He had then driven into the deserted bylanes of Jorbagh and had stopped the car. He had turned to face her. 'When can we meet again?' She had blushed and remained silent. His face had drawn close and she had felt him kissing her. For a few seconds she had struggled, determined not to give in as easily as she had a few days ago but had then caved in to the delicious wave sweeping her senses. She had returned his kisses. She had not even realised when he had unbuttoned her blazer. She had not realised as his hands had held her waist. As she had returned his kisses, his hands had begun opening the buttons of her shirt. True to intent, she had dressed in a conservative dark business shirt for the dinner date. His lips on her exposed waist had jolted her and she had made feeble attempts to unlock their embrace.

He had immediately stopped touching her and had landed one final kiss on her cheek. He had driven her straight home after that. As she lay in bed, she repeatedly asked herself the reason for her weak resolve. Had it been attraction or the lure of danger? She had vowed after that first amorous encounter that she would be cautious about this man in future. Yet she had almost slept with him again despite the fact that she was meeting him for only the third time in her life. She was aware that the first occasion had been pure lust but what was it now? Was she mistaking the break in her monotonous life for attraction?

It was close to midnight when Nigam called a halt to search operations at the RAW junkyard. His men had unearthed nothing of value. The experts from within RAW had been able to tell from the semi-charred remains of the scrap, that Mohan Bhargava had carried a briefcase on his last journey. There was no sign of the contents of the briefcase. A frustrated Nigam was aware that Agni had most probably been carrying information of great importance in that briefcase. Not a single sheet of paper had been found in the destroyed taxi. The only paper was the blackened scrap that Kaushik had found stuck to the metal framework of the front seat of the taxi. This scrap, merely three inches in length, was darkened by heat and did not offer any indication of having originated from the baggage of the deceased Bhargava. An irritated Nigam had pocketed the scrap as a souvenir of the dashing of the last hope he had harboured.

As he drove his Maruti 800 home, he cursed his luck. He had always trusted his instincts as a child and they had rarely deceived him. He had always scored more than his rivals when he had bowed to his instincts and his pre-dawn visions. He rued his luck. His mind went to the mythical tale of the ancient warrior Karna, whose prowess in archery had failed him during his last but fatal duel with the Pandava, Arjun. The Mahabharata explained the defeat of Karna as having been brought about by the human form of Krishna. Surendra Nigam wondered which gods had conspired against him to deny him that little slice of luck that a man as hardworking as him deserved. As he neared his home, he let out a little groan of despair. Home meant his mother, and his mother meant having to listen to tales about the virtues of thousands of prospective brides.

As he parked his car, he said a silent thanks to the director who had given him an opportunity to awaken from his inertia. While he dreaded his meeting with him the next morning, he was aware that the director knew that DCP Nigam had not lacked in dedication or perseverance. He had failed because luck had eluded him or because the Pakistanis had carried out a perfect murder. He prayed that Rajnish Mishra would consider him for a permanent deputation to RAW so that more challenges could come his way and shake his mind out of the intellectual morass it had fallen into.

As a tired Nigam dodged more attempts by his mother to show him pictures of potential brides, a tired Atreyee felt her eyelids begin to droop with sleep. Her last thoughts were of him, and the germination of the resolve that she needed to slow down the attraction and at least attempt to end this journey. She had decided not to meet him for at least a week, and then wait and see. Maybe after ten days they could meet, but only for lunch.

As she drifted off to sleep, the man who had dominated her thoughts began his research for one of the most important projects of his life.

50

ISLAMABAD, DECEMBER 4, 1995

The man known to Rajnish Mishra as Gabriel trembled with nervousness for the first time since the beginning of his espionage career. He read and reread the letter from the director of RAW. Although the letter indicated that it had originated from London, his fingers twitched with anxiety. The Indians had indicated that fresh information was required about the plans that had been revealed to Mohan Bhargava. Gabriel was also angry. He was angry at Agni, for having died without informing his superiors of Operation Karakoram. He had taken a huge personal risk and written to Agni about the entire plan and yet the Indian had been careless enough to have lost his life without letting his chief know about the operation. Agni's death only days after he had sent him the blueprint meant that his fellow countrymen believed that the leakage had ceased with the death of Agni.

Gabriel knew that his handler's murder had been planned by the ISI or rather the elite service within the ISI, the CFIO. He had been informed that the plan had been carried out by the CFIO chief, Brig. Nazir and Nazir's deputy, one Major Tariq. He himself had not been able to prevent Bhargava's murder. If he chose to now inform the Indians about the most ambitious project in the history of Pakistan and the ISI, he would surely increase the risk to himself. In any case he was aware of the spirited efforts Nazir and his entire team were making to unmask his identity. He had first-hand information of telephones being tapped, mails being intercepted, rewards being upped for Pakistani informers within the Indian intelligence services. The frenzy was expected, as the stakes for Brig. Nazir were tremendous. He knew that the failure of Karakoram would result in a purge that would begin with Nazir himself. Not only would the CFIO chief lose his post, he could lose his life.

He wondered whether the risk of getting discovered was worth the crores of rupees that RAW would pay him. His first payment of five crore for spilling the beans to Bhargava had already been deposited in his account abroad. Gabriel did not do his banking in Switzerland as did so many of his compatriots in Pakistan and India. According to him, Switzerland was too predictable. He had chosen the equally discreet banking industry of Monaco and the isolated islands of the Cayman. The small country, in addition to being a tax haven and an abode for gamblers, was also home to several small banks that were as discreet as the ones in Geneva and Zurich. While the money was, of course, an incentive, what finally helped him make his decision was the long-term goal of toppling Gen. Mehmood from his post of premier. And the first step would be the failure of Operation Karakoram.

He knew that he would need to move fast. Only twenty-four hours ago he had received word that the professional assassin engaged by the ISI had sent word that the operation would be carried out before December 15. Gabriel also had an idea of the money that was to be paid to the assassin. At that price, he knew there was a slim chance of the man bungling, as the local Indian assassin had on his amateurish attempt on Vijay Kapre. Gabriel had a strong belief in destiny. He had the feeling that even if the Indian authorities were informed of Karakoram, there was still a chance Kapre would lose his life. But the odds could be balanced and he would even out the odds for the Indians. He remembered that four years ago he had sent word to Agni that there could be an attempt on the life of Rajiv Gandhi; yet the former prime minister of India had been killed by an LTTE suicide bomber. Knowing Bhargava as he did, he was sure that Agni had conveyed the warning to the top levels of RAW but it had somehow got lost in the political red tape that was so typical of India.

As far as running the risk of discovery, he was confident that the sheer outrageousness of the idea was his security. If Operation Karakoram failed, he would have his several crores in addition to a chance of seeing the downfall of Gen. Mehmood; and if the ambitious operation succeeded, then he would certainly enjoy more power, as would every member of the Pakistani establishment. He had been born into a once affluent Lahore family: his ancestors had squandered the family fortune. They had once been amongst the feudal elite of Lahore, but were reduced to dire penury by the time he was a young boy. He had seen the struggle of the common Pakistani first hand. Everywhere he had been bogged down by red tape, the endemic corruption. Somehow he had summoned his reserves of inner strength and managed to become an integral part of the same establishment that he loathed so much.

Once his real objective of ensuring the return of a democratically-elected government in Islamabad was realised, Gabriel had made plans for a luxurious retirement. He had hopes of settling down in Australia, which he had once visited on a military training exercise. He had loved the villas overlooking the Sydney harbour.

He sat down to send a coded reply to Rajnish Mishra.

A few miles from Gabriel, in the same city, sat three men whose hearts were also trembling with nervousness and excitement. Maj. Tariq and Maj. Chaudhary sat in the inner office of Brig. Qayyum Nazir, at the CFIO headquarters. 'He has not given any reason for stating that the assignment will be carried out by December 15.'

'I think I know the reason,' said Maj. Chaudhary, who was now working closely with Maj. Azim Tariq and Brig. Nazir.

'What is it?'

'On December 16, Kapre leaves Delhi for a three-week whirlwind tour of the country.'

'And your source?'

'A friend in the BBC office in London,' replied Mushtaq Chaudhary.

An impressed Nazir nodded. Clearly Maj. Mushtaq Chaudhary had made good use of his time in London. 'Why can't he be killed after these three weeks?'

Both the Majors knew that Nazir was only doing a bit of loud thinking. 'For one, I suppose it may be too late for any damage to result from his death.' Tariq looked up for a reaction.

'It's possible, but that is a political thing which our man is not concerned with.'

'Yes, he has made his decision on the basis of certain logistics only,' added Chaudhary.

'And any idea about those logistics?'

'My source with the BBC has said that this three-week programme is the only fixed and confirmed news that they have of Kapre's campaigning. After these three weeks, Kapre's party managers have left his itinerary open. He will visit regions as per the feedback the party receives of its prospects for February 1996.'

'So, after three weeks we won't have any advance knowledge of his whereabouts?'

'That's right. And he won't stay long enough in one place for any action to be planned.'

'Clearly our man has done his homework.'

'He seems to be of Caucasian descent,' Brig. Nazir said, beginning to feel a little calmer. The magnitude of the personal risk he was taking was constantly on his mind. If the operation failed, he knew that Gen. Asad Mehmood could survive, Lt. Gen. Ghulam Hussain could survive, so could Mohd. Shujaat, and Lt. Gen. Waheed, but he would certainly not. His would be the first head on the sacrificial chopping block.

'Yes, his accent was most definitely English, specifically well to do, London,' commented Maj. Chaudhary who had heard the audio recording of the voice of the man they were talking about. Brig. Nazir's electronic experts had fitted cameras in all the available rooms of the hotel where the assassin was expected to stay during their first meeting. He had of course wrong-footed them by choosing to stay in an altogether different hotel in the distant suburbs of Islamabad. As both Nazir and Tariq had carried hidden recording microphones on their persons, a hazy and unclear audio recording had been captured. This recording had been heard by the audio experts within the ISI but other than speculating about the accent to some extent, they had no definite idea where the man was from.

'Why do you think he chose the name of 'Walker' to register himself in the hotel?'

'It's a common English surname,' volunteered Maj. Tariq.

'I'm sure that it is not the name on his passport, if his passport is genuine in the first place.'

'Such a man must possess many passports of different nationalities.'

'Well, the passport he used to enter Pakistan stated his name to be different.'

'And how would you know that?' asked an extremely curious Nazir.

'After he left, I installed special cameras at all check-in counters at our international airport.'

Tariq had saved this bit of information no doubt to surprise me, thought the chief of CFIO. 'And what name did his passport carry?'

'Only if you promise not to laugh Sir,' Tariq said, smiling.

'Yes of course, just tell me the name.'

'It was Derrick Jonathan Major.'

'So what's funny about that?'

'Nothing, except that it's also the full name of the Prime Minister of the United Kingdom.'

Both Brig. Nazir and Maj. Chaudhary burst out laughing. 'Well at least our man has a sense of humour, if nothing else. So did you follow up on Mr Derrick Jonathan Major?' smiled Nazir.

'Yes, a cursory enquiry of the London directory services indicated the presence of 485 DJ Majors in Greater London itself, leave alone the rest of the country.'

Brig. Nazir suddenly stopped smiling and became grim again. 'So, we have nothing to do except wait for news; hopefully good news.' His two subordinates were silent. They were both thinking of the danger that was still not past. A danger lurking under the benign name of Gabriel. Within minutes Nazir's face clouded with deep creases of worry.

'You are thinking of Gabriel?' queried Maj. Tariq.

'Yes, he can still derail this operation.'

'Uhmm,' Tariq cleared his throat and sought to allay the fears of the chief. 'Maybe not, because after that aborted attempt on the life of Kapre, security is already very tight, yet our man thinks he can pull it off, so what harm can Gabriel cause?' Tariq was aware that his argument was a feeble attempt to cheer up Nazir.

'Yes, but he is counting on the element of surprise; specific information to the Indians could change everything. As Maj. Chaudhary has informed us, Bhargava had received the detailed summary of the operations. Gabriel could send out that information again.'

Although both the Majors knew of the great threat Gabriel posed, they maintained an outward calm. 'Even if the Indians find out that a professional has been engaged to assassinate Kapre, they don't know his exact plans. After all, he doesn't charge millions of dollars to get discouraged by the world's most primitive security apparatus.' Maj. Chaudhary had decided that a bit of bravado could have the effect of lifting the sagging morale of the Brigadier.

'Yes, this operation may succeed, but his continued presence will eat up Project K2 from within. Don't forget the ultimate aim is to split India into pieces, as they did to us with Bangladesh. Remember Azim, if, God forbid, this operation fails, and I am not here to guide you—' Tariq and Chaudhry began to interrupt Nazir, but he gestured to them to let him continue '—then you must not forget the existence of Gabriel. Do not reveal his existence to anyone in the ISI, unless you are absolutely certain of the person's loyalties. Do I make myself clear? To no one in the ISI.' Tariq and Chaudhary nodded, proud that the officer holding one of the most coveted posts in Pakistan had chosen to trust them with the biggest secret of the Pakistani establishment. Of course Tariq had no idea that Nazir had at one time suspected him and had his house and movements watched. 'But do not forget that he exists, and always keep your eyes and ears open for him, for

340

he will always pose a threat to the eventual realisation of the goals of Project K2.'

Brig. Nazir was relieved that at least one burden had been lifted of his chest. Unknown to Chaudhary, or even Tariq, his men were also watching the movements of Mohd. Shujaat. After Col. Abbas's disclosures to Nazir, Nazir's men had questioned all of Shujaat's men and threatened them with summary executions without trial. Except for Abbas, all of Shujaat's informers had been on his payroll and had owed him no personal loyalty. Faced with the spectre of summary executions, most of Shujaat's men had quickly switched loyalties.

Immediately after the discovery of Gabriel and his treachery, Brig. Nazir had confronted Mohd. Shujaat through Col. Ashraf Abbas. Nazir had known that confronting Shujaat was extremely dangerous but after knowing of the existence of Gabriel, he had decided he could not let the possibility of Shujaat being Gabriel remain unexplored. He had decided that it would be safer to let Abbas break the news of Shujaat's defeat to him. Shujaat had expectedly blown a fuse and had almost murdered Abbas who had pleaded helplessness. The motive behind confronting Shujaat had been to ensure that the son-in-law of the premier did nothing to derail the operation in order to fulfill any personal agenda. Brig. Nazir was aware that Shujaat would approach Gen. Mehmood with a bagful of complaints against him but he was willing to negotiate with a furious premier rather than risk treachery at what could be Pakistan's finest hour. Col. Abbas had gently explained to Shujaat that Nazir was aware of his activities and he should not do anything that would reflect poorly on him. 'You can have your revenge on the Brigadier, but plan it after this operation,' Abbas had added conspiratorially.

Col. Abbas knew that if Gen. Mehmood remained in power, both Lt. Gen. Hussain and Brig. Nazir would have to face difficulties caused by Shujaat. He knew that the premier would continue to ignore Shujaat for as long as he could but he would relent some day. On that day, Nazir would have to use his skills to carve out a safe passage for himself. Abbas had served in the presidential palace and had seen the destruction of many a promising career and also the loss of a few lives at the unnecessary childishness of Mohd. Shujaat. He was also aware that Shujaat's hold over Rehana was complete; and the general-turned-premier of Pakistan could not say no to the beloved husband of his only daughter.

When that time came, Col Abbas planned to seek fervent pardon from Shujaat and bank on the old village connections to save his life. He also hoped that direct access to the premier would go a long way in aiding his attempts to protect himself from the wily Mohd. Shujaat.

51

He checked himself in the mirror. The dark blue overalls were
stained with patches of white and gray paint. He had added
dirty gray glue paint to his hair and his head now bore the
grimy look of an overworked painter. The workman's bag had
been provided by his efficient Nepalese Man Friday. On his
feet were worn out and stretched canvas shoes that were
freely available at roadside bazaars. He then moved to check
whether the Atlas cycle looked dated enough. Satisfied with
his meticulous handwork, he began pedalling towards his
destination. Although in peak physical condition, he was
careful to adopt a tired look. Within twenty minutes, he
reached the multistoreyed apartments at Pandara Park. He got
off the cycle and slowly wheeled it inside.

The two guards stationed at the entrance stopped him. In
Hindi he informed them that he, Vinod Kumar, was the
NDMC painter deputed by the local CPWD office to paint
the water tanks on the roof of the building. The guards
directed him to make an entry in the visitors register. He
dutifully obliged and signed his adopted name in the scrawl
of a semi-literate workman. As he waited for the lift to arrive,

he heard footsteps and turned. It was a middle-aged lady who the guards were greeting. She got off at the fourth floor and he proceeded to the roof. He reached the terrace and was unhappy to see that it was full of children with their domestic escorts.

He realised he had chosen the wrong time to make his inspection. It was close to four P.M. and well beyond school hours. Had he come earlier he could have done his task in solitude. His oversight made him accept that even the most meticulous bit of planning could go awry. Since he had taken the trouble to change his appearance, he trudged forward to the water tanks that were nearest to the outer ledge of the terrace of the building. He rummaged in his tool bag and brought out a paint-brush along with a can of paint. He began painting the tank in a manner that would give him a bird's eye view of Pandara Park. From where he stood, Prof. Kapre's house was clearly visible. He could see a crowd of political hangers-on assembled on the professor's neat lawn.

He made a quick calculation: the distance was about sixty yards, well within the range of a Parker-Hale or any comparable sniper's rifle. The house was also a solid target for any missile shot from the overlooking terrace. The other option was of course to use his Press card to get close to the quarry and use the brilliantly designed watch slug that had been couriered to him directly from London after modifications had been carried out on the original Peshawar design. That option would give him the satisfaction of seeing his target fall but at the same time would not be able to guarantee a safe getaway from the resultant mayhem. He knew that the failed attempt a few days ago had queered the pitch for him to be able to use the watch gun.

He had read the reports of the amateur attempt on Kapre. The newspapers had reported that within five minutes all exit points of Pandara Park had been closed. He prided himself on his elaborate planning of getaways and did not want to risk capture at the hands of a primitive security service. He was sure that the wide and extended terrace of the building provided him with the best chance of escape. He looked at the other side of the terrace. The drop was of six floors but with some support it could be done. The rear of the building opened on to a lane that connected the smaller houses in Pandara Park.

He was well aware that soon after the assassination a cordon would be thrown around the district of New Delhi. His option would be to lie low within New Delhi for a few days and then leave the country. He had escaped in similar circumstances so many times now that there was no reason why this time would present any difficulty. What had to be planned was the exact weaponry and equipment that he would use. He looked around to see if there were any places that could be used for hiding his tools; there was no way the building guards would let him walk in with suspicious-looking material. He would have to bring in his weapons over a couple of days.

It was now half past five and he realised that half the water tank had been painted. It was time for him to call it a day and ensure that he didn't stick out because of an extra dedication to work. There were even more children on the terrace now, some accompanied by parents.

He cycled back after informing the guards that he would return to complete the unfinished work.

He returned the next day before noon on the pretext of completing the paint job. The guards did not notice that his tool bag was longer and wider than a normal bag of a CPWD workman. He looked around the terrace and was happy to see that there was no one else there. He opened his tool bag and took out an oily leathery material. Within this thick material was wrapped, in two layers of plastic, one oiled and greased Heckler and Koch machine pistol and one standard bore AK-47 assault rifle. He opened the water tank. With several strips of duct tape he stuck the package to the underside of the tank's lid, closed it, and placed a small lock on the metal lid of the tank. He knew that, except in a case of extreme bad luck, no one would open the water tank nor would anyone notice the small lock placed on the lid.

Once his basic assault weapons were safely stored, he began repainting the tank for the next fifteen minutes before leaving. The next day the contents of his bag were stored in a water tank adjacent to the first one. These consisted of a custom-made Colt sniper rifle with special bullets that, in addition to exploding inside a human body, also spread nitrous cynide thereby ensuring death within two seconds of impact.

In addition to the special rifle was a made-to-order shoulder propelled rocket launcher. The specialty of this launcher was that instead of the standard length of four-and-a-half feet it was only two-and-three-quarters feet. The rocket was laser guided and could be off centre by a maximum of only four inches. The launcher was also fitted with a digital telescopic sight and the rocket itself had a destructive capacity of taking out an armored vehicle of standard specifications.

The only doubt that remained in his mind was the rocket launcher. All the other weapons had been used by him in previous operations. The launcher had been manufactured by a Swedish small arms manufacturer, ABB Jensen Corp., highly recommended by the harshest critics and analysts of the modern arms bazaar. He had stopped in Stockholm on his way back from Spain and had placed the order after hurriedly scanning their catalogues. The cost of the design and manufacture had been US$ 300,000 and it had been delivered to him disguised as an astronomical telescope. The claimed range of the launcher was over 1400 metres but he reckoned that a realistic estimate would be between eight and nine hundred metres.

Before every previous assassination he short-listed a variety of tools. There had been times when unscheduled changes in the plans of targets had necessitated a change in the choice of tool or the use of more than one tool. But such instances had been few and far between. The last time it had happened was in Oman when the prince was guarded at his desert retreat by more men than anticipated. The result had been the need to immobilise the guards and even kill one of them.

For Prof. Kapre he had decided that he would use the Colt sniper rifle. Although he had been reluctant to repeat it in India because he had used it in Spain, the failed attempt on the Indian leader and his enhanced security cover had forced him to alter his plans. He had also decided to wear on his person that day the watch sent to him from Peshawar. He would not be using it of course, but he felt like wearing it.

As he cycled back, his thoughts went over the direction his life had taken. He had of course long ceased to believe in God. God, he often said, was a mirage for the poor and helpless. Those who charted their own lives were their own lords and did not need to clutch at any third party divinity. At this stage, when he was at the top of his chosen vocation, he had no regrets. There was a part of him that loved playing God. Political leaders, lords and barons, royal princes, all were equally helpless before his long arm.

It was a little later than usual for the pre-dawn musings of Surendra Nigam. The scrap of paper that the lab at RAW had spent hours studying contained two lines of typed English. Nigam could hardly make any sense out of them. Hours of early mornings struggle had not helped him in cracking what was obviously a code. Only the word 'Gabriel' stood out. Nigam knew the significance of archangel Gabriel in Islam and he of course connected the code to Pakistan. As he began to be disturbed by the jarring notes of his mother praying loudly in her less than melodious voice, a stream of light began to bombard his mind. The nature of the information Bhargava had, had to be in keeping with his stature in the establishment. Nigam had concluded that Mishra's grief over Bhargava's death was not so much because of his personal relations with Agni but because of Agni's contribution to RAW. What contacts had Bhargava built in his time spent in Pakistan and which of them continued to send him information even when he had ceased to reside in that country? What dangerous game was being played by Pakistan now in assassinating Mohan Bhargava on Indian territory? What had made them so desperate?

Nigam waited impatiently till it was 8 AM. Then with trembling hands he dialled the residence number of the director. Although Nigam had no answers to the ever-deepening mystery, he had decided that he would share the puzzle with his director. Nigam also harboured a slim hope that Rajnish Mishra may know something about the source in Pakistan. If the director could add something to the disjointed bits some answer might emerge. After ten minutes he replaced the receiver. At the mention of the word 'Gabriel', Rajnish Mishra had become silent. The director had then told Nigam to be in his office by 10.30 AM. One thing was certain— 'Gabriel' did mean something to the director.

'You must have a hundred questions today.' Nigam remained silent at this half-hearted query from the chief. In answer he passed the scrap of paper to Rajnish Mishra. Mishra turned it over in his hand. His eyes flickered and his brow furrowed in some kind of understanding. Nigam waited for the director to regain his composure and tried to concentrate on the orange paperweight that lay on the table before him. From the corner of his eye he could make out that Mishra had pulled out a dossier marked 'top secret' and was gently opening the thread that bound the file. To keep himself busy, he then turned to look at the family photograph that lay on the side cabinet to the right of the director. Nigam knew that Mishra had bright and vivacious children. However, he found his attention diverted by the woman in the picture. He had heard whispers about Mrs Rajnish Mishra's beauty.

'What I am going to tell you today is known to very few people. The man known as Gabriel holds the key to Bhargava's murder.' Nigam looked up at his director. 'Gabriel is the Pakistani mole who was recruited by Agni in Pakistan. It is my feeling that Gabriel had sent such information to Agni that resulted in his death.'

'That is my feeling too,' said Nigam. 'But what is this information that Bhargava wanted to tell you in person?'

'That of course is the missing link. If I could find that out, the entire mystery would be solved.' Mishra did not tell Nigam that he was expecting the same information from Gabriel. He had decided that he would take that decision once the specific information was placed before him and he had had a chance to analyse it. He was not even sure if Gabriel would respond to his request. But if he did, RAW would be paying him Rs ten crore for divulging information that he had already sent to his recruiter.

52

It was 5.30 in the morning when he awoke. A simple breakfast of milk with cornflakes and two apples followed. He then put on a track suit. Prithviraj Road to Pandara Park was a walk of about fifteen minutes at his rapid pace. On that cold and dark winter morning there were not too many people on the streets. He moved steadily towards Pandara Park. He had memorised Prof. Kapre's routine. The REP chief's schedule—released to selected members of the accredited Press and special security members—had been unwittingly revealed to him by Atreyee Mishra. He turned into Pandara Park and paused for a split second before continuing, his mind working furiously. Instead of the usual Delhi police guard, the security presence seemed to have multiplied overnight. He could make out the distinct olive green colour of the uniforms. There were barricades all around the central park.

He continued to walk towards the multistoreyed apartment block. What had happened in one night? There was no one who could have tipped off the Indians of his plans for the simple reason that no one knew of them. As he crossed the entrance to the lane that led to Kapre's house, he saw the security men eye him suspiciously.

350

As he finished the round and retraced his steps, he saw an unmarked white Ambassador move towards Kapre's residence. It stopped at the barricade and a man in plain clothes stepped out to direct the security officers. On the night of December 13 Rajnish Mishra had finally received word from Gabriel that the ISI planned to assassinate Prof. Vijay Krishna Kapre and had hired a professional assassin to undertake the assignment. Gabriel had also confirmed that this information had been known to Mohan Bhargava whose murder had been planned in Islamabad by Brig. Qayyum Nazir and his dedicated subordinates. A freshly galvanised Rajnish Mishra had rushed to the cabinet secretary and the two had in turn called on the Prime Minister. Both Reddy and Hitesh Singh had directed that Prof. Kapre was to be protected at all costs. Hitesh Singh had called up Kapre and personally apprised him of the danger.

The amused Kapre had dismissed the threat, taking it to be a desperate ploy by the Congress, perhaps to prevent him from campaigning freely. An exasperated Reddy had then directed Mishra and Anand Kishore to ensure that no harm came to Kapre. The chiefs of RAW and IB had stationed the elite national security guard all around Kapre's Pandara Park residence. IB had deputed one of their senior deputy directors, L.K. Jha, to personally supervise the security arrangements along with Surendra Nigam and Madhukar Bhatt, deputy director of RAW. They had contemplated sealing the terrace of the apartment building near Kapre's house and then stalled at the instance of Jha who happened to reside on the third floor. He had two sons who, along with a few friends, practiced cricket on the terrace. Sunanda Jha had bowed to the entreaties of her wailing sons and requested her husband to intercede. 'You are the head of his security, can't you tell them to leave our building alone?'

Singer's sharp eyes noticed that access to the building was still open and a few servants had begun to materialise in the car park to walk their employers' pets. As he walked back to Prithviraj Road, he asked himself whether he should proceed as planned. If he waited till December 16, then he would have to track Kapre on his campaign trail all over India. That in turn would have its own logistical problems. The presence of the national security guard at Kapre's house could in fact add a further thrill to his assignment.

As Singer reassured himself that Kapre would waken to his last morning soon, a disturbed Nigam walked up to the officer-in-charge outside the REP chief's house. 'Has that terrace been sealed?' he asked, pointing in the direction of the apartment building.

'No Sir, Jha saheb has told us to leave the building alone. He feels there is no danger there.' So saying the officer lowered his eyes, aware that Nigam's concern was well founded.

'Any guards there?' The man nodded towards two guards at the entry to the terrace on the staircase.

'No, I mean on the terrace itself?'

'No Sir, Jha saheb says it will disturb all the children of the officers who live in the building.'

'Oh God!' an exasperated Nigam shook his head in disgust. As deputy director, L.K. Jha was equivalent to an additional commissioner of police and certainly senior to Nigam. Surendra decided to raise the issue with Mishra and Bhatt, the deputy director of RAW.

As a worried Rajnish Mishra read the *Times of India* to take his mind off Prof. Kapre, his wife debated whether to tell her husband what she had seen. But how would she explain her presence in the man's room? Perhaps it hadn't been so significant after all. As her daughter gave her a quick kiss before running out of the room, Atreyee's thoughts went back to the previous night. She had had sex with him again. They had met for dinner at the Claridges Hotel after which he had taken her to his home. He had then very deliberately and gently picked her up and taken her to his bedroom. She had responded to him eagerly as he made love to her repeatedly. She had wanted to stay the night with him but he had told her he had a business meeting in the morning. It was in the washroom that she had accidentally stumbled upon a file containing several newspaper cuttings on Prof. Kapre.

NEW DELHI, DECEMBER 15, 1995

Vinod Kumar, the CPWD workman argued in vain with the guards at the building in Pandara Park. *'Par main yaha roz aata hoon,'* he pleaded, trying to convince the guards that he had to apply a second coat to the water tanks on the terrace. The guards were unmoved. *'Ab koi kaam nahin hoga, aur agley baar apna security pass banwa ke lao.'* It was 10.15 AM and several of the officers who lived in the building were leaving for work. Two of the officers attracted by the row the security guards were making walked to the entrance and demanded to know what was wrong. The security guards explained that they were under strict orders to allow only the residents of the building inside. One of the irritated officers then summoned the regular building guards and asked *'Tum ise pehchaante ho?'* He gestured in the direction of Vinod Kumar. The guard said he did recognise him, and that he had been sent by the CPWD. 'This is too much,' exclaimed the officer, 'I am calling Lucky to protest.' He trooped back into the building angrily.

Lucky was how Jha was known to friends and colleagues. In a few minutes the first officer returned with the deputy director. Jha nodded to the salute and told the guards to allow the painter in. 'The CPWD sends workers with such difficulty,' he told the officers, laughing. The guards searched Singer's tool bag and promptly let him pass. Jha nodded and went back inside. At about the same time, Nigam was waiting for Mishra to be free from an important phone call so that he could convince the director to give orders to seal the terrace of the Pandara Park building. His conversation with Bhat had only resulted in two guards being posted at the entrance of the terrace.

It was these guards who stopped Singer for the second time. They let him go after searching his tool bag and after having received word on their wireless sets from their colleagues below. He entered the terrace and began rapidly painting the water tank. After awhile, convinced that the coast was now clear, he unlocked the tank and took out the Colt sniper rifle and the rocket launcher. He put his paint-brush aside and began to conduct a last-minute check on the Colt. It was three minutes past eleven and Kapre was scheduled to leave for the party office at ten past eleven. As he began adjusting the telescopic sight of the Colt, the door to the terrace was pushed open. He dropped the Colt and the ABB Jensen rocket and covered the weapons with the cloth that he had around his waist. It was one of the security guards who had been at the entrance to the terrace. The guard walked up to him. He had a cigarette in his mouth and looked bored. He moved closer to him and stood looking around lazily.

'So, who do you think will be the Prime Minister?' He gestured towards Kapre's house in the distance.

'*Bhaiyya*, what difference does it make to people like us?' He tried to sound disinterested to cut short the conversation. As his large watch showed six minutes past eleven, his sharp eyes saw the front door of Kapre's ground floor house opening.

'But who will you vote for?' persisted the guard, puffing on his cigarette. Singer shrugged and turned away. He could see Prof. Vijay Krishna Kapre emerging from his home and fervently hoped the guard would let up and leave. 'Don't you think Kapre will do a good job?' Singer noted Kapre move towards his car. He made his decision. He cupped his palms on the mouth of the stunned guard as small gelatin slugs discharged from the watch gun and detonated inside the guard's stomach. With his other hand he drew out his knife. One swing of the shining blade severed the aorta of the guard.

As the limp body of the guard slumped to the floor, he wiped his hand clean and looked at Kapre frantically. The REP supremo was now in his car and the engine of the Ambassador was gunning. His watch told him that the time was fourteen minutes past eleven. He could still use the Colt but he knew that sniper rifles could not be trusted with moving targets. He would have to use the rocket launcher. Or wait for another day. With the sigh of a gambler, he picked up the launcher and adjusted its electronic sight on the car that was now moving at a speed of twenty kilometres per hour towards Dr. Zakir Hussain Marg. He then adjusted the laser operation. His watch now showed seventeen minutes past eleven and the car was crossing the gate of the local government school of Pandara Park. As he released the trigger of the launcher, the guards at the ground floor of the building thought they heard a whizzing sound like that of a bird of prey. Twenty seconds later the Ambassador blew up in a huge orange-red ball of fire. One of the doors flew over the school boundary wall injuring four girls playing there.

Sure that there were no survivors, Singer packed his deadly cargo into his tool bag and hurried to the back of the terrace. The second guard, stunned as he was by the huge noise of the explosion ran down the stairs not even waiting for his colleague to join him. At the edge of the terrace, Singer swung a thick metal chain enclosed in nylon casing over the ledge. He then took out a small pulley approximately six inches in diameter. The pulley was clasped over the metal chain and he swung over the ledge of the terrace. His thick gloves grasped the long handles on either side of the pulley and he swung down the chain. Exactly one-and-a-half minutes later he landed on the ground and rushed towards the hedge of a neighbouring bungalow. Three nights ago he had hidden the uniform of a local Delhi police constable in the hedge. In another four minutes he had removed his overalls and stuffed them in his tool bag. At exactly twenty-four minutes past eleven, dressed in the uniform, he had crossed Pandara Road to enter the road to Khan Market. By this time all the thirty NSG guards stationed outside Kapre's house had assembled around the debris of the burnt Ambassador. No bodies could be found. Present in the car along with Kapre were his driver, Sitaram, his secretary Mahesh Prasad and his personal security officer, Akash Rajgarhia.

It was thirty-five minutes past eleven when Nigam, Jha and other officers reached the site of the carnage. The man responsible for the killing had by then reached his comfortable house on Prithviraj Road and was relaxing on his bed after having asked his servant to prepare a hot water bottle. Atreyee only found out about the assassination when her husband called to tell his wife and daughter to stay indoors. He had failed, he told her, despite having been forewarned. He told her that experts were still examining the site but it seemed that an assassin posing as a CPWD employee could have had something to do with the murder. Mishra had also told his wife that he felt personally responsible and that he would be resigning within hours. Atreyee was in a state of shock as she realised how she had been used.

She cursed herself repeatedly. She had given him details of Kapre's schedule. She had ignored the newspaper clippings in his room... With trembling hands she opened Rajnish's locker. She withdrew the fully loaded revolver from it and told the driver to take out her car. As she rushed out of the house, Nigam was also rushing to his official car. He was going to the RAW chief's residence. He had been directed by Rajnish Mishra to personally get the file in which some sketchy details of the hired assassin had been provided by Gabriel. As he was about to turn into the lane in Rabindra Nagar, his vehicle almost crashed into another car that he recognised to be the director's personal car. Nigam didn't know why he did it, but on pure instinct he chose to follow the car that was now moving at an unusual speed of ninety kilometres per hour through the barricaded zone in front of Lodhi Gardens and Amrita Sher Gill Marg. He knew nothing except that Mrs Mishra was at the wheel and was driving like a person possessed.

Within five minutes the wife of the director drew up outside the house at Prithviraj Road. Singer was trying to adjust the frequency of his radio to check if BBC had caught the news yet. At her footsteps, he turned and his face broadened into a good natured smile. 'You bastard,' she shrieked. She was trembling with rage.

He looked at her calmly. So she had figured it out. 'I'm sorry I had to do this, but I do genuinely admire you, Atreyee.'

'You're a killer and I'm turning you in,' she said, pointing the revolver at him.'

At this he smiled. 'Please calm down,' he said. He moved his left arm closer to his right hand. He felt the handle of his stilleto. It would take a few seconds for the knife to hit her but he had to aim it at her neck so that it would kill her instantly without causing her any pain. As he drew out the knife he was distracted by the sound of shattering glass. It was that sound that drowned the noise of the bullet that hit him below the left shoulder. Before he could react, DCP Surendra Nigam fired again. This time he slumped. Before all feeling left him Atreyee could swear that she saw a smile of relief flood his face.

Epilogue

The election results trickled in. Without the inspiring presence of their dynamic supremo, the REP failed to get a simple majority. It finished with a tally of 121 seats in the Lok Sabha. Though the figure was higher than the 103 seats that the Congress got, it was not enough to attract the crowd of regional parties that had reaped the benefit of Kapre's death so the REP failed to cobble together a coalition government. The Left alliance led by the two big parties, the CPI and the CPM, made huge gains and decided to push for a non-Congress, non-REP government at the Centre.

Brig. Qayyum Nazir was flooded with felicitations from Gen. Mehmood and the other top brass of Pakistan for the successful conduct of Operation Karakoram. The cross-border export of terrorism continued unabated as the third front government was preoccupied pleasing its various constituents. As a result, Project K2 hurtled on, every day inching closer to its goal. Mohd. Shujaat had his revenge when the dithering Col. Ashraf Abbas was court-martialled on the trumped up charge of corruption. Brig. Nazir and others managed to save his life but Abbas was stripped of his rank and slipped into ignominy. Though Shujaat was unable to cause any damage to Nazir because of the success of Karakoram, he attempted to harm him by attacking his subordinate officers. Nazir managed to save Maj. Azim Tariq also and ordered Tariq to maintain a low profile till Shujaat had got over his fury. Maj. Mushtaq Chaudhary was, however, shunted out to the ordnance factory in the town of Bahawalpur and did not return to the ISI for the next four years. He was reinstated by Nazir in his capacity as Lt. Gen and the chief of ISI at the time Pakistan conducted its retaliatory nuclear tests in 1998.

Rajnish Mishra took the success of Karakoram as a personal failure and put in his papers within days of the death of Kapre. An unhappy Reddy tried his best to persuade Mishra not to resign and even offered to move the RAW chief to a cushy gubernatorial post, as committed earlier, but Mishra refused. 'I have had enough. I want to spend some time with my family now,' he told the former prime minister. Before resigning, Mishra ensured that DCP Surendra Nigam was permanently absorbed into RAW. Nigam took to RAW with felicity and went on to carry out several operations with aplomb. Before leaving RAW, Mishra also revealed the identity of Gabriel to Nigam. Jha, the IB officer whose singular carelessness ensured the success of Karakoram, was placed under immediate suspension by his disgusted superiors; he began a long legal battle to be reinstated. Nigam, the only one who knew the truth about the man responsible for the success of Karakoram did not disclose it to anyone and earned the eternal gratitude of Atreyee Mishra.

A grieving David Steiner—who found out about his friend's death from his Man Friday—arranged for Singer's cremation and acting under his assumed name of Ray Darrel, collected his partner's share of money from Zurich and floated a charitable trust for orphans. He did not name the trust after his friend as he was not sure what name he would have been comfortable with. He held a memorial service for his old friend, but again, it was dedicated to an anonymous man who had finally found peace in death.

Aware that the success of Operation Karakoram had further inspired Nazir to resume the search for the traitor, Gabriel fled Pakistan at an opportune moment and did manage to retire into the opulent luxury of the Gold Coast and Sydney. Lt. Gen. Nazir never did manage to figure out that the retirement of his boss at the most glorious moment of Pakistani intelligence history was actually a desperate play for self preservation. The man was given a warm send off and none present, from the premier Gen. Mehmood to middle-rung operatives like Maj. Tariq, could fathom that the man they were seeing off was not leaving because he wanted to spend his old age with his sons. Though Lt. Gen. Ghulam Hussain had failed to prevent the success of Karakoram, the very fact that he managed to escape Pakistan with his life, despite being the most dangerous spy the country had ever had, was a victory for his alternative persona as Gabriel.